Coast-to-Coast Praise for

CONTINENTAL DRIFT

W9-BVD-884

CONTINENTAL DRIFT

Russell Banks

BALLANTINE BOOKS • NEW YORK

for Kathy
Yun seul dwèt pas capab' managé gombo.

The author gratefully acknowledges the generous support of the Ingram Merrill Foundation and the National Endowment for the Arts.

Library of Congress Catalog Card Number: 84-48137

ISBN 0-345-33021-8

This edition published by arrangement with Harper & Row, Publishers, Inc.

Printed in Canada

First Ballantine Books Edition: April 1986
Ninth Printing: May 1991

Contents

I am free. High above the mast the moon
Rides clear of her mind and the waves make a refrain
Of this: that the snake has shed its skin upon
The floor. Go on through the darkness. The waves fly back.
—Wallace Stevens, *Farewell to Florida*

Harper's Creek and roarin' ribber,
Thar, my dear, we'll live forebber;
Den we'll go de Ingin nation,
All I want in dis creation
Is pretty little wife and big plantation.
—Northrup, *Twelve Years a Slave*

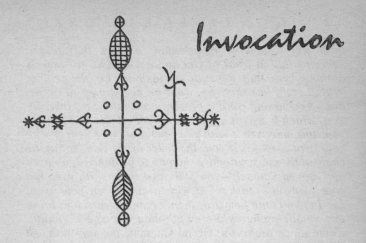

Invocation

It's not memory you need for telling this story, the sad story of Robert Raymond Dubois, the story that ends along the back streets and alleys of Miami, Florida, on a February morning in 1981, that begins way to the north in Catamount, New Hampshire, on a cold, snow-flecked afternoon in December 1979, the story that tells what happened to young Bob Dubois in the months between the wintry afternoon in New Hampshire and the dark, wet morning in Florida and tells what happened to the several people who loved him and to some Haitian people and a Jamaican and to Bob's older brother Eddie Dubois who loved him but thought he did not and to Bob's best friend Avery Boone who did not love him but thought he did and to the women who were loved by Bob Dubois nearly as much as and differently from the way that he loved his wife Elaine. It's not memory you need, it's clear-eyed pity and hot, old-time anger and a Northern man's love of the sun, it's a white Christian man's entwined obsession with race and sex and a proper middle-class American's shame for his nation's history. This is an American story of the late twentieth century, and you don't need a muse to tell it, you need something

1

more like a loa, or mouth-man, a voice that makes speech stand in front of you and not behind, for there's nothing here that depends on memory for the telling. With a story like this, you want an accounting to occur, not a recounting, and a presentation, not a representation, which is why it's told the way it's told. And though you, too, may see it with your own eyes and hear it with your own ears—as if you, the teller of the tale, sat in the circle of listeners, attentive, hoping to be amused, amazed and moved yourself—you still must see it with eyes not your own and must tell it with a mouth not your own. Let Legba come forward, then, come forward and bring this middle-aging, white mouth-man into speech again. Come down along the Grand Chemin, the sun-path, all filled with pity and hardened with anger to a shine. Come forward, Papa, come to the Crossroads. Come forward, Old Bones, full of wonder for the triple mystery of men and women clamped to one another, of blackness and of the unexpected arrival of gods from Guinea. And come forward eager to cast shame all about. Give body and entitledness and boldness to this white mouth-man's pity and anger by covering his shoulders with a proper cloak of shame, and give him pure, physical pleasure under the slow, close sun among people and gods whose evident difference from him and from his one big God brings him forward too, finally, unto himself and unto everyone present as well. And let this man tell what the good American man Bob Dubois did that was so bad in the eyes of God and les Mystères and in the eyes of the mouth-man himself that Bob Dubois got left lost to his wife Elaine, who had loved him for a long, long time, and his son and two daughters and his friend Avery Boone and the women Bob Dubois had made love to and the men and women who had lived and worked with Bob Dubois in Catamount, New Hampshire, and in Oleander Park, Florida, and on fishing boats out of Moray Key. Again, Legba, come forward! Let this man speak that man to life.

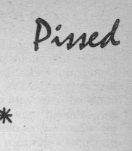

Pissed

1

IT'S DECEMBER 21, 1979, A FRIDAY, IN CATAMOUNT, NEW Hampshire. It's late in the day, windless and cold, bits of snow dropping from a dark, low sky. At this latitude at this time of year, the sun sets at three forty-five, and Catamount, a river town laid north and south between a pair of glacial moraines, settles quickly without twilight into darkness. Light simply gets replaced by cold, and the rest remains the same.

A half foot of old crusty snow has covered the ground since the first week of the month, followed by days and nights of dry cold, so that the snow has merely aged, turning slowly gray in yards and on rooftops and in heaps alongside the streets, pitted and spotted along sidewalks and pathways by dogs and mottled everywhere with candy wrappers, beer cans and crumpled cigarette packs. The parking lots and sidewalks, plowed and salted weeks ago, are the color of ash, so that new snow gently falling comes as a cleansing fresh coat of paint, a whitewash that hides the old, stained and tainted world underneath.

Robert Raymond Dubois (pronounced locally as "Doo-boys"), an oil burner repairman for the Abenaki Oil Company, walks slowly from the squat, dark brick garage where he has parked the company truck, walks hunched over with careful effort, like a man in a blizzard, though snow is falling lightly and there is no wind. He wears a dark blue trooper coat with a fur collar, and a black watchcap. In one hand he carries a black lunchbox, in the other an envelope containing his weekly paycheck, one hundred thirty-seven dollars and forty-four cents.

Dubois thinks, A man reaches thirty, and he works at a trade for eight years for the same company, even goes to oil burner school nights for a year, and he stays honest, he doesn't sneak copper tubing or tools into his car at night, he doesn't put in for time he didn't work, he doesn't drink on the job—*a man does his work*, does it for eight long years, and for that he gets to take home to his wife and two kids a weekly paycheck for one hundred thirty-seven dollars and forty-four cents. Dirt money. Chump change. Money gone before it's got. No money at all. Bob does not think it, but he knows that soon the man stops smiling so easily, and when he does smile, it's close to a sneer. And what he once was grateful for, a job, a wife, kids, a house, he comes to regard as a burden, a weight that pulls his chin slowly to his chest, and because he was grateful once, he feels foolish now, cheated somehow by himself.

Dubois parks his car on Depot Street facing downhill toward the river and tight to the tailgate of a salt-covered pickup truck. It's snowing harder now, steadily and in large, soft flakes, and the street is slick and white. Black footprints follow him across the street to a brick building where there are apartments in the upper two stories and a used clothing store, a paint store and a bar at street level, and he enters the bar, Irwin's Restaurant and Lounge. The restaurant is in front, a long, narrow room the size of a railroad car, filled with bright green plastic-covered booths and Formica-topped tables. The room is

brightly lit and deserted, but in back, through an arch-
way, the bar is dark and crowded.

The bartender, a muscular woman in her mid-fifties
with a beer-barrel body and a large, hard, lipsticked
mouth and a mass of bleached blond hair arranged carefully to resemble a five-and-dime wig, greets Dubois and
shoves an opened bottle of Schlitz across the wet bar to
him. Her name, unbelievably, is Pearl, and she is Irwin's help. In a year Irwin will die of a heart attack and
Pearl will buy out his estate and will finally own the
business she has run for decades.

These northern New England milltown bars are like
Irish pubs. In a community closed in by weather and
geography, where the men work at jobs and the women
work at home and raise children and there's never enough
money, the men and the women tend to feel angry
toward one another much of the time, especially in the
evenings when the work is done and the children are
sleeping and nothing seems improved over yesterday.
It's an unhappy solution to the problem, that men and
women should take pleasure in the absence of their
mates, but here it's a necessary one, for otherwise they
would beat and maim and kill one another even more
than they do.

Dubois is sitting at a small table in a shadowed corner
of the bar, talking slowly in a low voice to a woman in
her mid-thirties. Her name is Doris Cleeve. Twice divorced from brutal young men by the time she was
twenty-eight, Doris has nursed her hurt ever since with
alcohol and the company of men married to someone
else. She is confused about where to go, what to do with
her life now, and as a result, she plays her earlier life,
her marriages and divorces, over and over again. As in
certain country and western records on the jukebox by
the door, Doris's past never fails to move her.

Except for her slightly underslung jaw, which makes
her seem pugnacious, she's a pretty woman and not at
all pugnacious. She wears her ash blond hair short,
stylish for Catamount, and dresses in ski sweaters and
slacks, as if she thinks she is petite, though in fact she is

merely short. In the last few years she has put on weight, mainly because of her drinking, but she hasn't admitted it to herself yet and probably won't, until she discovers one morning after she turns forty that she is a fat woman, as fat as the rest of the women she works with down at the cannery. She has slender wrists, though, and small, delicate hands, which is why she still thinks of herself as petite, and having just lit her cigarette (actually, Bob lit it for her, with a flourish of his butane lighter), she jiggles and admires her bracelets while he goes on talking.

Bob Dubois in most ways is an ordinary-looking young man. You'd pass him in the Sears tool or sporting goods department without a thought, a tall, bulky workingman in good physical shape. Stiff, short, light brown hair that resists combing, square features, pale blue eyes, small ears and, because of his size and build, a surprisingly delicate mouth—Bob's face is an easy face to ignore, so long as he is ignoring yours.

But if he's not ignoring yours, if he's slightly curious about you or attracted, sexually or otherwise, or threatened, his broad face changes and becomes extremely expressive. Bob's face is like an intelligent dog's, unable to hide or effectively disguise his emotions, and it's forced him into being fairly honest. He's learned to disguise his thoughts, of course, his strategies, plans and fantasies, but not his feelings. He doesn't know this, however, because whenever he looks at himself in a mirror, he seems to have no feelings whatsoever. He wonders what he really looks like. Photographs can't tell him—he looks into a camera lens the same way he looks into a mirror, as if he were an actor portraying a corpse. If he truly were an actor and could portray a living man, then perhaps he would know what he looks like.

When he's not trying to act, when he's himself, he has a curious, good-humored, friendly face, or else he shows you a closed, hard, angry face. One or the other, with not much in between. Because this shift from open to closed, from good-humored to angry, from kindly to cruel, is abrupt and is wholly unchecked along the way by degrees of coldness, anger, and so on, the extremes seem extreme indeed, opposites, even though, as Bob himself feels and understands it, the shift from his being a happy man to an unhappy man is one of only slight degree.

It's the same regarding his intelligence—that is, how it appears, how it feels to him and how he understands it. One moment he looks positively brilliant and feels it and believes it; the next moment he looks downright stupid, and he feels and believes he is stupid. The shift from one to the other, however, seems to him only a matter of degree—mere inches.

"My wife doesn't understand me," he says to Doris Cleeve.

"You probably don't understand her, either."

Bob smiles and lights a cigarette. "I don't make enough money." To her, as he says this, Bob looks good-humored, friendly and smart. Better than anyone else in this place, who is in a bad mood, unfriendly, stupid or all three. Also, he's handsome, in a way.

"So? Tell me who does. Especially at Christmas. You wanna hear *my* problems?"

She has large, healthy teeth. A fleck of tobacco from her unfiltered cigarette clings to a front tooth, and for an instant Bob wants to lick it off. "I don't get enough sex," he says.

She laughs out loud and looks down at her drink, gin and tonic. As if satisfied, Bob peers across the smoky, crowded room and smiles at no one in particular. Someone has played the Johnny Paycheck song, "Take This Job and Shove It," on the jukebox, and at the chorus a half-dozen customers join in, singing loudly, happily along, slapping backs and grinning at one another.

IT'S DARK OUTSIDE. GIGANTIC RED AND GREEN ELECTRIC candy canes and wreaths dangle from lampposts while shoppers hurry anxiously along the sidewalks from store to store. The snow is falling heavily in fat flakes that turn almost at once to gray slush beneath the boots of the Christmas shoppers and under the tires of the cars.

Bob Dubois stands stiffly at the pay phone in the

hallway that leads back from the bar to the rest rooms. A burly, unshaven man in a checkered wool shirt and overalls squeezes past, touches him on the shoulder and says Bob's name, then hitches his pants and returns to the bar, as Bob goes on talking into the telephone.

"Yeah, I already been to the bank and cashed it. Listen, I'll . . . I'll get home in a couple hours or so; it's the only chance I got to shop. . . . I know, I know—white. White figure skates, size four. I'll try Sears first. I know it's late, I just haven't had a chance, you know that. . . . I dunno, a couple hours, maybe. . . . I'll get something to eat down here. Okay? Okay. . . ."

He hangs up and moves slowly down the hall to the men's room, where there is a small spotted mirror over the sink, into which he will gaze for a few seconds, wondering what he looks like, wondering if his lies show, or his fears, or his confusion. Giving up, he will try to comb his stiff hair, posing once or twice as the man he saw last night on television in a Christmas perfume ad, tuxedoed, dark hair graying at the temples, parking his Lancia on a moonlit street in Aix-en-Provence, leaning down to kiss the long neck of a lovely, smiling blond woman in an evening gown, whispering a compliment into her pink, perfectly shaped ear.

On the floor above the bar there are three apartments, two studio apartments facing Depot Street and a larger unit at the rear facing an alley, and on the floor above that three more. In the tiny kitchen of one of the studios on the top floor, Doris Cleeve, having served Bob Dubois a Schlitz, is fixing herself another gin and tonic.

"How many times you been here now, Bob? A dozen? How come I always hafta tell you to make yourself comfortable before you make yourself comfortable? Tell me that."

Bob draws the curtains over the pair of windows that face the street, and as they close, catches a glimpse of his car below, the roof and hood white with snow. "C'mon, Doris," he says. "You know how I feel about this."

"About *me?*" she asks. "You mean how you feel

about *me?''* She sits down at the table facing him. He is standing in front of one of the windows and next to an upholstered platform rocker.

"Well . . . yeah. I guess so. But I meant about being here, like this.'' He looks stupid again, and he knows it. Holding his beer in one hand, he tries knocking a cigarette free of the pack with the other and dumps a half-dozen cigarettes onto the floor. "Look,'' he says, kneeling to retrieve the cigarettes, "I love my wife. I really do.''

"Sure you do, Bob. Sure you do.''

He sits down in the rocker, sets the can of beer on the maple step table next to it and lights a cigarette. "Well . . . I do.'' He turns the can slowly with his thumb and forefinger, leaving wet, spiraling rings on the tabletop. "You and me, Doris, that's different. That's friendship. Know what I mean?''

The woman is silent for a few seconds. "Yeah. I know what you mean.'' And she does know, because at this moment their thoughts, though they cannot be uttered, are essentially the same. Both Bob and Doris are struck, amazed, even, that such a simple event as a man and a woman in a room together can turn out to be so complicated that neither is able to say why he or she is there. They have been in this room together enough times to know that it's not because they are friends, for their friendship is not the sort that demands privacy in order to thrive. And it's not because they are in love with each other, for Doris still loves her second husband, Lloyd Cleeve, who broke her nose and three ribs one night and on another gave her a concussion and on five or six more bruised her face, until finally she left him and he moved down to Lowell, Massachusetts, and started in on another woman. And Bob still loves his wife Elaine, who nags a little but is kind to him in all the important ways and most of the unimportant ways as well, who does understand him. And though Doris is more able than Bob to separate sexual pleasure from the pleasure of being loved by someone, neither of them has come to this room to satisfy his or her sexual needs. Elaine Dubois, after seven years of marriage, is still

attractive to her husband, and she thoroughly enjoys
making love with him and does so frequently and with
great, uninhibited enthusiasm, which enthusiasm happens to operate on Bob as a powerful sexual stimulant,
arousing him to levels of endurance and spontaneity he's
never reached with other women. And Doris, who, as
mentioned, is more able than Bob to separate sexual
pleasure from the pleasure of being loved, perhaps because she is thirty-five years old and has been living
alone since she was twenty-eight, frequently visits and is
visited by a tireless nineteen-year-old plumber's appren-
tice with a scraggly blond beard and shoulder-length
hair, a hard-muscled, dope-smoking kid named Rufus,
called Roof, who rents the studio directly beneath hers.
He usually shows up at her door, barefoot, in tee shirt
and jeans, late at night when she can't sleep and has
been pacing the floor. They smoke a joint together, and
then he goes to work on her, until, hours later, exhausted, she falls asleep against his hairless chest, and
when she wakes in the morning, he is gone.

Bob stands in the darkness by the bed that a few
minutes ago was an orange sofa and pulls off his clothing. Then, quickly, as if the room were cold, he yanks
back the covers and slips into bed, stretching his naked
body out and folding his arms behind his head.

In a few seconds, Doris emerges from the bathroom
wearing only her panties, which, when she reaches the
side of the bed, she daintily removes. Then she slides
into the bed next to Bob and puts her arms around him
and kisses him softly, gently, on the mouth, the neck,
the shoulders. Her mouth and her little moans, to his
relief, arouse him (not that he's not easily and regularly
aroused; it's just that once in a great while for no reason
he can name he is not able to convince his inert penis to
rise up and please, and the experience, painful, humiliat-
ing and bewildering, has had an effect on his self-
confidence all out of proportion to its frequency). To
Bob, Doris's body is more attractive naked than clothed.
She is round and smooth and soft to the touch, her
nipples are pink and hard, and her thatch of light brown

pubic hair is dense and surprisingly silky as he runs his hand over the swell of her belly and out along the inside of her thighs.

Soon she has her legs wrapped around his waist, her head turning from side to side on the pillow, her hands digging into his shoulder muscles, as he slides in and out of her, swiftly and smoothly, and then her breathing becomes loud and rapid, and she cries out and yanks her head forward to his face and kisses him frantically on the mouth, grinding and mashing her lips against his, while he goes on moving steadily in and out, as if nothing has happened, as if he were a machine. He knows, of course, what has happened—it's how it happens with Elaine—and sometimes, if he keeps on pounding steadily away, as if he can do this all night long, it will happen again, and that will make him a better lover to her. So he keeps on going. And yes, it happens again, and he's pleased with himself and begins to move against her more swiftly now, to take his pleasure almost as if it were payment for hers. He goes on, and it goes on. But nothing happens. On and on, with Doris trying to help out by moving around him, swinging her legs up his body, locking her legs against his back and shifting her buttocks higher. But still it goes on, and nothing happens. He feels no buildup of heat, none of the usual tightening in the groin and belly, and eventually he finds himself worrying about the time and thinking of his wife's face and his daughter Ruthie's ice skates, white, size four, and Sears, which will close at nine, until his penis, still stubbornly erect, feels as if it belongs to someone else, and he feels like a man out walking a stranger's large, energetic, badly behaved dog. He wants to stop, but she'll know—he's not sure what she'll know, but he doesn't want her to know it—so he goes on, only to discover, at last, that he's lost all his force and that his penis, still large and thick, is doughy. He has no choice now. He pulls his hips away from her, and she unlocks her legs and draws them down to the bed.

"What's wrong?" she asks.

"Nothing. Nothing. That . . . that was wonderful."

He rolls over onto his back and studies the luminous hands of his watch.

"Is everything all right?" She's not really interested or even curious; she's just being polite and isn't quite sure how to go about it.

"Yeah, fine. Of course," he quickly answers. Then, more slowly, "It's just that . . . I dunno. I was getting kind of worried, about the time and all, you know?" He lights a cigarette and inhales deeply and lets the smoke trickle from his lips. He's not really worried about the time, and he doesn't exactly feel guilty toward Elaine. After all, he's had up to a dozen occasions before this to test his capacity to feel guilt for having committed adultery, and it hasn't worked. All he's felt is fear of getting caught at it, like a child cheating at Monopoly. He knows he's supposed to feel guilty, but he simply does not feel guilty for sleeping now and then with other women than Elaine, so long as he knows that he is not in love with the other women and that, therefore, he has in no way jeopardized Elaine's position as his wife. That would make him feel guilty—to imagine another woman than Elaine, to imagine Doris, say, as his wife.

No, something else is oppressing him tonight. He's felt it physically, like a hard-skinned bubble in his gut, since he left work. He looked at his paycheck, and he felt it. He got into his car, studied for a few seconds the torn, faded upholstery, the clutter of tools, toys, food wrappers, kids' mittens and empty beer cans, and he felt it. And then at Irwin's, standing at the bar chatting with Pearl and nodding and listening to men he knows from work and others he knows solely from having drunk with them, workingmen and out-of-work men and a few old drunks who once had been workingmen, he felt that heavy bubble there, too. And he felt it when he first spotted Doris in the corner sitting alone, where he knew she'd be, because she was there almost every Friday night at this time, waiting, if not for him, then for the next-best man in the place. (Doris is not a whore, she's not even promiscuous; she's one of those women who are waiting and who once in a while get bored waiting, so she pretends for an evening that the man she is talking to is the man she happens to be waiting for.) And a few minutes later, when he found himself crossing the barroom toward her, again he felt the bubble, but now it felt painful to him, so that he wondered for a second if he was sick, and he tried to remember what he had eaten for lunch. But it went away as soon as he started talking with Doris, kidding her and being kidded for a while, then asking her if she had any beer in her refrigerator, to which she answered yes, did he want to come up?

And now, after making love to Doris, he feels the hard, metallic bubble once again, still located low in his belly, but expanding toward his chest and groin now and rapidly growing heavier. He suddenly feels frightened, but he doesn't know where to aim his fear—and that only makes him more frightened. What if he has cancer? He's panicking. Jesus H. Christ, what's wrong? He's pulling his clothes back on, slowly, carefully, as if nothing's wrong or unusual, but he's thinking in a wind: My God, I'm going to blow up, my life's all wrong, everything's all wrong, I didn't mean for things to turn out like this, what the fuck's going on?

Bob Dubois does not know what is going on, because, on this snowy night in December in a dark, shabby apartment over a bar on Depot Street, as he draws his clothes back on, he does not know that his life's story is beginning. A man rarely, if ever, knows at the time that his life's story, its one story, is beginning, especially a man like Bob Dubois. Until this night, except for the four years he served in the air force, Bob has lived all his life in Catamount and since high school has worked for the same company, Abenaki Oil Company on North Main Street, at the same trade, repairing oil burners. He is thirty years old, "happily married," with two children, daughters, aged six and four. Both his parents are dead, and his older brother, Eddie, owns a liquor store in Oleander Park, Florida. His wife Elaine loves and admires him, his daughters Ruthie and Emma practically worship him, his boss, Fred Turner, says he needs him, and his friends think he has a good sense of humor. He is a frugal man. He owns a run-down seventy-five-year-old duplex in a working-class neighborhood on the north end of Butterick Street, lives with his family in the front half and rents out the back to four young people he calls hippies. He owns a boat, a thirteen-foot Boston whaler he built from a kit, with a sixteen-horsepower Mercury outboard motor; the boat he keeps shrouded in clear plastic in his side yard from November until the ice in the lakes breaks up; the motor's in the basement. He owns a battered green 1974 Chevrolet station wagon with a tricky transmission. He owes the Catamount Savings and Loan Company—for the house, boat and car—a little over $22,000. He pays cash for everything else. He votes Democratic, as his father did, goes occasionally to mass with his wife and children and believes in God the way he believes in politicians—he knows He exists but doesn't depend on Him for anything. He loves his wife and children. He has a girlfriend. He hates his life.

2

BECAUSE THERE'S NOTHING DRAMATICALLY OR EVEN APparently wrong with his life (many men would envy it), and because Bob Dubois was raised as most poor children are raised (to keep a wary eye on those less fortunate than he, rather than to gaze hungrily in the opposite direction), he is not inclined to complain about his life. In fact, what he hates about his life is precisely what he usually points to with pride: he has a steady job, he owns his own house, he has a happy, healthy family, and so on.

The trouble with his life, if he were to say it honestly, which at this moment in his life he cannot, is that it's over. He's alive, but his life has died. He's thirty years old, and if for the next thirty-five years he works as hard as he has so far, he will be able to stay exactly where he is now, materially, personally. He'll be able to hold on to what he's got. Yet everything he sees in store windows or on TV, everything he reads in magazines and newspapers, and everyone he knows—his boss, Fred Turner, his friends at the shop, his wife and children, even his brother Eddie—tells him that he has a future, that his life is not over, for there's still a hell of a lot more of everything out there and it's just waiting for the taking, and a guy like Bob Dubois, steady, smart, skilled, good-looking and with a sharp sense of humor too—all a guy like that has to do is reach up and grab it. It's the old life-as-ladder metaphor, and everyone in America seems to believe in it. Bob has survived in a world where mere survival is insufficient, so if he complains about its insufficiency, he's told to look below him, see how far he's come already, see how far he's standing above those still at the bottom of the ladder, and if he says, All right, then, fine, I'll just hold on to what I've got, he'll be told, Don't be stupid, Bob, look above you—a new car, a summer house down on the Maine coast where you can fish to your heart's content, early retirement, Bob, college-educated children, and some-day you'll own your own business too, and your wife can look like Lauren Bacall in mink, and you can pick up your girlfriend in Aix-en-Provence in your Lancia, improve your memory, Bob, eliminate baldness, amaze your friends and family.

He stands in front of the Sears, Roebuck store, seem-ing to study the children's clothes worn by the manne-quins, but actually he's thinking about his penis and testicles. The children in the window, schoolchildren, are blond and clear-faced, happy and chic, all good students with bookbags and briefcases, dressed in crew-neck sweaters and corduroy pants, wool wraparound skirts and nylon tights. They're happy.

Snow is falling onto Bob Dubois's cap and shoulders, his hands are in his pants pockets, and he is taking care not to touch his genitals, because they feel large and sensitive to him and have driven away the feeling of that hard, heavy bubble, and he is afraid that if he touches his penis and testicles, they will suddenly feel small and merely functional, and that hard, pressing, stone-heavy bubble will come again. He jiggles his change and keys, reminds himself almost forcibly that he must buy ice skates for Ruthie and enters the store.

The sporting goods department is downstairs in the basement, with appliances and tools. Surprised, Bob finds that he is the only customer on the floor. A portly, red-faced salesman with dark, slicked-back hair and wearing a white shirt and a loud yellow tie crosses from the skis and says, "We're closing." Then, when Bob seems not to have heard him, he asks in a quiet voice, "Can I help you?"

Bob hesitates a second, looks slowly around at the hockey sticks, pucks, pads and skates, as if he has stumbled into ladies' lingerie, and mumbles, "I don't know . . . I'm looking for something for my daughter . . . she's only a kid, she's only six. . . ."

The salesman folds his arms across his chest. "It's nine-oh-five. We're closing."

"Do they still make those old Eddie Bauer skates with the wooden toes? You know the kind I mean? With the tendon guards?"

"Not for small children, no. And not for girls. Look, maybe you can do this tomorrow; we're open all day tomorrow," the salesman says, and makes a half turn toward the skis.

"I played defense, you know. In high school. I played for Bishop Grenier, me and my brother Eddie."

"I'm from Dover," the salesman says, reminded, no doubt, that he's got to drive twenty-eight miles in a snowstorm to get home to a stiff drink and stockinged feet on a hassock and the TV on. "Look, mister, we're closed. If you know what you want, and we got it out here on the floor, I can ring it up for you, but you gotta be quick, okay?"

"Yeah, right," Bob says. "I'm sorry. Skates, I'm looking for skates for my daughter." He squints and looks around him at the counters and displays, as if trying to think of a word. "Figure skates."

"Size?"

In his right front pocket, Bob's hand, as if with a will

of its own, reaches down and forward and cups his crotch, and what he feared would be true is in fact true—his penis is small, ordinary, a minor organ that urinates day and night and now and then ejaculates, and his belly feels full of slag again. "She's only a little kid. It's her first skates," he says.

Reaching forward, the salesman places one hand on Bob's shoulder. "You'll have to do this tomorrow," he says firmly.

Bob wrenches his shoulder away from the man's hand, but the man ignores the gesture and simply walks off. "Hey!" Bob calls. "Hey, pal! You know what?"

The man stops and turns warily back.

"You know what? I don't *want* your damn Sears and Roebuck ice skates! Your twenty-dollar specials! I want something *better* than that! Custom-made, maybe."

"We're closed," the man says in a low voice.

"Better. I want something *better*."

"I'm sorry," the man says, and again he turns away.

Bob looks at the bald spot on the back of the man's head. Bald as a baby's behind, he thinks, and suddenly he remembers deciding never to strike his wife and children, remembers it as if it were a precise fall of light or an odor, when instead it was a complex, clearly defined event that occurred one Sunday afternoon two summers ago, when he and Elaine took Ruthie and Emma out fishing on Lake Sunapee.

Bob had pictured the day differently: a family outing in which Dad teaches the older child to fish; he catches a half-dozen small-mouth bass and she catches a perch or sunfish and is excited and grateful; Mom looks on proudly; Baby coos and plays with her fat fingers. But instead, the bass weren't biting and the mosquitoes were, Ruthie thought fishing was a pointless activity and Elaine had to struggle to keep Emma, barely two that summer and downright annoyed with the project, from falling out of the boat. Though the sun was hot and the lake windless and still, they'd all dressed as if for a cool, breezy day on the water. By ten o'clock in the morning, after less than a half hour of it, they were sweating and wrinkled inside long-sleeved shirts, trousers, caps and jackets. First Bob and then Ruthie stripped to their tee shirts and jeans. A little later, Elaine pulled off her jacket and jersey and sat in the stern in bra and Bermuda shorts, and keeping an eye out for passersby, took off all Emma's clothing.

Finally, Bob gave up trying to fish, and to everyone's relief, started to pack his gear in. He raised anchor and after five or six tries, got the motor started and headed the boat toward shore. All the way in, he sat in the stern and studied his family, their bodies: Ruthie's stalk-like neck and large, dark, blossomy head, her narrow back and arms like twigs, her knobby knees, hard legs and long, bony feet—the body of a thoroughbred filly, it seemed to him, long and awkward now, a little brittle, but filled with promise of beauty, grace and power; and Emma's cherubic pink roundness, her smooth lumps of flesh, all spheres, moons and fruit, and creases where they joined, and her hair, blond and silky, laid over her crown in thin, spiraling loops—to Bob, she had the neatly shapeless, compressed body of a puppy, foolishly good-natured, utterly unconscious of its fragility; and Elaine's short, compact body, her muscular arms and freckled shoulders, her breasts, firm and, for a small woman, large and succulent-looking, her straight back and flat belly, her sturdy, lightly haired legs—Bob thought of the burro that carried Jesus into Jerusalem, a white one, large-eyed and sweet-tempered, diligent, patient, hardy and humble, but pretty too, a slightly glamorous version of an anciently rudimentary type.

All the way in to shore, Ruthie, seated forward near the bow, looked impatiently toward land, as the pine and spruce trees grew larger and more detailed and familiar, while Emma, her naked ass in the air, scrambled about on the flat bottom of the boat, and Elaine, eyes jammed shut, shoved her face, shoulders and chest toward the glow of the sun, until finally the boat scraped the gravelly bottom, and Ruthie jumped out and drew the bow onto land. Elaine scooped up Emma and stepped gingerly to shore and set the naked child on the grass.

Suddenly alone, Bob sat in the stern of the boat, and for an instant he saw these three female bodies in all their transience and fragility, their awful availability to pain and destruction. He was terrified for them, and he swore to himself that he would never strike their bodies, that he would never raise his stony male bulk and iron-hard strength against them. Then, at the same instant, he felt bubbling from deep within his chest a dark hatred for the very vulnerability he was swearing never to offend. He despised it.

Bob studies the bald spot on the back of the salesman's head. There's tissue, thin, pink skin, then eggshell bone, then fleshy brain, he thinks. And that's it. That's all there is between everything and nothing. "I'm sorry," he says in a low voice. "Hey, really, I'm sorry, pal. There's nothing wrong with Sears, you understand. Nothing. I like Sears. Shop here all the time. It's just . . . it's just that . . ."

The salesman has disappeared behind a tepee of skis stacked on their ends and has started to close out his register.

Bob's face twists on its axis, a big, square-faced man writhing on the pole of his own pain. He lets his hands flop uselessly at his sides. "I want . . . I want . . . I want . . ." This isn't going right; everything's coming out wrong. He's supposed to be talking nicely to this salesman, conning him, getting a good buy, a floor model with scuffs selling for wholesale, the way Eddie always gets things for his kid, one-third off and just as good as new, better, even, because new costs too much. Why can't he make this salesman *like* him?

From beyond the skis, the man calls, "They're locking the doors now!"

Bob says nothing, just stands there as if he were a mannequin.

The salesman peeks around the skis and sees Bob hasn't left yet. "Come back tomorrow if you want skates!" he shouts, as if he thinks Bob is hard of hearing or maybe simple-minded.

"Tomorrow?" Slowly Bob's face breaks into a grin,

and he laughs, once. "Hah! Tomorrow. It'll be the same tomorrow," he says. Still grinning, he takes a step forward, as if to explain. "What I want is . . ."

"Look, you better get outa here or I'll hafta call the manager."

Bob stops, and quietly, somberly, he says, "I'm sorry. I just . . . I'm sorry." Turning, he slowly walks away, plods past the copper-toned refrigerators and stoves, the pastel-colored washers and dryers, and up the stairs to street level. A janitor jangling a huge ring of keys lets him out to the sidewalk, where it's snowing heavily. No one else is on the sidewalks, though cars occasionally pass sloppily by on Main Street. Jamming his hands into his jacket pockets, Bob lowers his head against the flying snow and quickly walks the two blocks to his car on Depot Street.

He stands on the slippery sidewalk next to his station wagon, now a long white mound, and stares at the bar across the street, studies the small red neon sign flashing Irwin's name at him like a beacon through the falling snow, then gazes up at the darkened blank windows of Doris's apartment. His bear-like head droops, and glancing at the salt-covered pickup truck, cold and empty, still parked in front of his car, as if deserted in an old war, he looks down Depot Street toward the cannery and the river, and then back up Depot Street to Main. This is his whole world. He knows every square inch of its surface. For a second he studies the candy canes dangling from the lampposts, when all of a sudden, without a thought of it, he doubles up his right fist and holds it out in front of him, as if he were holding a hammer, or as if it were a hammer itself. His left hand remains in his jacket pocket, relaxed and warm, but his right hand is a fist raised against and extended toward the night, and he brings it heel-first swiftly down, smashing it against the windshield on the passenger's side. The blow shatters the outer layer of glass and sends silvery cobwebs across the windshield, the force of the blow spraying the snow in fantails, clearing the windshield instantly. Again, he brings the heel of his fist down, and again, until he has filled the windshield entirely with spiderwebs of broken glass. Then he attacks the side windows, and the snow shudders and falls like a heavy curtain to the street. First he hits the front window on the passenger's side, then the back, then the rear window, until he has worked his way around to the other side of the station wagon, where he makes his way forward to the driver's window, pounding as he goes, as if trying to free a child trapped inside.

Across the street, Pearl, one forearm curled protectively over her large chest, has stepped outside to the sidewalk. "Bob?" she calls. "That you?" Her voice is uncharacteristically small and frightened. She keeps the door behind her open, one hand on it in case she has to retreat quickly.

Bob stops himself and peers through the falling snow to the woman across the street. "Yeah. It's me."

"You okay, Bob?" She lets go of the door and it closes slowly.

Bob sighs heavily and lets his hands fall to his sides. "Yeah. I'm okay."

"You want someone to drive you home, Bob? You had a few too many?"

"No, I'm okay. I'm not drunk," he says. "Just pissed."

Pearl watches him silently and carefully, as if he were a dangerous animal with a leg in a trap.

"Pissed!" he says with a laugh.

"What're you doing?"

He laughs again, a hard, humorless laugh. "What am I doing? That's a good question." Then, suddenly serious, he says, "You don't understand, Pearl. No one knows what I mean. About anything. No one."

"You okay? You want me to get one of the boys inside to drive you home?"

Yes, yes, he's okay, and no, he doesn't need anyone to drive him home, he knows the way. He waves her off, as if she were foolish, and gets into the car and starts the motor. As soon as he turns the ignition key, the windshield wipers, still switched on, come to life and clatter bumpily across the shattered windshield glass.

Ignoring the noise, Bob drops the car into gear, backs slowly uphill away from the pickup, then pulls out to the street and heads down the hill toward the river, where he turns left toward home.

Pearl shakes her head and walks back inside to the bar. She's seen this kind of explosion a hundred times before, not usually this early on a Friday night, though, and never with Bob Dubois doing the exploding. But he wasn't really exploding, she thinks, blowing out of control like some of those guys do when they've been drinking and talking mean for hours, suddenly getting physical and smashing everything in sight. No, the way he walked around his car, pounding and breaking the windows one after the other, was methodical and almost calm. He said he wasn't drunk, and except for the fact that he was breaking the windows of his own car, he didn't seem to be drunk. It was strange. It's the quiet ones, she thinks. They're the guys you have to watch. But she's never thought of Bob Dubois as the quiet type. He's a gregarious man, by and large, generally cheerful and talkative, a man with an eye for the women, she thinks, a man who can please women, too, because he talks one way, kind of reckless and sexy, and behaves another, polite and restrained, so that the woman is left free to get a little excited without being afraid of leading him on too fast, and that way, in the end, when she decides to invite him upstairs for a drink or whatever, she thinks that she has made the decision freely. She thinks it's her decision, not his.

Two of the side windows are shattered completely, the others merely cracked. Hundreds of tiny cubes and chunks of glass lie scattered across the seats and floor. Silvery nebulae spattered over the windshield and rear window and the remaining side windows obscure Bob's vision as he drives, and a cold, snowy wind blows through the car, swirling around his face and chilling his bare hands. He clutches the steering wheel as if afraid he will fall over. To keep the car from slipping and skidding on the slick surface of the streets, he feathers the brake and gas pedal. Between the top of the dashboard and the windshield the wind steadily builds a small, powdery ridge of snow that the heater can't melt. It's dark, except for occasional streetlights, and no cars pass him either way. Bob feels he's riding in a horse-drawn wagon somewhere in Siberia, as if he were being carted late at night from one prison to another. That's how he pictures himself, a passive man, inert and shackled, huddled in straw against the cold and snow in the back of an open cart clattering over icy ruts behind a sick old horse. The horse is driven by a pair of stone-faced guards, brutal-looking men who speak an unknown language in grumbling voices, who seem not to know the name of the man they are hauling, or his crime. The guards, though peasants, are specialists in transporting prisoners from one place of confinement to another. There are hundreds, perhaps thousands, of these silent, impassive transporters with their wagons and tired old horses, men whose ultimate purpose is to keep the prisoners moving, keep them in transit from one cold, isolated place to another, so that at no time will all the prisoners have to be accommodated, housed, fed.

The snow, dry and light, flutters to the earth from a low, dark blue sky, blanketing the roadway and muffling the blows of the horse's hooves against the layers of ice and hardened snow beneath, hushing the creak of the wheels of the cart and cushioning the ride through the town. Silver strings of smoke curl upward from chimneys to the sky. Now and then, light from a window peers across a soft gray yard to the road, but there are no signs that the inhabitants of the town know or care that a new prisoner has arrived. Dubois wants to stand in the back of the cart, to raise his fists and shout, "I'm here! *I'm . . . here!*" but the chains on his wrists and ankles hold him down, forcing him to turn in on himself, as if to warm his cold body before a tiny, carefully tended fire located at the center of his chest.

3

WHEN BOB DUBOIS ENTERS THE HOUSE, HIS WIFE ELAINE is sitting in the living room on the couch watching *Hart to Hart* on TV. She's wearing her flannel nightgown, pink quilted housecoat, and slippers shaped like pink acrylic mounds, and in her hair, large blue plastic curlers. She doesn't look up when her husband enters but goes on watching TV as if she were still alone.

Quietly, Bob shuts the outside door behind him, locks it, shucks his coat and cap and tosses them onto a basket of dirty laundry in the front hall, then walks slowly into the living room, where he drops his body like a sack of potatoes into the slipcovered armchair. It, like the couch, is aimed at the television set, a large console color set placed against the wall opposite the rest of the furniture in the room. To the left of the TV is a skinny, gaudily decorated Christmas tree, its lights going on and off like channel markers. At the base of the tree a half-dozen brightly wrapped packages have been arranged with care, spread out from the trunk of the tree so as to give the impression of plenitude.

"I'm sorry I'm late," Bob says in a low voice, apologizing to the TV screen. His face is red and puffy, his blue eyes are still wet and his nose is running freely. With shoulders slumped forward and hands hanging limply between his legs like pendulums, the man looks like a thrashed and deserted dog.

Sitting back stiffly but still watching Mr. and Mrs. Hart get dressed for a party, Elaine says, "Did you get the skates?" It's an accusation, not a question. She's a small woman, almost tiny, with a handsome head, especially in profile. Her sharp Roman nose and crisp chin clarify a face that's otherwise ordinary and vague, made so by Elaine herself, because, despite what everyone has told her, she doesn't think she's especially pretty and works at hiding her face from other people's scrutiny.

Silent for a few seconds, Bob finally says, "No. I didn't get the fucking skates."

"Oh," she answers, and then, without looking away

from the TV, she touches her hair curlers, as if suddenly frightened, strokes the several strands of reddish-brown hair that lick the nape of her neck, quickly lowers her hands and locks them around her knees. "So, where'd you go? Since work."

"Irwin's for a while. That's where I called you from. Then Sears. The skates at Sears were lousy . . . and expensive."

"Oh," she says. "I was worried. Because of the snow and all."

An advertisement appears on the screen. A jubilant, pink-faced family in pajamas and plaid bathrobes gathered around a modestly decorated, dark green tree is being photographed by the father of the family with his new Polaroid camera. Elaine turns away from the screen and for the first time looks at her husband's face and realizes that he's been crying. He looks at her, and away. Then silence, and she goes on staring at him.

She says his name, as if not believing the man next to her is really Bob. Her hands move to her mouth, and she brushes her lips with her fingertips, as if trying to read unuttered words from them. In the nearly ten years she's known him, she's never seen him like this. She's seen him angry, hurt, glad or sad, but she's never seen him cry, though she has on a few occasions wished he would break down and cry. There was the time when his father finally died from the cancer, and the summer after that, when his mother died so suddenly, and the time Elaine confessed to having slept with Bob's best friend, Avery Boone, and when they thought Ruthie would die from the spinal meningitis and she didn't, and then they thought she'd never walk again but she did—all those times he had simply tightened up, like a man being photographed by the police, a man afraid of being identified later by witnesses as the rapist, the burgler, the driver of the getaway car.

Slowly, without looking at her, he lifts his swollen right hand, opens and extends it so she can see the swelling and discoloration along the heel of the hand. "I broke . . . I broke all the windows of the car."

"You *what?*"

"I said I broke all the windows of the car. Don't worry, I'll get 'em fixed. I'll tell the insurance company some kids vandalized it or something."

"Broke the windows? Why?" she asks calmly. This is her way. In a crisis she is calm and patient. She saves her rage and alarm, her joy and her grief, even, for later, when she has got all the information.

"I don't know, Elaine. I don't know, I just got . . . so damned . . . mad. You know?"

"Are you drunk?"

"No, no. I had a couple of beers at Irwin's, that's all. Nothing."

"Then why are you . . . why were you so mad? Did you get fired? What *happened*, Bob?"

"Nothing. Nothing *happened*." He finally turns and faces her. He knows she's not angry at him, she's only confused, and now he wants her to understand. He wants her to know what he knows, to feel what he feels.

Crossing from the couch to his chair, Elaine kneels and cups his injured hand gently in both of hers, as if confining a small, delicate animal there.

"I went to Sears. I went there and looked at the skates there, you know, for Ruthie, and came back to the car . . . and I got so damned mad . . . the skates were expensive . . . I got mad at everything, though, mad at everything . . . then I just got to pounding on the car windows, and they broke. And then coming home, I felt . . . coming home I felt worse than I've ever felt in my life. I can't even say it, how bad I felt. And then all of a sudden I just . . . I just started crying. *Me!*" he says, almost shouting, his voice breaking, his face forcing a grotesque grin over its surface. "I mean, I don't know what's the matter with me, what was the matter, I mean, because I'm okay now, but just like that, all of a sudden I'm crying like a baby. Me! Crying like a fucking baby!"

"Oh, Bob, don't," she croons. "Don't." She strokes his hand lovingly.

"No, no, I'm okay now. No kidding, I'm fine now. It's just that . . . it's just I was so *surprised*, you know?

Because I was so mad and all. And I have to tell you, I have to tell . . ."

"No, honey, it's okay. I understand. Don't worry, honey."

"No, you don't understand. I have to tell you how I felt."

"I know, baby." She goes on stroking his hand, soothing and trying to heal it with her touch.

"No, Elaine, you really don't understand," he says, pulling his hand away. "Listen to me. It's this place. This goddamned place. It stinks. And it's my job at Abenaki, that fucking job. And it's this whole fucking life. This stupid life. All of a sudden, this whole life came to me, it showed me itself. I had the feelings before I saw it, and I didn't know what the feelings came from, until I saw it, and then I saw this life, this whole fucking life, and I knew what the feelings came from. I saw that there's no way out of it for me. It's like I'm my father all over again. I'm all grown up now, and all of a sudden I'm my own fucking father over again. Just like by the time he was my age he got to be his father. The both of them, dumb Frenchmen down at the goddamned mill running a lathe, the both of them, their whole livelong lives! Only difference now, the mill is turned into a fucking pea cannery where only women work, so I'm fixing broken oil burners for Fred Turner, crawling in and out of boiler rooms and basements *my* whole livelong life!"

Elaine is silent for a second. Then in a quiet voice she says, "We have a good life, honey. We do."

Bob looks at his feet. "My father, when I was a kid, used to play a record over and over, I don't know where the hell he got it, he only bought the record player for Ma and me and Eddie to play, but he had this one record of his own, a forty-five by Frank Sinatra called 'Destiny's Darling,' a really stupid song. But he loved it, and he used to have a few beers and play that record over and over, until he'd get this kind of dreamy look on his face, sitting there in his chair listening to this song and pretending he wasn't who he was. And me and

Eddie, we'd see him doing that and we'd laugh, you
know? We'd laugh at him, because we knew we were
different, we'd never do anything so stupid as our old
man, work all day in a fucking mill and come home and
have a couple of beers and play a goddamned record by
Frank Sinatra about being destiny's darling. I mean,
Jesus! What an asshole, I'd think. I was only a kid, I
was in high school then, me and Eddie, but being such
hotshot hockey players and all, getting written up in the
papers and all, we thought *we* were destiny's darlings.
Only now it's fifteen years later, and here I am. Just like
my old man. Only instead of coming home and sitting in
my chair and playing 'Destiny's Darling,' I'm watching
fucking *Hart to Hart* or some damned thing on TV. And
if my kids were a few years older, they'd be laughing at
me, the way me and Eddie used to laugh at my old man.
Look at the asshole, they'd say, Ruthie and Emma,
bigshot cheerleaders in high school and all, look at the
asshole, he thinks he's Robert Wagner or somebody,
they'd say, he doesn't know he's half drunk and covered
with soot from other people's furnaces and doesn't have
a pot to piss in and never will.''

"Oh, honey, we have a good life. We do."

"Maybe *you* do. Or at least you *think* you do. Because you happen to be living the way you always wanted
to live, the way when you were a kid you hoped you'd
live. Because of your old man's taking off on you and
your ma like that, and your ma having to work herself
practically to death at the cannery by the time she was
forty-five. But me, I don't know, I thought it was going
to be different. Me and Ave Boone, we used to talk
about building a boat and going to Australia or someplace in the South Pacific and making a killing. We used
to say that, 'We'll make a killing.' If I said those words
now, it'd be like sand in my mouth, because I'd be lying
and I'd know it. No fucking way I'll ever make a killing.
Ave, he did it. He got out. He built his boat, just like he
always wanted to, and he got out. It took him till he was
almost thirty, but he got out . . .''

"Alone," she interrupts.

"Yeah, alone. But that's the way he is. He likes it that way. But he got out, that's the point, and Eddie got out too. Eddie made a killing too. Ave Boone in his boat on the Keys, and Eddie wheeling and dealing in central Florida, while I sit up here in the snow and ice and darkness and fix people's oil burners and wonder how the fuck I can afford a pair of ice skates for my kid for Christmas."

"But we have the kids, the house . . ." she says.

He doesn't hear her. "One time when we were kids, Ave came over to my house, and he had this advertisement he'd cut out of some fancy New York magazine he'd seen in the dentist's office, and we were sitting around in my bedroom talking about what we were going to do after school or something, we were maybe seniors then. And he pulled this ad out of his wallet and unfolded it and handed it to me. It was a whiskey ad, and there was this handsome guy wearing his trousers rolled up to his knees and no shirt on, walking ashore on some tropical island. And he's got this case of Haig & Haig on his shoulder and a dinghy on the shore behind him and a nice forty-foot catamaran sitting out in the bay. Eddie was out of school by then and was working at Thom McAn's on Main Street selling shoes, but he was already figuring out what he was going to do in Florida a few years later, and I was already thinking about maybe joining the air force so I wouldn't get drafted because I didn't have anything like Eddie's epilepsy to keep me out or Ave's belief that he could con the draft board into a four-F, because neither of us particularly wanted to go to Vietnam and get fucking shot. Anyhow, Ave shows me this clipping like it's a letter from Hugh Hefner asking him to spend a week with the Playmate of the Month or something, and he says to me, 'There. That's me,' he says." Bob is silent for a few seconds. Then he sighs. "You wanta know what I said? I'll tell you. I said, 'That's me too.' "

Elaine takes his hand in hers again. "Honey, honey . . ."

Bob brushes his eyes with the back of his other hand. "I just don't know what happened. Ol' Ave, he's probably right this minute walking ashore with a case of Canadian Club or Chivas Regal on his shoulder, and my brother Eddie is down there dancing cheek to cheek with his wife in a fancy nightclub while his accountant works late figuring out another tax dodge for him. And what am I doing? Sitting in Catamount in a fucking chair with the stuffing coming out so bad it has to be covered with slipcovers because I can't afford to get it upholstered or buy another one." He plucks at the arm of the chair as if clearing it of lint. "I sit up here feeling sorry for myself. Crying like a fucking baby. Just like my old man. Only he didn't have brains enough to cry or get mad and break all his car windows. He sat in his chair with the stuffing coming out and listened to Frank Sinatra tell him he was destiny's darling. Then he got old and then he died. And that's all she wrote."

"Come on, honey. It's Christmas . . ." she says.

"It sure as shit *is* Christmas," he snarls. Then, after a few seconds, in a low voice he says, "I don't know, Elaine, I'm sorry. Maybe I'm having a nervous breakdown or something. I've never felt this way before. I don't know, but I do know I can't take it anymore. Maybe I'm freaking out. It's this place, maybe, the cold and the dark . . . and no money. And it's because I've had this look at myself, at my life, you know? I've looked at it, and all I can see is my father all over again. And his father. And on and on. All the way back to the fucking Dark Ages. Since the beginning of fucking time. I thought . . . I thought it was going to be *different*. You know? Not necessarily like the picture of Avè Boone coming ashore with a case of whiskey on his shoulder, I mean. But different. But now, tonight, I saw it all. I saw myself. Clear as crystal. I saw myself, and I realized that it'll never be any different. *Never*. It's like all these years I've just been waiting around to win the state lottery or something. Like that's the only way my life, our life, can be different. The only way it can be the way I thought it would be is if I win the goddamned state lottery. You know what that means, Elaine?"

"No. But it's not true anyhow. We have a *good* life. We *do*."

Ignoring her, he says, "It means we're dead. That's what it means. Dead."

"No, honey. No, it doesn't. You're just depressed, that's all."

"You're right, I'm depressed. But for Christ's sake, Elaine, there's a *reason!* Don't you think people get depressed for a *reason* sometimes? That's what I'm trying to get you to understand, for Christ's sake. Try. Please try to understand. Because you're dead too. Not just me. You know you are too. Way down deep inside yourself, you know you're dead. And the girls too. They're as dead as we are, unless they get lucky. We're all dead. Like my father and mother, and like your mother too. We only *think* we're alive. We watch that fucking TV screen, and we think we're like those people there, fucking Hart and Hart, and that makes us forget that we're not like those people at all. We're dead. They're pretty pictures. We're dead people.

"I listen to Fred Turner down at the shop tell me how pretty soon he'll take me off night call so I don't have to go out nights and Sundays anymore to fix people's goddamned broken furnaces, and I think I'm alive. I start to thinking I'm like Fred and someday I'll be a big guy with my own company, even though I didn't have a father with a company to hand it to me like Fred did, and pretty soon I'll be driving around in a white Caddie with my company's initials on the number plates, DOC, Dubois Oil Company. But Fred went to fucking college, and I can barely balance my own checkbook, and besides, if he takes me off night call I won't get any more overtime and we won't be able to handle the mortgage payment next month, so I say, No, Fred, for Christ's sake, don't take me off night call, I need the fucking overtime. That's being dead, Elaine. Dead.

"And I come home to this house and see how if I don't paint it this spring the rot's going to get it by next winter, only I can't afford to paint the goddamned thing. And I can't afford to put storm windows on it so we don't have to burn so much oil, which I can't afford either anyhow, and then I look out the window at that damned boat I still owe money on and which I wouldn't have bought and built if my friend Ave Boone hadn't taken off for the Keys with his boat, and I realize that I can't afford to take off a week from work in the spring just so I can use the fucking thing anyhow.

"And every time I drive that car I still owe money on I realize I'll be lucky to get another month off the damned thing before the fucking transmission goes, which I can't afford to have fixed if it does go. And that's being dead, Elaine. Day and night, week after week, year in and year out, it's the same, until finally my body catches up with the rest of me, and it dies too."

He removes his hand from hers and lights a cigarette. She remains kneeling at his side, and the television goes on yakking in the background. "I listen to my brother Eddie on the fucking phone telling me about his new house on the lake in Florida and his new boat and how he sends his kid to horseback lessons, you know? And at first I want to kill him. But then I think, Hey, Eddie's my brother and he's only a couple years older than me, and he's not really any smarter than me or better educated, so I must be alive too, like Eddie, 'cause he sure as shit seems alive to me. So it's you and me and our girls, just like Eddie and Sarah and Jessica. Only it's Eddie and Sarah and Jessica in Oleander Park, and it's his liquor store that's doing so great he's going to open up a second store and trade in his boat on a bigger one—that's what he told me last time he called. And it's me in Catamount, New Hampshire, and it's Abenaki Oil Company, and me on night call because I can't meet my bank payments without the overtime. No . . . if Eddie's alive, I'm dead, Elaine."

"Honey, honey, honey," she says. "It's just because it's Christmas and all. You're worried. That's all. And you've been working too hard, all these nights and Saturdays and Sundays being on call. It's worse than being a doctor. You've just been working too hard. And we're not like Eddie and Sarah, you know that. We don't *want* to be, either. We *love* each other, Bob. We don't *need* all those material things they've got, to be happy. We've always said that."

He snorts and looks above the TV set at a spot on the wall, and though he is thinking of Doris Cleeve, he says to his wife, "Sure, we love each other. But if we had some of those material things Eddie's got, if I had a fucking future, then maybe there'd be some kind of chance for romance. Hah! A chance for romance! Maybe we could go on a little vacation in the Caribbean, you know? Make love in the moonlight, drink rum punches from a coconut. Actually *do* the things we just get to think about. I wish you could understand what I'm trying to say to you." He thinks of Doris Cleeve in her shabby apartment above Irwin's, her thick legs and belly, her weary melancholy, her alcoholism, and he says, "It all started with those skates. . . ." His shoulders sag, his eyes fill, and he shakes his head from side to side as if saying no.

Above and to the right of the television set, a small plaster crucified Jesus gazes sadly down. Bob studies the object, and as he does every time his gaze happens to fall on it, he wonders how he can improve the way it looks. By itself and because of its smallness, the crucifix looks isolated and pathetic. The way it looks now, has looked from the day years ago when Elaine first hung it on the wall, the thing bothers Bob. He'd change it somehow, but if he surrounded it with pictures or wall hangings, framed mottoes or bric-a-brac, he wouldn't really be able to respect it. It would be a decoration, like everything else. On the other hand, if he swapped it for a larger crucifix, one of those massive and detailed crosses with a Jesus so large you can see the awful expression on His face, it would be scary. He'd think he was in a church or a priest's house or a monastery. Better to leave the thing the way it is.

"Bob," Elaine says quietly. "Bob, let's move."

"What?"

"I mean it. Let's move, Bob. Let's start over. Let's move and start over." She's smiling up into his large, sad face. "Let's just sell the house, sell the car and the boat, and even sell the furniture, and start over someplace else. *Lots* of people do it."

Bob screws his face into a question mark. "Move?" He's never really put the possibility to himself, never truly thought about it. Moving was what other people did, people who were just starting out in life, like Eddie back when he left for Oleander Park, or people without family responsibilities, like Ave Boone, or people who had no choice. "Now? Sell everything?" Would it be giving up, admitting defeat to everyone? "Not the boat," he says. "I've only got three more payments on the boat."

"Okay, fine, honey. Not the boat. And not the car, if you want. Things we need. But everything else. Then we can take the money and go to California, or go down to Arizona, if you want. Anywhere. I don't care. Anywhere, so long as it's somewhere else, where there's a future for us. We're not dead," she says. "We're not. It's this *place* that's dead."

"I don't know about California. I don't know anybody out west, you realize. I mean, you can't just wander into a town and start your life over," he says. "What about Florida? Oleander Park. With Eddie. You know."

Elaine lapses into silence and scowls slightly. She says, "Well . . ." then stops.

Elaine does not like Eddie, even though he's her husband's only brother, and she pities Eddie's wife Sarah, because of the way Eddie treats her, and she thinks their daughter Jessica is stupid and a little on the homely side. Bob always insists that Eddie means well, and Sarah gets her kicks from suffering, she's a whiner, and though whiners drive him crazy, that's all she is, so he can ignore her, and Elaine should too, and Jessica, poor kid, she's just going through an awkward stage. Consequently, Elaine rarely voices her feelings about them, and until now she has felt immense relief whenever, after Eddie has made his annual pitch, Bob has turned him down. The pitch runs like this: "Listen, Bob, you move the fucking wife and kids down, I'll put your French ass to work tomorrow morning managing the fucking store in Oleander Park while I set up that new cocksucker I been planning over in Lakeland, and also I got a few cute little real estate deals on the back burner I can keep myself busy with and maybe cut you a piece of, and then in a few years, if you're still interested, we can work out a partnership deal, maybe open a goddamned chain of stores, like Martignetti's down in Massachusetts, and get cocksucking big, you know? Big. The fucking Dubois brothers. Like those Dunfey brothers from Hampton who run all those hotels now. The Dubois Boys. Right? Just like the old days, only now it's palm trees and all that tanned pussy in bikinis. Sand in your shoes, Bob. Think about it. That's all I'm asking, just think about it. Because if you ever get sick of shoveling all that fucking snow, all you got to do is call me up, brother, and you got a job in Oleander Park, a job that a hell of a lot of guys'd give their left nut for. So think about it, okay?''

Bob, as recently as a month ago at Thanksgiving, when Eddie last called, has always smiled and said thanks, but he spent ten years learning how to fix oil burners, a trade there wasn't much call for in Florida, and besides, he was happy. He had a good job, a nice house, a loving wife and two healthy kids, a future too, one that was connected to his past and made sense to him. Throwing all that away and starting over in Florida didn't make sense to him.

"Well what?" Bob asks his wife. "Eddie's doing all right in Florida, you know that. He has from the first down there. And he wants me to come down. You know that.''

"Yes, sure, I know. It's just . . . we've talked about all this before. The Florida business and Eddie's offers, and you were the one . . . it was always you, you were the one who said Eddie would be hard to work for, and the idea of running a liquor store always seemed boring to you, I thought.''

She stands and walks to the TV and snaps it off, and

the room suddenly seems vacant, as if they have wandered into it in search of someone not at home. "Let's go to bed, Bob."

"I'll get the skates for Ruthie tomorrow," he says. "First thing in the morning."

"I know, honey. I know." She extends her hand, and he leans forward in the chair, takes her hand in his and rises. Together, they switch off the lights and slowly walk up the stairs to bed.

4

BEFORE BOB AND ELAINE DUBOIS SLEEP ON THIS SNOWY night in December, they have one more conversation that is of significance to them both.

They are lying on their backs side by side in darkness, he in his underwear, she in her flannel nightgown. She has wrapped her curlers in a nylon net. When, in a familiar form of invitation, he lays one leg over hers at the thigh, she quickly slides her hip against his.

Bob speaks first. "You know something? Ever since we were kids, I was the big silent one and Eddie was the little guy who did all the talking. But actually, I was a lot smarter than Eddie. In school, I mean. I was even smarter than Ave Boone, but he just never tried, he didn't give a shit then, just like now. But I *got* things faster than Eddie did. He was always just this side of flunking, and I did okay in school. And he knew I was smarter than he was, so he was kind of jealous of me and got a real kick whenever he could make me look stupid, which was easy for him when we were kids, because he was almost two years older than me, even though he was only a grade ahead of me in school. But I was jealous of him too, because he could talk so good, and all I could do was stand there like a big dummy.

"The only time we were even, when we were really equals, was when we both skated for Bishop Grenier those three years before he graduated. He was a forward, and I was a defenseman, and we were the best combination in the state for three years running. The Dubois brothers. Remember? The Granite Skates, they called us in the Boston papers. That was the year I was a junior and we won the New England Championship down in the old Boston Arena. If it was today instead of 1966, we'd both have gone to college on scholarship. UNH, probably. But hockey wasn't such a big college sport in those days. Anyhow, we were a team then, me and Eddie. And we were real close then. You know? Real close."

"You want to move to Florida, don't you?"

He sighs heavily and says nothing for several seconds. "I didn't before"

"But you do now."

"Naw, I just don't want to buy Ruthie's skates," he says. "If we move to Florida, I won't hafta buy her any skates for Christmas."

"Be serious. You do want to move to Florida, don't you?"

"Well . . . yes, I do."

"Right away? Right after Christmas?"

"No. No, there's something I want to do first." He slides his leg down her thighs to her knees, then back again.

"There is? What?"

"You know what I want to do first. And I'm not moving to Florida till I do it."

"Now?"

"Is it okay? You wanta check the calendar?"

"It's okay."

Bob turns, places one hand between her legs and kisses his wife on the mouth, gently, gently, then more intensely, and when she starts to move beneath his hand, he kisses her fiercely, until he can feel himself huge and stiff, and then he finds himself fucking her with marvelous, thrilling force, while she turns and writhes under him, pushes her pelvis back at him more and more rapidly, in their old, familiar, utterly natural rhythm, the rhythm it took them years to discover, a rhythm they'll never lose, they know, because it belongs to them alone,

Bob and Elaine, his body and hers, in the one clear linkage either body can make to the other. They push smoothly on, one against the other, until first she sighs, and then seconds later he feels himself spread warmly out from the center of his body, and they stop.

For a few moments, they lie face to face in silence together, she on her back with her nightgown around her waist and her legs snaked around his waist, he with his weight resting on his elbows, and she says in a tiny voice, "Don't ever do it with anyone else."

"I won't."

"I don't think I could bear the idea. I could bear the reality, but not the idea. You know what I mean?"

"Yeah. I know. Me too. I couldn't bear the idea. I don't think I could even bear the reality," he adds. "If I knew about it, I mean."

"Good," she says. "Me neither." Then she brings her legs down, easing him from her.

Battérie Maconnique

1

IT'S AS IF THE CREATURES RESIDING ON THIS PLANET IN THESE years, the human creatures, millions of them traveling singly and in families, in clans and tribes, traveling sometimes as entire nations, were a subsystem inside the larger system of currents and tides, of winds and weather, of drifting continents and shifting, uplifting, grinding, cracking land masses. It's as if the poor forked creatures who walk, sail and ride on donkeys and camels, in trucks, buses and trains from one spot on this earth to another were all responding to unseen, natural forces, as if it were gravity and not war, famine or flood that made them move in trickles from hillside villages to gather along the broad, muddy riverbanks lower down and wait for passage on rafts down the river to the sea and over the sea on leaky boats to where they collect in eddies, regather their lost families and few possessions, set down homes, raise children and become fruitful once again. We map and measure jet streams, weather patterns, prevailing winds, tides and deep ocean currents; we track precisely scarps, fractures, trenches and ridges

39

where the plates atop the earth's mass drive against one another; we name and chart the Southeast and Northeast Trades and the Atlantic Westerlies, the tropical monsoons and the doldrums, the mistrals, the Santa Ana and the Canada High; we know the Humboldt, California and Kuroshio currents—so that, having traced and enumerated them, we can look on our planet and can see that all the way to its very core the sphere inhales and exhales, rises and falls, swirls and whirls in a lovely, disciplined dance in time. It ages and dies and is born again, constantly, through motion, creating and recreating its very self, like a uroborous, the snake that devours its tail.

Seen from above, then, the flight of a million and a half Somali men, women and children with their sick and dying beasts out of the drought- and war-shattered region of Ogaden in the Horn of Africa would resemble the movement of the Southwest Monsoon Current, for instance, which in the heat of July moves slowly, almost imperceptibly out of the Red Sea just north of Ethiopia and Somalia, across the Gulf of Aden to the Indian Ocean, where it joins the Northwest Monsoon Drift and dips southward along the subcontinent, by winter looping back again toward Kenya and Tanzania, bringing rain to Mombasa and Dar es Salaam and filling the great inland waterways and lakes. The movement of the Somalis would seem inevitable, unalterable and mindless; and because we would have watched it the way we watch weather, it would seem tragic. We could not argue over who was at fault or what should have been done; ideology would seem a form of vanity, a despicable self-indulgence. We would rise from our shaded seat in front of our hut alongside the dusty road that leads from the treeless Damisa hills in Ethiopia to our village near the trading town of Samaso in Somalia, and we would step forward onto the road with a cup of water and a small bowl of millet and whey for the family we have been watching approach for the last hour, a man, tall and gaunt, ageless, leading a half-blind camel with a pack of sticks tied to its back, and, coming along behind, a

woman with a scrawny child in her arms, and behind her
yet another cadaverous child. We let them sleep under
their thin blankets beside our hut, and in the morning, as
the sun breaks across the brown plain, give them bread
and water and point the way southeast to Samaso, another thirty kilometers, and say the name of the man
who is said to own a truck for transporting to the coast
and the refugee camps there the people who come down
from the hills, the Somali-speaking nomads who have
raised cattle in that wilderness for a thousand years and
who now must flee famine, drought and the war, the
endless war between the Ethiopians with their Russian
guns and Cuban allies and the soldiers of the Western
Somalia Liberation Front. The man, his black skin cut
through almost to the bone of his face with worry and
fatigue, nods and repeats the name of the man with the
truck. He will take you to Kismayu, we say,just as we
told the others, for nearly every day they come. The
camps are there, on the coast. There is food and shelter
there, and people who will know how to cure your
children of their sores. The man asks if there will be a
price for this transportation. We shrug, as if we don't
know. He nods. He understands. Perhaps he will be able
to sell his wretched camel. If not, he knows that one
night soon, on the cold ground outside the tiny crossroads village of Samaso, they will die. First the children
will die, then probably the man, and then the woman.
And tomorrow or the day after that, another family will
come down from the hills and will cross the dry, hot
plain along the rutted road, will stop for the night beside
our hut and in the morning will move on to the same
fate.

IN THESE YEARS, THE EARLY 1980S. MOST EVENTS AND
processes that have been occurring for millennia continue
to occur, some of them silently, slowly, taking place an
inch at a time miles below the surface of the earth,
others noisily, with smoke and fire, revolution, war and
invasion, taking place on the surface. We measure the
geological change in millimeters per annum, feel nothing

move beneath our feet and conclude, therefore, that nothing has happened. By the same token, when we read in newspapers and hear from the evening news broadcasts that there is revolution in Iran, war in Iraq, foreign soldiers and tanks in Afghanistan, because each new day brings a surfeit of such news, blotting out the news of the day before, news of Israelis in Lebanon replacing accounts of Russians in Afghanistan, Americans in Grenada replacing Israelis in Lebanon, we conclude here, too, that nothing has happened.

The metabolic rate of history is too fast for us to observe it. It's as if, attending to the day-long life cycle of a single mayfly, we lose sight of the species and its fate. At the same time, the metabolic rate of geology is too slow for us to perceive it, so that, from birth to death, it seems to us who are caught in the beat of our own individual human hearts that everything happening on this planet is what happens to us, personally, privately, secretly. We can stand at night on a high, cold plain and look out toward the scrabbled, snow-covered mountains in the west, the same in a suburb of Denver as outside a village in Baluchistan in Pakistan, and even though beneath our feet continent-sized chunks of earth grind inexorably against one another, go on driving one or the other continent down so as to rise up and over it, as if desiring to replace it on the map, we poke with our tongue for a piece of meat caught between two back teeth and think of sarcastic remarks we should have made to our brother-in-law at dinner.

While we stand and think of trivialities on the plain in Baluchistan, the crust of the earth, in plates, diverges, carves long, bottomless trenches beneath the sea between India and Antarctica and shoves the last, lost child of Gondwanaland north into Eurasia, attaches India and Pakistan to China, Afghanistan and Iran with such irresistible force that the subcontinent bends and dips down at the line of convergence, buckles and crumbles at the edges and heaps up, as if with the blade of a colossal shovel, the Himalayas and the Hindu Kush, a thousand miles of mountain peaks twenty and twenty-five thousand feet high, the very mountain peaks and passes we can see in the distance and have watched night after night all our brief, distracted lives.

And while we wait with one son, the eldest, and a brother-in-law from Peshawar who has told us of the money to be made leading rich Afghans down from the passes to the refugee camps, we hope that he is right, we hope that the Afghans will indeed be wealthy and will be eager to pay us handsomely for escorting them down the mountain pathways, where thieves hide and wait. But at the same time, we know the brother-in-law is wrong, for we have heard for years that the Afghans who flee into Pakistan are poor. It is the Iranians, we have heard, who are rich, the merchants who, crossing their border at Kuhak, face the desert and then the mountains of the Makran Range and turn south, heading for Karachi and the sea and eventually to America. Those who live down there, near the Iranian border, they are the ones who grow fat from escorting refugees, while we risk our lives up here with the Afghans for nothing.

But the brother-in-law, an arrogant man who has played professional football in Lahore and therefore believes he knows what we do not, has insisted that we can make a year's money from a few days' work with little risk, and to convince him that he is wrong (or so we have said to him) we have agreed to come up here with the boy, who is old enough to carry a rifle and walks behind us. Bandits, murderers, madmen—they live up here near the snow year-round and prey on travelers without guns, so we, the boy, and even the brother-in-law, make a show of our weapons.

As we climb closer and closer to the snow, we know that now they are watching us from behind rocks and from cliffs overhead. Then, after a long while of climbing, we emerge from a narrow defile, and before us, beneath a long, pale yellow ridge and in a large wedge of shadow, there is suddenly a mound of snow in the path, hard, old snow the shape and size of a collapsed tent, and we see the bodies in the snow, a woman and two men and a child, throats slashed, old blood pinking the whiteness around them, clothes partially wrenched off and torn back from frozen bodies, bags and cases opened and scattered, papers, clothing, household utensils tossed aside in an angry hunt for coins.

You see now, we say to the brother-in-law. They are poor.

He pulls thoughtfully at his mustache, and the boy comes up alongside him and sees the Afghans lying in the snow, and frightened, he turns in a slow circle, searching the rocks and crevices around us.

There are plenty more Afghans coming, the brother-in-law says in a low voice. But . . . perhaps another day would be better, he adds, and we turn and commence making our way back down the mountain to the village.

The brother-in-law is a fool. And we are a fool for not believing what we know is true, what we know with our deepest brain, the one embedded in the very center of our skull, where we know that forever, from the beginning of time, the only outsiders who have come through here and have needed us to help them have been poor, sad, frightened creatures running from some army.

Yes, there are more coming, we say, when soon the descent is not so difficult and we can walk alongside one another again. And they will keep on coming until after we are gone and the boy is gone and even after that. And they will always be poor. You cannot help the poor, not when you also are poor. Let the bandits have them, we say.

I suppose you are right, the brother-in-law murmurs, which pleases us, but we say nothing of it to him.

SYSTEMS AND SETS, SUBSYSTEMS AND SUBSETS, PATTERNS and aggregates of water, earth, fire and air—naming and mapping them, learning the intricate interdependence of the forces that move and convert them into one another, this process gradually provides us with a vision of the planet as an organic cell, a mindless, spherical creature whose only purpose is to be born as rapidly as it dies and whose general principle informing that pur-

pose, as if it were a moral imperative, is to keep moving.
Revolve around points and rotate on axes, whirl and
twirl and loop in circles, ellipses, spirals and long curves
that soar across the universe and disappear at last at the
farthest horizon of our human imagination only to reap-
pear here behind us in the daily life of our body, in our
food, shit and piss, our newborn babies and falling-down
dead—just keep on moving, keep breeding and pissing
and shitting, keep on eating the planet we live on, keep
on moving, alone and in families and tribes, in nations
and even in whole species: it's the only argument we
have against entropy. And it's not truly an argument;
it's a vision. It's a denial in the form of an assertion, a
rebuttal in the form of an anecdote, which means that
it's not a recounting, it's an accounting; not a representation, a presentation.

The universe moves, and everything in it moves, and
by transferring its parts, it and everything in it down to
the smallest cell are transformed and continue. Water,
earth, fire and air. To continue, just to go on, with
entropy lurking out there, takes an old-fashioned, Bibli-
cal kind of heroism. That the seas move, that the waters
flow from gulfs across whole oceans along continents
and back again, is marvelous. That the continents themselves move, that they separate from one another, re-
group and gather themselves into mountain ranges,
plateaus, vast savannas and grassy veldts, is a wonder.
That far beneath the deepest seas the grinding of the
plates that carry those continents generates sufficient
heat to melt rock and erupt in fiery volcanoes, making
high, conical islands appear in the North Atlantic and
South Pacific where, before, dark waters for millennia
rolled uninterruptedly, this is truly worthy of admiration. And what is marvelous to us, what fills us with
wonder and admiration, we must emulate, or we die. If
the stubborn determination of the Somali tribes to find
food, water and peace, even though they must cross
deserts alone to get there and must often perish along
the way, seems to us marvelous, and if the Afghans'
willingness to face ice and snow and murderous bandits

in the high passes of the Hindu Kush rather than let government soldiers enter their villages and shoot them for having given shelter one night to a few ragtag local mujahedeen guerrillas, if their decision to move away and start over elsewhere seems wonderful to us, and if the flight of a half-million starving Khmer peasants out of Kampuchea into Thailand, where they are greeted by sympathetic but terrified Thai officials who drive the Khmer back to where the Vietnamese army wages war against the scattered remnant of Pol Pot's suicidal regime by burning the few remaining rice fields, if that persistent, relentless determination to go on knocking at the Thai gate until someone finally opens it moves us to admiration, then we must do the same. We must cross deserts alone and often perish along the way, we must move to where we can start our lives over, and when we get there, we must keep on knocking at the gate, shouting and pounding with our fists, until those who happen to be keepers of the gate are also moved to admiration and open the gate. We are the planet, fully as much as its water, earth, fire and air are the planet, and if the planet survives, it will only be through heroism. Not occasional heroism, a remarkable instance of it here and there, but constant heroism, systematic heroism, heroism as governing principle.

A CURIOUS TRAIT IN HUMANS, ONE THAT GIVES AID AND comfort to the dark angels of entropy and makes it all the more difficult to establish here on earth once and for all a Heroic Age, is the ease with which we take everything personally. At sea level, we cannot even see the Gulf Stream; yet if it benefits us, we think it's only right it does so. And standing on the earth, we cannot feel it move beneath our feet, but if we could, we would wonder what we had done wrong this morning and say ten Hail Marys, just in case. All the more, then, when a hurricane, named familiarly Jean or Hattie or Allen, spins slowly north from the coast of Guyana, gathers force and moisture from the warm waters off Trinidad and Tobago, crosses the Lesser Antilles, destroys everything in its path and chews its way toward us, here, in the Greater Antilles, let's say, for this we *can* see, this we *can* feel: the skies in the southeast darken slowly as ten-mile-high towers of cumulonimbus clouds cross the horizon, the air pressure drops so rapidly our heads ache, seabirds fly inland and disappear behind dark green jungle-covered hills, and the onshore breeze replaces the offshore breeze as if rushing from the island to greet the approaching wall of gray clouds: and it's because we can see the hurricane with our eyes and feel it with our bodies (though it's caused by something no more concerned with us and our individual and paltry fates than is the rotation of the earth) that we nevertheless take it personally. We make it "our" hurricane, and when we talk with tourists from America, we speak of "our" weather, just as the New Englanders among them speak with wry pride of blizzards and Californians brag about sunshine.

If, however, we are a poor, middle-aged woman with five children living in a daub-and-wattle cabin in the hill country of Haiti a few kilometers west of Port-de-Paix on the north coast, we know the hurricane comes because the loas have not been properly fed. It's not that we have been bad; it's that the quality of our attention has waned. We've forgotten the dead, *les Morts,* and *les Mystères,* we've neglected to feed them, and it's not we alone who have been neglectful, this poor, solitary woman, let's say, a woman with a husband gone off to America in a boat, not we alone, but all *les serviteurs,* all of us who serve the loas. It's true, for a long time now we have not fed the loas, so today the hurricane comes to remind us that it is we who live for the dead and not the dead who live for us.

In early August our side of the island was struck by a hurricane. We learned too late that it was coming—not that we would have done anything differently had we known about it sooner, for it was too late to stop it, the waters had already been stirred. We would deal with the loas later, we said, for that is how it has been done in the past. There have been other hurricanes, and after they have passed over us, even before we have patched up our houses and repaired our gardens, we have fed the loas. This year, however, when the hurricane came, it was different, for things got confused. And though we did not think we were a part of the confusion, we watched it and slowly got drawn into it and soon began to behave as if we, too, were confused. Here is how it happened:

Our settlement is called Allanche and it is located behind the first line of hills on the northwest coast a few kilometers off the road from Port-de-Paix to Saint Louis du Nord, which, because Allanche is too small to be a market town, is fortunate, for the women can carry their baskets of yams, mangoes and breadfruit, their apricot mameys and jamelacs, over the ridge on narrow pathways down to the coast road early on the morning of market day, and if they cannot hail a truck or car or wagon for a ride into Port-de-Paix, it is still not too late to walk the other way to the smaller market town of Saint Louis du Nord and arrive there in time to sell most of their goods.

First it rained for several days, a breezy, late summer rain, warm and various, turning the leaves of the trees, like wet, silver-palmed hands, this way and that, as the breeze off the sea tumbled against the hills. All the wood got soaked through, and when their cookfires went out, the people slept long and late inside their houses and shops, waking to talk in low voices and to peer out the door again and again at the red ground still riddled and puddled from the stoop to the lane, dribbling down the lane and down the hillside in new streams that ran red as blood all the way to the sea. These were long, boring days of waiting, gossiping, thinking of food and of the past, fussing with children's hair and guessing and arguing lightly about when the rain would stop and wood dry out so cookfires could be lit and yams baked again, damp clothes dried, bedding spread in the sunlight, children sent scurrying to the fields for greens and to the shop for a can of tinned beef or a box of yellow cheese. A few people in the settlement, Aubin, the police chief, Chauvet, the shopkeeper, and Placide, who owns a small truck, have kerosene stoves and were able to cook inside their houses. Soon the smell of their food cooking in the morning and again late in the day drifted through the settlement and set our stomachs to grumbling and made it difficult to keep our hearts from tightening with anger against everything—against our neighbors with their stoves, against our restless children, against the pair of uncooked yams in the corner on the floor, against the pair of chickens under the cabin scratching in the dirt and clucking quietly to each other, against the cold chunks of breadfruit crumbling in our mouths. We smelled a stew, a dense tangle of threads of tomato, chicken, onion and greens, and we looked across the dark room at each other's faces, the small children lying on the bed, the boy by the window, the sister-in-law and her baby in the chair by the window, and it was difficult for us not to hate the world so much that we hated even each other, we who must live in this world.

Then the rain stopped. The wind died, and the sky seemed to lift and lighten to a milky white. We smiled and stepped to the open doorway and looked at the yard, where everything dripped and glistened, as if the entire valley had all at once been plucked from under the sea by a gigantic hand and set down there between the blue-green mountains inland and the pearly sea beyond the hills. It was beautiful and newborn.

Then, before we could stop him, the boy darted around us and ran down the path, quickly gone, eager to see his friends and walk with them to Port-de-Paix, where they follow older boys and men who teach them how to make a little money doing things we will not permit them to do here in Allanche. We cannot keep them here, where they have no land to raise a crop and yet have no other way than farming to earn money for their families or themselves. These days all the boys soon go away to the towns and cities, even to Port-au-Prince, where, without their mothers and fathers, they become drunkards and pimps and beggars and even worse. Most of them never come back.

Aubin—the chief of police, he's called, though he has

no assistant—came down the lane from his office, which is also his home, and as he passed the cabin, he called out, You should shutter your window, ladies, and lock your door! This is the start of a hurricane!

He came to the window and peered in at us. He was wearing his cap and the jacket of his uniform, so we knew this was official business, this warning, even though he often called on us or shouted hello when he passed by, for the sister-in-law, Vanise, is the mother of his child and he enjoyed keeping track of the child, although he no longer cared for the mother, who, despite her youth, had grown thin and sour-faced and silent, except when she talked to us or to her baby.

It's a big one, a strong blow, he said, and puffing his round brown cheeks, he blew a gust of wind into the darkness of the cabin—*pfff!*—and laughed.

Then he was serious, for he saw we were frightened and alone, and he said he'd heard it on his radio. Everyone should just stay inside their cabins and wait out the storm, he said. It'll pass over the island in a few hours. Where's your boy? he asked us, and when he learned that the boy had left as soon as the rain stopped, he seemed concerned for a second. The roads have washed out, he said. He'll have to turn back. There's no road to Port-de-Paix anymore, it's buried in mud off the hills, he said. I heard it on my radio.

We listened in silence to him, and so he said, Pray he gets back before the hurricane strikes. Or he'll come home dead in a box. He said this with a cheerfulness we have grown used to, for he does not want the boys to come back at night, or ever. He wants them to disappear into the towns and not cause him trouble anymore.

And your husband, do you hear from him in America? Aubin asked. Does he send you money still? He smiled like a snake, no lips, no teeth. He's been gone a long time now, eh? Must be a rich man by now. He laughed, as if he had told a joke. Or else in jail. They put Haitians in jail in America, you know. I heard that on my radio too.

We said nothing, for though it was true, we had not

heard a word from the man in over a year, we also knew he was not in jail, for he had sent us money, American money, for almost two years, which we had hidden away, as he wanted us to do, for the time when we would be able to go to America to join him there. We knew that in the last year someone had been stopping his letters and removing the money from the envelopes, someone in the settlement, probably, who had learned somehow that he was sending us the money he earned taking care of a golf course in Florida. We had brought his first letter, after taking the money from it, to Berthe Moriset, a woman in the settlement who reads letters for people, and she had read his instructions to us to save the money and to spend it only "in emergency," which we understood to mean only when we were ready to come to America, but when we heard those words from Berthe's lips, we knew we had made a mistake in taking the letter to her, for now everyone would know. After that, we took out the money and burned the letters unread. Two more letters came, and then, for a year, no more. But we knew, even so, the man was not in jail.

What about you? Aubin asked Vanise. She sat in a clump of shadow in the far corner of the cabin, looking down at the infant in her lap as if its father were not present. She did not respond, so he shouted her name, *Vanise!* What about you? Does the baby do well?

We explained for her that there was no food, for we had been inside since the rain started and had not been able to find dry wood for the fire to bake the yams or cook one of the chickens.

Aubin looked at us as if we were all children and said that we should have stored wood under the house, but when we tried to explain that it was very difficult to find enough deadwood to store it against the future, he waved us silent. He's a busy man, Aubin, and does not want to be troubled by our difficulties.

Go to my office, he told the eldest of the daughters on the bed. Fetch an armful of sticks from under the building so your mother can make a fire and cook food for you. This is shameful, he said. A house with no man in it . . . , he muttered in disgust. We did not hear the rest, for he was gone.

But it did not matter what Aubin thought or said, for we knew, with the hurricane coming, with the boy gone and the road washed out, with all the danger and with the suffering yet to come, after the suffering we had already gone through, it was clear that the loas were hungry, and we said to one another that as soon as the hurricane was over, we would go to Cabon or Bonneau with one of the chickens and make a service for their feeding.

This seemed to lighten Vanise's load of woe. She stood, placed her infant son on the bed with the other children and made for the door, saying she would kill the remaining chicken, the one not saved for the *houngan,* and pluck it, and when the daughter returned from Aubin's with the sticks for the fire, we would cook it and have food to eat during the hurricane.

But this was not to happen. The girl quickly returned from Aubin's house empty-handed and weeping, for she had been greeted there by Aubin's wife, who knew of his child with Vanise. Aubin's wife, a sharp-tongued woman, shouted at the girl that she would not feed her husband's mistress and bastard and sent her away with threats of a beating.

Swiftly, Vanise descended into gloom again, and despite our wishes to remain optimistic, we followed her there, and before long, we were all once again sitting in the damp shadows of the cabin staring at the ceiling or looking out the door and window, lost in the floating world of our thoughts, as if the world where there was a hurricane coming and our son out somewhere in it and where there was no food to eat, no dry firewood, no dry clothes or bedding, as if that world did not exist.

But, of course, it did exist, and soon the sky darkened again and the rain returned, furiously now, as if angered by delay, pushed by a strong wind out of the sea, until in a short time the rain seemed not so much dropped from the sky above as driven straight at us, a pressing, milky wall of rain that bent the trees, turned the palms inside out, ripped palmettos and stripped shrubs from the ground and pitched them against the bowed trunks of the larger trees, the cabins and the rocks, where they clung for a few seconds, then got torn loose and sent flying in pinwheels over the rough ground to the next tree or outcropping in their path. The noise was immense, a howling, like a beast made nervous and then frantic, a beast crazed by the drumming of the rain against the tin roof and shuttered window and closed door of the cabin. The children cried, and we adults tried to calm them, but we, too, were frightened, because it did not seem to us that the cabin could hold itself against the force of the wind and rain, even though it had stood against many hurricanes over the years. The children knew we were frightened, despite our soothing, reassuring words, so they wept all the louder, their small wails swallowed instantly by the howl of the wind.

The day became night, and we lit a candle, though we had nothing to see. The wind continued as before, but slowly it shifted the direction it came from, moving from off the sea around to the north, until by midnight it was raging like a huge river down the valley that runs between the hills on the east and the mountains on the west. It was pummeling us from the front now, instead of from the side, and the trees that had been bowed in one direction were bent in another and, weakened, even the large thatch palms began to break off and fall. The children by this time were asleep, exhausted by their fear and weeping, and we were glad they could not hear the trunks of the trees snap and split, the ongoing roar of the wind and rain, the hammering on the roof and against the shutter and the door.

We woke, though we did not know we had fallen asleep, when suddenly the door was thrown back, and the wind seemed to toss the shadow of the boy, our son, into the room. He shoved the door shut again and tied it, then turned to us and said for us to light another candle, he wanted us to see what he had brought home. He was soaked through, dripping and shiny in the flickering yellow light of the room, and his face was bright and smiling.

Vanise lit a candle and came close to the boy, and when he held a bundle out to her, she said, *Oh!* She said it strangely, a mixture of relief, surprise and fear. When she stepped back, we could see that the boy was holding a large ham, the entire smoked leg of a pig, the kind of ham we had never seen before except in the pictures in magazines that people sometimes get from tourists or when they go to Port-au-Prince. A ham! An American ham!

And here is where we made our mistake, for we woke the children and immediately set to cutting off chunks of the ham, adults and small children alike, devouring it like starved animals. We laughed and grabbed and stuffed the salty meat into our mouths with our hands. Then, as our hunger lost its rage, we slowed and found ourselves nibbling and picking at the pink, grainy ham, now and then drinking water from the gourd, and we began to ask the boy where he had found the ham, who had given it to him?

He showed us a face that knows a secret, and for a while, despite our jokes and coaxing, would not tell us, for he was proud that he had brought this food home and wanted to enjoy our gratitude as long as he could. Finally, when we commanded him to tell us where he got the ham, he told us that he had taken it from a truck turned over in a mud slide on the road to Port-de-Paix, and then, as he expected, we were not as happy with the gift as before.

What truck was this?

A truck. Just a van. A van upside down in the mud, with the doors wide open and the rain coming in.

And where was the driver?

Gone, *Maman.*

Gone? He left his van and this American ham behind?

There were many hams, he said. Other kinds of meat too. All wrapped in paper and scattered all over the place, inside the van and falling out into the mud and rain.

Where did the driver go? Did you see him?

We saw him . . . He was dead. He was inside the van on the floor in front, and his head was all bloody from where he'd hit the windshield when the van turned over from the mud. It must have been hit by the mud when the side of the hill above the road loosened and came rushing onto the road.

Are you sure he was dead?

Yes, the boy said quietly.

Where is the rest of the meat, all the other hams and packages? And who owns them?

Some are still there. We only took what we could carry. There's nothing wrong. The driver was a stranger, he's dead.

But who owns this meat? we asked the boy, who was now afraid that we were angry with him. Whose van is it? What did it say on the sides? Whose sign is on it?

The boy did not know whose van it was, and even if there had been a sign on it, he could not have read it anyhow. He just looked up at us, wide-eyed, and shrugged and said, It's all right. It's all right, *Maman*.

But it was not all right. The ham belonged either to a rich man or to someone in the government or possibly to a hotel or restaurant in Port-de-Paix or Cap Haitien, and now we had eaten fully half of it. The white circle of bone that ran through the center of the meat stared from its pink nest like an accusing eye.

Vanise said in a low voice, Aubin will find out. He'll find out, and he'll come here and take away your son to punish him and you. And he'll take away my baby to punish me. She began to tremble and then to weep.

The boy said, No, it's all right. It's all right! he insisted, but his eyes were wet with fear now, for he, like all of us, knew that such things happen easily. There was his friend, Georges Le Rouge, who had asked the American family he worked for one winter to intercede with the police so he could take his driver's test for a chauffeur's license without paying the bribe, and Georges had disappeared the week after the Americans left. Aubin said they had taken him to America with them, but we all knew the truth. And there was the sad affair of the family of Victor Bonneau, whose eldest son went to Port-au-Prince and got mixed up with the people who ran the newspaper that people were not supposed to read. And we all knew Adrienne Mérant before her brothers ran off to Santo Domingo, knew her when she was pretty, and knew her afterwards, when the soldiers brought her back to Allanche from Port-au-Prince. People disappeared, or people were changed, and though sometimes it was clear that there were good reasons, it was also clear that sometimes it was only because they had made a mistake no greater than ours. And sometimes it was only because they happened to know or be related to someone who had made a mistake no greater than ours. The boy was wrong to insist that we had done nothing wrong, and he was right to be afraid, and Vanise was no doubt right to weep, and we, we were right to do what we did then.

We had not noticed it, but the storm had gone silent. The wind and rain had stopped, and the only sound was the drip of the water off the roof and the gurgle of the candle in the dish. It would come again, we knew. The hurricane always stops midway like this, as if to catch its breath, and then the wind turns and continues for another few hours, until, exhausted from having beaten the earth so long, it moves reluctantly away.

Our voices and the sounds of our movements suddenly sounded loud and harsh. The smaller children and Vanise's infant slept in a heap on the bed, while we sat around the small table next to the shuttered window, with the candle and the half-eaten ham and the gourd between us, and whispered, trying not to offend our ears with the crackling sounds of our own voices, lips and teeth.

Vanise, though seated at the table, was a bundle of short movements, her bony chest with its oversized, new mother's breasts heaving, her fingers tying and untying themselves rapidly as if she were at once knitting and tearing apart a baby's cap. Aubin will come tomorrow and take us away, she said in a thin voice. His wife will make him, even if he himself does not wish to do it. Or the police in Cap Haitien will make him do it, or the soldiers. They will find the van, and they'll know. As soon as Aubin remembers that the boy and his friends were on the road during the storm, he'll know they took the meat from the van. They'll all know, and then he'll come here, and no matter what we tell him, he'll know the truth.

She was right. When you deal with people like Aubin, people who have power over you, it's not enough to lie. You also have to be believed. We could bury the ham deep in the earth way back in the bush, and Aubin would still know that our son had come home in the hurricane with stolen meat and we had eaten it. The only way we could both lie and be believed was if the son was not at home, if, when Aubin arrived, the boy was gone, never to appear at home again. Then, though Aubin would be angry at the boy, he might leave Vanise and her infant and the rest of us here to ourselves. Of course, if he ever found the boy afterwards, if he saw him accidentally in Port-de-Paix some night or caught him walking along the road to Cap Haitien early one morning, he would arrest him, because the boy's not having come home immediately after the hurricane would mean that any lie he later told concerning the meat would not be believed.

There was nothing else to do, it seemed. The money was pressed between the two layers of floorboards under the bed, as thin as a newspaper between two short boards that came up easily, though they had not been lifted in over a year, not even to count. We used to count the money often, once a month, even. We would go over the stacks of green paper, ones, fives, tens and twenties, hungrily in late night candlelight with the door tied shut and the window covered, counting it and adding it up and dreaming over it, while we waited for the distant moment when we could go down to the fishing villages west of Port-de-Paix and make our arrangement with the men who own the boats and carry people over to the Bahamas and then to America and be there with our husband.

The candle fluttered, and we noticed that the wind and rain had resumed and were building to a roar again. The boy sat limply on a stool by the wall, his chest collapsed and his hands resting heavily on his knees. His face was blank, dark and withdrawn to a secret place of shame way inside him.

Lift the boards under the bed, we instructed him, and bring the money. Quickly.

He looked up, not understanding.

You heard. Do it.

He got up and crawled under the bed and soon was grunting and yanking at the boards there. Vanise studied him patiently, as if she were a grand lady and he retrieving a piece of dropped jewelry. She understood what he was doing and why, though he did not, and she seemed almost ready to smile. But that is because she had suffered more than he. He was merely for the first time in his life truly afraid. It was different for Vanise. Long ago, when her mother had died and then her father, and then all her brothers and sisters had died except the one who was the father of the boy, she had ended up living alone in a cabin outside Saint Louis du Nord letting men visit her and pay for her time and laughter and young girl's body. She had passed through fear then as if through flame to the other side, where resignation abides, and then she had become Aubin's favorite *jeunesse* for a while. He brought her back up here to Allanche, where he got a baby on her, and for a while she stepped back from resignation and began to learn how to be a *serviteur* and feed the loas, until Aubin grew tired of her, and a new, worse thing happened to her spirit, for she stood now on the further side of resignation, where people, especially women, laugh and cry too much and too often, where nothing matters and a second later everything matters. She was emptied out, and although we could love her, we could not trust her. All of us, even Vanise herself, knew that we would live better if we sent her away, but we also knew that she would not leave now unless for a better, safer place.

The wind and rain returned and beat on our heads until morning. We knew we would survive the hurricane, but we prayed to the Virgin and to our *mait'-tête*, while Vanise and the boy put their few articles of clothing and the uncooked yams and the remainder of the American ham into two small baskets, as if they were going to market in Port-de-Paix at dawn. We prayed on our knees with all the proper words we could remember, which were not so many as we would have liked, for we were no *mambo* or *houngan* or even a bush priest, a *prêt' savanne*, nor could we go out in the storm and find one to pray for us, nor would we have done so, even if the night were serene, for what Vanise and the boy and Vanise's baby were about to do could not be told to anyone yet.

The rain stopped, and the wind turned to gusts that came and went, and soon it was silent, and we began to hear hungry seabirds returning from the hills, crossing overhead toward the sea. We opened the door, and a gray block of light from the east fell into the cabin. It was morning. The hurricane had passed, and there was a sudden swelling of joy in our bodies, a warm, filling breath of pleasure, even though we knew that, with dawn, the boy and his aunt and her baby would leave us and that, no matter what happened to them in their journey, we would not see them again. We wrapped the money in a square of scarlet cloth and handed it to Vanise.

The fisherman named Victor in Le Môle is the one that people say carries people over to America. That is how the others left. That is how your brother got to Florida.

The girl looked down at her baby in her arms and smiled a strange, grim smile.

The boy said, *Maman?* When will you come?

Soon. When there is more money for it. Soon.

He looked at his sisters on the bed and crossed to them and silently patted each on her sleeping head.

Then he went to stand by the door. Come on, Vanise. We'll have to pass a lot of people on the road, and the sooner we pass them the better.

Vanise turned away from us and strolled toward the door as if she were going to a dance. Then they were gone. The boy, who was stepping into manhood sooner than he was ready, was gone. The girl and her baby were gone. The money was gone. We remained, and the small children, they remained. The storm was over. Under the house the chickens fluttered and scratched. Aubin had dry wood he would give us if we promised to repay him quickly, but we could not go there, not yet. We would stay hungry a little longer, and perhaps by evening some of our own wood would be dry enough to burn. Then we would kill a chicken and cook it and eat it.

Making a Killing

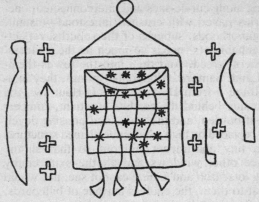

1

BOB DRIVES, AND ELAINE, SEATED BESIDE HIM, HOLDS THE road map in her lap, and the two of them keep their eyes away from the horizons and close to the road ahead and the buildings and land abutting the road. They avert their gaze from the flat monotony of the central Florida landscape, the palmettos and citrus groves and truck farms. They ignore, they do not even notice, the absence of what Bob would call "real trees." They look right through, as if it were invisible, the glut of McDonald's and Burger Kings, Kentucky Fried Chickens and Pizza Huts, a long, straight tunnel of franchises broken intermittently by storefront loan companies and paved lots crammed with glistening Corvettes, T-Birds, Cameros and Trans Ams, and beyond the car dealers, surrounded by chain-link fences, automobile graveyards, vast and disordered, dreary, colorless and indestructible. On the outskirts of every town they pass through are the miles of trailer parks laid out in grids, like the orange groves beyond them, with a geometric precision determined by the logic of ledgers instead of the logic of land, water and sky. And after the trailer parks, as the car nears another town, they pass tracts of pastel-colored cinderblock bungalows strung along cul-de-sacs and interconnected, one-lane capillaries paved with crushed limestone—instant, isolated neighborhoods, suburbs of the suburbs, reflecting not the inhabitants' needs so much as the builders' and landowners' greed. And then into the towns themselves, De Land, Sanford, Altamonte Springs, they lumber down Route 4 from Daytona, the U-Haul swaying from side to side behind the car like a patient, cumbersome beast of burden, and the tracts and housing developments get replaced by high white cube-shaped structures stuffed with tiny apartments laid out so that all the windows face other windows and all the exits empty onto parking lots. Bob and Elaine cannot see, nor would you point out to them, the endless barrage of billboards, neon signs, flapping plastic banners and flags, arrows, and huge, profiled fingers pointing at them through the windshield, shrilling at them to Buy, buy, buy me now! Instead, they see gauzy wedges of pale green, yellow and pink, and now and then dots and slashes of red, orange and lavender—abstract forms and fields of color that, once seen, get translated into rough notions about efficiency, cleanliness and convenience, and these notions comfort them. For they have done a terrible and frightening thing: they have traded one life for another, and this new life is now the only one they have.

The white people they see in the towns, in cars and alongside the roads and streets resemble the people of New Hampshire, except that they wear brightly colored clothing and their skins are tanned. But for the first time in their lives, Bob and Elaine Dubois see many people of color. Hundreds of them, thousands! Not the one or two they have seen before, noticed without comment just this week, in fact, waiting on their table in a Stuckey's outside Raleigh, North Carolina, or pumping gas into their car on the New Jersey Turnpike. (They missed seeing them in the Bronx because Bob was so afraid of losing his way as he passed through New York City that he made Elaine watch the signs for I-95 and shout out the turns while he watched out for the cars, trucks and buses beside, behind and in front of them, the U-Haul in the rearview mirror, the bumps and potholes in the road.) Back in Catamount, there was the bald, muscular black man who ran the rug-cleaning company, and there was the tall, good-looking guy in the three-piece suit that Bob saw once in Concord, the capital, a man who was probably a lawyer working for one of the agencies housed in the Federal Building, a man he'd mentioned several times to Elaine, but she had never seen him herself. Way back, when Bob was in the service, there were many young black men and even a few black sergeants, but for Bob, who was only a kid and hung out with the kids from Maine and New Hampshire, the blacks he saw then were abstractions called niggers that frightened him the same way whorehouses in Boston and gambling in the barracks frightened him—he didn't know the rules, and he didn't want to embarrass himself by asking, so he kept away, kept entirely to people like himself, learned how to fix oil burners, got stationed in New England despite the war and hitchhiked home on his leaves to visit his parents and his girlfriend Elaine and lie to his buddies in the taverns.

It was still possible at the time this story takes place, the late 1970s, to grow up in America without having known a single black person well enough to learn his or her name, without having seen a black person, except on television or from a great distance, even when that person happened to be standing right next to you in line at the bank or in a cafeteria or on a bus. Bob Dubois and his wife Elaine grew up that way. But now, suddenly, as they near Oleander Park, Florida, their new home, after having sold their house in New Hampshire, after Bob's having quit his job, after having sold everything they could sell, even Bob's beloved Boston whaler, after having said and waved goodbye forever to everything familiar, known, understood, they come up against and are forced to see many people of color, more of them, or so it seems, than there are white people. They see them working in gangs in the orange groves, riding in the

backs of trucks, mowing lawns, striding along the highways and sidewalks, and though Bob and Elaine are
safely removed from these people, protected from direct
contact by their car and all their possessions and by
each other, the people of color seem up close and ines-
capably real, as if they are suddenly banging on the
windshield, yanking at the door handles, climbing over
the roof and hood and shouting to one another, "Yo,
man! Come on an' check out the white folks!"

These black- and brown-skinned people, the American blacks in the department stores and supermarkets,
the Jamaicans and Haitians in the fields, the Cubans in
the filling stations—these working people, who got here
first, belong here, not Bob and Elaine Dubois and their
daughters Ruthie and Emma. It's Bob and his family
who are the newcomers at the Florida trough, and Bob
is embarrassed by his lateness. He feels ugly in his
winter-gray skin, ashamed of his wife's plain looks and
his children's skinny arms and legs, he feels poor and
ignorant in his noisy, dented station wagon and orange
rented trailer with all their possessions jammed inside,
the furniture and clothing they couldn't or wouldn't sell
in their yard sale or through their classified ad in the
Catamount Patriot. He feels embarrassed—that is, ex-
posed, revealed to the world for what he is—and perhaps for the first time in his life, his entire body fills with
fear.

Elaine looks quickly over at him and nervously, as if
she has been reading his thoughts, says, "All those
black people working in the fields and everything, they're
not really Americans, right?"

Bob says nothing, just keeps on driving.

She adds, "I've read they're from Cuba and those
kinds of places."

For a moment they are silent. Then Bob says in a low
voice, "Thank God for Eddie."

"Yeah," she says, reaching for the road map.

2

ELAINE HATES THE WAY EDDIE TALKS. "HE HAS A FOUL mouth," she says.

Bob, his head and both hands in the refrigerator reaching for more beer, turns and looks at her. Didn't the man find them this trailer they bought on Lake Grassey, didn't he give them an almost new Sony portable television as a house present, which the kids are happily watching in the back bedroom instead of hanging around in the kitchen and living room, whining and bothering the grownups, who want to talk business because tomorrow is Bob's first day on the job, a job that his brother Eddie, for Christ's sake, gave him? Is she unhappy here? They haven't been in Florida a week, and already she wants to go home? *This* is home now.

"It's just the way he talks, that's all," Bob explains. He whispers his words to her—Eddie and Sarah are sitting silently in the living room not ten feet away, smoking cigarettes and looking in opposite directions, Eddie at one end of the couch peering out the open screened door at the packed-dirt yard, the pink trailer across the lane, then the marsh and, beneath the soft purple shadows of dusk, the dark blue surface of Lake Grassey. Sarah, her long, thin legs crossed at the ankles, looks out the window beside her at the pale blue exterior of the trailer next door and examines it as if it were a picture of a trailer instead of the real thing.

"Eddie has a good heart," Bob whispers. "It's just he's still a kid in some ways. He talks the way we did when we were kids—'fuckin' this,' 'fuckin' that'—that's all. You know." He holds three cans of Schlitz in one hand and swings the refrigerator door shut with the other.

"Yeah, I know, I know. I just don't want the girls to have to hear it, that's all. . . ."

"For Christ's sake, Elaine!" he hisses, and he places the cans of beer on the counter, as if to free his hands. He stares at her, willing her to be silent, to be happy, to be proud of him, to love his brother and his brother's

wife and child. To be grateful. "We'll talk later," he says, and returns to the living room.

Elaine goes on peeling the potatoes. It's nearly dark, and the kitchen, facing east, settles into shadow first. Crossing the room to the light switch by the door, she comes to stand at the threshold, where she watches and listens to the others, who are staring at an object placed in the middle of the coffee table. Surrounded by empty beer cans and ashtrays, cigarette packs and butane lighters, the Sunday newspaper and a copy of *People,* settled in the midst of the clutter but organizing and diminishing it, lies a large, dark blue pistol. Sarah, her legs still crossed, stares at the gun as if it were a small, dead, slightly repulsive animal. Eddie looks at it proudly, as if he has just killed it, and Bob looks at it with confusion, as if he has been asked to skin it.

Eddie reaches into the side pocket of his seersucker jacket and draws out a small green package of bullets and places the box on the table next to the pistol. "You'll want these," he says. Eddie, who people sometimes say resembles the actor Steve McQueen, snaps his curly blond head to attention and, with his lips pursed, studies his younger brother's face for a second.

"Is it loaded?" Elaine asks from the doorway.

"Not now," Eddie answers. "But it will be tomorrow."

From the sofa, Sarah glances quickly up at Elaine, fails to catch her eye and goes back to the staring out the window at the side of the trailer next door. "I don't know why you need a gun," she says to the window.

"You mean you don't know why Bob needs a gun," Eddie says cheerfully. "Me you know." He grins up at Elaine, still standing in the doorway, and pats his jacket under his left arm.

"Are you carrying a gun? Right now?" Elaine asks. "Here?"

"Sure."

Bob reaches over and plucks the pistol off the table, turns it over in his hand and examines it carefully. He releases the magazine, slaps it back, hefts the gun in his right hand. He studies the hand with the gun in it, as if memorizing it.

"Why do you have to carry a gun?" Elaine asks.

In a swift, unbroken motion, a practiced move, Eddie lifts his butt from the couch, darts his right hand into his back trousers pocket, brings forth his wallet and flips it open, revealing an inch-thick stack of bills. *"That's* why, honey. I'm in business here, seven fucking days a week I'm in business, and a lot of what I do gets done in cash, or else I wouldn't be in business very long. You understand," he says, winking at Bob.

"I guess so," Bob says. "You mean because of taxes and so on?"

"Yeah . . . yeah, that, sure. There's a lot of stuff I have to keep off the books. Your fuckin' salary, for instance. Which is all to your advantage, you understand; all it saves me is bookkeeping. But there's a lot more things I gotta worry about that you don't hafta even think about, like deliveries, for instance, and working with the fucking trade unions trying to get that new store over in Lakeland set up and built . . ." he says. "All you got to worry about for now is selling booze across the counter, keeping the shelves stocked, putting in your weekly orders and making your nightly deposits at the bank. I take care of the rest."

"So why does Bob need a gun?" Elaine asks.

The others, even Sarah, look at her as if she is simple minded. "Elaine, honey," Eddie says, smiling. "You are not in Catamount, Cow Hampshire, anymore, sweetie."

"Don't call me sweetie. Please."

"Okay, okay. Sorry."

"Things are different here, Elaine," Bob says.

"You bet your ass things are different here. We got niggers with guns and razors here," Eddie says, suddenly serious. "We got Cubans who cut your balls off. We got Haitians with their fucking voodoo sacrifices and Jamaicans with machetes as long as your fucking arm. We got dark-skinned crazies of all kinds, all hopped up on their fucking pot and cocaine, riding around in brand-new Mercedes-Benzes without enough pocket money to put gas in the tanks. We got Colombians, for Christ's sake, with fucking *machine guns!*"

"Oh, come on, Eddie, you're going to send them back to New Hampshire scared out of their wits. It's not that bad," Sarah says. "Honest." She unfolds her legs and takes a slow sip of her beer. "It's not like Miami," she adds, stretching her arms overhead and arching her back like a cat. She's wearing a beige pantsuit that accentuates her tan and the long angularity of her body. Bob once saw her naked and was surprised at how closely her body resembled an adolescent boy's body, long, tight, smooth, with tiny breasts, like white circles on her chest. He was also surprised by how attractive he found her body. It was in his and Elaine's own bedroom in Catamount one hot summer afternoon a few years earlier, when Eddie, Sarah and Jessica had come up for a week in June to visit them and examine summer camps in New Hampshire for Jessica. Because of the unusual heat, Bob came home from work earlier than usual, and finding the house empty, guessed everyone had gone to the lake for a swim. When he strolled into his bedroom he caught Sarah there, naked, sitting on the edge of the bed painting her toenails. She looked up as he entered and made no attempt to hide herself from him. Her dark hair, cut short, was wet and brushed back like a swimmer's, and to Bob she looked so clean and precise, so apparent and without mystery or guile, that he felt a great longing to make love to her, which surprised and frightened him and sent him back down the hall and rapidly down the stairs. At the bottom of the stairs, he turned, looked up and waited, as if he expected Sarah to appear there. After a few seconds, he took a long pull on his beer, swallowed and hollered, "Hey, I'm sorry, Sarah. I thought nobody was home!"

"That's okay," she called. "Everyone's gone swimming. I stayed home to take a nap and a shower. I'm sure I'll end up feeling better than they will."

"Yeah," he said. He knew from the music in her voice that if he went back up the stairs and entered the bedrom, took off his clothes and started kissing her along her throat, she would not even pretend to stop him, and afterwards she would never say a word about it to him or anyone else. That is the moment he remembers now whenever he looks straight at Sarah. He still can't decide whether his decision to sit in his chair in the living room until Sarah was dressed and cheerfully downstairs was the right decision, for, like most people, Bob finds it difficult to know right from wrong. He relies on taboos and circumstances to control his behavior, to make him a "good man," so that on those infrequent occasions when neither taboo nor circumstance prohibits him from satisfying an appetite and he does not satisfy that appetite or even attempt to do so, he does not know what to think of himself. He doesn't know if he has been a good man or merely a stupid or scared man. Most people, like Bob, unchurched since childhood, now and then reach that point of not knowing whether they've been good, stupid or scared, and the anxiety it provokes obliges them to cease wondering as soon as possible and bury the question, as a dog buries a bone, marking it and promising to themselves that they will return to the bone later, when they have the time and energy to gnaw, a promise never kept, of course, and rarely meant to be kept. One of the more attractive aspects of Bob's character, however, is his reluctance to bury these bones, his willingness to go on gnawing into the night, alone and silent, turning it over and upside down, persisting until finally it is white and dry and, in certain lights, a little ghastly. His memory is cluttered with these bones, like a medieval church basement, and it gives to his manner and bearing a kind of melancholy that attracts people who are more educated or refined than he is.

Turning away from Sarah, Bob asks his brother, "What the hell am I supposed to do with this gun? I haven't shot a handgun since the service."

Eddie laughs. "I don't give a flying fuck what you do with it, so long's you keep it with you when you're at the store. The niggers know you got a gun in the store, believe me, they know, they get the word out. Least-ways the niggers in this town do, because they all know each other. Then on a Friday night when they're out looking for easy cash, they'll keep on moving down the line. You'll never have to use it. Just keep it with you when you go back and forth to the bank, and under the counter by the cash register the rest of the time, and if some nigger's stupid enough to want to knock off the place, you blow the sonofabitch away. Like I said, I got a license."

"I don't like it," Elaine says. She walks abruptly back to the kitchen.

"Who the hell does?" Eddie calls after her. "But what the Christ are you supposed to do? Some guy comes in, says, 'If you have a minute, Mister White Motherfucker, give me what's in the cash drawer, as I happen to have a chance for some excellent cocaine tonight and I'm a little low, and besides, I'm two pay-ments behind on my BMW,' so you say, 'Certainly, sir, Mister Colored Gentleman, and would you like a case of cognac to go with that?' Come on, Elaine. You blow the bastard away!"

"What if he blows *you* away!" Elaine yells back.

Eddie is silent for a minute.

"Elaine," Bob says. He keeps looking at the gun.

"We've had this same damned argument a hundred times," Sarah says in a weary voice. "He won't listen. He thinks he's God."

As if to himself, Bob says quietly, "I don't want to shoot anybody. Christ, I don't even like hunting." He's a fisherman, not a hunter. When they were boys, both he and Eddie tried to enjoy deer hunting with their father. Eddie, after a few years, gave it up, because of the scarcity of deer and the difficulty of killing one, but Bob continued to go out year after year with the old man and his cronies, although whenever one of them shot a deer and bloodied the snow with the carcass, he found himself slightly sickened. In New Hampshire, most men who hunt deer do it in groups of three and four, driving pickups and four-wheel-drive vehicles to the end of a dirt road and as far into the woods as the vehicle will go. Then they walk all day through the snowy woods in the cold, sipping at a bottle of Canadian Club every now and then, when finally one of them catches a glimpse of a terrified buck darting uphill through chokecherry and birch and starts blasting away, until it leaps, somersaults and collapses in a heap. Then the other hunters gather around and talk while the man guts his deer. Later, with the carcass of the deer lashed to the front fender of the pickup, they stop at a roadhouse and buy drinks all around and finally arrive home, tired, drunk and very happy—except for Bob, whose only pleasure came from having got through another season without being obliged to take a shot at a deer.

Fishing, however, for Bob, is a solitary, carefully organized, slow and nearly silent activity. He loves the buoyancy of the boat when, a half hour before dawn, he first steps into it, the lap of the waves against the gunwales, the trajectory and sweet hum of the line going out and its geometry, the point-to-point-to-point relations it draws from his hand to the world above the waterline to the world below. Since childhood, he's fished with bait, hand-tied flies and lures along hundreds of the streams, rivers and ponds of New Hampshire. In canoes, borrowed boats, rented boats, and finally his own Boston whaler, he's fished most of the state's larger lakes and the bays along the coast, even fishing out at sea in Avery Boone's trawler, miles beyond the Isles of Shoals in search of bluefish in July. Sometimes he's left New Hampshire waters for salmon in Maine and Quebec, and on a few occasions he's found himself, his car parked beside the road, surfcasting in moonlight on the sandy beaches of Cape Cod. Since childhood, fishing has satisfied his need to be alone and in the natural world at the same time, his deep, extremely conscious need for the presence of his own thoughts coming to him in his own voice, which rarely happens in the presence of other people, his need for order and, perhaps his most tangled need, his need for competence. Hunting for deer, the only hunting he knows about, denies all those; to him, it's social, chaotic and impossible to feel competent at. When his father died, it was with great relief that he sold both his and the old man's rifles to a gun dealer in Keene.

"Don't be a pansy, Bob," Eddie says. "And anyhow, it's not like you're going to have to shoot anybody. Just so long as the bastards know you got a gun, they'll leave you alone. That's all. It's like dealing with the fucking Russians. The second those suckers think you're not ready for them, ready and able to nuke their eyes out, you're a dead man. You got to let these people know you're serious, Bob."

"Yeah," Bob says quietly. Then, smiling, "I'm just not sure I am serious."

"Sure you are," Eddie says, and he gets up from the sofa, stretches and heads for the kitchen. "Hey, Elaine, sweetie, when's supper, for Christ's sake? I'm so hungry my stomach feels like it's got a hard-on."

"Eddie, please," she says. "Your mouth. The children."

"Sorry, sorry, sorry," he says, nuzzling her neck until she draws her shoulder up and pushes his face away.

"Eddie, please, I'm trying to peel potatoes!" she says, and laughs.

Eddie pats her on the ass and opens the refrigerator for more beer. "Sorry, sorry, sorry," he sings. "Sorry, sorry, sorry."

3

CENTRAL FLORIDA IS CRATERED WITH SMALL, SHALLOW, smooth-shored lakes, mile-wide potholes in the limestone subsoil scattered from Gainesville in the north to Lake Okeechobee and the Everglades in the south. For thousands of years, water has eroded the soil from below as much as from above, until finally the simple weight of the land can no longer be supported, and one morning an entire meadow disappears, leaving in its place a pond, which, as the months go by, grows larger, as if it were eating the land that surrounds it, becoming at last a fairly large, nameless lake with a temporarily stabilized shoreline. In a few years, the ecology of the neighborhood will have accepted the lake's presence, and if human beings have been living in the area, they, too, will have accepted and adjusted to the presence of the lake, will have forgotten the recent date of its arrival, will name it and treat and think of it as if it has been there since prehistory. In time, the lake will appear on maps, and roads and streets will circle the lake and bypass it, towns and neighborhoods will be laid out along its shores, water will be pumped from it to irrigate the citrus groves and fields, to flush the toilets and sprinkle the lawns and wash the cars, and if the lake is large enough, a marina will open for business on one shore, and soon motorboats will draw girls in bathing suits over its sparkling surface on skis, while the water table drops half a foot a year. Then, late one night, in the middle of a marshy field across town and well in sight of a housing complex still under construction, a cow will break through the ground, and attempting to escape from the widening hole, will drown. By morning, half a hundred square yards of land will be under water. Mothers will instruct their children to stay away from it, as if it were alive and warm-blooded, but even so, the children will come out to the edge of the hole and stare at it, exchanging risk for wonder, tossing sticks and small chunks of limestone into the water, their tight, high voices crossing through the morning air like swallows.

It's not until Bob has been in Oleander Park for over a full month, however, that he is able to look out his car window on the way to work one morning and for the first time actually see these lakes that surround him. It's as if, a passenger on a bus, he has been reading a book for hours, and closing the book, looks around and realizes that he's in a bus station in a strange city surrounded by strangers. He thought he was alone, that the privacy of his dream was his waking reality as well, and suddenly he sees that the wall around him, made for him by his fears and anxieties, is very close to him indeed, and stretching beyond that wall for miles and miles, all the way to the horizon, is a brand-new world.

He is driving to work one cool morning, past the Cypress Gardens airport, and turning his gaze away from it toward Lake Eloise on his right, he observes for the first time a golden haze lifting slowly in thick swirls from the surface of the lake and drifting toward the trees along the far shore, bald cypress and locust and live oak trees with liana vines and Spanish moss drooping like memories from the branches, and he is struck by the soft, warm ease of the scene, and he wants to enter that scene.

Bob Dubois is a sensual man—that is, most of his deeper responses to his presence in the world make themselves known to his body before moving eventually on to his mind, a condition he learned early in life to trust and respect. If he were more articulate, more like his older brother, perhaps, and words did not so often feel like a tasteless paste in his mouth, he would probably, like most people, mistrust the information regarding the world that gets brought to him by means of his body's delight, or else he would hold the world so revealed in contempt. But he's not like Eddie, he's not like most people, and consequently, a beautiful sound makes him want to listen more closely, a beautiful meal makes him hungry when he wasn't, a beautiful woman makes him tumescent, and the sight of a morning haze rising off a still, dark lake makes him want to row a small, flat-bottomed boat quietly along the shore, to raise the dripping oars every now and then and cast a line among the knobby cypress roots for bass. His desires, then, reveal the world to him. His fears and anxieties, his aversions, obscure it.

Until this morning, he has not arrived at work feeling happy. Each day has brought a new disappointment, disillusionment or the kind of frustration you have to lie about to keep from blaming on anyone but yourself, because if you do blame it on anyone but yourself, you will be very angry at that person. And Bob cannot afford

to be very angry at his brother Eddie; he is too dependent on him.

He works twelve hours a day, six days a week, and
except for the part-time stock clerk, a black man in his
late sixties named George Dill, he is alone in the store.
Though he's paid in cash, with no taxes or other deduc-
tions taken out, his weekly pay is only seventy-five
dollars more than it was in Catamount. Eddie calls him
his future partner, though, and has promised Bob that
when the new store is open, Bob will be running both
stores and will be paid a share of the profits—assuming,
Eddie tells him carefully, he demonstrates a knack for
this kind of business, which of course Eddie is sure he
possesses, because, after all, isn't he one of the Dubois
brothers, and haven't the Dubois brothers always been
able to do whatever they set out to do?

Bob's main problem in life, Eddie tells him, is that
he's never set his goals high enough. Until now, that is.
"You got no experience at anything except fixing fucking oil burners." He told this to Bob one noontime when
he happened to drop by the store, and Bob, after having
worked at the store for ten days, took the opportunity to
complain lightly about the utter boredom of the job.
"That's because you're not learning anything," Eddie
said. "And the reason you're not learning anything is
because your goals are too low. All you want to do is
learn how to do a simple job, which you have done, and
now you're bored. What you got to do is learn about
what you want to know about, which should be money.
You don't know anything about money, honey, and
money-honey is what makes the world go round, so if
you want to go around with it, you better learn a little
about money-honey, brother of mine, or your ass will be
brass and somebody else's golden."

Bob isn't sure he'll be able to learn much about money
while standing behind a counter selling whiskey and
beer to servicemen—the store is located on Route 17,
halfway between Winter Haven and Shure air base—
keeping inventory, stocking shelves, unloading delivery
trucks and crushing and stuffing the empty cartons into

a Dempster-Dumpster out back, but Eddie reassures him that one morning he's going to wake up and everything will be clear to him. It happened that way to him, Eddie says, only he was just a kid when it happened, one year out of high school and working in the Thom McAn's shoe store in Catamount, wondering how come he was selling shoes instead of buying or making them, because it seemed to him, he tells Bob, that the people who were buying shoes and the people who were making shoes had a lot more money than the people who were only selling shoes. That's when it all came clear to him.

"What came clear?" Bob asks. He's begun to fear that maybe Elaine is right, that Eddie is a little crazy—"off the beam," is how she likes to put it—which makes Bob picture his brother as a cartoon character walking happily on air while the rest of them cling terrified to a tree trunk laid between two cliffs across a bottomless chasm.

"It came to me that money is what makes the world go round. Like I said. I know, I know, everybody with a mouth says it, but most people don't really *believe* it, which is why they don't really *understand* it. You have to believe something before you can understand it. Anyhow, that's why most people end up ignoring the facts, and the most important fact is that the guys with most of the money are always doing at least two of the only three things you can do in this life, which happen to be making things, selling things and buying things. The really big guys, your Rockefellers, your Fords, your Du Ponts, they do all three. Because that's all you can do in life anyhow, three things. If you do at least two of those things, and one of them happens to be selling, then your ass is golden. Simple. It came to me when I was eighteen, and it's been my guiding light ever since. My philosophy of life. My religion. I buy things and I sell things. All *you* ever done, up to now, is buy things. And the only way that takes you is downhill. Sure, you sold your time and your skills when you were fixing people's broken furnaces in the middle of the fucking night in the middle of the fucking winter, but in the real world, the world that money makes go round, time and skills, brother, are not *things*. A trade is not a thing. So I buy land and I buy booze, which, as you know, *are* things, and then I sell them for more than I paid for them, and then I take the difference and buy some more land and some more booze, and maybe I build a couple houses too, which I sell, and so on up the hill, all the way to pig heaven. That's the only way to beat the system, kid.''

''What is?'' What in hell is this man talking about? Bob wonders.

''You make things and you sell them, or else you buy things and you sell them. Which means that you can never really work for someone else. You alway got to work for yourself.''

''Well, I work for you.''

''Hey. No, you don't, Bob. Only temporary. Only until you catch hold of the system. Then we're partners. Then you'll be out there making yourself a fucking killing, man. A killing.''

Bob presses his brother for details on how, exactly, and when he will be transformed from employee to partner, from being a man who merely sells things to one who both buys and sells things, but Eddie, like a badly schooled priest explaining the mass, grows vague and dogmatic, until finally, since Bob persists, Eddie reminds him that it all comes down to trust in him, personal trust. Faith. Belief. After all, they are brothers, aren't they, and if you can't have faith in your brother, who can you have faith in? Strangers?

THIS MORNING, A COOL, EARLY MARCH MORNING, BOB DOES have faith in his brother and in his brother's system as well, his system for beating the system. After all, Bob now has a house for his family, even if it is a trailer, which at first made him feel slightly ashamed, but after a few weeks he began to look around and saw that the only people who did *not* live in trailers seemed to be either the kind of people he has always envied, doctors, lawyers, successful businessmen, or the kind of people he has always felt superior to, the poor whites ("crackers," he has learned to call them), the blacks and the foreigners, Cubans mostly, but also Haitians, Jamaicans and other West Indians, though he hasn't yet learned to tell them apart from the black Americans. He feels *normal,* which pleases him. His daughter Ruthie has been enrolled in school in Oleander Park, and they have figured out the school bus schedule so that every morning he is able to drink his second cup of coffee and watch her from the kitchen window as she walks down Tangelo Lane between the facing rows of trailers to the highway, where she stands with the other children from the park waiting for the bus. When the bus has picked up the children, Bob drains his cup, places it in the sink, kisses his wife goodbye, checks in the kids' bedroom to say goodbye to Emma, if she's awake, and leaves for work. An old ritual in a new place has been established, making the place seem familiar.

Though he works from nine to nine, and it's dark by the time he gets home, it's also true that the work is not difficult or especially tiring, so that when he does come home from the store he has more energy than when he got home from work in Catamount. He came home in darkness there too, at least from November till April he did. Exhausted, he usually emptied a couple of king-sized cans of Schlitz, ate supper, and fell asleep in front of the television set, only to be wakened by Elaine at nine to kiss the girls before they went to bed. He barely had enough energy or interest in his life or hers to stay awake with his wife, unless they were watching a television show that amused him. Then, finally, she would grow sleepy herself, and bored, and around eleven the two of them would climb the stairs to bed, where once or twice a week they made love, happily enough but lethargically, and fell asleep.

Since arriving in Florida, however, he helps put the girls to bed, often reading them a story, and then sits in the kitchen with his wife, talking intently to her, listening to her descriptions of her day's events and encounters and telling her his. Even later, after they have made love, which they do more frequently now, they go on talking. All the trivia of their daily lives seem strangely significant to them—the route taken by the bus into downtown Oleander Park several miles away, the funny woman in pink hot pants at the supermarket, the cortisone cream Elaine bought at the drugstore for Emma's rash; and on Bob's part, the trouble he has understanding what old George Dill is saying to him but how it's getting easier every day, so that now he not only understands George almost all the time, but he also understands the Cubans and the Haitians pretty well too, at least most of the time, and only when they speak English, of course, and so long as they know the name of what they want; and the kids with phony ID's from the base that he can spot before they cross the parking lot by the careful, self-conscious way they walk, as if they think they're on stage; and a long, rambling phone call from Eddie, half drunk at four in the afternoon, checking on the day's receipts before he floats a check for a part of a tract of marshland out near a town called Yeehaw Junction (Bob swears that's what Eddie said) that he and "some very big guys from Miami" plan to drain and cut into house lots and have a half-dozen cinderblock houses going up by the end of summer that they'll sell by fall to generate enough cash both to pay off the note for the original purchase and get started on a second half-dozen houses, which by Christmas will have generated enough cash to finance a shopping center right there in Yeehaw Junction, a report whose coherence makes Bob feel that he really is beginning to grasp the way the system works, both the big system and Eddie's smaller one, which feeling gives Bob, for the first time, the belief that before long he, too, will have a new, large house with a pool out on Crump Road near the yacht club and a big new air-conditioned car, a Mercedes, maybe, not an Eldorado like Eddie's, and his kids, too, will learn how to ride horses English style and go to summer camp in New Hampshire.

He thinks, as he pulls his Chevy wagon into the lot in front of the liquor store, that tonight he'll tell Elaine about that mist he saw rising from the lake on the way to work, how beautiful it was, and how it made him want to buy a canoe or maybe a small rowboat or another Boston whaler to replace the one he sold in New Hampshire, so he can go fishing for bass one Sunday morning soon while she and the kids are at mass.

EDDIE'S STORE, LOCATED NEAR WHERE THE OLD SEABOARD Coastline Railroad tracks lean in and run alongside the highway for a few miles, is named Friendly Spirits Liquor Store, the words in gold gothic letters painted across the single plate-glass window in front. It's a small white cinder-block building with a flat roof, which faces the highway and is hugged on three sides by citrus groves. Across the highway from the store squats a housing development for the families of enlisted men stationed at the air base, a gray, barracks-like complex of a dozen two-story buildings, parking lots and treeless, packed-dirt yards owned by the government and built by local contractors, one of whom happened to have been Eddie Dubois, who briefly established himself on paper as a painting contractor, then jobbed out the work to some students from the community college who'd advertised in the paper for house-painting work. Somewhere along the tangled line of contract negotiations and bidding for the construction of the housing project, Eddie came out with title to a house lot chopped out of the fields across the road, and with that in hand, he borrowed the money to build and stock his store, after which he absorbed his painting company into Friendly Spirits Enterprises, Inc.

Turning off Route 17, Bob notices, parked at the rear of the lot next to the Dempster-Dumpster, a red Plymouth Duster with a black woman and man sitting inside. Bob parks his car in front by the entrance, where Eddie instructed him always to park (so that he'd never seem to be without a customer), and sits at the wheel for a moment studying the couple in the Duster. On the seat next to him, inside a small canvas Barnett Bank money bag, is three hundred dollars in cash and rolled coins.

If they want the money, he decides, they can have it.

All they've got to do is ask, and it's theirs. He's relieved that the gun is inside the store, on the shelf below the cash register. Defying Eddie's instructions, Bob decided in the beginning not to carry the gun back and forth with him. Elaine pleaded with him to leave it at the store, made him picture Ruthie or Emma dead of accidentally inflicted gunshot wounds, and he said, "Okay, fine, you're right. Just don't mention it to Eddie, okay?" And then, having tucked it way in the back of the shelf beneath the counter, he forgot about the gun, until now, when he realizes that if he had the gun in his glove compartment, as Eddie expected him to, and if the black man and woman in the Plymouth got out of their car and strolled over to his car, he'd have to get out the gun, and when they yanked open his door and told him to give them the money bag or they'd blow his head off, he'd have to open fire, maybe hitting the man in the chest before the woman shot him in the face, killing him instantly. She'd take the money and drive away, leaving her partner lying on the parking lot, bleeding heavily and dying before the police got there to surmise that Bob got killed fending off an attempted robbery by a lone bandit.

Then he realizes that the Duster is parked next to the back door of the store. They must have broken in! There must be at least four of them, and waiting inside the store are three huge black guys, Jamaicans, probably, with machetes (he's heard Jamaicans are particularly vicious, especially when they smoke that strong Jamaican ganja), and as soon as he unlocks the front door and shuts off the alarm, he'll be a dead man, lying by the door in a pool of his own blood while the Jamaicans bring in the van they've rented for the occasion and empty the stockroom. Around ten, someone from the project across the highway will come in, a lonely housewife with three kids home from school with the chicken pox, and looking for a pint of vodka to get her through a lousy day, she'll find instead the body of a white man hacked insanely to pieces.

Bob shudders. What the hell should he do? Make a dash for the front door, lock it behind him as soon as he's inside, go for the gun under the counter and come out blasting? Or turn his car around and drive off, have a cup of coffee in town and check back later, after they've cleared out all the stock they can carry? Or pretend that nothing is wrong, as they clearly want him to do?

He decides to leave. Putting the key back into the ignition, he starts the engine as quietly as possible, but also does it casually, as if he has forgotten something at home and has to return for it. But when he pushes the gearshift from park to reverse gear, it stops, blocked, refusing to engage reverse—it's happened before, twice last week, and to free the gear he has to step outside and climb onto the front bumper and rock the car violently while someone else jiggles the gearshift. He's sweating, and casting a glance toward the Duster, he sees that the black man, dressed in a dark suit, has got out of the car and is coming toward him. Frantically now, Bob shoves at the gearshift, whispering, "Come on, you sonofabitch, come on, come on!" while the black man, like a dark cloud, draws closer to his car.

Suddenly he's at the closed window on the passenger's side, rapping on the glass, and Bob turns and sees the round, dark brown face of the stock clerk, George Dill, an intense, worried cast to his eyes, with new, deep lines crinkling his broad forehead.

Swinging open the door, the black man peers inside at Bob and utters a string of words. Bob, who can't understand the words, stares wildly at the man, open-mouthed and sweating.

"I thought . . . I thought . . ." Bob says, and George interrupts, blurting out the same string of incomprehensible words.

"George, I . . . I didn't reognize you . . ." Bob tells him. "The suit . . ."

Shutting off the engine, he pockets the key, picks up the money bag and steps from the car. He forces a smile onto his face and shows it, over the roof of the car, to George. "Whaddaya all dressed up for, George, a funeral?" He notices then that the woman in the Duster has got out of the car on the driver's side and is walking quickly across the lot toward them. She's a tall, slender woman, darker than George, wearing high heels and a long black chiffon dress, and on her head a broad-brimmed black hat. She's attractively made up, with lipstick and bright red earrings and necklace, and she's calling Bob's name, "Mister Dubois," in a friendly, familiar way, as if she knows him, though he is sure he's never seen her before. He would have remembered, he knows, because she's extremely pretty, with a wide, pleasant face and the kind of slender but sexy body, like Sarah's, that he's been thinking about a lot lately.

"Yes?" he says, smiling easily, as the woman comes around the front of his car and stands before him. She's nearly as tall as he, he notices with pleasure, and she's about his age, though he thought at first that she was younger, still a girl.

"Let me explain. Daddy's all upset, Mister Dubois."

Bob looks over at the old man and sees that the fellow is peering off toward the orange groves. The dark, pin-striped three-piece suit he's wearing is way too large and hangs loosely around his bent body. He's hatless, and Bob notices for the first time that, except for a thin belt of matted gray hair, George is completely bald. His shining brown head looks fragile, like a ripe plum.

"George," Bob calls to him in a cheery voice. "Where's your hat? I've never seen you without that Miami Dolphins cap of yours."

The old man doesn't respond.

"Mister Dubois," the woman says in a low voice. "I'm his daughter, I'm Marguerite Dill. He lives with me."

"Is he okay? Is something wrong?" Bob is serious now. He understands that he doesn't understand, but he knows that no one will hurt him for it.

Carefully, in her soft, warm Southern voice, the woman explains to Bob that her father's only brother died last night, and her father has taken the death badly. Except for her, the old man has no one else, not around here anyhow, because she brought him down here from Macon, Georgia, five years ago, when her mama died. "Since he was a young man," she says, "he's needed somebody to take care of him." The brother, who lived in Macon, loved him, but he had his own family to take care of, so it was only right that her daddy come to Oleander Park to live with her. Now she is taking him back up to Macon for the funeral, which means that he won't be able to come in to work for the rest of the week. She knew he'd understand, but her daddy insisted on coming over this morning to explain it to Bob himself. "He likes you very much, Mister Dubois, and he likes his job here. I told him I'd phone you and explain, but he insisted, he just kept on saying he wanted to face you himself, about his brother and all . . . but he's in a kind of a shock, and he has trouble talking right normally, he gets all nervous and forgetful, you may have noticed that . . . but especially now, with his brother and all . . ."

"Oh, damn, I'm really sorry," Bob says. "That's okay, he can take all the time he needs. Tell him . . . Hey, George," he calls, and he walks around the woman and comes up behind the old man, putting an arm around his sagging shoulders. "Hey, listen, George, I'm awful sorry about your brother."

George turns his face up to Bob's. "Thank you, Mistah Bob."

"No problem. About your job, I mean. We need you, sure, but we can get along for a week or so without you. You just go on up there to Georgia and . . . just do whatever you have to do, George."

"I will. You is the one man in the worl' can understand," George says. " 'Cause of you an' your brother Mistah Eddie."

"Right, you're right. I do know how you must feel, George, so you just take off as much time as you feel you need, and when you come back to work, why, you just show up here at the store, and your job'll be waiting for you." Bob gives the old man's narrow, slumped shoulders a hearty hug.

"Thank you, Mister Dubois," the woman says. "Come

on now, Daddy, we best be going now.'' Taking the old man by an elbow, she leads him toward the car.

"Are you driving up to Georgia?" Bob asks.

"Yes."

"Well . . . drive carefully, then."

"Thank you, I will." She leads her father around to the passenger's side and opens the door for him.

Bob takes a few steps toward them. "That your car?" She looks up. "Yes."

"Nice car. V-eight or six?"

"It's a V-eight."

"Burns a lot of gas, I bet."

She smiles and opens the door on the driver's side. Then, without answering him, she slides into the car and closes the door.

Standing in the middle of the parking lot, Bob watches the woman and her father leave, turn left at the highway and head north. And though it's not the first time since leaving New Hampshire that he's thought of Doris Cleeve, it's the first time he's missed her.

4

WHAT KIND OF MAN IS BOB DUBOIS, WHO, ALTHOUGH married, keeps for himself the secret privilege of sleeping with women other than his wife? A more sophisticated man than Bob would instantly recognize the lie, and if the lie persisted, if it refused to get itself corrected, would name it a symptom, and before too long, the marriage might be dissolved. But for men like Bob Dubois, it's different.

For Bob, the facts are these: he loves his wife; he loves other women too, but not as much as he loves his wife; if he betrays his wife by sleeping with other women, and she does not discover it, then he has not been cruel to her. And, naturally, he does not want to be cruel to her, for, as said, he loves his wife. Also, he knows that the facts are the same for her, that if she sleeps with other men and he does not discover it, so long as she loves him as deeply as he loves her, then she has not been cruel to him. And he knows she does not want to be cruel to him. Of course, everything changes if he discovers it. As with Ave.

It's a very painful and delicate balance, and one cannot be neurotic and hold it, because it depends for its sustenance on a willingness to endure mutual suspicion, jealousy, watchfulness and now and then a deliberate averting of one's gaze when one's mate has been careless with evidence of transgression. It might be said that acceptance of these facts is immoral or, at best, self-destructive, but it's better said that acceptance of these facts indicates a mature realism, especially among people for whom the continuation of marriage has a higher priority in life than establishing one's personal integrity, higher even than believing in the personal integrity of one's mate, and higher, too, than the utter luxury of making public a private truth. Privacy, the secret knowledge of oneself, is, for the poor and the ignorant, that is, for most of the people in this world, what publicity often is for the rich and the educated. It's their best available way to keep their lives from disappearing into meaninglessness.

For this reason, even though his wife has recently learned that she is pregnant with their third child, Bob does not feel particularly guilty or even secretive, but merely private, when, in the presence of Marguerite Dill, he imagines and longs to be making love to her and says and does everything he can think of to make that possible.

He learned of Elaine's pregnancy before George Dill returned from his brother's funeral in Macon, and for a few days he forgot about the man's lovely daughter and spent his hours at the store lost in fantasies focused on the future exploits of his son, for he knew the child would be a son. He had never heard of a man fathering two daughters and then a third, though he knew, of course, that it sometimes happens, the way any kind of bad luck sometimes happens. But when it has never happened to someone you know personally, you have difficulty believing it will happen to you. Thus, until the day George returned, accompanied by his daughter, Bob used his long, boring hours at the store to imagine his life with a son. And though his imaginings were common and sentimental—his son fishing from the bow of the boat, his son playing baseball, hockey and basketball, his son winning the spelling bee—many of the details through which he visualized these scenes were sufficiently vivid and personal for him to remember details and episodes from his own childhood that he had forgotten.

He caught glimpses of himself as someone else, as perhaps his own father might have seen him. He saw his hair, at first wavy and blond and then, by the time he started school, straight and chestnut brown, like Ruthie's. He saw the fear and sheer envy in his blue eyes of his father's great, iron-hard size, the wonder of it, his awestruck gaze when, at his father's urging, he punched the man in the tightened belly with all his force, and the man went on laughing until the boy hurt his hand and had to stop, which only made the man laugh all the harder. And he saw the terrible tremble of his lips when his father told him that to teach him to swim he and Uncle Richard were going to toss him from the dock into the lake, which they did, and indeed he did learn to swim that day, gasping and spitting water, slashing at it as if it were a beast, until he got his body close enough to the shore to feel the pebbly bottom against his feet. And then he saw his bizarre grin as he scrambled back to the dock and full speed ran its length, his skinny arms pinwheeling, and threw his body into the water himself, over and over again, slashing his way back to shore, rushing to the dock and racing to the end of it and tossing himself into the water, until finally the men stopped laughing at him and walked back to the women at the picnic table in the pine grove. And gradually Bob began to see his unborn son as he had never seen himself, for he saw the boy as pretty and frightened and sad. This confused him somewhat, muddled his fantasies, because he did not know what he should do to keep his son from being like that, from being like him, pretty and frightened and sad. Bob knew his own father had loved him and that he had been a kind, gentle, good-humored man, and with his son, Bob would have no choice but to try to be the same man his father had been with him. Any other kind of man, any other kind of father, was unimaginable to him.

The morning George Dill returns to work, he comes accompanied by his daughter. Bob has already opened the store and is sweeping the floor with a push broom, when he looks up and sees the tomato red Plymouth drive into the lot, Marguerite at the wheel. Her father, wearing his usual blue cap, white short-sleeved shirt and khaki trousers, looks small and fragile next to the woman, as if he were her child and she were driving him to school. Bob quickly puts the broom behind the stockroom door and walks to the cash register, pulls out his pen and order book and bends over the book, dropping deeply into the intricacies of the retail liquor business.

The woman enters first, wearing a nurse's uniform with a light, pale blue cardigan sweater over it. "Well," Bob says, "you're safely back. That's good."

"We are." She smiles lightly. Her dark brown face shows her fatigue. She has ashen circles under her eyes, and when she smiles, the skin over her high cheekbones tightens.

"I've missed you, George," Bob says heartily. "You never realize how much you need someone until they take a vacation. 'Course, I know this wasn't a vacation."

"No, Mistah Bob, it weren't no vacation. Dead and buried and resurrected and up in the Kingdom of Heaven now . . ." George says, his voice trailing off, his gaze starting to wander across the store.

"Daddy wants to come back to work right off, Mister Dubois. He's not really . . . right yet, you know, but I thought, if it was fine with you, that it would be good for him to come back to work, maybe get his mind off his brother that way." She ends her sentences with a lilt, a slight upturning of tone, so that she seems to be asking a question, a question that Bob feels compelled to hasten to answer.

"Oh, yes, sure, of course. I understand. Beautiful. Let him get right back to work. Be good for him. George," he says, "the broom's back by the stockroom door. You might's well take over where you left off."

The woman watches her father hurry off, her expression an odd mixture, odd to Bob, of relief and irritation. Bob has never seen an attractive black woman up close before. That is, he's never really looked into her eyes, never studied the curve of her lips and let his gaze fall along her long, tense throat. He's never allowed himself the pleasure, never subjected himself to the threat, of her beauty. In the past, whenever he's happened to find himself standing next to an attractive young black woman in line at the supermarket, for instance, or facing one of the two black women tellers at the bank in town or a customer, a housewife from the project asking for a six-pack of Colt 45, he's either dimmed his gaze or else has turned away altogether, embarrassed and frightened.

He hasn't been aware of that, of course, until now, when he unexpectedly finds himself staring at Marguerite, examining her boldly but nonetheless innocently, for at last his curiosity has overcome his fear and at this moment, but only for this moment, he has not yet made himself sufficiently familiar with her darkness to begin to long only for her, to touch and hold her, lick and kiss her, to lie down and fuck her and her alone and not just any tall, slender, attractive black-skinned woman, which is the way it has been until this moment, impersonal, abstract, pornographic and racist. Here I am on a white shag carpet fucking a beautiful black woman, me, Bob Dubois, for God's sake, pale and hairy, muscles tensed, cock swollen, red, stiff, while the beautiful, smooth-skinned black woman shakes her round buttocks in my face and peers back at me and offers me some more of her marijuana cigarette.

George has started sweeping in the far corner of the store, out of sight beyond the head-high shelves of gallon jugs of cheap wine, and the woman turns back to

Bob. "I think I'll be picking him up and leaving him off
for a while," she says thoughtfully, biting her lower lip
with large, widely spaced upper teeth. "He's still not
. . . like he was yet. I'm a little worried about his getting
the right bus home and all, you know? And getting off at
the right stop? You know?"

"Oh, sure, sure, I understand. I mean, it's a hell of a
shock to his whole system, probably." Bob feels himself
stumbling after the words he wants to say. He wants to
be both suave and consoling, as reassuring as he is
seductive, but he knows he sounds instead like a man
who's busy and hasn't quite heard what's been told to
him.

"So . . . you're a nurse," he finally says. Her hair,
cut in a short, loose Afro, is black and shiny and prematurely flecked with gray.

"Yes, I work for three doctors, out at the Westway
Clinic."

"Ah," Bob says, as if gaining an insight.

"You know it? You live out there in Auburndale?"

"No, no. It's just . . . that's a nice job, a nurse in a
clinic. Better than a hospital, right?"

"Better hours. But that's about all," she says. Then,
"You got a nice smile, you know that?"

"Ah," Bob says again. Suddenly he asks her, "Are
you married? I mean, George never mentions a son-in-
law. Only you. He talks about you a lot. So I wondered
. . ." Her skin is clear, unblemished and roan-colored,
dark brown with a slight reddish tinge brought forward,
Bob notices, by lipstick and the makeup on her cheeks.
She's wearing perfume, lilac, and when he sniffs for
more of it, he looks at her nose, broad, symmetrical,
functional. A true nose, he thinks. Not a large, pointy,
phony nose like his, not a dog's nose. Elaine's nose he
hasn't looked at for years, although he used to wonder
at it, because it was so perfectly shaped, or so it seemed
to him then—slightly curved, short and narrow, giving
to her small face the look of a fierce bird, like a falcon or
hawk—but now he can't recall it. His memory is only of
having paid attention to something that has disappeared,

swallowed by her eyes, so that now, when he looks at
his wife's face or remembers it, all he sees is the center
of her eyes, as if her face has somehow gradually become invisible without his ever having noticed until after
it was gone, lost to him, he is sure, forever.

Marguerite answers his question as directly as he asked
it, as if she is used to having white men she barely
knows ask her if she is married. She was, she tells him,
but not now, not for over five years. Her husband was
in the air force and stationed here at Shure. "But," she
says, shrugging, "that didn't work out so good. But I
liked it here, and I had a better job than the one I used
to have in Macon, so I stayed. And the next year my
mama died and Daddy came down."

"It doesn't make sense, your being alone," Bob says
with great seriousness.

She laughs. "Yes, it does, Mister Dubois . . ."

"Bob."

"Okay, Bob. Yes, it does make sense! A lot of sense."
Then, turning to leave, she smiles and says, "Besides,
I'm not alone, you know."

"You're not? I thought . . ." He doesn't know what
he thought.

"I got my daddy!" she calls from the door. Then, to
the old man, "Bye, honey! I'll pick you up at five,
okay? You remember, now, y' hear?" And then she is
gone, leaving Bob Dubois standing at the cash register,
his heart thumping, head abuzz, hands, he suddenly
notices, wet with sweat.

ON MONDAY, WEDNESDAY AND FRIDAY, BOB LOOKS FOR-
ward to seeing Marguerite twice, in the morning when
she brings her father to work and again in the late
afternoon when she picks him up. She could more easily
drop the old man off in the morning, and later, sitting in
her car outside, signal with the horn for him to come
out, but she doesn't. She gets out of the car and comes
into the store and talks with Bob. Bob believes she does
this because she is falling in love with him. He believes this
because he thinks he is falling in love with her, and

just as his days have now taken on an unexpected yet longed-for significance, at least his Mondays, Wednesdays and Fridays have, so, too, he believes, have her days, once tedious and bland as boiled potatoes, now come to seem intense, shapely, piquant.

At home, Bob merely waits for time to pass. He withdraws from his nightly conversations with Elaine, leaves off, or treats as a chore, reading stories to the girls before they go to bed, and usually ends up falling asleep on the couch before the eleven o'clock news comes on. Naturally, Elaine resents and then quickly fears the change in him, for she does not attribute it to anything other than to the change in her, that is, to her pregnancy, which, she thinks, has made her more sensitive than usual, more demanding and more easily hurt.

So she tries to avoid criticizing Bob for depriving her and the girls of his attention, and really, that is all he's guilty of so far, so why should he be criticized? He's working sixty and seventy hours a week at a demeaning, boring job that he was led to expect would be something quite different from what it's turned out to be, he's cut himself off from everything that's familiar to him— landscape, manners, friends—and except for Eddie, around whom he's never able to rest, he has no one he can simply enjoy himself with, no one to go out for pizza and beers with, no one to go fishing with, no one to go with him on a Sunday morning to Chain-O'-Lakes Park in Winter Haven, where the Red Sox hold their spring training rites and play their exhibition games, where, if he got out there before they went north in late April, he could get, he told her, Carl Yastrzemski's, Jim Rice's and Freddie Lynn's autographs for their son, because someday, he said to her, those guys will be dead and buried and Bob junior won't believe that his dad saw them in the flesh and actually had a conversation with them.

Elaine feels sorry for her husband. She suggests hiring a babysitter and going out together to the Okie Doke, a dance club she's heard about from one of the wives she's befriended at the park, a woman named Ellen

Skeeter, but Bob says, "Naw, that's just one of those cracker joints where the music's too loud and everybody gets drunk and ends up stomping on your feet if you try to dance or picking a fight with you on the way to the men's room."

So she urges him to take a Sunday and pack a lunch and drive with her and the girls to New Smyrna Beach on the coast, but he sighs and says, "Just what I need after a hard week, a day spent in the car fighting the traffic, with the kids fussing in back, a bunch of sandy sandwiches in the sun, and a sunburn to boot. Besides, this time of year the beaches are jammed with all those noisy Canucks who couldn't afford to come down in January and February. God save me from the Frenchmen. It's the same kind as used to drive us nuts in July at Old Orchard Beach in Maine."

Well, maybe he could go fishing with Eddie one Sunday, take a ride in the boat he's always bragging about, learn how to water ski, since Eddie's so eager to teach him.

"Fuck Eddie," Bob grunts, leaning forward on the couch to switch channels on the Sony.

Naturally, then, though neither of them intends or desires it, Bob and Elaine fall to quarreling. At first it's snarl and countersnarl, followed by a sullen silence that fades in an hour or two. But then her insecurity and attempts to please him, colliding almost nightly with his desire to be left alone with his fantasies and depression, make him feel entrapped as well, a feeling that makes him act like a man who thinks his guilt is being exploited, even though he believes that he has done nothing to feel guilty for, which only increases his resentment. Confused and angry, he lashes out at her, until she, too, is confused and angry. Weeks go by marked only by their quarrels and the silent, solitary periods in between, a sad time for them, since neither of them knows what is happening to them or how to stop it.

Until finally, one morning in late May, following a particularly vicious argument the night before, a shouting, name-calling fight that began when Bob arrived home from work without the half gallon of milk she'd called and asked him to bring, and he'd stomped to the refrigerator for a beer and found none there, which meant she'd been drinking his beer in the afternoon with her fat friend from Georgia, the redhead whose name he refused to remember because he hated her voice. They'd gone to sleep shuddering with rage and the knowledge that they both were becoming ugly people.

The next morning, Elaine, as usual, wakes first, showers and dresses quickly and wakes the girls. An hour later, showered, shaved, barefoot and wearing a clean pair of khaki pants and a tee shirt, Bob enters the kitchen, passes the girls at the table and Elaine at the sink without acknowledging them, as if the three are familiar bits of furniture, two chairs and a pole lamp reliably in their accustomed places. He opens the refrigerator door and studies its foggy interior, settles finally on tomato juice and closes the door. He has to step around his wife to get a glass from the cupboard, and as he passes her, he looks down at her high, rounded belly.

"Morning," he says in a low voice.

"Good morning," she answers, and she looks at her children as if for approval. Wasn't Mommy polite to Daddy?

Squinting, Emma watches her father carefully. Her puffy, round face is covered with purple jelly. White underpants and a tank top cling to her sausage-like body, making her look more like a miniaturized sumo wrestler than a Caucasian female child. Ruthie, opposite her at the table, ignores her father altogether. Dressed for school in clean corduroy jeans and a striped short-sleeved jersey, she pretends to read the advertising on the back of the Count Chocula box.

"Hi, kids," Bob says, pouring himself a glass of juice.

Emma continues squinting up at him, as if he were the sun, while Ruthie seems to go on reading about adult daily nutrition requirements.

Bob puts his face next to Emma's and, grinning, bugs his eyes out. "What're you so serious about, Flowerpot?"

When the child lets a tentative smile creep over her

thin lips, Bob stands up, tousles her thin hair with one hand and empties the glass of juice into his mouth. Then, to Ruthie: "Hey, don't you say good morning to your father?"

Slowly, like peeling back a gummed sticker, Ruthie removes her gaze from the cereal box and looks into her father's eyes. Then she looks down, almost shyly. "Hi, Daddy."

"You want breakfast?" Elaine asks him.

"Sure. Whatcha got?" He's at the stove, pouring himself a cup of coffee.

"Eggs, if you want. Bacon's all gone." She squeezes the words from her mouth like tiny, dry seeds.

"Fine." Pushing open the screened door, Bob steps outside and, coffee cup in hand, strolls barefoot from the trailer across the driveway and gets the *Ledger* from the box. Opening it to the sports section, he checks out last night's major league baseball scores.

"Sonofabitch. They're on a tear," he says as he enters. "They do this every fucking spring. Go on a tear and get me all lathered up, then blow it in August to the fucking Yankees." He sits at the table next to Emma and spreads out the paper.

"You swear too easy."

"Huh?" He takes a sip of coffee and goes on reading.

"You swear too easy. I wish you wouldn't." She stands with her back to the sink, holding one egg in each hand, as if about to juggle them.

"Do you still love Mommy?" Ruthie suddenly asks, somber, unafraid, but deeply interested in his answer. Emma looks up and watches his face. Elaine too. They all watch him. What's going on? Have they made some kind of bet on it?

"What're you telling her?" Bob asks Elaine.

"Not a thing. She asked me the same question. Before you came out."

"And what did you say?"

She looks at the eggs in her hands and taps them lightly against one another. "I said I don't know."

Bob glares at his wife, then turns to his daughter. "Why do you want to know a thing like that, Ruthie?"

"I heard you and Mommy yelling last night. You woke me up."

Bob closes the newspaper and crosses his arms in front of him. "Aw, honey, I'm sorry about all that. Of course I still love Mommy."

"How come you said you didn't?"

Bob looks at Elaine, who turns away and cracks first one egg into the skillet, then the other. He feels emptied out, a metal drum. He doesn't want this. No man wants this.

His daughters wait for his answer. He looks down at Emma beside him. What can she know? "Did we wake you up too, Flowerpot?"

Nervously, Emma opens and closes her hands, squeezing jelly between her fingers.

"How come you said you don't love Mommy anymore?" Ruthie repeats.

"Well, honey, it's like . . . sometimes grownups say things they don't mean. That's all. They get a *little* mad about one thing, and then they act *real* mad about another. It's like when we first moved here, some of the kids at school were mean to you, and now they're your friends. They didn't mean it."

"But it's different. They're not s'posed to love me. You, you're s'posed to love Mommy. What did you get mad for?"

Elaine turns away from the stove and waits for his answer.

"You still love *Daddy*," Ruthie says to her mother. It's an announcement, but it wants confirmation.

"Yes," Elaine says. "I love Daddy." She turns back to the stove.

"What did you get mad for?" Ruthie asks him again.

Bob sighs and looks at his wife, as if for guidance, but she's holding her back to him. "I . . . I don't know, honey. I don't know why I got mad last night. It was late, and I was tired, and worried. In a bad mood, that's all. Now eat your breakfast and let me read the paper, okay?'' He smiles wearily, and the child returns her gaze, brow furrowed, to the cereal box.

He reads the Red Sox box score, notes with pleasure that Yaz went three for four with two doubles and Torrez pitched seven innings and struck out five. "Sonofabitch. Yaz is forty and he's playing like a kid. I love that sonofabitch."

"Will you please watch your language!" Elaine says, hands planted on hips. "This is a whole new habit of yours, this swearing all the time."

"Sorry, sorry, sorry," he says. He takes another sip of his coffee, and to win back her favor, smacks his lips noisily. "Good coffee."

"Thanks," she grunts. "Here's your eggs."

He breaks the yolks with the tip of his fork and rubs a piece of toast through them; it's the way he has eaten eggs all his life. If by accident he were served eggs well-done, he'd try to break the yolks, and failing, he'd react with confusion. They wouldn't be actual eggs to him. They'd be vegetables or cheese or fish. Eggs run and make a lovely mess that you can clean up with a piece of buttered toast.

"I can't believe Yaz," he says, still poring over the paper. "He's almost ten years older than me, but he's playing like a kid. If I tried to do what I did as a kid, I'd break my ass." When Bob was a kid, large and fast and tireless, he was a graceful bear sweeping the puck away from a three-on-one rush to his goal, skating the length of the rink alone, long, graceful, powerful strides, with the puck swirling ahead of him across the blue line, where he ducks to one side and fakes the defenseman, cuts to the other, jerking the puck along as if it were attached to his stick by a piece of string, charging the net, driving the puck with the force of his rush a half foot above the ice over the goalie's desperate slash, and as he glides past the goal, he watches the puck smack against the net, watches it drop softly to the ice, watches the goalie angrily whack his stick against the ice, and Bob smiles, skates slowly, smoothly, back to his end of the ice, barely out of breath.

"Y' know," he says to Elaine, "I'm really sorry we didn't get down here for spring training. I'd have loved to watch the Sox work out, over there at Chain-O'-Lakes Park, over there in Winter Haven. It's only a couple miles. Now," he says, lowering his voice, "now they've all gone north, it's all up north. I used to go to Fenway with my dad once in a while when I was a kid. I haven't been to Fenway in years. . . ."

"We were here in time. You could've watched them play."

"Well, yeah, I know. But we were still getting settled and all." He looks up from the newspaper and peers out the window above the sink at the flat roof of the trailer next to theirs and the tops of the palm trees and the bright blue sky beyond, and he says, "It's hard, I sort of didn't believe they were here. In Florida, I mean. I've known it all my life, the Red Sox do spring training in Winter Haven, Florida, and here I am living ten miles away, only I can't picture it, so I just sit around, like I always did, waiting for them to come home to Fenway and begin the season. Only, when they do begin the season, here I am in Florida. It's strange. I probably would've got Yaz's autograph. Its real easy in spring training to get to talk to the players and all. They walk right over to the fence and talk to you."

"I know," she says.

Ruthie comes up next to him and says, "Bye, Daddy," and purses her lips for a kiss.

Instead of kissing her, he stands and says, "Wait a minute. I'll walk out to the bus stop with you."

Surprised and pleased, she claps her hands together, then flips one hand for him to hold. Together, they step out the door into the bright sunlight, and holding hands, cross the yard and driveway to the paved lane, where, looking back at his station wagon, he notices once again his New Hampshire number plates and says aloud to himself, "Jesus, I've got to get Florida plates before they pick me up for it."

The car looks peculiar to him. He's owned it for almost three years and has only got five more payments to mail north to the Catamount Trust, at which point, as he's said to Elaine many times, he knows the transmission will go. But this morning, as he walks past the car with his daughter and moves down the lane to the highway, he turns and studies the car and wonders why it looks so strange to him, as if it has been cut out of a black-and-white snapshot and pasted onto a color picture of pink hibiscus and bougainvillea, green patches of grass, pale blue mobile home, dark green star-shaped thatch palm behind the trailer, citrus groves beyond the crisp, cloudless blue sky above. He's walking backwards, barefoot, sucking on his upper lip and no longer holding his daughter's hand.

"What're you looking at?" she asks, peering over her shoulder.

"Oh, nothing. The car. The house."

"We should get a new car."

"You think so, eh?"

"Yeah. A red one. To go with the new house." Ruthie skips ahead of him, ponytail flying, and he turns from the car and walks quickly to catch up.

"Yeah!" he calls after her. "A new car to go with a new house to go with a new job! A whole new life!"

She slows and waits for him, and when he catches up, he takes her hand again, and they walk on in silence to where the school bus stops at the side of the highway.

By the time he returns to the kitchen, he's sweating, and his tee shirt has large wet circles under the arms. The kitchen is empty; he assumes Elaine has taken Emma to the bathroom to wash her face, hands and arms before putting her outside to play. He checks his watch, eight twenty-three, and dropping his weight onto his chair, leans over to finish reading the paper.

"Aw, Jesus," he says, looking with disgust at the purple smears and globs of jelly on the paper. "Jesus H. Christ," he murmurs. He stands quickly and grabs the newspaper at the sides, as if to lift it, but then, looking down on it from above, he notices for the first time a photograph in the center of the page opposite the box scores. It's a wirephoto of a base runner sliding head-first, sliding into second, Bob thinks, or possibly third, though he knows right off that it's Carl Yastrzemski, number eight, doing the sliding. It's Yaz at forty, stretching a long single into a double by running ninety feet full speed and hurling his body against the ground, diving and stretching his arms for the base as he twists his body hard to the right to avoid the tag, spikes, shinbones and knees of the second baseman.

For several seconds Bob studies the picture, then, in a violent move, his face stiffens and he crumples the entire newspaper into a large, loose bundle, pushes, crushes and crumples it again and again, until he's made a dense, crinkly ball of it. He steps around the table and opens the cupboard under the sink, tosses the ball into the plastic trash bucket and closes the cupboard door.

Facing away from the kitchen, through the living room to the hall beyond, he hears Emma's angry cry, almost a howl, as her mother rubs the child's cheeks and chin, arms, hands and belly, with a rough, wet washcloth, and he hears Elaine order the child to be still, hold still, it'll be over in a minute if you'll only hold still and stop squirming.

Bob knows he loves the woman properly. And he loves the children properly too, though he's never had to ask himself that one, thank God. Those are facts, though, and a man has to give himself over to the facts of the life he finds himself living, no matter how he's living it.

He walks quickly back through the trailer to the bedroom he shares with his wife, to get ready for work.

5

NEVERTHELESS. BOB IS OBSESSED WITH MARGUERITE DILL, who is not at all as he imagines and supposes her to be. It would be difficult, if not impossible, to say here who or what she is, exactly, and probably beside the point as well, except to observe that Bob knows very little of what it is to be a woman, nothing at all of what it is to be

black. He's honest and intelligent enough to admit this
and behave accordingly, but like most white men, he's
not imaginative enough to believe that being a woman
is extremely different from being a man and being black
extremely different from being white. If pushed, and he
has been pushed now and then, at least by Elaine, he'd
go only so far as to concede that the differences are
probably no greater than those between child and adult,
and because he bears within him the child he once was,
and the child he once was carried within him the seed of
the man he would someday become, then understanding
between the two is an easily arranged affair of one's
attention. To understand your children, you attend to
the child in you; and all your children have to do, if they
wish to understand you, is project themselves twenty or
thirty years into the future. Therefore, to imagine Elaine
and Doris and now Marguerite, the three women who in
recent years have mattered most to him, all Bob has had
to do is pay attention to the woman in himself. It's
harder in the case of Marguerite, but all the more interesting to him for that, because with her he has to pay
attention to the black man in himself as well.

When Bob talks to his wife, he is thinking about
Marguerite. When he looks at his wife's reddish hair,
pale skin, rounding body, he thinks of Marguerite's hair,
skin, body—but not to the disadvantage of either woman.
It's just that hair, anyone's, reminds him of Marguerite's
hair; skin, if he happens to notice it, reminds him of
Marguerite's skin; and breasts, belly, thighs and so on,
remind him of Marguerite's. Which aspects, of course,
he's never actually seen and therefore must imagine,
relying for components on the occasional *Playboy* and
Penthouse black centerfold he's seen.

Elaine tells her new friends at the trailer park and her
sister-in-law Sarah that Bob is distracted, preoccupied,
worried, and she adds that she's concerned. But in fact
she's more than concerned. She's frightened. She believes he doesn't love her anymore. And to make matters worse, she believes that it's because she is pregnant.
The sad truth of the matter, however, is that Bob often

forgets she is pregnant, and when he remembers, it's as if he's remembering something that was true long ago.

His obsession with Marguerite has become his sole companion. He talks to it, argues with it, admires and respects it, gives it all the attention and time he can steal from his family and job. He's almost grateful that he has no friends here and that his job, where he's often alone for hours at a time, blocks him off from the voices and needs of his wife and children. Though he is not aware of it, he has recently taken up humming a tuneless tune, hour after hour, whenever someone else is within hearing range. As soon as that person, George Dill or Elaine or one of the kids, leaves his proximity or closes the door between them, he ceases humming and lets his obsession loose, as if it were a dog wanting exercise, to leap and run about the room, dart out the door and gallop in wild circles in the parking lot and across the marshy fields, until it's almost lost from sight, where it wheels about and comes racing happily back to him, leaps into his arms and licks his face with joy.

Months pass, and little changes. Elaine's body has gone on swelling steadily, and Emma, knowing something threatening is going to happen, has become sullen and withdrawn, not exactly a behavior problem, but not pleasant to be around, either, and Ruthie has complained increasingly of school, even feigning sickness to stay home, until it turns out that she has what's called a learning disability, which, the school nurse tells Elaine, and Elaine reports to Bob, may be merely emotional or she may be slightly dyslexic. Time will tell, but not to worry, many children pass through phases like this, especially when adjusting to a new environment. But if it persists into the second grade, when reading is essential for learning, special instruction will be necessary. Bob barely hears the report, for he's suffering from a learning disability of his own, a disability fed and encouraged by his Monday, Wednesday and Friday visits from Marguerite, which have become part of her weekly routine too, possibly rationalized as, but nonetheless essential to, her caring for her father, a man who drifts through his days as lost in his private past as Bob is lost in his private future.

Bob and Marguerite have become close friends. They gossip together. She tells stories about the three doctors she works for, calls them Winkum, Blinkum and Nod, a lecher, a crook and a lazy man. He counters with complaints about his brother, his job, his boring family life, and then one morning remembers Ruthie's learning disability and shoves it into the conversation so as to elicit Marguerite's professional opinion, which turns out to confirm the school nurse's opinion, a fact that impresses Bob with Marguerite's intelligence and education.

Now, for the first time, Marguerite seems genuinely curious about Bob's wife and children. They've talked of many things before this, often matters of considerable intimacy, at least for Bob, such as when and how his parents died, which parent he resembles more, and how he is both different from and very much like his brother Eddie. She even asked him once if he had played any sports in school, which Bob took as a clear indication of her interest in his body, and as a result, he went into elaborate detail about the kind of body you needed if you were going to excel as a defenseman in hockey. "Lots of endurance," he told her. "You gotta have lots of endurance. And big bones, it's good to have big bones and flat muscles. You can't have one of those muscle-man bodies, you know the type, muscles like grapefruit glued to skinny bones. 'Cause you really get banged around, playing hockey. You go into the corner, digging for the puck, some big guy'll come at you full tilt and lay a body check on you that slams you into the boards, and it's legal, all legal, so you gotta keep on playing. No time to lie there and clear your head and check for broken bones. I still skate," he told her, lying. "Leastways I did till I left New Hampshire. Pickup games, you understand, nothing organized. I'm still in shape for it all right, but I don't have the wind anymore. Cigarettes," he said ruefully, lighting one up.

Marguerite asks him what his wife is like. She's genuinely curious; his answer will help her understand what she herself is like. Her father is in the stockroom, cutting cartons and stacking them into neat bundles. He knows she's here and it's past quitting time, but he's grown accustomed to her chats with his boss, which leave him standing in the background, pulling at his earlobe and waiting, like a bored child, for her to finish whatever obscure adult business she's up to.

"Well, first off, Elaine's a lovely lady," Bob says. "Very much the mother," he adds, leaning forward with both hands on the top of the cash register, as if it were a lectern.

"And you, are you very much the father?"

Bob looks intently into her eyes, drops his gaze for a second and says in a low voice, "No. No, not really. And I got no excuses, either. It's just . . . it's just that I'm all the time too worried about myself. She's not like that, Elaine. She doesn't worry about herself all the time, like I do, so she's free to think about other people, the kids, mainly, and me. It's not selfishness, I don't think. It's different. I'm not really selfish. I'm just all the time worried about myself. . . ."

"Why don't you stop worrying about yourself so much, then?"

"It's not like that. You can't just decide and do it, or else you end up worrying about that too, and you're right back where you started from. It just has to happen. You just have to be born a better person than I happen to be, that's all."

"Oh, come on, you're not a bad person. You're really not."

"Not *bad*, maybe. But not *good*, either. See, you, you're good. You think about your father and worry about him more than you worry about yourself. Like Elaine does. Me, I worry so much about whether I'm any good or not, or what I ought to do or shouldn't ought to do, or whether I'm smart enough or work hard enough, all those things, that there's never much room in my head for anyone else's problems. Even somebody like my brother Eddie, for instance, who, even though he's selfish, really selfish, and I'm not like that . . . still, he's a good man, because in the end he doesn't worry about himself too much. I don't know, it's a kind of vanity, you know? What I've got. I mean, Eddie's free to be good. I'm not, almost. He's more the father than I am, and more the husband too. More the brother, even. He sees somebody's got a problem, and he tries to solve it, even though he's selfish, which only means that he won't solve it if the solution is going to hurt him somehow, and most solutions won't do that, you know. Especially if you've got some money, like Eddie does. But me, I don't even notice it that somebody's got a problem, not even when it's staring me in the face. I don't know what makes me this way, but it's the way I am, and I can't stop being the way I am just by wanting to. Any more than Eddie can, or Elaine, or even you, can stop being the way you are just because you want to. If you want to.''

"I suppose,'' Marguerite says, stretching wearily. "It's hot out there. Nice in here.''

"You got air in that car, though.''

"Yeah. But it's getting from here to there that bothers me.'' She laughs. "That's the trouble with air-conditioning. Nobody missed it till after they got it. Anyhow, when that thing in my car starts up, all it blows out at first is more hot air. It's worse'n a heater.''

Bob watches the woman carefully, as if she were prey. "Are you . . . are you going straight home from here?''

"Yeah,'' she says. "I got to fix supper for Daddy.''

"Then? Then what?''

"Then . . . nothing, I guess. No big date. No nothing.'' She smiles with slight embarrassment, as if coming up empty-handed.

"Don't you have any boyfriends?''

"Nope.'' With a sudden movement, she stabs at her hair with stiffened fingers. "No boyfriends. You never heard me mention none, did you?''

"Well, I wondered. You know, since you're so good-looking and all, and single. But I never asked before, because I figured you'd just say yes.''

She smiles. Her teeth are large and gapped. To Bob, they're sexy, forthright, passionate teeth. "And you didn't want to hear me say so?"

"Right." He smiles back.

"What about you, mister?"

"Well. I'm married, you know," he says, suddenly serious.

"Yeah. But that don't stop people."

"I'll tell you the truth."

"Uh-huh. You tell me the truth."

"I have . . . I *did* have a girlfriend. In New Hampshire. A nice woman, though. I used to see her once in a while. No big thing, though. We weren't in love or anything. You know. Just friends."

"Uh-huh. Just friends. What about your wife? Did she know about this friend of yours?"

"Jesus, no! No. It was just a once-in-a-while thing, me and Doris. That was her name, Doris."

"Uh-huh. Doris. Well," she says, "I've got to get Daddy and go home."

"Is your house air-conditioned?"

"I got me one unit in the living room, and it cools the rest of the house down pretty good, except when I'm cooking or there's a whole lot of people in the house. But it's fine for me and Daddy." She looks toward the back of the store, as if in search of her father, who sits in the stockroom on a crate, waiting for her call.

"Ah, listen, Marguerite, I'd like to go out for a drink with you sometime. Would that be okay with you?" He exhales slowly.

Screwing up her face, as if trying to remember his name, she studies his eyes for a few seconds. "You sure? I mean, there's places we could go. Over in Winter Haven or up in Lakeland. You're married, you know. In case you've forgotten." She pauses. "And we'd stick out."

Bob takes shallow breaths quickly and his voice comes out higher than he'd like. "Of course I'm sure. Just go out for a few drinks, you know, some night after I close the store."

"You know what you're doing," she informs him.

"Oh, yeah. No problem. I could pick you up at your house, if you wanted, or we could meet someplace."

She is silent for a second, then smiles and pats his hand. "Tell you what. I'll pick you up here at the store some night. My car's got air, remember? That ol' thing of yours, that's a Yankee car." She smiles warmly and calls her father.

Folding his arms across his chest, Bob steps back from the register, as if he's just completed a big sale. He leans against the shelf behind him and watches the woman and her father head for the door. Just as she reaches to open it, Bob calls to her, "How about tonight? I close at nine."

Without looking back, she says, "I don't know," opens the door and steps into the heat.

At seven, she calls him, and sounding slightly frightened, speaking more rapidly than usual, she says that she'll meet him at nine, then hurriedly, as if late for another appointment, gets off the phone.

Bob immediately calls Elaine at home and tells her he's made a new friend, a Budweiser salesman from Lakeland, who's asked him out for a drink after work, so he'll be home a little later than usual tonight.

This relieves Elaine. A new friend is what Bob needs. Someone to brag to, someone he can talk fishing and sports with, someone he can complain freely to, especially about Eddie, because she knows he won't complain about Eddie to her, no matter how much Eddie, that bastard Eddie, bothers him.

THREE TIMES IN THE NEXT THREE WEEKS BOB AND MARguerite drive out in her car for drinks at the Barnacle in Winter Haven. That first night, when they returned to the store, Bob leaned over from the passenger's side and kissed her on the cheek, nicely, then got out and waved good night. The second time she drove him back from the Barnacle, they sat in her car for a few minutes talking about the stupidity of one of the doctors she worked for at the clinic, and Bob reached over and kissed Marguerite full on the mouth in midsentence, passionately ground his mouth against hers, and she let him slip his tongue between her big teeth and on into her mouth. The third time, they sat in the car making out like teenagers for nearly an hour, before Bob finally pulled himself free, zipped his pants and stumbled from her car to his. They didn't go to the Barnacle after that; they drove straight to the Hundred Lakes Motel out on Highway 17 north of Winter Haven.

Compared to most men his age, Bob has made love to few women, so if he no longer thinks of himself as inexperienced, it's mainly because of the frequency with which he has made love over the years. He lost his virginity when he was seventeen in the back seat of Avery Boone's Packard when he and Ave crashed a beer party at a New England College coed dormitory, and by pretending to be sophomores from Dartmouth, talked a pair of beer-drunk freshman girls from Fairfield, Connecticut, into leaving the party and driving to Lake Sunapee with them.

"Older wimmen!" they hollered afterwards, all the way home to Catamount. It had been Avery's idea, so he did most of the hollering, but Bob gleefully shivered with excitement for hours.

The next summer, Bob joined the air force to avoid being drafted into the army and sent to Vietnam to be killed, and the fear of venereal disease, embarrassment for his ignorance and a country boy's shyness kept him celibate for most of the next four years, until, home on leave, he took Elaine Gagnon to the drive-in theater in Concord and promised to marry her. She had just graduated from high school, and when her mother died that same month, thought originally of going to hairdressing school down in Manchester, to get away from everything, she said. But she fell in love with Bob Dubois, who had been a senior at Bishop Grenier and a hockey star when she had been a withdrawn, insecure, plain-looking freshman whose father had disappeared years before and whose mother worked on the line down at the cannery. Elaine counted herself lucky to be able to stay in Catamount and wait for Bob to be discharged from the air force so she could marry him and take care of his house, have his babies, wash his clothes, cook his food, laugh at his jokes, share his anger, and comfort and reassure him, and in return obtain for herself the family she never had and always felt she both needed and deserved. She got a job in bookkeeping at the cannery, and they did it the first time in the bedroom she had shared with her mother in the tiny apartment over Maxfield's Hardware Store on Green Street, and both Bob and Elaine thought it was the most exciting thing they had ever done. So they did it again, and then they did it as often as they could, which, for the next two years, until Bob had saved enough money for a down payment on the house on Butterick Street and they could get married, was only once or twice a week, usually on Saturday nights at her place. He was living with his parents then. After they got married, they did it four and five nights a week.

Despite this clearly focused attention, over the next four years Bob fucked five women other than his wife, all of them customers of Abenaki Oil Company, one time each. He had a hard time distinguishing between making love on the run to these women, covering their shoulders and arms with oil burner soot, and masturbating. He felt a similar kind and quantity of guilt for both. Even while doing it, he felt stupid and young, adolescent again, the way he used to feel when he was in the air force. He'd wake up in his barracks bed and remember that the night before he'd spent several sleepless hours contemplating deliciously obscene fantasies while masturbating slowly into a handkerchief or sock. He'd look in his shaving mirror, and he'd see the weakness in his eyes, and he'd loathe himself for about a half hour.

In his late twenties, he stopped masturbating, which was no easier for him than quitting smoking would have been, and stopped responding warmly to the flirtatious words and looks of lonely women with broken oil burners, and he concentrated all his sexual attentions on Elaine, which for a while pleased him, made him feel strong, disciplined, clean. Then one night he learned from Elaine that she had slept with his best friend, Avery Boone. The announcement came a week after Avery had sailed south on the inland waterway in his converted Grand Banks trawler, the boat Bob had helped salvage and redesign and that he'd used freely for several years fishing out of Portsmouth, alone on some days and with Ave and anyone else who wanted to come along when the bluefish were running.

With Ave gone, Elaine had felt free to confess what had been bearing down on her conscience like a stone, what she had confessed to three different priests and what all three had urged her to confess to her husband, which is that one day when Bob was out on the boat, the *Belinda Blue*, gone alone for mackerel, Avery had come over to the house, and they had got drunk together and had ended up in bed together. Avery had been horrified afterwards, as had she, and made her promise never to tell Bob, it would destroy their friendship, which was more important to Ave than anything else, except, of course, Bob's relationship with Elaine.

Bob had taken the news stoically, grimly, and when she was through confessing, he told her he understood *her* crime, but he couldn't understand Ave's. Several times over the next few years, Ave wrote from Moray Key, Florida, where he'd established himself as a charter fisherman, but Bob never answered, and then all they heard from Ave was an annual Christmas card, signed with his full name, first and last, as if to admonish his friend for his silence.

Bob had not forgotten Avery Boone, but he figured he had forgiven him. Elaine's obvious faithfulness and her shame for her one aberration helped him forgive his old pal, but so did his own affair with Doris Cleeve, which started shortly after Elaine's confession and continued haphazardly until the week before Bob and his family left Catamount for good. He never even said goodbye to Doris Cleeve, never even told her he was leaving.

And that's it, the entire sexual experience of Bob Dubois. On the face of it, it's not much, but in a way,

Bob made up for his paucity of actual experience by thinking about sex constantly and, for the most part, clearly. His good fortune, and perhaps hers, is that he enjoyed sex with his wife and she enjoyed it with him, so that despite his constantly thinking about sex (remembering past encounters fondly, visualizing future couplings with unusual vividness) and his use of an unexpected, if somewhat naive, gift for narrative, his thoughts rarely turned in on themselves, where they could easily have bred feelings of deprivation, self-pity and resentment. But all that, of course, was before he met and fell in love with Marguerite Dill.

THEY ENTER, MARGUERITE FIRST, BOB HOLDING THE door open for her, and commence kissing in the middle of the room. Bob thinks that maybe he'd like to have the lights on, but he can't figure out how to say so without sounding a little weird, so he lets it go and continues kissing her and fondling her long body. She's wearing designer jeans and a gray tee shirt that advertises Disney World with the head of Mickey Mouse, whose black ears spread like a diva's breastplate across her large, round breasts.

She's very passionate, he thinks, as she bites, sucks, licks his face and lightly moans. Stepping her back to the bed, where she kicks off her sandals, he lays her down and proceeds to draw her jeans off, first one leg, then the other, and then her panties, while she shrugs her way out of her tee shirt and unsnaps her bra.

Standing, Bob unbuckles, unzips, unbuttons and unties his own clothing, until he, too, is naked, and hugely erect, he knows, for he can feel the weight of his cock swaying in front of him, out there in the breeze and spray like a bowsprit, and as he comes forward onto her, his mouth reaching in the darkness for her mouth, his hands reaching for her breasts, he has a quick vision of himself as a white boat, a skiff or maybe a flat-bottomed Boston whaler, sliding easily onto the hot golden sands of a tropical beach, with dark, lush jungle ahead of him, the burning sun and endless blue sky above, and behind him, the sea, surging, lifting and shoving him up and forward onto the New World.

"Go easy," she whispers. "I'm not ready." She holds him by the shoulders, spreads her legs and grinds her pelvis and groin against his, while he goes on kissing her along the neck, down and across her shoulders, until her moans and the heavy thrust and rub of her groin start to get to him, and he makes his first attempt to enter her.

"Easy, easy," she warns. He's gentle, but persistent, a man knocking lightly at a locked door, determined to wake his lover and not her maid. Wetting his fingers with spit, he reaches down and strokes her lightly with his fingertips. She arches her spine first toward him, then away, and lifting her pelvis, she opens like a flower to him. Again, he drops down and moves to enter, but again he finds himself ejected.

"Wait, wait. Kiss me. Please kiss me."

He kisses her, starting at her face and ears, tangling his fingers in her dense hair, then down along her neck to her breasts, where he feathers her large, erect nipples lightly with his tongue, while she twists beneath him and coos with evident pleasure. Moving his mouth off her breasts to her belly, he draws his hands to her breasts and strokes her nipples with precise care, drifting with tongue, teeth and lips downward, over her hips, along the inside of her thighs, and when she spreads her thighs, he moves his mouth quickly against her cunt, prods and probes it with his tongue, until he knows its shapes, and begins licking hungrily, noisily, with gentle precision, his heavy arms laid across her belly, his fingertips fluttering over her breasts. She has brought her naked feet together, sole against sole, and when he starts to run his prick slowly against her feet, she moves them away, as if frightened. A third time, lifting his weight onto his elbows, he attempts to enter her. A third time, he fails.

"I want to make love to you, Marguerite."

"You are. You are. Do what you were doing. Do that."

He lowers his mouth to her breasts and moves quickly down her body. Soon she is quivering beneath him, and after a few moments, she lifts her pelvis against him, shudders and says, "Ah-h-h!" In seconds, she has drawn him up and forward, has turned him onto his back and has buried her face in his groin, licking and sucking on his penis. Almost before he knows it is happening, it has already happened, and she leaves him for the bathroom, where he hears from behind the closed door the sound of water running.

By the time she returns, he has got under the covers of the bed. She joins him there, and wrapping her long arms around his body, she snuggles against him and says, "That was wonderful. Real nice."

"Yeah," he says. "No, it really was."

"I'm sorry. I guess . . . I guess I'm sort of nervous and all. You know?"

"Oh, yeah, well, I didn't even notice. I mean, that's okay. It was really great. No kidding. You've got a beautiful body," he says softly, though he hasn't actually seen it yet, except for a glimpse as she flicked on the bathroom light and quickly closed the door behind her, a flash of brown buttock and back.

"Thanks. You're not so bad yourself."

6

A HALF HOUR LATER THEY LEAVE THE MOTEL AND DRIVE BACK to Oleander Park, chatting about the Boston Red Sox, promising each other that next spring they'll have to go to some of the exhibition games together, since, to their mutual surprise and pleasure, they both happen to be Boston fans, or so they insist.

They kiss goodbye passionately, and she says, "I love you." Bob steps from her car and, once outside, says, "Me too."

But when she has gone, and he has got into his own car and has started the motor, he drops into deep confusion. What happened? What did he expect to happen? What did he want? What did he get? What did he give? As he asks the questions, one by one, he realizes that he can't answer any of them, not a one, and consequently he does not know how he should feel now. Happy? Sated? Disappointed? Ashamed? Angry? Proud?

The only thing he does know, he tells himself, is that he loves her. Yes, he, Bob Dubois of Catamount, New Hampshire, has fallen in love with Marguerite Dill of Auburndale, Florida, by way of Macon, Georgia, where she was a Southern black woman married to a Southern black man. This means, of course, that he no longer is in love with his wife Elaine. Or so he insists.

When he moves the gearshift lever, it jams, refuses to slide into reverse. He jiggles it, wrenches it, sneaks up on it and flips it, but nothing works. He checks his watch. Ten forty-five. The only way he can get the car into gear now is to have someone sit inside the car and jiggle the shift lever while he jumps up and down on the front bumper. The highway is deserted and dark, and across the street at the housing project, everyone's inside watching TV.

He shuts off the motor and gets out of the car, slamming the door shut. "Shit," he says aloud, thinking of the five-mile walk ahead of him. "Shit, shit, shit." It means walking in darkness along the gravelly shoulder of Highway 17, past Lake Louise and the moss-shrouded cypress trees and tall pines, then south on 520 past the marshes to Lake Grassey and home, unless he can talk someone into coming out here to the store at this hour to help him free the transmission. He'd call a garage, but that would cost him twenty-five bucks at least, and he spent his last few dollars on the motel room, insisting on it, despite Marguerite's polite suggestion that they split the cost.

Who can he call? Who does he know in this place? His brother Eddie would tell him to call a cab and then would tell him where he could buy a Chrysler Cordoba demonstrator with only 3,500 miles on it for two grand off list. A steal. Elaine would borrow a car and drive out eagerly, but she'd come with one of her friends from the trailer park, probably Ellen Skeeter, that nervous, red-headed Georgian with the sudden, loud laugh and the three-hundred-pound husband named Ron who works at the Dairy Queen in Cypress Gardens. And Elaine would wake the girls and bring them too. A big production. Lots of talk. He doesn't want lots of talk tonight. Not now.

His brother or his wife, then. Or Marguerite. Yes, he can call Marguerite. She should be nearly home by now. Auburndale's not that far. Unless she didn't go straight home. Unless she stopped off for a nightcap at a bar on a corner a few blocks before her house, a dim, smoky tavern filled with black men and black women and soul music on the jukebox, and she'll meet and drink and talk black talk with a guy she knows from the neighborhood, a tall, slim, goodlooking guy named Steve or Otis, with a pencil-thin mustache and long black eyelashes, and she'll leave with the guy and go back to his apartment, smoke some marijuana and have wild, Negro sex with him. Afterwards, they'll lie back on his purple satin sheets, and she'll fondle his huge prick and wonder why on earth she tried to make it with the liquor store clerk when, any time she wanted, she could have *this*. The guy will shrug and say, "Beats me, baby. Everybody know honkies got small dicks."

He unlocks the door and enters the store, stopping at the threshold to flick the switch for the light over the cash register, so he can read the telephone book. Locating the name M. Dill, he starts to dial the number, when he hears a soft male voice behind him. "Hang up the phone."

He glances over his shoulder and sees two black men, one a few feet behind him and carrying what appears to be a shotgun, the other standing in the shadows over by the door, locking it.

Bob hangs up the phone.

"Hit the light," the man with the shotgun tells the other. He's young, in his early twenties, and the other is even younger. They're both wearing nylon shirts with silver-and-black geometric patterns flashing over them, tight double-knit bell-bottomed slacks, and jogging shoes.

"What you want to kill the lights for, man? We gotta see."

"Hit the fucking light. We got enough light from the sign." The man with the shotgun speaks in a slow, patient manner, as if worried about being misunderstood. The light goes out, and the store drops back into soft, gloomy semidarkness. "Now, what you got to do," he says to Bob, "is let us make your deposit for you tonight. You understand me?"

Bob nods his head up and down, but doesn't move the rest of his body. His feet feel bolted through to the floor, his arms bound to his sides. His heart is pounding like a pile driver, but his blood is congealed in the veins, thick and heavy, moving like cold syrup, sluggishly, reluctantly, against the frantic, terrified beat of his heart.

The man with the shotgun regards Bob quizzically. "Did you *hear* me, man? We going to make your deposit for you tonight." The man has delicate, small, excellent teeth, and his skin is a yellowish color, the dimly golden shade of a pair of Italian loafers Bob was thinking of buying as soon as he got paid.

"I . . ." Bob carefully clears his throat. "I already made the deposit tonight. Earlier."

The man with the shotgun motions with his head for the other man to come forward. This one's chinless, with skin the color of brown glass, and his head is covered with tiny plaited cornrows laid in parallel strips from his forehead back to the nape of his neck, an elaborate hairdo that, to Bob, looks more like a skullcap than hair.

"Look, man," the first one says to Bob. "Just open the fucking register, don't be cute, and nobody gets hurt. We in a big hurry, so if you cute, motherfucker, we just going to blow you away. Now gimme the fucking money. All of it. Checks and all."

"I really did. I already made the deposit. Early, at nine."

"Blow 'im away," the younger man says. His hands open and close quickly, as if he'd like to get them around Bob's throat. "Go on, blow the sucker off. I *hate* the sucker already. I hate the way he looks." He laughs suddenly. "I *hate* 'im!"

"Shut up. Get busy and find us a case of Scotch, a case of Dewar's. I'll take care of . . ."

"Fuck 'im, fuck the pig! Just blow off his fucking head!"

"Look, I'm telling the truth. I came in to make a phone call. My car . . ."

"Oh, man, you are so fucking stupid!" The man lifts the barrel of the shotgun and places it lightly against Bob's chest. It's a twenty-gauge pump with a choke, Bob notices. He looks down the long black barrel to the man at the other end. The safety is off, and the man is handling the gun firmly, but with ease. He is familiar with the gun. The stock is buried snugly under his right arm, and his right hand curls around the trigger guard, index finger laid against the trigger, while his left hand carries the weight of the gun.

The man with the cornrows has taken a step away and is watching his partner excitedly. *"Do* it! Go on, *do* the motherfucker! We can get the money without him."

"Shut the fuck up and get the Scotch."

"Listen, I'll give you whatever you want, everything in the store. I don't give a shit, it's not my store. I'll help you load up, even. But the register's empty. You gotta believe me. I already made the deposit, and then I went out with my . . . with my girlfriend for a while, and then my transmission got jammed, it does that a lot, so I came in just to make a phone call, that's all. We closed up at nine."

"You're closing now, man. We *seen* you closing up, which is why we come in here. But I don't want to argue with you, white man, I just want to stop a minute in my travels, get me some change and a case of Dewar's, and keep moving. But you making it hard for me. We in a hurry. You understand me?" He pokes Bob's chest with the muzzle of the gun.

"Yeah, sure, okay, fine."

He'll kill me if I argue, Bob decides. The information comes to him like the rule of a game he has been struggling to understand.

"Here, look," Bob says, waving an arm in the direction of the cash register. "See, cash drawer's wide open. Empty. Nothing. You want my watch? It's a fucking Timex, but you're welcome to it." He peels off his watch and slaps it onto the counter, smashing the crystal. "Here's my wallet. Empty too. Not even any fucking credit cards. I just *work* here! I'm a peon, a clerk, a *nobody!*"

Holding the gun level with Bob's chest, the man steps carefully around the counter and looks down its length at the cash register. "Gimme the bag. You know, the night deposit bag. I don't want your fucking tin watch, man, so don't get so excited. Just gimme the bag." Glancing toward the back of the store, he calls to his partner. "You got that case of Dewar's? Hurry the fuck up, man!"

"It's too dark. Ask the guy where the fuck is it."

"In the stockroom in back," Bob says in a low, almost confidential voice. He and the man with the shotgun, the man who will kill him, are alike, Bob thinks. They're different from the man with the crazy hairdo and the wild eyes. "No shit, mister, I really did already make the deposit tonight. I left the store at nine because I had to meet a girl." Bob wants to tell him that his girlfriend is black, that she lives in a black neighborhood and knows lots of black people, and even though she's a nurse, she comes from a poor family. "My girlfriend . . ." he starts.

"I don't give a *fuck* about you, man! Or your girlfriend! Just gimme the bag!"

"Forget it!" the other man hollers. "I found it. Dewar's." Then, after a few seconds, he says, "Shit! Empty. These're just empty cases here, man. Ask whitebread where the fuck the Dewar's is. Do you got to have Dewar's? They's some other kinds here on the shelfs. I could fill one of these empty cases with one of these kinds."

"Look in the fucking stockroom!" the man shouts, angry now. "And hurry the fuck up!"

"It's dark back here, man. I can't see no Dewar's, I can't see nothing."

"Where's the light switch for the stockroom?" the man asks Bob.

"On the wall on the right, by the door."

The man relays the information. Then he raises the shotgun and aims it directly at Bob's forehead. He says, "I'm going to blow your fucking head all over that wall behind you." His voice is as cold and calm as the ground. "I'm going to splash your fucking brains, you white sonofabitch, unless you get me that money bag right now."

"All right, all right. Relax. I'll get it." Bob moves slowly to his left, keeping his eyes on the muzzle of the shotgun, as if planning to duck when it goes off. "I'll get it." He reaches under the counter by the cash register, gropes around, finds the gun and flicks the safety off with his thumb. He draws it slowly out, inch by inch, thinking, in a howl, Oh, Jesus, Elaine, my poor babies, I'm going to die now. The man is going to kill me because I lied. But I had to lie, he wouldn't believe me when I told the truth and he was going to kill me for that. So I lied. And now I'm going to die for lying. The man will kill me, and maybe I'll kill him too. Oh, Elaine, oh, my babies, oh, Jesus, I love you, Elaine, I don't love the nigger girl, I never did, I just love you, Elaine, you and my babies. I'm a good man.

He half faces the silhouetted figure of the man cradling the shotgun. Crouched over the pistol, as if shielding it from rain, Bob squeezes the trigger, hears the explosion, hears Silhouette's roar of pain, then hears the deeper explosion as the shotgun goes off, hears glass behind him shatter, and suddenly notices the sweet taste of gin on his mouth, all over his face, or blood, he can't tell, because it's warm like blood and he's never tasted warm gin, but there's no pain, just a numbness in the hand that fired the .38 and a ringing in his ears, broken suddenly by the sound of the shotgun firing again, and at the same time there's a yellow flash near the door, and smoke and the smell of gunpowder and burning cardboard and the clatter of broken glass above and behind him. Then silence, except for the slosh and trickle of liquor spilling from broken bottles down the shelves to the floor. He hears a noise from the stockroom—Cornrow bumping against cases in the dark—and from the front of the store, the sound of the door latch, Silhouette trying to unlock the door. Bob stands and holds the .38 out in front of him with both hands, the way he's seen it done on TV. He aims through the rear sight and fires. Silhouette grunts and gurgles and slams against the door. The shotgun falls, and then the man falls too.

Bob races alongside the counter and darts across to the back of the store next to the open stockroom door, where he presses against the wall and listens to Cornrow on the other side struggling in the dark to escape, bumping walls, smacking against head-high stacks of beer, knocking over George Dill's broom, panting, pushing, groping for an opening in the unpainted cinder-block wall, until, finally, there's silence. Then Bob hears it. First a whimper, then the awful bawl of a child. And he smells it. Human shit.

He steps through the doorway, flicks on the overhead light and sees the shuddering boy huddled on the floor against the far wall, inches from the back door. The boy looks up, eyes wet, large mouth loosely open, his whole body trembling in terror. He looks around him and sees how close he is to the door, sees that one push on the crash bar would open it. Escape. Freedom. Gone from him now. "Don't kill me, please don't kill me!" he blubbers. "Let me go, please let me go! I didn't do nothin', honest. Please, mister, don't kill me!"

Bob holds the gun out in front of him with both hands and aims it at the boy's head. "You black sonofabitch. I oughta blow *you* away."

"Aw-w-w!" the kid bawls.

"You're disgusting." Bob lowers the gun. He wrinkles his nose. "You stink like shit too." He takes a step backwards. "Whew! Jesus H. Christ! You just lie there, shitpants. Lie there and stink. I don't want your smell near me. And don't move a muscle, or I'll blow your fucking brains out. I'll do you the same favor you wanted to do me."

Slowly, Bob backs out to the counter and picks up the telephone, and laying the gun flat on the counter, punches the number for the police. "This's Bob Dubois out at Friendly Spirits on Route 17," he declares. *"D-u-b-o-i-s.* Yeah, Dubois. Spelled like that. I know, I know. Yeah, listen, I just shot a guy trying to rob the place. Friendly Spirits. Route 17. Yeah, and I got his buddy too. Got 'im right here. No, no, just one of 'em, the other guy shit his pants. Yeah. The other guy? I don't know, I might've killed the guy. Yeah, Friendly Spirits. On Route 17, opposite the housing project south of the base."

Hanging up the telephone, Bob walks with a bouncy step back to the stockroom, and when he enters the room, he sees at once that the back door lies wide open, and the boy has fled. Bob stands there, shocked, looking at the wet spot against the wall where the boy lay, then at the open door, then at the parking lot beyond.

Exhaling slowly, he suddenly, and to his surprise, feels relieved, and when he looks down at his hand and the heavy gun in it, discovers that he's bleeding. His white short-sleeved shirt is spattered with blood, and the back of his neck and arms are laced with tiny glass cuts. They aren't painful, but Bob knows that bits of glass are still embedded in his flesh, so he's careful to avoid touching them.

When he checks on the man he shot, he sees immediately that the man is dead, shot twice, once in the shoulder and once in the mouth. The crumpled body lies like an island in a large, spreading puddle of blood. Suddenly nauseous, Bob jogs his way back through the store to the stockroom, then out the open door to the parking lot, where he glances at the robbers' car, a dull, pale blue Dodge Charger with battered New York plates, and vomits onto the asphalt.

When the police arrive, he is seated cross-legged on the counter next to the cash register with his gun laid beside him, feeling giddy and swilling on a bottle of Dewar's while light skeins of blood run down his back and arms.

À Table, Dabord, Olande, Adonai

A YOUNG HAITIAN WOMAN, WITH HER INFANT IN HER ARMS and her adolescent nephew standing beside her, watches the sea behind them slowly swallow the Haitian hills. The small, crowded boat plows northward through a choppy, slate-blue sea, toward America, Vanise believes, toward Florida, where everything will be different, where nothing except the part of her that's inside her skull will be the same, and gradually even that will change. First the village of Le Môle at the base of the green hills is devoured, then the low slopes checkered with cane fields and coconut palms go under, gone to where the dead abide, and at last the familiar dark green hills succumb. There is no known place peering back at her from the horizon, and now she faces only a point on the compass, an abstraction called south, *Adonai,* that refuses to speak to her in any voice but her own.

This is a new kind of silence for Vanise, one that frightens her, and she begins to chatter at the boy, Claude, scolding him for having stolen the ham from the wrecked truck, pointing out his stupidity in having brought it back to the cabin in Allanche, his deceit in not telling them immediately where he found the ham, before they had eaten at it, so that he could have put it back uneaten before anyone discovered that it and the rest of the meat had been stolen and Aubin came looking for him, and not finding him there would punish his mother and her and her baby, unless Aubin did find him there, in which case Aubin would have taken him off to jail. We would still be at home in Allanche, she reminds him, cooking a chicken and yams on the fire, if you were a good boy. You would have your mother, and we would all have each other, if you were not a thief.

The boy looks down at the rising and falling deck. Slowly he turns away from the south and faces north. Yes, he says, but now we are going to America.

Vanise feels the weight of a huge, swelling stone in her belly. She sighs, turns away from the southern horizon to the north and starts waiting for the sight of America rising from the sea.

FOR CENTURIES, MEN AND WOMAN HAVE SAILED THIS PASsage north of Hispaniola waiting for the sight of one idea or another rising all aglitter with tangible substance from the turquoise sea. Columbus approaches from the east in search of Cathay, and Ponce de León cruises north from Puerto Rico looking for the fabled Bimini, and now comes Vanise, huddled by the low rail in the bow of a small wooden fishing boat out of Haiti, scouring the horizon for a glimpse of America. None of them is lost. All three know they'll recognize the substance of their idea as soon as they see it, Columbus his Cathay, Ponce his Bimini, Vanise her Florida.

And so they do. Columbus, with a globe in his mind half the size of Ptolemy's, knows at once that he has reached the fringes of the Empire of the Grand Khan. Ponce, coming upon an island he believes has not been seen before, in his excitement brushes too close to the uncharted reef and has to beach his ship for repairs on the shore of what, for several days, he knows is the Island of the Miraculous Waters. And Vanise, sighting a finger of green land just before sundown blots it out, knows that she has seen Florida.

Columbus, of course, has merely reached part of an archipelago that extends from continents he does not know exist, an unbroken land mass emerging from ice in the north and ice in the south and creating an almost insuperable barrier between old Europe and old Cathay. Ponce has merely landed accidentally on a small, uncharted, brush-covered island where the Indians, though peaceful, will not come out and speak to him of Bimini while he waits for his men to repair the ship.

Vanise has come to North Caicos Island, an easy place to locate exactly. With a map in hand, you can sit at a table in a city in North America, and by marking a point at 21 degrees 55 minutes north, 72 degrees 0 minutes west, you can locate where the Haitians will land tonight. Or you can draw lines, 100 nautical miles north from Cap Haitien, 400 nautical miles south-southeast from Nassau, 575 nautical miles southeast from Miami and 150 nautical miles northnortheast from Guantánamo Naval Station in Cuba. The four lines will converge over North Caicos Island, where there are a few tiny villages, Kew, Whitby and Bottle Creek, a small hotel and miles of deserted white beaches.

VANISE WAKENS. THE AIR HAS CHANGED; SHE CAN SMELL trees. She raises her head, moving with care so as not to waken the boy or her baby, lifts her body at the waist, looks over the rail into darkness. The engine chugs slowly belowdecks, and she can hear waves breaking nearby.

They have arrived! America! Opening her eyes as wide as she can, she stares intensely into the darkness, but she can see nothing. No lights, no hills outlined blackly against a lighter sky—nothing. But she knows, despite the blackness peering back, that they have come to America, and smiling, she lowers her body, lies on her side and lets herself drift into peaceful, trusting sleep.

If a man believes he is happy, he is. If not, not. And if a woman, a young, illiterate Haitian woman in flight from her home with her infant son and adolescent nephew, exchanges all her money for a boat ride to America, and without knowing it, gets dropped off instead at North Caicos Island, six hundred miles from America, and believes that at last and for the first time in her hard life she is happy, then she is happy. The truth of the matter, the kind of truth you would get with a map, compass and rule, has no bearing on her belief or its consequences.

Until, that is, she gets her own map, which at first would resemble one of Columbus's early, wildly speculative drawings of where he thought he was. A person's map tells more about where that person thinks he is than about where he is not, which is, of course, everywhere else. Columbus, when he drew this, thought he was in the Philippine Sea:

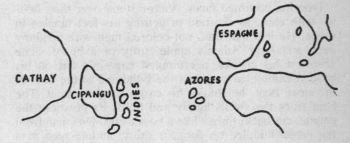

Vanise, believing she was a hundred yards off the beach at Coral Gables, Florida, would have drawn something like this:

On Vanise's map, you are ten hours off the north coast of Haiti, and Florida is on the horizon, or would be, if you could see the horizon. It's a dark, moonless night. Victor, whose boat this is, comes forward to where Vanise and the boy, Claude, encircle the baby like the halves of a clamshell. They lie surrounded by a crowd of eight or ten people, who are also lying down or seated hunched over, men mostly, dressed in their best clothes, shoes, hats, and clutching battered suitcases and rope-tied baskets and bundles.

Ignoring upturned faces, Victor steps over their bodies with care, as if afraid of getting his feet tangled in ropes. He is a tall, thin, nut-colored man with a skinny neck and large Adam's apple, tufts of a beard, acne scars on his cheeks, a crumpled captain's hat on his head. Leaning back against the bulkhead in the bow of the small boat, he studies his cargo for a moment. The boat rides the swells lightly and holds its position; the engine, cut back, throbs like a bass drum. One man from the group huddled on deck, a short, middle-aged man with a cane cutter's body, lifts his head and broad shoulders and peers over the starboard rail. They hear waves breaking nearby.

Keep down! Victor barks, and the man drops to the deck as if shot.

Vanise believes she is happy, and she almost laughs out loud at the poor man, his sudden, wide-eyed motion, his face that of a little boy who stole someone's pie and unexpectedly saw the victim coming along the road.

That's comical, she whispers to her nephew, who smiles also. She squeezes the boy's hand. She is very dark-skinned, the color of freshly ground coffee, and she is short and in the shoulders and hips small as a girl. Because of the baby, her breasts are large and full and seem to push against her blouse. Her thick black hair is wiry, chopped off a hand's width from her skull and wrapped in a band of scarlet cloth that brings her high, strong cheekbones, broad nose and full mouth forward toward the light, giving her the appearance of a serious, powerful woman. A man would not confuse her with a girl, or with a woman he could fool easily. If she gave anything to anyone, it would be because she wanted to. Or had to—and then it would not be a gift. Back in Le Môle, when she first appeared at Victor's pink cinder-block house, led there by the old man from the docks who does that work for him, sorting from the crowds of supplicants the few who have both the money and the need to get away, Victor looked her over carefully, first to be sure that she had the money and would give it to him, but also to see if she might be fooled into giving him something extra, to see if, like many women, she confused her need with his worth. But no, she saw Victor for what he was, despite her need, and so he had not bothered to try to fool her. He would take her money and treat her like the rest.

Beyond the reef, Victor informs his passengers, is Florida. Biscayne Bay. He says the words slowly, lingering over the consonants and lengthening the vowels, making the words sound like the name of a powerful and beneficent loa. Now, you must pay attention to me, he tells them. It is very, very difficult to get through the reef. We must do it quickly, when the tide is at its highest, which is very soon now, and then we will drop you at a landing on the shore and quickly return. Or else we cannot get back through the reef. Someone will be there to guide you to Miami. He says this word slowly also—Mee-ah-mee—and several of the people at his feet make broad smiles.

I must collect the money now, he says abruptly. There will be no time later. Because of the tide's turning. And the reef.

There is a general groping into pockets and scarves, parcels and bags, while the captain moves among the crowd, reaching down, plucking and counting out the bills, moving to the next one, and on, until soon he has accounted for everyone. They seem relieved to have paid him, less tense than before, as if, by taking their money from them, five, six hundred dollars per person, sometimes more, sometimes less, depending on the bargain struck back in Le Môle, he has taken from them an anxiety, a burdensome responsibility, for now they are smiling easily at one another, whispering and nudging shoulders and thighs. They seem to feel less alone than when they possessed so much money.

The captain has moved to the cabin and has climbed up to the controls, and his mate, a shirtless, shiny, Rasta-locked youth, has replaced him in the bow of the boat, peering over the rail and down at the water. He waves to the capain like a pilot, turns and searches the water below. The engine spins faster now, and the boat moves forward, while the mate waves the captain on, holds him suddenly back, gestures to the starboard side, then to port, then leads him straight ahead again, and the wet, rattling sound of the waves breaking on the reef grows louder.

All the people on the deck are up on hands and knees now, peering over the rail, studying the white foam where the water gets slashed by the reef, looking in vain for the deep, dark cut that the captain must know is there, that the dreadlocked youth in the bow, too, must know is there, for haven't they made this journey many times, isn't this the knowledge and skill that Victor is famous for all over the north coast? He has taken hundreds, maybe thousands, over to Florida, and each time he has done it, he has had to cross through this reef to Biscayne Bay, they tell themselves. Even so, they pray. They pray to the loas, to the Virgin and all the saints, to their *mait'-tête*, if they have one, and to their parents, if they are dead. They pray to anyone who has the power to slide this small wooden boat filled with people between the shark's teeth of the reef into the calm, deep waters of the bay.

> *Prié pou' tou les morts:*
> *pou' les morts 'bandonné nan gran bois,*
> *pou' les morts 'bandonné nan gran dlo,*
> *pou' les morts 'bandonné nan gran plaine,*
> *pou' les morts tué pa' couteau,*
> *pou' les morts tué pa' épée,*

*pou' tou les morts, au nom de Mait' Carrefour et
    de Legba;*
pou' tou generation paternelle et maternelle,
ancêtre et ancêtere, Afrique et Afrique;
*au nom de Mait' Carrefour, Legba, Baltaza,
    Miroi. . . .*

Then, suddenly, they are through. The reef and the
white crashing waves are behind them, and before them
lies the land, extended like a dark wall beneath velvet
sky, with a white seam of beach between the water and
the low palmettos. A rickety pier reaches like a bony
arm from the beach, with a clearing in the trees beyond
and what looks like a sandy road or lane leading inland.

The captain cuts quickly from the reef across the bay
and brings the boat around and against the pier. He
shuts down the motor, and the mate leaps from the boat
and swiftly ties the bow and then the stern to the pilings.

Be quick! Be quick! he says, and the people scramble
from the boat, lugging suitcases and baskets, shoving
one another to get free of the boat. Quickly! the mate
repeats. Already he is untying the line at the stern.

Suddenly, with one arm curling her baby against her
breast, Vanise steps away from the group of refugees
and touches the mate on his naked shoulder.

Eh? What do you want?

With her chin, she points toward the shore and the
bush beyond. This, she says. This is not Miami.

He's silent for a second. Over there, he says at last,
pointing east along the beach. Then he runs forward to
untie the bow of the boat. They're ready to depart. The
captain races the engine impatiently.

But Vanise has pursued the mate, and when he stands to
leap aboard the boat, she grabs his wrist and yanks him
back. Where is the man to help us? she demands. Where?

Soon! Let go of me! he shouts. Then, suddenly, his
voice changes, goes soft, and looking way down at her,
he says, Don't worry, miss. Miami's not far. We land
you here to avoid the American police. It's not so easy
now as it used to be. Just don't be afraid.

She releases him, and he takes one long stride and is aboard the boat. The captain guns the motor, the propeller churns a foamy wake behind it, and the boat wallows a moment and pulls rapidly away from the pier. Vanise watches the small, dark boat cross in a straight line the silky waters of the bay and slow briefly before the low white ridge marking the reef, where it picks its way through, and is gone.

Then, slowly, in silence, the people walk one by one down the narrow length of the pier toward land, step to the hard-packed beach and begin their wait. Some lie down on the witchgrass and watch the sky, star-pocked, circle overhead, some stroll slowly up the beach a ways and talk in low, nervous voices to one another, some sit on the pier and dangle their legs over the edge. Vanise and her baby and the boy, Claude, walk to the end of the pier and look out to the sea, to where the boat has gone, back to Haiti.

This is not America, she says in a low, cold voice. The boy places the basket down, and Vanise sits on it, opens her blouse and starts nursing her baby.

Are we lost? the boy asks, his voice about to break.

No! she answers. Then, more softly, No. But this is not America.

VANISE, LANDED, DROPPED OFF, ABANDONED ON THE NORTH coast of North Caicos Island, a nearly empty, flat, impoverished island six hundred miles from where she'd expected to land—what's one to say to her now? Sit down, Vanise, be rational and find out where you *really* are, Vanise, and then find out where America *really* is, and then Haiti, Le Môle, Allanche, your sister-in-law's hurricane-battered cabin up on the ridge. Get it all in perspective.

No, Vanise, don't. Don't find out where you *really* are. That will only make you believe that you are indeed lost. To the boy's frightened question, Are we lost? you would have to say, Yes, Claude, lost.

To be lost is not to be able to return or go on, for the world is not lost, you are. It's the fear behind the old joke told by parents about their child, who, they say, got lost, and when they found her, the child calmly said, No, I wasn't lost, you were. And the parents chuckle gratefully, knowing that if the child had not believed that, she would have fallen into terror.

In one sense, Vanise knows where she is. She just doesn't know where America is. She's standing on a hard white beach at high tide in the Caribbean. The wind blows from the east. Immediately before her is a lane that winds into the low bush, and when she walks along the lane, she discovers that it connects to a marl-paved road, chalky white, now that the moon has risen. As she walks, her map gets extended ahead of her to the horizon, which keeps receding in the distance. Her map is a living, coiling and uncoiling thing, moving in undulant waves before her the way a manta ray sweeps the bottom of the sea. Her map is a process, the kind of map you must keep moving into, if you want to read it.

BY DAWN, VANISE AND HER INFANT AND THE BOY ARE WITHIN sight of the inland village of Kew. Though they do not know the name of the place yet, they do know that this is still not America. There are goats here, tethered in the gutters alongside the road, and roosters crowing, and tin-roofed cabins the same as in Allanche, set off the road a ways, with tiny outhouses and laundry lines in back, patchy vegetable gardens, pole beans, yams, spindly corn stalks. A scrawny brown dog yips at them as they pass, and Vanise hurries the boy along ahead of her, looking back over her shoulder.

What are we going to do? Claude asks his aunt. Where are we?

Don't worry! she snaps. We'll find out soon what we're to do. She clicks her tongue against the roof of her mouth, as if to scold the boy.

The sky is turning pearly white, like the belly of a fish, and the palm fronds, the glittery leaves of mahoe trees and the pebbled sides of cabins stand sharply forward from the shadows. It's a familiar light to Vanise, falling at the same crisp angles with the same clear intensity as at this hour and season in Haiti. But the soil is different, pale gray here instead of blood red, and the houses seem more scattered, less clustered against one another, with narrow, unpaved roads instead of footpaths leading from one house to another.

The roosters arch their short backs and cut the still air with harsh calls from the edge of town down to the square in the middle and back out to the opposite side, and soon the dry, clean smell of new woodsmoke reaches Vanise and the boy, and they realize at once that they are hungry.

The boy speaks of it first. Should we stop to eat? he asks. We have the ham. And the yams, he reminds her, and the rose apples and guavas they picked on the walk from Allanche to Le Môle—when was it? Only yesterday morning? Is the last dawn they saw yesterday's, and that on Haiti? Has it all happened so quickly? How did they move so soon from a known world to an unknown one, and why aren't they more frightened than they are? The boy cannot understand this. He can ask the questions, but he cannot answer them, and that frightens him more than any answers might. He feels like a boy in a dream, not quite responsible for his actions. If something appears in the dream that can kill him, he knows he will just fly up and over it.

At the center of the town there is a crossroads and a low wall encircling a cottonwood tree. Here Vanise stops and sits. The boy stands before her, looking around him at the four roads that seem to come from above to this low place in the middle, there to cross and rise up on the opposite side. A half-dozen houses, mostly unpainted masonry buildings tacked onto smaller, older, daub-and-wattle cabins, face the several roads, with overgrown yards in front and here and there an old American car, dented and rusting, parked beside the house. Doors open now and then, and a person, usually a child, appears, runs to the outhouse and returns slowly, languidly, walking barefoot across wet grass, opens the door and disappears into the warm darkness inside. Little girls in short cotton smocks march out and back, little boys in white saggy underpants, lean shirtless men wearing jeans or gym shorts, fat women in sleeveless, baglike dresses.

It's as if no one sees the young Haitian woman in the red headscarf and blue-gray skirt and blouse, her baby in her arms, and the boy, a lad slightly taller than she, wearing a short-sleeved white shirt and dark pants and black sneakers. Their baskets lie at their feet next to the low marl wall, and while the woman sits on the wall and nurses her infant, the boy gropes through the baskets in search of breakfast—fruit, a pair of egg-shaped, pale green *jambosiers* and a pair of lemony *goyaviers*. It's almost as if the strangers are invisible in this tiny town, for though no one stepping from his door could fail to see them at the crossroads in the milky dawn light beneath the tall cottonwood tree, no one calls them or even hails them with a tentatively raised hand.

Vanise and Claude hear them call and hail one another, however: *Tyrone, you fetch me wood now, bwoy, or me beat you!* And: *Get dat dog from out de house! G'wan now, get im from de house, y' hear?* There's a familiar enough roll to the words, the grumpy, early-morning sounds they themselves make back in Allanche, but Vanise and Claude can't understand the words. It's garble to them, as if the people are speaking backwards. The boy's eyes open wide in wonder, and Vanise cocks her head, listens more closely. She hears music from a radio, not Haitian music, certainly, and nothing like it, either, not calypso or reggae or salsa. It's a twangy, slow music, and though thinned by the cheap transistor radio inside the cabin, it's unmistakably American country and western music. They've heard that sound before, now and then, from the radio and on records brought back on holidays from Port-au-Prince by cousins returning to the country intent on impressing those who refused or weren't able to move to the city.

The boy says, Maybe this *is* America. Only not Miami, that's all. Miami's probably someplace near here, that's all.

Vanise looks at him with scorn. America doesn't look like *this*, she says in a low voice, almost a whisper.

But where are we, then?

. Vanise shoves her face close to the boy's and hisses, We're in the center of a village, at a crossroads, and we're eating our breakfast there! Anybody can see that. You can see that. She's not angry at the boy, but she sends her words to him as if they had been heated and cast into cold water. Give me the *jambosier,* she says.

He passes her the fruit, and she tears off a fleshy chunk with her teeth. The baby, finished sucking at her breast, has fallen asleep and lolls back against her shoulder. Holding the rose apple with her teeth, Vanise buttons her blouse quickly and resumes eating. She hadn't realized how hungry she had become, with all the excitement—first the fear of the boat ride and the sea, then the joy at the sight of land, and then the disappointment and anger, and now the complex fight to stave off being lost—and she's almost startled by the intensity of her own hunger and the pleasure she takes from satisfying it. The boy, too, eats ravenously and with sudden joy.

When they have finished the fruit, the boy decides to risk another question. What are we going to do, Vanise? He wipes his mouth with the back of his hand and studies the door of the house across the road from them.

We shall wait. She says it firmly, as if waiting were an action, like hiding or running away or building a house. She passes the boy the sleeping baby, which he holds expertly in the crook of his skinny arm, and she breaks off a leafless branch of the tree behind them, squats in the dust and begins to draw. As she draws, she prays in a broken way that she knows is amateurish and incomplete, but it's all she can remember from her sister-in-law's teaching. She knows the names of the cardinal points, and she addresses them properly: to the east, *A Table;* to the west, *Dabord;* in the north, *Olande;* and in the south, *Adonai.* She draws a long horizontal line from east to west in the dust, then two verticals, one long and one short, that cut the horizontal into three parts. She crosses herself, and while she draws elaborations and curls, circles and lines around the crossbars, she salutes the two trinities, first the Christian God, his son Jesus and the Holy Ghost, then *les Mystères, les Morts*, and *la Marassa*, the sacred twins.

Standing, she crosses her arms and examines the drawing at her feet, a *vever* for Papa Legba. Now, she says, we wait.

The boy relaxes and sits down on the low wall, the baby still in his arms. He's no longer afraid. He did not know that his Aunt Vanise possessed so much *rada* knowledge, that she was a *mambo*, or he would not have been frightened before, when he did not know where they were. They will wait now, here at the crossroads under the sacred cottonwood tree, for old Papa Legba to help them.

The sun rises above the trees, and soon the day is dry and hot. A car rumbles down the lane to the crossroads and slows as it passes; the driver, a skinny black man wearing a painter's cap, does not seem to notice them. A few minutes later, a boy on a red Honda putts by, changing gears and gunning his motor at the intersection, spinning his rear wheel as he turns to the left and heads up the rise and over it out of sight. Soon schoolchildren emerge from the houses and from the woods on narrow pathways. They are dressed in white and blue uniforms and carry books and papers under their arms and in satchels. Behind them, on the far side of the crossroads, a store has opened to the street, and several of the children stop there in the shade for box milk or Coke. They ignore Vanise and Claude and the baby as they pass, but look back at the trio when they have got behind them.

At the tops of breadfruit trees and utility poles, turkey buzzards perch and show their backs and stretch dewwet wings to the sun. Doves coo in the crackling underbrush, and long-legged egrets stalk the marshes and gutters and now and then rise awkwardly from the moist ground and soar, suddenly graceful, against the cloudless blue sky. The sun moves slowly higher in the sky, and the shadow of the cottonwood tree in the center of the village of Kew shrinks until it is no larger than the circumference of the tree itself, a blot on the dusty gray ground. Vanise and the boy are thirsty now, and the boy, Claude, finally, after thinking about it for close to an hour, asks his aunt if he can try to buy a Coca-Cola at the store behind them.

No, she says. We must wait for Papa Legba. We cannot leave. Besides, we have no more money. She reaches down and plucks from the ground next to the *vever* a smooth round pebble she has suddenly spotted there, as if it were a new plant that broke through the ground a second before. There, she says, passing the pebble to the boy, who puts it into his dry mouth. You see, Old Bones is looking after us.

The lad smiles and sucks contentedly on the stone. After a moment, he, too, reaches to the ground and retrieves a smooth pebble, which, with a broad, understanding smile, he gives to his aunt.

The hours pass, and as the afternoon comes on and the day begins to cool slightly, women and older girls emerge from the darkness of their houses and stroll down the road past the cottonwood tree to the store, to the butcher over the low rise beyond, to their neighbors' houses. All of them ignore the strangers, the boy and the woman and her baby. They see them, of course, but this is a shy, careful people, a patient people as well, not like Jamaicans or Bahamians, not like Cubans, either, all of whom would have accosted the strangers by now and demanded to know why they were sitting in the center of their town, where did they come from, what do they want here.

It's nearly four in the afternoon when a yellow, three-legged dog, steps with precise delicacy from the brush at the top of the rise in the road facing Vanise and Claude, looks toward them, turns and approaches them at a lopsided trot. Vanise saw the dog the instant it emerged from the trees and recognized him at once.

With the baby asleep in her arms, she stands, pulling the boy off the wall to a standing position beside her, and together they watch the yellow dog draw near. He has an intelligent, slightly cockeyed face, one ear perked, the other flopping, and he moves on two front legs and one hind more easily, it seems, than if he had all four. He walks with a slightly airy lope, as if gravity did not hold him quite the same way other creatures are held.

A few feet away, the dog stops and stares orange-eyed up at them, one eye looking straight at Vanise, the other studying the boy. He sniffs the air, then suddenly darts toward the basket at the boy's feet.

Feed him! Vanise whispers hoarsely. He wants to be fed!

The dog pokes his muzzle at the bottom of the boy's basket and then looks up and says in a smooth voice, What have you got in there? I want what I smell in your basket.

The boy looks wonderingly over at his aunt. Feed him! she commands. He wants the ham. Feed him.

Quickly, the boy yanks the top from the basket and reaches down, gropes past the clothing and comes to the ham his mother carefully wrapped two nights ago in Allanche. He draws it out, unties the knot in the red kerchief and lays the meat and bone on the ground next to the drawing in the dust. The dog watches warily.

Put it at the top, above the cross, Vanise says in a calm voice.

The boy obeys, moves the ham and stands, and the dog leaps upon the offering, grabs the meat with his mouth near the smaller end, sinks his teeth deeply into it and lifts it, the heavy end dragging the dog's head down on one side like a man with a pipe in the corner of his mouth.

Then the dog turns away from them, takes a few steps and looks back. He puts the ham carefully down in the middle of the road and says, Come along now. Hurry. Then he grabs onto the ham again, lifts it and starts trotting quickly up the road in the direction he came from. Vanise and Claude reach for their baskets, hoist them to their heads and follow along behind.

The dog moves swiftly, and they can barely keep up. At the top of the hill, he stops a second, looks back at them and steps into the bush. Then it's down into a tangle of liana vines and low, dense mahoe trees and macca, with the yellow dog darting up and down and over limestone outcroppings and underbrush, the woman, baby and boy with their heavy baskets scrambling along behind, panting in the heat, lashed in the face and on the arms by vines and low branches, losing sight of the dog for an instant, then spotting him again and clambering over stones and fallen trees after him. The baby is awake now and crying, frightened. Vanise ignores the child and scolds Claude, telling him to hurry, run on ahead, don't lose sight of him!

Soon they find themselves running along a sandy pathway that winds down a narrow defile between two limestone ridges. The dog stops ahead of them a ways and watches them stumble along behind. He drops the ham again, as if to rest a moment, and says loudly, with tricky laughter in his low, smooth voice, Come on, now, Vanise! Don't tell me you can't keep up with an old, three-legged dog! He laughs and grabs up the ham and races on, suddenly leaving the path and scrambling up the steep side of the defile to the top of the ridge and over. They follow, out of breath and wet with sweat, Vanise pushing the boy from behind, urging him on. Hurry, Claude, don't lose sight of him! Get to the top and find him.

At the top, they stop for a second and search the underbrush beyond, low palmetto all the way to a turquoise streak of sea in the distance. They see the tin roofs of scattered cabins and small, cleared patches of ground here and there. He's gone! the boy wails. I can't see him. Then, a second later, No, there he is! and he points ahead at a yellow flash of fur on the ridge fifty yards beyond.

When the dog at last picks his way down the rocky side and enters the palmettos, they leave the ridge and in the palmettos come upon a mud flat, circle it halfway, following the dog's three-legged tracks in the gray mud when they cannot see the dog itself. Then, beyond the mud flat, the ground rises slightly and opens to a grassy field, and they see at the far end of the field a small, unpainted cinder-block house. The dog heads straight for the house, through a corn field, old, dry corn stalks clattering in the afternoon breeze, across a packed-dirt front yard and around the side of the house to the back.

Vanise and Claude run along the windowless side of the house, their breath rough, their clothing wet and stuck with burrs and leaves, and they suddenly come upon the dog lying in the center of the backyard, gnawing at the ham with deep concentration, as if he has been there all afternoon.

There is a door and stoop on the back side of the house, closed, curtainless windows on either side of it. Beyond the dog there is a shed or henhouse made of old doors and roofed over with green corrugated plastic, and beyond the shed, a garden plot with yam poles stuck in the ground and tiny, bright green corn shoots peeping through the dirt. In the distance is a field, then woods, then sea.

Vanise sits heavily down on the stoop, and the boy sits next to her. Before long, their breathing slows, their hearts stop pounding, and their clothes, in the cooling breeze off the sea, loosen and dry. The yellow dog goes on chewing at the ham quite as if they were not present. Beside them squats a large metal drum, a rain barrel with a spout leading to it from the low roof. Lying on the ground next to the barrel is a white enameled cup, and the boy grabs it up, fills it with water and hands it to his aunt, who drinks and hands the cup back in silence. The boy drinks, then sits down again next to Vanise, and they resume waiting.

Will Papa Legba speak to us again? Claude asks.

Just be silent, she whispers. See, even the baby knows how to behave, she adds, looking down at the infant asleep in her lap. Give him water, she commands, pointing toward the dog with her chin, and Claude quickly obeys, filling the cup and placing it with great tenderness a few feet in front of the animal.

The dog studies him, and when the boy has returned to the stoop, lets go of the ham, steps warily toward the cup and slurps at the water. Returning to the ham, the dog curls around it, and holding the meat with his front paws, tears at it with renewed concentration, getting down to the white bone now, licking and chewing, gnawing against it and poking his long pink tongue after the marrow.

Suddenly, they hear from the other side of the house the sound of a car, loud and blatting, a car without a muffler approaching the house rapidly, bumping across rocks and ruts and coming to an abrupt stop. A door slams, a man shouts, a harsh, loud voice that carries no sense to Vanise and Claude but is filled with the sound of anger and impatience. *Robbie! Where de fuck you at, mon? Come get you out here, mon! You goddamn bumba-clot, me gwan tan you hide, mon!* Then silence again, until the front door squeaks open and is flung shut, and the man hollers again, this time from inside the house. *Robbie! Lazy sonofabitch! Me cyan leave dis house a minute widdout trouble.*

Vanise and Claude do not move. They hear the sounds of someone rummaging through the house, hear pans clatter behind them, then silence. A moment passes, and the screened door at their backs opens, bangs against them, forcing them quickly off the short stoop, and when they turn, they face a large, coal-black man, balding on top, with a thick, bristly gray mustache and wearing a bright green safari shirt and khaki trousers. He puts his fisted hands on his hips and stares down at them. His large brown eyes are covered with a film, as if behind a pane of yellow glass, and several shiny scars lie across his cheeks and upper arms, raised and thick, like serpents. Vanise sees the cross-eyed dog peer across the yard at the man and flop its thin tail against the dusty ground.

Wal, now. Who dis? The man's voice is low and comes rumbling from his chest, and he smiles with the expression of a man who has unexpectedly won a small prize. His two front teeth are rimmed in gold, his wide, full lips shiny like his scars.

Vanise and Claude examine the ground at their feet. The dog gnaws at the hambone, hurriedly now.

You Robbie's woman?

Vanise knows he is speaking to her; she looks up and says nothing. The baby has awakened and turns uneasily in her arms.

C'mon, gal, talk to me. Where Robbie at? Him send you over here to say him sick again? Ras-clot, dat mon, me cyan deal wid him no more! Him s'posed to work dat patch by de salt flats, an' me check him all day, an' him never show once, lazy, simple sonofabitch. You tell him, sister, you tell him find himself another job. Me cyan deal wid him no more.

The man turns and swings open the screened door, stops and looks back at the woman. *G'wan, now, nothin' more to say. Go home, sister, and tell Robbie him fired.*

Vanise stands there in silence, looking away from the man, waiting.

What your name, gal?

She says nothing, shifts her weight and looks down at her baby's face. The man lets go of the screened door and takes a step toward her. For several seconds he studies the people before him, a young and pretty black woman with a baby in her arms, and a boy, and two baskets on the ground.

Suddenly, he smiles broadly. He knows everyone in town, practically everyone on the whole island, and he's never seen this woman before, or the boy. He drives a taxi between the landing strip in Bottle Creek and the Whitby Hotel, and he moves around the island a lot, and these faces are new to him. They are strangers' faces. *You one of dem Haitians, dat's what.* Putting out his hand, he places it heavily on her narrow shoulder and says loudly into her face, *Haytee? You from Hay-tee, gal?* He removes his paw from her shoulder and turns to Claude. *Hay-tee? C'mon, bwoy, you can tell me. Me na gwan do you no harm, bwoy. Me a fren,* he says, pointing to his beefy chest. *Me like Hay-shuns! Sonofabitch, fucking Haitians, dem, dey cyan understan' English, even.* Then to Vanise, *Hay-tee, gal?*

She nods her head slowly up and down. Haiti.

Ah-ha! The man flashes his gold-rimmed teeth. He swings open the screened door again and this time waves the woman into his house, but she stands rooted to the ground. Giving up, the man walks inside alone and returns a second later with a bottle of white overproof rum in his hand. He takes a long slug from the bottle, sighs as if relieved of a burden and sits down on the steps, looks back and forth from the boy to the woman. *So,* the man says to no one in particular, *me kotched me a coupla Haitians.* He takes another drink, extends the bottle to Vanise, who shakes her head no. *You gotta name, gal? What dem call you?* he tries.

Silence. Claude, wide-eyed at the sight of the large, loud man, clings to the side of his basket with both hands. Vanise's face is expressionless, impassive, as if she has turned herself into a stone.

The man points to his thick chest. *Me George. George McKissick. George,* he repeats, stabbing himself with his finger. *All dem other Haitians, your frens, dem, dey got kotched already, got 'em dis mawnin' near Bellefield Landing. Jus' sittin' on de beach, thinkin' dem in America. Now dey in de jail over on Grand Turk. What you think o' dat, gal? You lucky, dat's what. Lucky.*

Vanise listens closely, but nothing the man says makes sense. Now and then a word or string of words sounds familiar, but she loses the meaning instantly. She can read the man's face, however, and his body and the tones of voice he uses, bass tones, not harsh, not sweet, either, but rising and falling in a low range, as if he were trying to tell her a funny story.

He's playing with them, she knows, treating them like babies. And he likes to drink, drinks quickly and deeply with obvious pleasure and need. He lives alone: the house and yard are of a man alone; no signs of a woman or children here; no clothes drying on a rope, no toys scattered in the dirt, no curtains in the windows. Except for the yellow dog, no animals, either. The henhouse seems empty, and there are no chickens or roosters in the yard scratching and pecking in the dust. No pigs or goats. The man probably doesn't even eat here much; he comes home to drink alone and sleep and go out again. His scars tell her what happens when he is out at night in the bars. Another man must tend his crops, she decides, because this man is too bulky to be a farmer, too quick and nervous in his movements. And he has a calculating look, the look of a man who likes to buy things low and sell them high, who likes to haggle with people, not with the ground, the rain and the sun. And despite his playfulness, she can tell that he is not a kind man.

George goes on talking to Vanise, almost as if she understands his words. He tells her about the other Haitians from the boat, how they'll be kept in jail until they can be shipped back to Haiti, how stupid they were for trusting someone to bring them all the way to America in a boat small enough to get through the reef off North Caicos. The police are used to Haitians coming ashore here, and most of them get caught and sent right back. A few hide out, they're good farmers and stonemasons and sometimes metalworkers, and they work cheap, because they'll be turned over to the police if they don't, same as up north in the Bahamas. The Haitians who got caught this morning, he points out, were not as smart as Vanise. They stayed bunched up like cattle at Bellefield Landing, where they were bound to be seen. They should have separated and run into the bush, as she did, where they might have been lucky enough to meet up with someone like George McKissick, who would be willing to help them. Instead, they're in jail tonight, and she and her baby and little brother are here, with George McKissick, on his farm.

He goes silent for a few seconds, scratches his belly, swigs from the rum bottle, stands and takes up the white enameled cup from in front of the dog. He fills it from the barrel and drinks. Refilling the cup, he passes it to Vanise, and she drinks, hands it back. Then the boy. George sets the cup afloat in the rain barrel and studies it for a moment.

He's decided not to turn them in to the police, he announces. At least not tonight. He smiles, faces them and goes inside.

The sun has edged close to the horizon beyond the

field, and the sky is splashed with long, broad, plum-
and silver-colored streaks of cloud moving in from the
east. The sea breeze has shifted and become a land
breeze, bringing with it the smell of cassia trees and
heat-dried corn stalks from the meadow in front of the
low house.

What's he going to do? Claude asks.

Vanise looks over her shoulder at the yellow dog, who
lifts his pointed head and stares at them a second, then
resumes working at the hambone. Don't worry, Vanise
says to the boy.

A moment later, George kicks open the screened door
and comes out carrying a small, stained mattress. He
motions with his burly head for them to follow and
hurries across the yard past the dog to the shed. Hefting
the mattress onto one shoulder, he unlocks a rusty pad-
lock on the low door and yanks it open. Then he tosses
the mattress inside. He stands away and points into the
darkness and says, *Dere, gal, nobody gwan fine you
dere. Put you in de house, but someone soon come
an' fine you, turn you in first chance.*

Vanise leans forward and peers into the darkness and
heat of the hut. She smells chickens of long ago, the
remnants of dried, powdered droppings ground into the
dirt floor, old feathers and tufts, bits of grass and seeds,
yellow hulls of ancient corn in corners, dust motes floating in the air.

The last time he used this shed, George explains, he
stored some marijuana for his brother-in-law, who made
heaps of money off it and went to America and never
paid him a shilling for his troubles. Ever since then, he's
kept the shed locked and empty, because every time he
went near it, he got mad all over again. He figures if he
lets the Haitians use it awhile, he'll forget about his
brother-in-law's betrayal.

George points to their baskets, then inside the shed.
Vanise understands, swings her baby onto her left arm
and drags her basket into the darkness. Claude follows
her example, and when they emerge they find George
seated back on the stoop, his bottle in his lap, waving

them over. Like obedient children, they go and stand before him.

He explains loudly and slowly what the arrangement will be, and though they do not understand a word of what he says, they know a bargain has been struck. In a few days, it will become clear to them that George will provide shelter and food for them, yams and corn meal, rice, chicken backs, sometimes pork and maybe fish, when he can get it cheap, and they will work for him, in the fields, house and yard, and when George drives home from town in his taxi, drunk, loud and angry at the world, he'll stumble through the kitchen, grab his bottle and cross the backyard in the silvery moonlight to the henhouse, where he'll swing open the door and enter. Pushing the boy off the mattress, moving the sleeping infant aside, he'll yank down his trousers and make Vanise open up to him. The first time this happens, the boy will sit shivering all night on the stoop. After that, he will crawl into the man's car and sleep on the back seat until daylight wakes him.

Vanise and Claude and the baby, whom they soon start to call Charles, will stay on the island of North Caicos hidden away like this for many months, before they have learned enough of George McKissick's words to speak to the young man they replaced, Robbie, a thin, lazy brown man who comes around every week or so (more often after the morning he accidentally discovers Vanise in the yard) to make vain attempts to collect his pay.

Robbie is a kindly but stupid man, and it does not occur to him that this silent woman and boy are Haitians, until finally the boy speaks to him, asks in a halting, garbled way how to find a man with a boat to take them to America. To hurt McKissick, who now believes he will never have to pay Robbie for the work he did, and also to get his old job back, he will help them escape, he says, not to America, which is probably impossible to arrange without money, but straight to the Bahamas, where boats go all the time. There are plenty of small wooden cargo boats shipping salt for food, with captains not at all averse to carrying a pretty young Haitian woman belowdecks in a corner of the hold. If she must bring along her child and nephew, no matter. They can be shoved aside when necessary.

COLUMBUS STAYED ON THE ISLAND FOR ONLY A FEW DAYS, when, no longer afraid of being lost, certain of where he had landed, he departed for Cipangu, Japan, which "the Indians here call Cuba." North Caicos itself became lost. The admiral's landing and brief stay here went recorded as having occurred way to the north in the Bahamas, at Watling's Island.

Ponce de León, after fourteen days ashore, set sail and headed north from Whitby, where a small stream parted the beach and entered the sea. Glad to be rid of the place, his head once again filled with visions of a new youth, a new life, a new old age, he quickly forgot the island. He would not even have marked it on his chart, had it not been for the reef on which his ship had foundered and were it not, therefore, a place to avoid.

A Man's Man

1

BOB DUBOIS'S FIRST CALL, AFTER TREATNENT AT THE WINTER
Haven Hospital overlooking lovely Lake Martha, is to his
brother Eddie. It's one thirty-five in the morning, he's shot
and killed a man, been rushed in a wailing ambulance
through the night, had twenty-seven slivers of glass removed from his flesh and a pint of pink antiseptic daubed
over half his torso, and now, in blood-stained shirt and
pants, as he stands in the lobby of the emergency ward
of the hospital, two car-crash victims hurtling past on
rubber-wheeled stretchers, a drunken middle-aged black
man with stab wounds in his bicep arguing with the nurse
at the admitting desk, a white teenaged mother and
pimply-faced father sitting warily in straight-backed chairs
while their baby undergoes tests to determine the extent
of internal damage caused by the beating they gave her,
Bob calls his brother Eddie, and all Eddie wants to
know is how the hell the other nigger got away.

"Whaddaya mean he ran out the back while you were
calling the cops? Why didn't you bring the bastard out
front by the phone, just keep him covered?"

"Look, the kid shit his pants, he was so scared. He stunk. I didn't want to get near him. I don't know, I just didn't think he had it in him to try anything, not after the way he was scared."

"You shoulda shot the fucker in the knees. Then called the cops."

"Christ, Eddie, he was only a kid. Maybe fifteen or so. I mean, for Christ's sake, I was a little rattled, y' know. What the hell do you want? I mean, I never shot a guy before. I never even got shot *at* before. I mean, the guy's standing there with a fucking twenty-gauge aimed at my head. I'm lucky I'm alive. You woulda had a heart attack."

"I woulda shot *both* niggers."

Both men are silent for a few seconds. Then Eddie says, "Look, I'm sorry. It's just that I hate those bastards. Fucking coons sit around taking welfare while we work our asses off, and then they come around with their fucking shotguns telling us to give 'em all our money. You know?"

"Yeah."

"No, you did good, kid. I'm proud of ya. No shit. You swacked a nigger and saved the day's take."

"Well, I'd already made the deposit anyhow," Bob explains. "There wasn't any money there. The register was empty."

Eddie doesn't quite understand. What was Bob doing at the store, then, if he'd already made the deposit?

"I . . . well, I went out with someone, for a couple of drinks. Friend of mine. Then the transmission, the throw-out bearing, I think it is, got jammed. You know, like it does. So I went into the store to call Elaine or somebody to come get me."

"Oh, yeah? You getting a little on the side, kid?"

"Oh, no, no, nothing like that. A friend of mine, guy I know." He can't use the story about the Budweiser salesman on Eddie.

"Sure, sure. I don't give a shit you're ripping off a piece of poon now and then. Just don't do it on *my* time, okay? You get all the pussy you want on your own time, but I ain't paying you to wet your dick, you know."

"Yeah."

"Who's at the store right now?"

"Cops. State and local."

"Okay, I'll get right out there," he says. "You, you go on home and get some sleep. I'll see you in the morning. Is the place a mess?"

"Yeah. Lots of broken bottles. I got cut. . . ."

"Okay, I'll be there in the morning too. Don't clean up until the insurance guys get there. You understand. It's better for a big claim if the place looks like it got hit by a shit storm."

They say goodbye and hang up, and for several minutes Bob stands by the phone trembling, as waves of rage, fatigue, horror and regret run through him, one hard upon the other, until he can no longer distinguish between them. He barely knows what part of the country he's in, and he no longer remembers why he came here, why he left the place where he knew who he was, knew what he felt and why, knew how he felt about the people he lived with—his wife and children, his friends, his boss, his girlfriend, all of them living in the place where all the people were white and spoke the same kind of English and wanted the same things from life and knew more or less how to get them.

For the first time since he came to Florida, he lets himself say to himself that he has made a terrible mistake. He should have endured the sad frustration of his life, should have been patient and waited, because it would have passed, probably once Christmas had passed, and in a few years he would have got ahead, he would have been promoted at the oil company, maybe even ended up with a desk job as a supervisor or an estimator for new work. He would still own his house on Butterick Street, his boat, the dining room set they sold for one hundred dollars in the yard sale. He'd still be able to fuck Doris Cleeve when he got a little depressed or bored, and he'd know exactly how she felt about him and how he felt about her. He wouldn't worry if his prick was too small because he was a white man. He wouldn't worry about how well or badly he made love, because Doris always got wet right away and sucked him right into her with obvious excitement and joy. Good old Doris Cleeve. And he wouldn't have to think about the yellow-skinned black man lying in his own blood with a fist-sized hole in his face where his mouth and all his pretty teeth used to be, or the boy huddled in his shit against a cinder-block wall begging him not to kill him, or Eddie wondering why the hell he didn't kill him. He wouldn't be the man he has become, and then the man he has become would be free to go on and be someone else, some guy Bob Dubois would never miss knowing anyhow, some nervous, unsure liquor store clerk who tried and failed to make love to a pretty black woman and then almost got himself killed and had to shoot a robber because the man was black and he was not and as a result did not have the wit to talk his way out of it, when, if the robber had been white, Bob would have explained easily and nothing bad would have happened to the sad-eyed liquor store clerk working for his older, smarter brother while his wife gets more and more pregnant and life gets daily more complicated and difficult and all he can think about in the face of it is how can he redeem himself as a lover with the black woman he failed to make love to successfully. This man is not the sort of man Bob Dubois would want to know if Bob Dubois were the same man he was six months ago.

Looking around at the strangers in the waiting room, the nurses and attendants and the occasional intern passing through, Bob suddenly feels lost to himself, as if the man he once was has been destroyed and replaced by someone he can't recognize. It makes no difference what he does now, Bob decides. He can walk out the door to the breezy night, to the smell of magnolia and honeysuckle, to the anonymous cars passing by on their sleepy turns toward home, empty buses hissing to a stop to pick up late-night stragglers after the bars have closed, card games shut down, tempers and passions cooled enough to take back to living rooms and bedrooms—he

can walk out to that world and join it, and with no one
the wiser, drift on out to Highway 17, hitch a ride north
as far as Atlanta, where, along about Wednesday, the
police will pick him up for vagrancy. He pictures himself
slumped in the back of the police car, two thick-necked
young cops in front on the other side of an iron mesh
barrier smoking cigarettes and talking in low Southern
voices about bets they've placed on the All Star game
this weekend. Bob doesn't know what sport the All
Stars play, or where the game is being held. He barely
knows what city he's in, what season it is (late spring,
early fall, tropical midwinter?), or how he got the cuts
and slashes on his neck and the backs of his arms, so
that when at the police station the desk sergeant asks
him about the cuts, he makes up a story, tells him he got
rolled by a couple of black kids in Macon who cut him
with their razors for the fun of it, and he's believed,
booked and taken to a highway work camp near Wood-
bine to spend thirty days cutting and burning kudzu
alongside Interstate 95. After that, when he's released,
he rides with a friend from the work camp, a pickpocket
who steals a car five miles from the camp, to Nashville,
where the friend says they can both get work as bartenders . . . or he talks a local peanut farmer into hiring him
as a fork-lift operator at the warehouse . . . or he phones
his wife in Oleander Park, Florida, and tries to explain
what happened to him, so that she will borrow a car
from a neighbor and will pick him up and drive him
home to where he used to live, with her and their two
daughters and unborn son.

He tries to explain to Elaine what has made him feel
that it no longer makes any difference what he does. He
tries and tries, first on the telephone from the hospital
and then, beside her, in the car driving home. But he
fails. First she understands too quickly and feels sorry
for him; then she can't understand at all and feels inade-
quate and guilty; and finally she pretends to understand
and says she has felt the same way herself. It's how it
was that night in New Hampshire, little more than six
months ago, when he came home weeping and they

decided to move to Florida. In New Hampshire, he could weep like a child and cry, "I want . . . I want . . ." and she could respond by saying, "A new life! A fresh start! Florida!" and it didn't matter that she didn't understand him, or that she understood him too easily and therefore not at all. He could dream his way back to life, could make love to her and fall asleep with a smile on his face and wake the next morning believing that what he was about to do would make a difference in his life and in the lives of his wife and children. Their lives would soon be better than they had been, not because of chance or dumb luck or just rewards handed down from heaven, but because he, Bob Dubois, had decided to leave his old life behind and pack up and head south. Everything was going to be different, and better. That, most of all. Better.

Now, however, when he cries to his wife, "I want . . . I want . . ." there is nothing she can say to make him forget that she can't understand him at all or else thinks she understands him all too well. Consequently, his mind turns to the woman Marguerite Dill, whose love for him, if he can acquire it, will make him different from the man he is, the man who cries, "I want . . . I want . . ." Men do that to women, use them to remake themselves, just as women do it to men. Men and women seek the love of the Other so that the old, cracked and shabby self can be left behind, like a sloughed-off snake-skin, and a new self brought forward, clean, shining, glistening wetly with promise and talents the old self never owned. When you seek to acquire the love of someone who resembles you, in gender, temperament, culture or physical type, you do so for love of those aspects of yourself, gender, temperament, culture, etc.; but when you seek the love of someone different from you, you do it to be rid of yourself. And so Bob, who more than anything desires to be rid of himself, falls to contemplating the love of a Southern black woman and the kind of Northern white man it will make of him.

Once again, he decides that he no longer loves his wife. He's not sure what the implications of that decision are, but he hopes they don't mean separation and divorce, breaking up the family. He's not ready for that, and even so, she, more the Catholic than he, would not permit it, no matter what the cost. They no longer quarrel, he and Elaine; that scratchy period passed the day he decided Marguerite was only a passing fancy. Since then, his days and nights with his wife and children have been peaceful, if somewhat boring. Since then, he has not had to fuss with himself to rub out the guilt he felt in the company of his children, who wanted to know, did he still love Mommy? Now, however, he fears that the nasty and exhausting quarrelsomeness that plagued them for several months in the spring will return and will quickly escalate, until he's forced to make an impossible choice between his love for his children and his love for a woman not their mother. Bob's no psychologist, but he knows how things go.

On the other hand, he believes that the kind of man he will become, by virtue of his acquiring Marguerite's love, is the kind of man who can locate with ease the excluded middle between his love for his children and his love for a woman not their mother. The man is handsome, of course, and sexy and good-humored; he's not rich, not yet, but some men don't have to be rich in order to seem it; he's kind and gentle, tender to women, children and animals, without being sentimental, however, because, after all, he's a "man's man" as well; he's a stern yet jocular father to his children, and he can take care of his wife too, can assume a custodial role in her life, honoring and attending to all her needs, even her sexual needs, while at the same time making plans to leave the house later, after he's satisfied her sexual needs, to drive in his Lancia convertible across the towns of central Florida in the humid summer night to meet his beloved where she waits for him, seated elegantly at a table for two in the small back room of a restaurant that overlooks a dark, star-dappled lake, where the sound of small waves lapping tawny sands and the seductive smell of orange blossoms fill the night air. That's the kind of man Marguerite would love.

*   *   *

HE IS SEATED ON THE EDGE OF A SHORT, WIDE DOCK. HE'S wearing dark blue swimming trunks and a yellow life vest, his feet tucked into water skis and his hands grasping a bar attached to a tow rope which in turn is attached to Eddie's new boat. Late afternoon sunlight glitters off the lake in sheets and planes, and the still air ripples in the heat, distorting the tall, dense, gray-green live oaks and cypress trees along the grassy shore. From where Bob is seated, the shoreline loops and spreads gradually into an approximate O three miles wide and long. They are on the grounds of the Lakes Region Yacht and Country Club, he, Elaine, Ruthie and Emma having been admitted at the gate earlier as guests of Edward Dubois, and after meeting Eddie, Sarah and Jessica at the clubhouse bar, where the grownups drank mint juleps on the terrace under a Cinzano umbrella, they strolled across the clipped, pale green lawns from the clubhouse and marina to one of the half-dozen small, secluded coves on the club grounds where there are picnic tables, fireplaces, boat landings and short, shallow beaches. It's a Sunday, Eddie's thirty-third birthday.

Last week, when Bob and his family were invited by Sarah to come to the club and help celebrate the day, Bob instructed Elaine to find out what they should give Eddie for a birthday present. "The sonofabitch's already got everything he needs," he muttered. Elaine asked her sister-in-law what Eddie needed. Sarah suggested they get him something to go with her gift to him.

"What *is* your gift?" Elaine asked. They were talking on the telephone, Elaine standing in her kitchen, Sarah lying in coconut oil next to her pool. Bob sat on the couch in front of the TV watching the New York Yankees, in a late season game, thrash the Red Sox, who once again had betrayed him in August after having seduced him, almost against his will, in May.

"Fucking Reggie," he grumbled, taking a quick pull on his beer. "I hate the way he struts. Look at the bastard, like a goddamn rooster."

Sarah spoke slowly, almost coyly, though Elaine

couldn't imagine why she wouldn't simply come right out and tell her what she'd bought for her husband's birthday. "You'll *never* guess what it is," she said. "I'm almost *ashamed* of myself, and I *know* I'll be sorry later."

"Well, what should we get him to go with it?" Elaine asked, her voice cooling. "Whatever *it* is."

Sarah giggled. "Seat cushions."

"What?"

"Seat cushions."

"Seat cushions? Like, for sitting on? For a couch?"

"No, no, silly. For a boat!"

"A boat? You bought him a boat? Another one?"

Bob groaned, "Jee-sus H. Christ! Another fucking boat!" and Elaine shushed him with the flat of her hand, and he went back to staring at the TV screen, hating Reggie Jackson with renewed fury.

"Oh, it's real cute, he's gonna love it," Sarah said. "Wait'll you see it. He's been talking about this one in particular for months, and he's dropped a few hints, but I know he doesn't think I'll go out and do it, actually go out on my own and buy him a twelve-thousand-dollar boat."

"Twelve thousand dollars!" Elaine gasped.

Bob looked up from the TV screen and stared at his wife as if he suddenly felt sick and wanted sympathy.

"Where'd you get that kind of money, Sarah? Won't he be mad when he finds out? I mean, I can't imagine . . ."

"Oh, Eddie's been putting money into an account in my name now for a long time, in several accounts, actually, and I never touch it, even though he tells me I should go ahead and spend it when I want to and not let it sit there where anybody who wants to can see it. It's some kind of tax thing. I never understand that sort of thing. Anyhow, he'd rather have me buy things with the money than leave it in the bank like that. Jewelry and stuff. I don't know *how* he'll feel about me spending money on a boat, though. But as long as it's in my name, I think it's all right. I checked with his accountant, and he said it was okay, though I hope he didn't tell Eddie—I really want to surprise him. He's been so worried the last few weeks. Actually, since the robbery, though I don't think that's what's got him down.''

Cushions, then.

Bob stopped one morning at Wiggins Boat Yard and Marina in Winter Haven, where Sarah had bought Eddie's boat, and bought four large, square, unsinkable cushions, rust-colored, to match the boat, a Regal Empress 190XL, a twenty-foot-long, arrow-shaped speedboat with a 150-horsepower Johnson motor and a top speed of over forty-five miles per hour. Bob lugged the set of cushions in a large, gift-wrapped box from the car out to the terrace behind the clubhouse and then across the rolling lawns to the picnic grounds by the shore, where Sarah had arranged to have sandwiches, beer for the adults and lemonade for the kids, birthday cake and ice cream sent down from the clubhouse, and where Eddie, who had received his gift earlier that morning and had been playing with it ever since, had tied his new boat. When Bob saw the vehicle sitting low and sleek in the water, saw its abundance of chrome and curved glass and glistening deck, saw the snug interior fitted out like a sports car, he set the box of cushions on the ground by the picnic table and stood awkwardly in front of it, as if to hide it from sight, and wished he had bought something like a Swiss army knife instead.

Later, after eating the sandwiches and drinking several Heinekens, and after Eddie had blown out the candles on his cake (eleven of them, one for each three years, Sarah explained), Elaine presented the box to him, with her apologies. "It's not much, Eddie," she said, lifting it with difficulty to the front of her huge belly and passing it over the table to him.

Bob looked out at the lake and let his gaze fall on the new boat tied to the dock, where it moved on the rippling water like a thoroughbred racehorse trembling in a shifting breeze.

Eddie tore open the box like a child, then beamed happily at the sight of the cushions inside. "Hey! Thanks, Elaine! Bob! Thanks a lot. This's great. Look, honey, *cushions!* They match the boat," he said, genuinely pleased. He'd figured on renting cushions today at the marina, he said, or hauling over the small yellow cushions from his old boat, which would have been okay, he explained, but not perfect. "And everything should be perfect on a maiden voyage, right, Bob?"

"Right. Perfect."

Now, as if to atone for his feeble gift, Bob agrees to water-ski behind Eddie's new boat, while his wife and sister-in-law watch from the shore and his daughters and niece, hugged by life vests and seated on the new cushions, watch from the boat. He's never skied on water before; in fact, he's never skied on any kind of surface, despite having been raised where people drive from cities hundreds of miles away just so they can spend a few hours careening down mountains on slats strapped to their feet.

With the motor burbling and spitting behind the boat, Eddie looks back at Bob and asks if he's ready. Sitting next to her father in the cockpit, Jessica, looking sadly like a plucked chicken in her purple tank suit, seems profoundly bored. Emma stares at the gauges on the glittering dashboard in front of her, while Ruthie examines the tow rope where it's clipped to the swivel at the stern, follows its coiled, half-submerged length to the dock, fifteen feet away, where it's attached to a short bar that her father, grim-faced, extends chest-high in front of him and clings to with both hands.

"Be careful, Daddy," Ruthie says.

Eddie laughs and revs the motor. Emma delightedly follows the needle on the tachometer with her index finger, and Jessica peers off to her right, as if at a photographer specializing in preadolescent girls. She skied first, expertly circling the lake twice, then on the second pass letting go of the rope twenty or thirty feet from the landing dock and sinking slowly into thy water, rising again and languidly floating the skis to shore ahead of her. She had looked good to Bob out there, swooping from one side of the wake to the other, riding over the waves and sending a high, white fantail behind her. It looked easy.

Eddie agreed. "But not as easy as it looks," he warned. "Don't get pissed if you fuck it up at first." He offered some basic instruction, assured Bob that he'd start off slowly and told him to be sure to let go of the tow rope when he went down; he'd come back and pick him up right away.

"What do you mean, 'when'? '*If*' I go down is what," Bob corrected him.

"Yeah, sure," Eddie said, grinning.

The skis feel comfortable to him, like rubber slippers. He nods to Eddie that he's ready and lifts the rope from the water, flicking it like reins on a horse.

Eddie guns the motor, the stern squats and the bow lifts, and the boat leaps forward, instantly straightening the rope, yanking Bob from the dock into the water. He sinks like a stone, then suddenly rises, standing, the skis rushing over the skin of the lake, and he's doing it, he's water-skiing! Eddie, glancing back, grins and raises his fist and cheers. Ruthie claps her hands with joy, and Emma follows, and even Jessica seems pleased.

As he whizzes away from shore, Bob lets go of the tow bar with one hand and waves triumphantly. He draws the rope to him, tests its tautness, then lets it back out, feels the water pounding against his feet, the wind in his face, and discovers that he can shift his weight on the skis and move himself to the left or right of the boat. On and on they go, straight out toward the middle of the lake, faster and still faster, and Bob feels wonderful. He decides to imitate his niece and cross the wake, and a second later the water is smacking loudly against the bottoms of the skis, but he holds on, keeps his legs bent slightly at the knees, his back straight, his arms outstretched, and he's over, way out on the starboard side, almost parallel to the boat, as if he were racing with it. He knows he is grinning foolishly, but he doesn't care. He's happier at this moment than he has been in months, happier than he can remember having been for years, mindless and moving fast and barely in control, concentrating mightily on all the quickly shifting elements—water, boat, towline, skis, feet, legs, back and arms—creating and sustaining a balanced tension between them that surrounds him like an ether and brings him wholly to life.

Soon they have circled the lake and are making a pass by the dock. Bob can see Sarah, tall in her white jogging suit, standing on the dock, behind her Elaine, large and lumpy in pink maternity shorts and smock, seated at the picnic table. Eddie cuts back a bit and slows slightly, but Bob waves for him to go on, take another turn, so Eddie hits the throttle, and as they pass the dock, Bob leans to his right and skids over the waves to the left of the boat, swinging closer and closer to the dock. The skis bump over the water as if over rutted ice, pounding loudly against it, and Eddie, looking quickly over his shoulder, sees the danger and turns the boat slightly shoreward and increases speed to straighten the line and get Bob back behind the boat and away from the dock. But it's too late. Bob's headed straight for the dock now. Sarah sees what's happening, knows what's about to happen, and her hand goes to her mouth and she starts backing quickly off the dock toward the safety of the land. Elaine gets awkwardly but rapidly to her feet and rushes forward.

"Let go!" Eddie shouts. "Leggo the fuckin' rope!"

Bob sees the collision that he cannot avoid. He sees his body, wet and nearly naked, smashed against the wooden dock, and suddenly his knees buckle, the skis dive nose-first into the water, and then his feet are free, he's underwater, still holding to the rope, being ripped through the water and to the surface again, while Eddie screams back, "Leggo! Leggo! Leggo, you dumb asshole!"

The boat is roaring away from the dock now, hauling Bob behind it, banging his body against the rock-hard water. Eddie, with one hand on the wheel, has stood up and is gesturing wildly at Bob to let go of the rope. Bob can't hear anything but the roar of the water and the boat, can't feel anything except the pounding against his body, as if he were being kicked by a dozen boots at once. He rolls his body on its side, trying to escape the pounding. His hands seem frozen to the tow bar, and he can't let go, he can't pry his own fingers loose, until, at last, Eddie cuts the motor, and the boat slows and stops, the rope coils and sinks, and Bob releases the bar, rolls over onto his back and, arms loose, legs dangling, head lolling back, waves washing over his body, he floats like a dead fish, a large white carp.

Eddie turns the boat and slowly approaches him. "You stupid sonofabitch!" he screams. "Why the fuck didn't you let go the rope? You coulda got killed!"

Bob grabs the gunwale and says nothing, just holds on.

"You all right?" Eddie asks. The children are gray-faced, and Ruthie has jammed her thumb into her mouth.

"Why . . . why the fuck . . . didn't you kill . . . the motor?"

"I couldn't, you asshole! You were s'posed to let go the rope, I kept waiting for you to let go, that's why!"

"You . . . bastard. You . . . coulda killed me."

"Me!" Eddie screams, his eyes bugging out. "Me? Me? *I* coulda killed you?"

"I forgot . . . I forgot to let go. I couldn't think. It was the first time. You coulda killed me," Bob says again. "Help me get into the boat," he says grimly, raising a hand from the water. "You're a real bastard, Eddie. No shit."

Eddie turns away and tells Jessica to pull in the tow-line. She stands and draws the rope quickly in, dumping it in a snarl behind the seat. Reaching down, Eddie grabs a rust-colored seat cushion and tosses it into the water. "Here," he says. "Ride *that* to shore, you stupid sonofabitch. *I* coulda killed you," he sneers. "I shoulda just kept on going, till you finally figured out to let go the fucking rope. But I probably woulda run out of gas first, you stupid asshole. You can ride your goddamned cushion home." He hits the throttle, and the boat churns the water, turns, and heads roaring toward shore.

Bob watches it get smaller, sees his daughters looking

back in fearful confusion, and when the waves subside, he paddles to the bobbing cushion and grabs onto it. Then, shoving it out in front of him, he kicks his legs and starts moving slowly in the direction of the dock and picnic grounds and his family.

2

THE NIGHT ELAINE WENT INTO LABOR AND HAD THE BABY, Bob was with Marguerite at the Hundred Lakes Motel. It was a Thursday, October 16, and the baby, a boy weighing six pounds fourteen ounces and named Robert Raymond Dubois, Jr., was born three weeks ahead of schedule and, despite Elaine's rapid weight gain in the last few weeks, had shown no signs of arriving prematurely, and so Bob, as he had for months, treated the forthcoming birth of his third child as an event in the distant future, almost as if it were an event in someone else's life.

For Elaine, of course, the baby was already an active member of the family and had been since late May, when she first felt him kick against her ribs from inside. But it's often this way, that the mother and father regard the birth of their child as taking place at dates months apart, especially after the birth of the first child and almost always when the mother and the father have made their life together one thing and their lives apart different and separate things, which has been increasingly true of Bob and Elaine since Bob discovered Marguerite Dill and, more emphatically, since the robbery.

At eight-fifteen that night, Bob telephones Elaine from the store to say that he'll be home late, he's going out for a drink with the Budweiser salesman. Business is light tonight anyhow, it's a Thursday, so he may even close the store a little early. He'll be home before midnight, he assures her, while outside in the parking lot, Marguerite waits for him in her car, the motor running, windows open to the cool fall night, tape deck playing Isaac Hayes.

Elaine whines briefly and in a thin voice, but after all,

Bob, unlike most husbands, always calls her when he's going to be late, and he's seldom late more than once a week, and besides, he has no other friends, and, she reasons, a man needs friends, especially a man who has become, as Bob has, such a loner. Go ahead, she tells him, and have a good time, she had planned on going to bed early anyhow, she wasn't feeling too great today. She probably shouldn't have tried to do all the house-cleaning in one day. She's already in bed, or at least on it, with her swollen feet up, her huge belly looming in front of her, her bulging slacks unzipped at the sides to ease her thick, soft flesh. Across from the bed on the dresser, the Sony jabbers in Spanish. She flicked it on just as the phone rang and hasn't found her program yet.

At nine-oh-eight, she chuckles at one of Gary Cole-man's smartaleck remarks on *Diff'rent Strokes,* feels the first, light contraction and suddenly turns serious, because she recognizes it immediately, does not for a second confuse it with indigestion or heartburn or just her imagination. Elaine knows her body, can read all its signals accurately, and she has been through this twice before and recently enough to have retained a clear, physical memory of it. She knows at once that she's going to have her baby tonight. Picking up the phone next to the bed, she dials the liquor store, praying silently that her husband won't have left yet.

The phone in the store rings an even dozen times, then stops. Bob is already at the Hundred Lakes Motel, smoking marijuana for the first time in his life. He mentioned to Marguerite the last time they were together like this that she might relax if she got drunk enough, and she suggested they get high together sometime. Did she mean marijuana? Grass?

"Sure. Why not?"

"Well, yeah, why not smoke a little grass? It can't hurt you, can it?"

She was surprised he'd never tried it, she even thought it was cute, or so she said, and she promised him she'd bring a couple of joints with her the next time they went out.

Now, in the darkness of the room (which she seems to prefer, though he just once would like to leave the lights on when they are naked, but he still can't figure out how to propose it without sounding slightly perverse), Marguerite lights the joint and sucks the smoke into her lungs noisily and passes it to Bob.

He tries to hold it casually, almost drops it, quickly recovers and inhales deeply. He likes the sucking noise she makes when she smokes, likes the odor, likes the way his thoughts suddenly soften and liquefy. His skin feels crisp and tingly, but everything enclosed by his skin feels densely soft and warm. Like oatmeal, he thinks. He giggles and tells her what he was thinking.

"More like grits," she says. "With gravy."

"Pancakes with hot maple syrup," he suggests.

She says, "No, more like hushpuppies. I feel like a hushpuppy."

"Ah," he exclaims, he has it now. "Corned beef and cabbage."

She laughs a long time, or what seems like a long time. "Chitlins!"

"Yorkshire pudding, that's it exactly!"

"Nope. It's rice an' field peas!"

"Baked beans . . . with molasses and salt pork."

"Beaten biscuits. You ain't never had no beaten biscuits, I bet. Sometime I got to make you some. With red gravy on 'em."

"Boiled lobster!" Bob says he feels like a boiled lobster, red and hard on the outside, sweet and meaty on the inside. "Um-m-m," he says, smacking his lips. "There's nothing as good as that sweet, white, lobster meat sucked out of the hard, red claw and dipped in melted butter."

They are silent for a few seconds, and then their hands touch, and they lie down beside one another and place mouth, breasts, belly, thighs and feet against mouth, breasts, belly, thighs and feet, and then he moves into her, swiftly and easily.

At nine thirty-five, Elaine's water breaks. Too early, she thinks. Too soon. This is going to be a quick one, not like the others, and the contractions, now about five minutes apart, are heavy and deep, as if her uterus were a giant fist opening and closing. The pain is cold, not hot, and comes in waves, but it's not as strong as when the others were born, she thinks, at least not as strong as she remembers. But they were big babies, and Emma was ten days late, and this baby is going to be early and probably small. Another girl, she decides. Oh, Jesus, not another girl, though it'll be easier if it's a girl. Easier and nicer. Except for Bob. Where the hell is he? The bastard. Oh, Bob, you bastard, where the hell are you? She grunts and turns to the phone and dials the number of her friend Ellen Skeeter, who, thank God, answers right away.

They shower together, and for the first time Bob sees Marguerite's naked body, long, dark brown and shining, like polished sandalwood. He soaps her slick back and buttocks, rubs her shoulders and neck with one hand, her ass and the back of her thighs with the other, and when, like a strung bow, she arches backwards and spreads her thighs, he slides his hand into her from behind, one finger, then two, then three, and she gasps, leans forward and lays her weight against the tile wall of the shower, lets the warm water splash over her soapy back, gush between her buttocks and down his stiff, pumping arm. Shoving her ass against him, she drives his fingers deeper and deeper into her body, until her cunt is sucking at his hand, reaching for it and grabbing, letting go, then reaching and grabbing again, farther in each time, snapping and letting go, over and over, deeper and deeper, and then she's swirling his thick fingers around inside her, twitching them, whirling her ass in wet circles, and soon she starts to moan, low and steady, and flailing one hand back around in search of his prick, finding it, she pulls away from his fingers and jams his prick in, and he grabs onto her thrashing hips and rides, rides, rides, while the water splashes warmly over their faces, shoulders, chests and bellies.

By ten-eighteen, when Elaine arrives at the emergency room of the Winter Haven Hospital and is met by her doctor, swiftly examined and rushed upstairs to a delivery room, she's deeply into hard labor, and her cervix has dilated sufficiently that the doctor, a gaunt, red-eyed, rumpled Mississippian named Tucker Beacham, escorts her stretcher to obstetrics himself, in case he has to deliver the baby in the hallway. Ellen Skeeter, frightened and excited, joggles along behind the two, calling out to her friend, "Don't you worry 'bout a thing, honey, your chil'ren goin' be fine. Soon's I get you taken care of, honey, I'll call home an' tell Ronnie to stay right there at your place tonight. Ronnie'll take good care of the chil'ren till Bob gets home, honey, an' he'll tell Bob everything, so don't you fret, now."

In the parking lot by the store, Bob kisses Marguerite softly on the lips, says he loves her more and more every day, and steps from her car. "Wait a second," he says, closing her car door. "Wait till I make sure I can get my car into gear." He slides into his car, starts the motor and drops the car into reverse. It makes a clunking noise, but it goes in. "Okay, it's fine," he says happily. "I don't need you no mo' for *nuthin*. Not for *nuthin!*" he says, laughing.

She smiles out the open window of her car and purses her lips at him. "You will soon, honey. Jus' wait." Then she spins the wheel and drives off.

Slowly, Bob draws out a cigarette and lights it, inhaling the smoke the way he inhaled the grass, tamping it down into the furthest recesses of his lungs. Grass is great, he announces to himself. Switching on the radio, he fiddles with the tuner until he finds a country and western station, and for a few seconds he listens to Kenny Rogers and Dottie West sing "Don't Fall in Love with a Dreamer."

Abruptly, he cuts them off and flips the tuner down the band, until he picks up the rumbling, wet voice of Barry White. Then he backs the car, cuts the wheel, and slowly, smoothly, oozing sexy confidence like ol' Barry himself, Bob Dubois drives onto the highway, turns left and heads on down the road to home.

At eleven-twelve, Bob's son is born, tiny, cheesy and

blue, and because this is the first time Elaine has seen one of her children born—with Ruthie and Emma, she exhausted herself in labor, and the pain grew so great that finally she asked to be knocked out with gas—she believes the baby is born dead, and she starts to sob uncontrollably.

Dr. Beacham grins behind his mask. "You got yourself a baby boy, Miz Dubois," he says, handing the baby to the nurse. "Now," he says, patting her still large belly, "let's see if we can get the rest out as easy as he come out."

"It's okay?" she asks in a plaintive voice. "It's alive?"

"Sure is. Soon's we get him a little cleaned up, he's all yours. Now, let's bear down hard one more time," he says softly.

"It's a boy, then," Elaine says. "And he's alive!" She wants to see him, to hold him to her breasts, to examine him all over, his mouth, nose, ears and eyes, his tiny fingers and toes, and his penis, oh, especially his penis! It's the strangest thing that's ever happened to her—to have a male body, a body with a penis on it, emerge from her female body! It seems beyond belief, almost nonsensical. In a sensible world, females would give birth to females, and males would give birth to males. How can this funny miracle be?

She does what she's told and pushes her abdomen down and out, and when the placenta is driven from her, it feels like a wonderfully liberating bowel movement, and she almost laughs aloud. Then she reaches her arms toward the nurse, who places the baby boy on Elaine's stomach with its tiny red face facing hers, and suddenly Elaine is weeping with love for this blind, wet infant, this sweet chaos lying limp as earth on her belly, this incredible, terrifying, godlike innocence.

At eleven-thirty, Bob drives into his yard and parks the car, gets out and strolls slowly in the moonlight across the dew-wet plot between the driveway and the trailer. He hitches up his pants, unlocks the door and walks inside, and stops short in the doorway when he sees Ronnie Skeeter spread out on the couch, the Sony flickering on the coffee table before him. Ronnie's huge body takes up nearly the whole couch. Though it's a cool evening, and all he's wearing is a Dairy Queen tee shirt and Scotch-plaid Bermuda shorts, Ronnie, as usual, is sweating ripely. He's sprawled from the center of the couch on out to the ends, his meaty arms flung over the back of the couch, his huge beer gut, like a weighty sack of flour, billowing out in front of him and swooping smoothly down to his pinched crotch, where enormous red legs merge like turnpike ramps.

He looks up brightly as Bob enters. "Hidie, Bob!" he says. "Elaine ain't here. She . . ."

"What's going on?" Bob interrupts, sensing disaster. "Where're the kids?"

"Oh, they're jus' fine. Sleepin' like bugs in a rug." Ronnie goes back to watching Johnny Carson, his message delivered. With the flat of one hand, he rubs the top of his blond crew cut, patting it affectionately, as if it were a pet.

"Where's Elaine? What's going on?"

Ronnie looks back slowly, reluctantly. It's hard to watch the Johnny Carson show when you keep tuning out. You miss a lot of the jokes because you don't know exactly who Johnny's guest is or what Johnny or Ed said last. He tells Bob that his wife Ellen took Bob's wife Elaine to the hospital.

"Hospital! Why?"

"Well, if I was to guess, Bob, I'd say it was so she could have her baby."

"Oh, Jesus! Oh, Jesus! Jesus H. Christ! When, Ronnie? When did she go?"

"Couple hours ago. Hey, listen, I hope you don't mind I drank a couple of your Colt 45's. I didn't want to leave the kiddies here alone and get some from home."

"No, no, fine, fine." Bob opens the door to leave, then abruptly turns back. "She went to the hospital?"

Ronnie answers without looking away from the TV screen. "Yeah. Couple hours ago."

"Alone?" Bob feels his blood wash down his body. His face is stiff and white, a hardened plaster mask, and his hands are shaking. Alone? Oh, not alone. Please, not alone. Oh, my sweet Jesus, what an awful thing to happen. That poor woman. Alone.

"Naw. Ellen drove her. She tried to get you, Elaine did. But you was out, I guess."

"Yeah, right. With a friend. From work. Had a couple of beers. You know."

"Right. Well, she's in the hospital. . . ."

Bob turns to leave again. "What hospital? Winter Haven?"

"Yeah, that'd be the closest one. Same as the one you went when the niggers cut you." Ronnie leans forward, grunting with the effort, and adjusts the sound. His broad forehead is slick with sweat. "You . . . you oughta get yourself one of them remotes. I got me one, and they're real nice."

"Oh, Jesus, what if she already had the baby! I better phone the hospital. Right?"

"Suit yourself."

That won't change anything, Bob thinks. What's done is done. If she's had the baby, his calling won't help her; and if she hasn't had the baby yet, she's probably stuck away in a room without a phone. "No, I'll go right over now. If she calls, Ronnie, or if your wife calls, say I'm on my way, okay?"

"Sure enough. Hey, I might tap me a couple more Colts, if it's all right with you."

"Sure, sure, help yourself. Take all you want. And thanks for watching the kids. I'll call you from the hospital, soon's I know what's happening."

"Suit yourself," he says, working himself free of the couch, his eyes already moving toward the refrigerator. "I'll just sleep here on the couch till you get back. I don't have to work till tomorrow noon. Friday night's busy, after the movies let out and all, so I stay late an' don't go in till noon."

Bob doesn't hear him. He's already out the door and running for his car. As he runs, he punches his fist against his thigh, curses himself through clenched teeth. If he could beat himself up, he would. If he could slap himself around, punch himself in the stomach, throw himself to the ground and stomp on his back, kick himself in the kidneys, break his ribs, he would. But he can't. Elaine needs him, so he can't punish himself yet. But he will, goddammit, he will.

BOB PUSHES OPEN THE DOOR FROM THE HALLWAY AND ENters the nearly dark room, walks carefully past the other beds, two of them with women sleeping in them, one empty, to the bed at the end, and as Dr. Beacham promised, Elaine is there, all in white, like an angel, or at least a saint, covered with a sheet and wearing a cotton nightie, her face washed and smooth, her damp hair pulled back by a pair of Ruthie's white plastic barrettes. She's lying slightly propped on pillows, peacefully asleep.

Stopping beside the bed, Bob stares down at his wife, looks down the length of her body to where the baby was and on to her feet. Her left hand dangles from the bed, as if pointing to the floor, and her thin wrist, circled with a plastic cord and name tag, is like a child's, and to Bob, at this moment, tells everything. Her slender white wrist carries to him the long, sadly relentless tale of her strength, her patience and her trust. It tells him what he's been shutting out for months, perhaps for years. Purely and simply, it tells him about the woman's goodness.

His jumbled thoughts and feelings suddenly clarify and separate, and he realizes in a rush that *this* is what he loves in her. And this is what he's been denying himself, keeping it from himself so that he could go on thinking he didn't love her, so that he could go on trying to love a different woman, a woman he thinks is probably not good, or at least she's a woman whose goodness he's incapable of seeing, as he sees Elaine's goodness now, simply by looking down at her wrist.

Shame washes over him, and he feels suddenly cold. He knows, for this brief moment, what he's done, and the knowledge makes him feel naked. To keep his options open, a man has kept himself from loving his own wife. This is a terrible sin. It's the kind of sin, worse than a crime, that Satan loves more than a crime, because it breeds on itself and generates more sin. Because of the nature of his sin, it's been impossible for Bob to see goodness in Marguerite or Doris or anyone else he might like to love. Yet until now, to keep his options open, he's been willing, he's even been eager, to trade off the years it took him to lose sight of Elaine, all the years of living with her day in and out, eating, working, sleeping with her, night after night, season after season, until she finally became invisible and he no longer knew what she looked like, until her voice became as familiar and lost to his ears as his own is, until, when he wished to see her, truly see who this woman was, he could only look into the exact center of her eyes and see the exact center of his own eyes looking back and know that he still had not seen her—until finally, now, years and years later, after what he's done to her tonight, and perhaps only because of what he's done to her tonight, Bob is able, when Satan isn't looking, to glance at the woman's thin wrist and at last see the woman's goodness, which is the very thing, the only thing, a man can truly, endlessly, passionately love.

Her eyes flutter open, and she smiles. "Hi, honey."

Bob can't speak. He pats her shoulder, then leans over and gently kisses her on the lips.

She brushes his cheeks with her fingertips and whispers, "The baby's a boy, Bob. It's a boy."

He nods. He knows, he knows.

"Have you seen him? He's real pretty."

He shakes his head no, turns away from her face and lays his head on her breast.

Tenderly, she runs her fingers through his hair.

"I . . . I'm sorry," he says in a muffled voice. "I . . . I'm sorry I wasn't able to . . . to help."

She smiles and says that she knows he's sorry, but he shouldn't feel guilty, the baby came early and quick. "It was real easy," she says. "Not like the girls. I almost had him in the car on the way over. Poor Ellen, she thought she'd have to deliver him herself." She laughs, and he laughs a little too.

He stands and clears his face with his fists, like a child, and they smile at one another. "A boy, huh?"

"Yep," she says proudly.

"Bob junior?"

"Bob junior."

"Wow. A son."

"Going to grow up and be just like his daddy," she says sweetly.

A shade passes over Bob's face. "No."

"Oh, come on, honey. Be happy."

"I am, I am. I just . . . no, I'm happy, really. A son!"

She tells him he can see his son in the morning, the nurse will bring him in early so she can feed him, and if Bob wears a face mask, he can see him and maybe hold him too. Then she asks about the girls.

Ellen Skeeter's going back to Oleander Park to be with them now, he tells her, and she said she'd stay all night and get Ruthie off to school in the morning, if he wants, which he does, because he plans to sleep out in the waiting room tonight. "Thank God for Ellen and Ronnie," he says.

She smiles and tells him to go on home and get some sleep and come back early tomorrow. "You're going to be busy the next few days," she tells him. "I'm on vacation, me and little Bob, but you and the girls, you got to take care of business as usual, you know."

He understands. She's right. She's always right. He does have a lot to do in the next few days. He kisses her lightly, pats her wrist gently and backs from the room.

3

LATE THE NEXT AFTERNOON, GEORGE DILL SPOTS HIS DAUGHTER's car as it lurches out of traffic into the parking lot of the liquor store and pulls up by the Dempster-Dumpster in back, and he shuffles forward to the front door, waves good night to Bob and starts out.

"Hey, George!" Bob calls from the register. "Isn't Marguerite coming in?"

"No, sah, Mistah Bob, she tol' me this mornin' she gon' be in a hurry tonight, so I better be ready." The old man nods emphatically, as if agreeing with himself, and his Miami Dolphins cap slides forward on his bald head.

"Really?" Bob says. He didn't see her this morning. He was at the hospital, viewing his son and namesake, and got to the store later than usual; by then Marguerite had already dropped her father off and gone on to the clinic. He wasn't able to tell her, as he'd planned, that he would not be able to see her anymore.

Bob steps around the counter and peers back through the side window at her car. He can't quite see who's inside, though it is clear to him that there is someone other than Marguerite inside the car. A man, evidently. In the front passenger's seat. A black man.

"George, tell Marguerite I need to speak with her about something, will you? Tell her it's important. It'll only take a minute." He returns to the cash register and starts totaling the day's sales.

Seconds later, Marguerite appears at the door, opens it and sticks her head in. She's wearing her nurse's uniform, looking tired and a little perturbed. "I can't talk now, honey. I gotta rush. I'll talk to you later, okay?"

"No. It has to be now."

She doesn't understand.

"Come inside and close the door."

"Only a minute?"

"Yeah. Only a minute."

She steps inside and lets the door close behind her, then walks carefully across the floor to the register. "Is somethin' wrong?"

"No, nothing's wrong. But . . . but Elaine, she had her baby last night. Our baby. She had a boy."

Marguerite's face breaks into a quick smile, a flash that catches itself and turns serious again. "That's real nice, Bob. A boy. Is she okay and all, Elaine?"

"Yeah, she's fine, fine. But . . . well, listen, she had

the baby when I . . . when I was with you last night. I got home, and . . . well, you know.''

"Oh."

Bob looks down at the cash register keys and drums his fingertips nervously across them, as if trying to type out a message.

"You couldn'a known she was gonna have the baby, honey. Those things happen on their own. The baby don't know or care what his daddy's doing at the time." She tries a faint smile.

"Yeah, well, I know that. But even so, I naturally did a whole lot of thinking last night . . . and this morning. I thought a lot about the way things have been going for me."

"Uh-huh." She crosses her arms over her breasts and takes one step backwards.

"Yeah, well, I decided we shouldn't see each other anymore, Marguerite." There. It's said. He looks into her eyes hopefully, but they narrow and harden.

She swallows with difficulty, then speaks in a dry, high voice. "You feeling guilty is all. With the new baby and all. And you not being there last night, being with me and all . . .''

"Well, yeah, of *course* I'm feeling guilty!" he snaps. "I should, for Christ's sake. Guilt's important, you know. It tells you when you've done something wrong. And what I've been doing lately is wrong. Wrong."

"No, it ain't. It just makes you feel all guilty inside, especially right now, with the new baby and all. That don't mean it's wrong, Bob. We got to talk this over. We can't just walk off like this."

"No," he says, shaking his head slowly. "There's nothing to talk over."

As if she hasn't heard him, she brightens slightly and says, "Yeah, we got to do some talking, honey, that's all. Maybe we take a break, and you just take care of your wife and babies for a while, and don't worry about me none for a while. Don't worry about nothing for a while. Then we can do some talking later on."

"Listen, we can't."

She looks into his blue eyes steadily. "You just don't know what kind of woman I am, do you?"

"Well . . ."

"And I guess I don't know what kind of man you are, either." She extends her right hand toward him, and her eyes fill, and quickly she blinks to cover it and withdraws her hand. "I hafta run," she says. "I got to work tonight." She turns abruptly and starts for the door.

"Marguerite."

She stops but doesn't turn around. "What you want?"

"Nothing. Go on."

She leaves at once, yanking the door shut behind her. He stands at the register, staring after her, and when the car passes, he sees the man in the passenger's seat, sees him clearly. It's a young man, slumped down in the seat and facing away from Bob and toward Marguerite, who is looking straight ahead. The man has his arm out the open window and is wearing a light blue shirt with geometric designs crisscrossing the billowy sleeve. His hair, Bob sees, is plaited in tiny cornrows from front to back, from forehead to nape of neck, neat, tightly rolled tubes laid parallel to one another and raised against the dark brown skin of his scalp like thick black welts. It's the kid! It's Cornrow!

My God, Bob thinks, she *knows* him, she's known him all along, and now she's brought him *here!* No wonder she was in such a hurry and didn't want to come into the store! She *must* have known he was the same kid who tried to rob the store.

No, she couldn't, he decides. She couldn't have known. It's just an awful coincidence. She's just giving the kid a ride home or something, they all know each other anyhow, and she's just giving him a ride home.

But she doesn't know the kid is a killer, then, a thief. She *can't!* Or she wouldn't be giving him a ride home. She's in danger, but she doesn't know it. By now Bob has got the .38 out from under the cash register and is running wild-eyed toward the door, car keys in hand.

The highway is clogged with cars at this hour, but by weaving between lanes and cutting into openings as they appear in the stop-and-go traffic, Bob is able to get in sight of Marguerite's red Duster by the time it reaches Eagle Lake, a few miles south of Winter Haven. He falls in line three cars behind hers, turns left onto Route 655 north, bypassing downtown Winter Haven and heading toward Auburndale. He's never been to her house and knows nothing of the town, so he's careful not to lose her. At the same time, keeping two and sometimes three cars between them, he's careful not to be seen by her.

His mind is a stream of thoughts and emotions suddenly thawed and flowing, a gushing, ice-cold torrent that mixes fear for her safety, anger for her having betrayed him, disgust with himself, desire for Eddie's approval, rage at the boy who wanted his friend to shoot him with a shotgun, and a strangely impersonal, generalized desire for a clarifying act of revenge. If you ask him what offense or crime he wants avenged, he won't be able to say, but even so, the desire is there, powerful, implacable, righteous and cruel. He will shoot that boy with the fancy hairdo, and he'll do it in front of Marguerite Dill, too. In front of her father. He'll just walk up and pull the gun out of his belt and fire point-blank at the kid's chest. Then he'll turn around and walk away, maybe call the police and tell them he caught the guy who tried to rob the store last summer, maybe call Eddie and tell him, maybe call Elaine and tell her. Maybe do nothing, just drive on back to the store and open it up again till nine and then go home and see his daughters and go to the hospital and visit his wife and new son—it doesn't matter what he does afterwards, as long as he has done it, done the one thing that right now needs doing more than any other thing needs doing, which is shooting his gun at the black kid in Marguerite's car. The knowledge rides high in his chest, bracketed and bolted there like a steel block, an ingot of desire around which the rest of his body and mind and all the time he has left to live and all the time he has lived so far have been organized and ordered. It's the absolute clarity of the desire that makes it irresistible to him, and now that he's engaged it, committed himself to its satisfaction, he can't turn back. He's in the wind now, in a kind of free-fall, a rushing, exhilarating plummet toward the very ground of his life.

The traffic has diminished somewhat, and they have entered the town of Auburndale, bumped across the railroad tracks that pass through the center of town, driven past the rows of citrus warehouses, on to the outskirts, where the narrow side streets are faced by small, shabby bungalows with low porches, where the streets are dusty and cluttered, yards are packed dirt, slash pine and locust trees are scrawny and tired-looking, and where all the people on the sidewalks and sitting on porch steps and driving home in their cars are black.

Unexpectedly, Marguerite turns left off Polk City Road, and just as the car between her Duster and Bob's station wagon reaches the intersection, the light turns red, and Bob has to stop. He cranes his neck and watches her reach the end of the block, cross and drive on. Then, about halfway down the second block, her car pulls off the street into a driveway by a small brick house with metal awnings over the windows. He draws his shirt out of his pants and covers the gun handle, and when the light changes, turns left.

By the time he reaches the driveway where Marguerite parked her car, the kid has left. Marguerite is on the cinder-block steps unlocking the door, while behind her, George hugs a grocery bag. Bob peers down the sidewalk past Marguerite's house and spots the kid jogging along about a block away. Slowing his car in front of Marguerite's, Bob turns to his right and catches a glimpse of her surprised gaze. Then he passes her and accelerates. She watches after him, one hand shielding her eyes from the dusty yellow glare of the low sun, then shaking her head as if disbelieving her eyes, goes inside.

At the corner, Bob catches up to the kid, who, when the car draws abreast of him, turns, and for the first time, Bob sees the boy's face up close, and yes, it is the same one, it's Cornrow, only he's older than Bob thought, in his twenties, maybe his late twenties, or at least he looks older now, out here on the streets, than he did cowering in the stockroom three months ago. Bob knows it's the same person. There's no way he could be mistaken. He recognizes the hair, of course, but also the skin color, the high cheekbones and almost Oriental eyes, the wide, loose mouth and receding chin, and the way he wears his shirt unbuttoned to expose his brown, hairless chest, and his bony frame and the jumpy lope of his stride. He knows this person. He's had his image burned into his memory, and there's no way on earth he would not recognize him instantly.

Bob leans over to the passenger's side and calls out the open window. "*Hey! You!* Come here!" He reaches under his shirt and grabs the handle of the gun.

Cornrow stoops a little and peers inside, sees Bob's twisted face and breaks into a run. He streaks down the sidewalk, passes a market and a Kentucky Fried Chicken outlet and darts to the right into a bar.

Dropping the car into first gear, Bob guns the motor and jumps it into the traffic, yanks the wheel and pulls over in front of the same bar. A few people passing by on the sidewalk, startled, stop and watch the white man leap from his car and rush through the door to the bar.

Inside, it's suddenly dark, and Bob sees only a long counter on the right with human shapes leaning against it and a line of narrow booths along the other side. A small crowd of people is gathered at the rear, and somewhere back there the blat of a television set cuts across the thick noise of a half-dozen male conversations.

Bob stands at the end of the bar, still by the door, next to a pair of middle-aged men silently studying their bottles of beer, and looks down the length of the bar, searching the unknown faces for the known one. But they're all strangers, old men and young men, a few fat women, all of them ignoring him, going on with their quiet conversations as if they hadn't noticed the sudden appearance of a breathless white man.

The bartender, a gaunt, extremely tall man with an Afro and wearing a yellow short-sleeved shirt, tan Bermuda shorts and red jogging shoes, strolls slowly toward Bob. The customers follow the bartender with their eyes and watch Bob by watching the other man, who leans across the counter and says, as if he knows Bob from somewhere else, "How're you doin' *today,* mister?"

Bob tries to see around the bartender and over the heads of the customers near the bar to the crowd standing at the back. "I'm looking for a kid, he just ran in here." His eyes have adjusted to the darkness, and he can make out the faces in the rear now. None of them is the face he's looking for; all of them, the dozen expressionless black and brown male faces looking back at him, are interchangeable.

The bartender puts a toothpick into his mouth. "Ain't no kid jus' run in here. Not so's I'd notice. You sure?"

"Yeah, I saw him. I followed him. He came in a few seconds ahead of me. He's here," Bob declares.

The man looks silently down at Bob. Then he says, "You a cop, mister? I gotta see some ID."

"A cop?"

"Yeah." He switches the toothpick from one side of his mouth to the other. " 'Cause if you ain't, you probably oughta look somewheres else. If you is, you welcome to look around all you like," he says, sweeping a long arm over the bar. "But I gotta see me some ID."

Bob slips his hand under his shirt and rests it against the gun. Now everyone in the bar seems to be staring at him. A wall of large, dark faces peers down the bar at his blue eyes, his peach-colored skin, his brown hair, his long, pointed nose. "Is there a back door?" he asks the bartender. He suddenly hates his own voice, high and thin, effeminate, he thinks, and his clipped, flat, Yankee accent.

"Yes, there is a back door." The bartender studies him for a second, then smiles wittily. "Maybe you the fire inspector?"

"No, no. I'm just looking for this kid, see, he ran . . ."

"Ain't no such kid run in here, no such kid as I seen, anyhow," he interrupts. Then abruptly he turns away from Bob and walks back down the length of the bar, and everyone else goes back to drinks and conversations.

Startled, suddenly alone again, Bob takes a step backwards, and as if watching himself from a spot located in a high corner of the room, he sees himself pull the gun from under his shirt. Holding the gun in the air next to his head, he aims it at the ceiling. At once, the bar drops into silence, except for the television in the rear, where Dan Rather intones the news. A few men say, "Hey!" and "What the fuck?" and then they see Bob and go silent, waiting. The pair of middle-aged men in front and a few others step back. Everyone watches him, and he watches himself, as if he has just turned into a writhing serpent.

Bob backs to the door and stops. *"Kid!"* he yells into the stunned crowd. "I *know* you're here! You're safe now, but not for long! I'm going to *get* you, kid!" he bellows. "I'm going to *get* you!" Then he backs through the door to the sidewalk, jams the gun into his belt and runs for his car, leaving everyone in the bar shaken but with something strange to tell about and wonder at for days.

In minutes, Bob pulls up in front of Marguerite's house. He steps quickly from his car, flings the door shut, strides up the steps and raps loudly on the door. When old George opens the door, Bob walks past him and in. George slowly closes the door behind him, and Marguerite, barefoot, her white uniform unbuttoned at the throat, emerges from the kitchen.

"I *thought* that was you," she says flatly. "What you doin' way over here?"

"Howdy, Mistah Bob," George says from behind him. "Sit down, sit down, make yourself to home."

Bob waves the old man away with the back of his hand, and George steps from the room quickly and purposefully, a man with better things to do than hover around a white man he has no particular fondness for.

"I followed you from the store," Bob announces. He says it as if it were an accusation.

"Yes?"

"I saw who was in your car when you left the store."

"Did you now? Fancy that." She pads back to the kitchen and yanks open the refrigerator door. From the grocery bag set on a small, oilcloth-covered table, she pulls out lettuce, tomatoes, frozen lemonade, bologna, and places them one by one in the refrigerator.

"I recognized the kid in your car."

Marguerite turns and squints her eyes at him. Then she shakes her head slowly from side to side and goes back to putting away her groceries. "That kid," she says, "is as old as you."

"Yeah, sure. And I suppose you don't know how I happen to be able to recognize him."

"No. And frankly, mister, I don't know as I care much about all that. I don't particularly like the way you talking to me. What you got on your mind, anyhow? You didn't come all the way over here just to tell me you think you know who I give a ride home to. Whyn't you just let me know what you got on your little mind and stop all this dancing round the subject. All of a sudden you sounding a little too cute to me."

"That kid in the car. You know 'im?"

"What's it to you? Who you think you is, my husband?" She takes a step toward him. "What the hell you think you doing? One minute you whining about how you gotta not see me no more 'cause of your wife had a baby, and then you come running in here and start to asking me all about someone I give a ride home to, like you own me or something! Listen, mister, you can just take it somewheres else." She turns away and folds the emptied bag, folds it carefully, meticulously, along the edges, and slides it between the refrigerator and the stove. "I don't know," she says in a low voice, as if to herself. "I just don't know anymore." She hides her face from him and stares out the kitchen window, at the back of another small brick house.

"I'm gonna *tell* you who that kid is," Bob says. "And I know he's a kid. He's no more than twenty or twenty-one—I seen him up close. That kid is the same one who tried to rob the store and got away while I was calling the cops. That kid is the one I shoulda shot, not the other guy. That kid wanted me dead, the other guy didn't. The kid kept telling the other guy, the guy with the shotgun at my head, to go on and blow *me* away! Don't you understand? Don't you *get* it? That sonofabitch was laughing at the idea of me dead! He kept trying to get the other guy to pull the trigger. The only reason I'm alive now is because the guy with the gun had enough brains or decency or whatever not to pull the trigger. But when *I* didn't pull the trigger, when *I* left that kid lying there in his own shit on the floor, crying like a baby, begging me not to kill him, he turned around and ran away. You know the story. So *I* end up looking like I don't have any brains, or else too much decency, which amounts to the same thing nowadays. No. I want that kid."

She is squinting into his face as if trying to understand a man speaking a language she's never learned.

"I want that kid," he says quietly, a child selecting a teddy bear from a shelf crowded with teddy bears.

"You crazy, Bob."

"I want that kid. He wanted me dead. Now I want him dead. If not dead, then scared shitless and in jail."

"Yeah, well, that guy in my car ain't the kid you want. You crazy, is what I think. Now get outa here," she says, and she brushes past him into the living room, crosses to the front door and opens it. "That guy in my car is husband to my cousin."

"He's a thief. Probably a killer."

"The guys who robbed your store was from New York anyhow," she says. "Read the papers. You know, when it comes right down to it, Bob, you just like every other white man."

"Don't give me that shit! *Don't!* I know who the hell tried to rob me! I know who the hell tried to get me killed! And I know who I saw in your car. I saw him just a minute ago, too, at the bottom of your street, and I called to him, and he took off running. Naturally. He knows who the hell he is, and he knows who I am, too. It's you who doesn't know who's who. Not me."

"You just now called out to him?"

"Yeah, I followed him to the end of the block."

"What'd you say to him?"

"Nuthin. I just hollered for him to come over to the car, and he saw me and recognized me and took off running. He ducked into a bar, and I ran in after him, but the guy in the bar covered for him, they all covered for him. . . ."

"You hollered for him to come over to your car? What for? If you so sure he's the one robbed your store, whyn't you call a cop? Tell me that. Whyn't you just ask me his name and then call the cops to come pick him up so you can identify him down to the police station?"

Bob looks stonily into Marguerite's brown eyes for a few seconds. Then he sighs heavily, and as if he's taken off a mask, his gaze softens. "Oh, God," he says. "Oh, God damn everything. I fucked it up. I fucked it all up, didn't I? Everything. Everything. All of it. Done."

Marguerite is still standing firmly by the open door, like a guard. If she's seen his face shift or heard his words, she shows no signs of it. "You looking like a crazy white man, you come down here, and you drive up and holler for a black man to come over to your car like that, and he takes a look at you and runs off, and you wonder why? You worse'n crazy. You dumb."

"I fucked it all up." He drops his weight onto the sofa, and leaning his head back, closes his eyes. "That's it. Everything. Done."

"What'd you plan on saying to him? That woulda been a real interesting conversation."

"Nuthin."

"So what'd you call out to him for, then?"

Slowly, Bob lifts his shirtfront, then drops it.

Marguerite's face, at the sight of the gun in his belt, doesn't so much drop as slide warily to the side. "Oh-h-h," she moans, a sound signifying both pain and insight, as if the name for the mysterious cause of the pain came to her only at the moment of feeling it.

George enters the room from a back bedroom, and Marguerite rushes to him, leaving the front door open and unattended. "Daddy," she says, "you get on back now. We almost finished, you gonna have your supper soon. Just you go on back and watch some more TV till we done.''

The old man peers across the room at Bob, then up into his daughter's face. "Somethin' wrong out here?" he asks in a firm voice. "I heard you gettin' upset," he says to Marguerite.

"Nothing, Daddy, nothing. Now go on back."

George looks coldly at Bob. "I know you got yourself a gun there, Mistah Bob. You got it under your shirt there. I seen it. Seen it when you come in. I sure don't want nobody gettin' shot now, and I know you is a good man, and you don't want nobody gettin' shot neither, no matter how mad you gets at 'em at the moment. Come tomorrow, Mistah Bob, things'll cool down some and you won't be so mad. You don't want to shoot no one, Mistah Bob. Marguerite, now, she makes her mistakes, sure, but she's a good woman. And she loves you, Mistah Bob, really loves you. Tol' me all about it. You don't hafta worry none about that. I can tell you, she been good to you right from the beginnin'. Ain't no one else come round here. She been good to you right from the start, so you got no call to get mad.''

"Bob," Marguerite says coolly. "Go home, Bob. Just go home."

Bob looks from the woman's face to her father's, then back again. "Don't be afraid," Bob tells them. "I'll go."

"We not afraid of you, Mistah Bob. We jus' worried 'bout you, that's all."

"No, I'll go. I'll go."

He stands, looks down in shame, and leaves.

Marguerite closes the door behind him, quickly locks it and does not look out the window after him. Instead, she walks immediately to the kitchen and commences preparing supper. She and her father never speak of the event again, not to each other and not to anyone else. There's nothing to say about it to each other that is not already fully understood, so they remain silent about it, almost as if it never happened.

4

BOB LIFTS HIS SHIRTFRONT WITH ONE HAND AND PULLS OUT the gun with the other, releases the loaded magazine and lays the gun and magazine down on the glass table in front of Eddie. Eddie looks at the gun, then up at his brother's somber face, lowers his gaze to the gun again, then moves it back to the *Wall Street Journal* on his lap.

"You wanna drink, Bob?" he asks without looking up. He's wearing salmon-pink trousers and a cranberry-red short-sleeved shirt and white Italian loafers, sockless. On the tile floor next to his chair is a ceramic pitcher half-filled with gin and tonic. "Sarah!" he barks. "Bring a glass!"

"No, forget it. No drink." Bob lets himself down slowly into the redwood chair opposite Eddie, who continues to read his paper, or pretends to read it.

Sarah appears at the sliding glass doors of the living room, spots Bob, smiles and crosses the patio to him. "Bob! It's wonderful about the baby! A boy! Congratulations!"

"Yeah," Eddie says. "Great about the kid. Congratulations." He looks pointedly at his watch.

"Thanks."

"I was over at the hospital this afternoon," Sarah reports, "to bring some presents and all, and I saw him, and he's just adorable, Bob! Adorable. I'm glad it was a boy. After all the girls in this family."

"Yeah. Me too."

"You want a drink, Bob? Let me bring a glass; Eddie's got himself a pitcher of gin over there. His nightly dose. I'm sure he'll share some with you." She's suddenly serious again, and she and Eddie exchange looks, quick, superficially wounding slashes, before she gushes on. "And Elaine, she just looks marvelous! Marvelous!"

"Sarah," Eddie growls, "Bob don't want a drink."

Sarah glares at her husband, then, glancing over the low table in front of him, sees the handgun and magazine, and steps away. "Oh, I'm sorry," she says, suddenly confused. She looks down at Bob. "Are you all right, Bob?"

"Yes, fine," he says. Then, "No. No, I'm not fine, Sarah," he says, staring straight ahead at his brother, who continues to look at the paper in his lap as if he were intently reading it.

"Sarah, leave us the fuck alone," Eddie says.

Turning quickly, she strides from the patio and disappears into the house. Behind Eddie, the pool glimmers in the twilight, and a thatch of palmettos beyond the pool, in a parody of a postcard, raises a silhouette against an orange- and lavender-streaked sky. Folding the paper in half, Eddie slaps it onto the table next to the gun and says, "Too fuckin' dark to read anyhow."

Bob says nothing.

Eddie grunts and leans down to the pitcher beside him and refills his glass. "Okay, let's hear it. Let's hear why you're here on a Friday night at seven thirty-five instead of at the store. I know it ain't because your wife had a baby last night, because you're here, where I live, not at the hospital, where your wife and new kid are. And you're not at home, where you and your other two kids live. So there must be some other, some very fucking good, some really extraordinary reason why you're here and not at the store. Right?" He speaks through clenched teeth, his blue eyes cold and angry. "And I suppose that when you plopped that gun in front of me, like it was catshit or something, I suppose that has something to do with why you're here and not at the store on a fucking Friday night, where you could be selling a thousand bucks' worth of booze for me, which right now happens to be very important to me and therefore in the long run should be very important to you too, asshole, since your livelihood depends very much on my livelihood."

"Don't call me an asshole anymore, Eddie."

" 'Don't call me an asshole, Eddie,' " he says, mocking him. He's speaking more and more rapidly now, his face red with anger. "I really love it, Bob—no shit, *I really love it*. The way you go around with a long face all the time, like you got worries or some kinda hair across your ass, when all you got to do, for Christ's sake, all you got to do is get up in the morning and get to work on time and come home and drink beer in front of the fucking TV screen till you get sleepy and then go fuck your wife for fifteen minutes and pop off to sleep. I really love it. You come in here like you got fucking troubles, and I'm supposed to sit here and hold your hand and listen sympathetically and say, 'Aw, Bob, it must be tough out there at the store, having to think about keeping a gun around in case the niggers want to rob you again. Gee, it really must be a burden on you.'"

"No, Eddie, that's not it. It's just, I gotta keep the gun away from me. That's all."

"What're you talking about?"

"You wouldn't understand. You don't hafta understand. It doesn't matter. It's like I'm afraid of heights, that's all, so you stay away from heights when you're scared of 'em. It's not a burden to me, like you said. And I'm not complaining about my life or anything. The job's fine. It's just, I got to keep the gun away from me."

"That so?"

"Yeah."

"Listen, Bob, let me tell you something, okay?" His voice is calmer now, and his face has returned to its normal shade of parchment brown. "I got problems, Bob. Real problems. Not like this candy-ass shit you're talking about. I mean, what the fuck do I care about you gotta keep a gun away from yourself? What do I care you're scared of heights? Save that shit for your wife when she gets outa the hospital. Save it for a shrink. I gotta run a business. I gotta do a certain volume every week, week after week, or one of these mornings you're gonna find me sleeping in the trunk of my car and my car'll be in Tampa Bay. I mean it. You, all you gotta think about is taking care of your mouth, your prick and your asshole. Me, I gotta come up with a certain amount of money every fucking week, Bob, or I won't have any mouth, prick or asshole to worry about. You understand what I'm telling you?"

Darkness has fallen on them like an attitude. The two

men sit across the round, glass-topped table from each other and watch each other gradually get absorbed by the darkness, as if they are backing away in opposite directions, and their words to one another drift aimlessly into space, unheard, unattended, unconnected.

"Is it because of the guys you're working with in these housing projects?"

"Your trouble is you think all I do is sit around counting my money and playing with my toys, like that boat. You think the difference between us is that you're unlucky and smart and I'm lucky and stupid, so you mope around all the time feeling sorry for yourself and pissed off at me. Well, let me tell you, Bob, I'm not lucky. And I'm not stupid. And you're not unlucky. And you're not that fucking smart. Things are a hell of a lot different from what you think they are."

"I'm not really complaining about the gun, Eddie. I just figured I could leave it with you, since you owned it anyhow, and take my chances down at the store, you know?"

"If I don't come up with a very definite amount of cash every fucking week, the next week after that I hafta come up with twice as much again, and so on down the line, until the only way I can meet my fucking obligations is go out and rob a fucking bank. Do you think Sarah understands any of this? Do you? Fucking broad. She thinks money comes from heaven. She thinks credit cards are money, for Christ's sake. You think I can go to a bank with this and take out a loan? Everything's paper, Bob. Everything."

"See, if I don't keep that gun away from me, I'm afraid I'll end up shooting someone. Not someone robbing the store, but someone else, a stranger, maybe. I don't trust myself anymore. I think I may be a little crazy or something. I don't know how it's happened, but I think sometimes I lose control of myself. Especially when it comes to women, you know? I get so pissed off at the world, so angry, that I'm liable to kill somebody by accident if I don't keep that gun away from me. It's not women, really, but they've got something to do with it. Somehow.''

"I've worked hard for this. For over fifteen years I've been working hard. I got an ulcer. Did you know I got an ulcer? My ass is bleeding too. Did you know that? I'm thirty-three years old, and I got holes in my stomach and a bleeding asshole. And now my epilepsy is coming back. I had two fucking seizures this month. First in five years. You figure it out.''

"I don't want to kill anybody, see. I didn't want to kill that nigger that robbed the store. I don't know even how I did it. Or why. I knew, the second time I shot at him, that he wasn't going to kill me anymore. I'd already at least winged him. I knew that. The worst he was going to do by then was get the hell out of there. But I killed him anyhow.''

"I'm not pissed at you, Bob. I just got a lot to worry about lately. I hate my fucking wife. I wish she'd just get herself royally fucked, have a hundred orgasms, and run off with the tennis pro or somebody. I don't even like my kid anymore. All she does is sit up there in her room getting stoned and listening to records of guys with safety pins stuck in their cheeks. I don't know why the hell I'm even doing this, working this hard. I should be like you.''

"It's probably only a temporary hard time, Eddie. It'll pass. It's probably the recession. You know, from the energy crisis and the fucking Arabs and all, and fucking Carter. It'll pass. You just gotta hold on to what you got for a while.''

"Yeah." They are silent for a moment, and then Eddie says, "If you leave that gun here, Bob, I'm just gonna hafta haul it back in to the store tomorrow morning and put it right back where it was.''

"I got to keep that gun away from me.''

"The gun stays at the store.''

Bob looks down at the table and tries to make out the shape of the gun, but it's too dark now. "No, I got to stay away from the gun. At least for a while. I'm too shaky these days.''

"The gun stays at the store."

Bob says nothing, shifts his position in the chair, then says, "Well, I guess I quit."

Eddie remains silent for a few seconds. Finally, he sighs and says, "Okay. Fine. Quit. Just fucking quit."

"I mean it, Eddie. I quit."

"Yeah, I hear you. You can pick up your pay tomorrow after noon at my office downtown. My secretary'll have it ready for you by three. Don't even come in to work tomorrow. I'll get a temporary for a few days. By Wednesday I'll have a replacement full time out there. That's the least of my worries right now, replacing you."

Bob stands up and faces his brother's lumpy shape in the chair below him. "Okay, then. No hard feelings?"

"No. No hard feelings. I think you're an asshole, of course. Worse, actually. Since you got a new baby and no job and probably no savings. But no, Bob, no hard feelings."

"I'll get another job. I can do lotsa stuff."

"Yeah. Jobs're falling outa trees around here."

"Listen, I'm sorry."

Eddie doesn't respond, and Bob takes a step away. "I mean it, Eddie," he says. "I'm sorry."

"No, you're not," Eddie says, his voice coming from the darkness. "You're not sorry. You're glad."

"Well, I'll be seeing you."

"Yeah."

Bob leaves, walking through the living room to the carpeted front hall, out the huge oaken door and down the long flagstone walkway to the street. As he walks, he listens for the sound of the gun, but it doesn't come. It's not until he reaches his car and has got in and slammed the door that he realizes he has been listening for the gun, and then he realizes why, for he knows that if his brother can't find his way out of this maze he's built, he will put the barrel of the gun into his mouth and pull the trigger and blow off the top of his head.

Bob turns the ignition key, starts the motor, and drives away.

5

THE GIRLS ARE FINE, HE TELLS ELAINE, FINE, AND AS SOON as he gets off the phone, he's going home to tuck them into bed. Then he'll drive out to the hospital to see her and the baby again. Where is he right now? At a pay phone. On the way home from work, he lies. He didn't call her from work, he explains, because . . . well, because he didn't realize how late it was until he got halfway home. So he pulled off the road at the first pay phone he' saw and called her to tell her he'd be a little later getting over to the hospital than he'd said this morning. It's been a real busy day, he explains. Yes, he, too, is grateful to Ellen and Ronnie Skeeter. They couldn't have done this without them. Yes, he promises that he'll do something nice for them. Maybe bring home some kind of fancy expensive liqueur from the store, she suggests. Galliano, maybe, or Kahlúa. Okay, sure, why not? He can buy it with his discount, she points out, and that way it won't cost any more than a regular bottle of whiskey would. Right, right, he says, cringing as he talks, drawing his body into itself, shrinking it away from the rapidly expanding world of lies he's created. He feels himself being squeezed small and pressed against an invisible wall, until he has begun to imagine his body moving through that wall and becoming invisible itself, leaving behind nothing but lies, leaving behind the life of another man, the one who calls home to check on his kids, while this other Bob, off on his crazy mission to Auburndale with the gun and then to Eddie's in Oleander Park, forgets all about his kids, forgets that he is the father of three children, two of whom are at home in the care of kindly neighbors; he's left in the visible world the life of a man who has a job in his brother's liquor store, when the man who's just become invisible has no job at all, has in fact quit his job without a second's hesitation or fear and has no regrets or second thoughts; he's left out there in the real world an invented, unreal man who's dutiful, prudent, custodial, faithful and even-tempered, while here in the invisible world, where Bob

now lives, he's feckless, reckless, irresponsible, faith-
less and irrational—so that the invented man, the one
everyone but Bob believes exists, is the father of the
real man, who is the man no one but Bob knows exists,
the man who is a boy.

He pulls off Route 17, and before he's halfway down
the lane to the trailer, he sees the van that's parked in
front of it, a large, metallic-green Chevy van with mag
wheels and one-way mirror glass on the side and rear
windows, and his first assumption is that it belongs to a
friend of the Skeeters. But when he draws abreast of the
van and sees the lettering on the driver's door, *Moray
Key Charters,* he knows the van belongs to Avery Boone.

This information should astonish Bob, since he hasn't
heard from Avery in almost a year, and then only by
means of a Christmas card mailed to him in New Hampshire. Bob never answered the card, not, however, because he was still angry with Avery for what happened
between him and Elaine (that, after all, was a long time
ago, and both parties felt properly ashamed of themselves immediately afterwards, and who knows, maybe
in some unconscious way Bob wanted it to happen,
especially that first summer after Ave and Bob finished
rebuilding the trawler, and Bob, as if to repay himself
for all the work he did on Ave's boat, treated the boat
pretty much as if it were his own and went out on it
almost every weekend, frequently alone). But the sight
of Avery's van parked on the grass outside his trailer
doesn't surprise Bob in the least. That is, the sudden
appearance of Avery Boone doesn't surprise the invisible man, Bob Dubois, though it would indeed astonish
and unsettle the visible one, the invented man. The
invisible version of Bob Dubois, the one who is feckless,
reckless, irresponsible, and so forth, that man finds it
perfectly natural that Avery should show up at this
moment in his life, both natural and desirable, because,
with Avery as with no one else, Bob can tell the truth
and in that way can make the visible and the invisible
man one.

Avery hasn't come alone, he's brought a girl with

him, the two of them driving south from a month-long
visit to New Hampshire, "to see the leaves turn color,"
Avery explains, an annual phenomenon that in Avery's
three-year absence from New England has taken on
mystical significance, like a total eclipse of the sun or
the return of a long-gone comet, a significance rein-
forced by the reaction of the girl, who, as a native
Floridian, has never seen the leaves go from green almost overnight to scarlet, gold, purple and orange and
then for weeks hold their color crisply, cleanly, as if at
the peak of health instead of the verge of death, and
who, as a young woman in her early twenties with a
somewhat mystical turn of mind anyhow, believes that
in the 1840s in a previous incarnation she lived in Concord, New Hampshire, where she was the mistress of
Franklin Pierce, U.S. senator, general in the Mexican
War and fourteenth President of the United States. She
first learned this from a Ouija board, but many events
and signs have confirmed it since. Her belief regarding
her previous existence has lent enormous significance to
this trip with her "lover," as she calls Avery, to his
home town and state and has caused her to elicit from
her lover any information regarding his present existence and actual past that he is willing to give, for she is
convinced that an apparently coincidental connection
with a man from New Hampshire, from a town not
twenty-five miles from where Franklin Pierce was born
and first practiced law, is no coincidence at all, but is in
fact part of a cosmic plan intended to connect her past
and future selves through the agency of this present self,
if only she allows herself to read the signs properly.
Avery Boone, she now realizes, is the most important
sign, as well as the vehicle for her actual, physical
return to New Hampshire, where there was, she reports
to Bob, a "rush of signs," including Bob Dubois himself, whose name came up often in this visit as she and
Avery drove along in the van late at night, and Avery
rambled on about his childhood and adolescence and
young manhood, all shared with a person named Bob
Dubois. When, after much prodding, Avery confessed to

having had a falling out with Bob, the girl, whose name
is Honduras (not her real name, of course, which is Joan
Greenberg—the name Honduras, she says, was given to
her when she was sixteen by her first lover, who happened to be a full-blooded Arawak Indian from the hills
of Jamaica), convinced Avery that he should take this
occasion to visit his old friend Bob Dubois in Catamount, to reestablish their bond, which would be good
for their karma, she pointed out, and when they learned
that Bob and his family had moved to *Florida,* well, she
just knew, oh, yes, man, she *knew.*

"Knew what?" Bob asks, because what the hell could
she know from that piece of information, except the
facts, and why does she keep calling him "man," and
where does she get off talking all the time in front of
Ave and him when they haven't seen each other for over
three years and obviously have a lot to talk about, and
why does Ave just kind of smile and lean back with his
hands folded behind his head and watch the girl rattle
on, as if he thought she was the most interesting person
he's ever met, although Bob does have to admit that she
is sexy, with that huge pile of orange curly hair bushing
out from a tiny face, and high cheekbones and tight wide
mouth, flared nostrils and pale green eyes and shapely
breasts, braless and pointing good-naturedly from behind a tie-dyed tee shirt, and tanned, muscular legs,
tight and smooth, practically leaping out at him from
dark green gym shorts, which she wears without underpants, so that when she sits cross-legged on the sofa, as
she is now, Bob can see light brown pubic hairs and a
neat little vertical roll of vaginal fat, which of course
excites him sexually and makes him pay much closer
attention to what she is saying than he might otherwise
pay.

The kids, Emma and Ruthie, seem to be fond of
Honduras, and though Emma was only a baby when
Avery left New Hampshire on the *Belinda Blue,* and
Ruthie only pretends to remember him, they both treat
him as if he were a favorite uncle, which is as he prefers
it and the model he adheres to anyhow, expressing eager

interest in Ruthie's schoolyard adventures and Emma's toys, while Honduras rattles on in the living room with Bob, telling him, as people in their late teens and early twenties are wont to do, what kind of person she *really* is, something Bob feels incapable of doing, so that her doing it, telling him that she's the kind of person who can't stand dishonesty in a lover, the kind of person who loves to travel, the kind of person who thinks a lover should not have to tell everything he or she knows about him- or herself, the kind of person who believes in privacy, the kind of person who needs to have a sense of belonging somewhere, the kind of person who thinks everyone should be encouraged to discover the life he or she was meant to live, all subjects of interest to Bob—love, truth, destiny—nevertheless, her talking this way finally irritates him, and he says so. "You're too young to know anything about yourself," he says. "If you got any brains at all, you'd know the only thing you can know about yourself is nothing, which is what it's taken me till now to find out," a pronouncement that Honduras says is "Far out, Bob, that's really very far out, you are really a very together person," she says. "No shit, a really very together person." And so when she asks if it's okay to smoke a joint, he says sure, why not, and when she lights up and passes him the joint, he takes a long hit, and when Avery strolls loosely into the room, passes him the joint, which Avery smokes the rest of the way down, causing Honduras to roll another joint for her and Bob, and when that's gone, Bob lays his head back on the couch next to Honduras's head, looks over at her green eyes, her long, blond lashes and dark eyebrows, and he smiles and says, "I really like you, Honduras," to which she responds by sitting up perkily and poking him on the point of his doggy nose with a fingertip, because she knows that this is not the time to encourage Bob Dubois, not with his two little girls in the back bedroom watching TV and his old friend and her lover Avery Boone rummaging through the kitchen in search of something to eat and Bob's wife and new baby in the hospital waiting for Bob to get there before the end of visiting hours. . . . "Hey, aren't you supposed to go to the hospital, isn't that what you said when you came in? Or is that what those people told us, the fat guy and his funny wife, what's their name?"

Bob says Skeeter, and they all laugh, but then he remembers his promise to Elaine and his new son, so he gratefully accepts Honduras's offer to baby-sit while he and Avery go to the hospital, an offer made, Honduras says, only because she knows she'll see the new baby and meet Bob's wife tomorrow when they come home from the hospital.

"All the pieces in this puzzle," she says, "are falling together." She looks up appealingly at the two men, who stand side by side at the door, and she spins on her butt, leans back on the arm of the couch, spreads her legs provocatively toward them and throws her head back, exposing her long white throat to them. "When you see Elaine," she says, "you tell her that I'm taking care of the girls and the house for her till she gets back. Tell her I love her and her new baby, and I love her daughters too, and I love her husband too. Tell her . . . oh, you'll know what to tell her," she says, suddenly laughing. "In*cred*ible," she says. "Really in*cred*ible."

Bob leaves first, feeling a little dizzy, and Avery follows, though once outside, Avery takes the lead, and they are soon inside his van, heading north toward Winter Haven on Route 17. This is an experience, riding in a customized van, new to Bob, and to his surprise, he finds that he enjoys it. It's a rather deliberately sensual experience, what with the carpeting, the padded swivel seats, the flicking lights of the dash and the CB scanner, the lush throb of an Earth, Wind & Fire tape on the stereo. "This is *some*thing," Bob says. "Really *some*thing."

He gives the directions, telling Avery where to turn right and left, and then, because the easy parts are coming more easily than he'd expected, Bob decides to try the hard part and tell Avery the truth about his life, so he says to him, "Ave, a lot's happened to me lately.

I'm in trouble, but you got to hear me out. There's nobody else I can talk to."

Avery nods silently; it's an old ritual, he knows: you don't say anything, not when the speech and its subject have been formally announced like this. You just nod and shut up and listen.

"Okay, first off," Bob says, "a few months ago, I went and shot a nigger, a guy trying to rob the store, Eddie's store. That's one piece of information."

Ave purses his lips and lets out a long, low-toned whistle.

"Then you oughta know that for the last six months or so, I been sleeping with a woman, a girlfriend, I guess you'd call her, not a 'lover,' really. And she's a black woman. A nurse," he adds.

"A black woman. No shit."

"Yeah. But that's not really the important thing about her. Anyhow, I blew the relationship today, I was kind of breaking it off with her, you know, because of the new baby and all, and I was feeling guilty and complicated about the whole thing, but I just wanted to pull back a little, to ease up while I thought things out . . ."

Avery interrupts to ask if Bob is in love with this woman, "this black woman," and Bob says yes, he is in love with her, but he doesn't know how much he's willing to give up for that. But the real problems aren't there, he goes on. The real problems grow out of this robbery somehow, when he shot one of the guys and let the other guy escape and then unexpectedly spotted him this afternoon, or thought he spotted him, the guy who escaped, with Marguerite . . .

"The black woman? Your girlfriend?"

Right, Bob says, repeating her name so he won't have to keep going through this "black woman" business, which is starting to irritate him, though he's not sure why. He plows on with his story, telling Avery about his having chased Cornrow to the bar and the confrontation there and the one in Marguerite's living room, his sudden realization that he was likely to kill somebody for no good reason and his decision to deliver the gun to Eddie, since it was his gun anyhow, and then his decision, when Eddie insisted on his keeping the gun at the store, to quit his job.

He doesn't know what's happening, he tells Avery. He's a changed man somehow. Maybe it doesn't show, but inside, he's a changed man, Bob insists, and it all started last winter, just before Christmas, when out of the blue he got himself turned around one night and ended up taking a hard, honest look at himself and his life, and what he saw made him so angry that he ended up punching the shit out of his car, which was lucky, he realizes now, because it could just as easily have been a perfect stranger he was punching, or Elaine, say.

"You took a hard look at yourself and your life and didn't like what you saw? So you decided to come down here and work for Eddie? Ol' Fast Eddie," Avery says, smiling and shaking his head slowly from side to side.

"Well, you know Eddie," Bob says, and he explains how he was led to expect that his brother would be making him a partner in his business here, liquor stores and real estate development. "And some other stuff he's got his fingers in. Shopping centers. I don't know."

"Eddie's a dealer, all right. A real horse trader. This place is made for him. Or he's made for it."

No, Bob says. Not true. And he tells about Eddie's fears of being killed, his involvement, Bob is sure, with the Mafia, "or somebody a whole hell of a lot like the Mafia, somebody he owes a lot of money to. And if he can't pay it back on time, he says he'll end up in the back of his car in Tampa Bay."

Avery is impressed. And his quick advice to Bob is to stay clear of his brother altogether. He tells him that he quit his job just in time, because if Eddie goes, so long as Bob is working for him Bob will go too, especially if he's running around with a gun on him. "You don't have a chance to explain much to these guys, Bob. They are definitely not your Catamount Savings and Loan types. What they are is very serious businessmen who enforce verbal promises by having big, ugly guys from Providence and New Jersey fly down just to break your arms and legs very slowly. I shit you not. I've been down here three years now, and I've seen a lot and heard a lot more, especially being down on the Keys, and there's two things you end up getting killed for down here, real estate and drugs, and that's because those are the two things you can make a killing at here. You can be a millionaire overnight, but you can get dead overnight too."

Bob points to the turnoff for the hospital, and Avery wheels the large, glistening vehicle smoothly off the ramp, turns left at the stop sign, then pulls into the hospital parking lot and stops.

"What about you?" Bob asks.

"What do you mean?"

"Well, how are you making it down here? You're obviously doing okay," he adds, gesturing to the car that surrounds them.

Avery slings one arm over the back of his chair and faces his friend. "Hey, Bob. *I* haven't changed, not inside, not out. You may have changed, but I haven't."

Bob studies him for a few seconds. True, he hasn't changed, Bob decides. Physically he's the same, a little heavier, maybe, but only through the face and neck, and that's natural enough when a man hits his thirties, especially if he's a drinker. No, he's the same man he was three years ago—as tall as Bob, but because of his smaller head and face, narrow shoulders and hips, seeming even taller; his hair is still reddish blond, though perhaps a shade or two lighter from the year-round sunshine and a few inches longer in back and over the ears, but that's the style now, especially here in Florida, and in fact Bob has been thinking of letting his hair grow out some too; Ave's blue eyes are still narrow, nearsighted, squinty, with a fan of crinkles in each corner, and his teeth still buck out slightly in front, making his face look perpetually adolescent, almost mischievous; his freckled pale skin looks as freshly sunburnt now in October as it did summers when he was a kid, peeling and pink across his nose and forehead no matter how much time he spent in the sun and no matter what precautions he took, hats, lotions, sun shields. No, it's the same Avery Boone he's always known, at least outside it's the same man, and that's usually an indication that inside he's the same as well, that he's just as good-natured and easygoing as he always was, just as lazy, just as easily amused and easily bored as when he was a kid, just as loyal and affectionate, but just as detached and impenetrable too, just as honest as he was, yet just as dishonest, just as careless with his life, as if it meant nothing to him, and just as careful not to risk it for anything less than a sure thing.

"I don't guess you have changed," Bob says somberly. "You get by okay with just the boat, taking out groups and stuff?"

"Yeah."

"It's a good life?"

"A good life."

"The old *Belinda Blue*, eh? She worked out fine down here? That old Maine trawler?"

"Yeah. She's a beautiful boat. Solid. Slow, but solid."

"You still running that old Chrysler diesel?"

"Yep."

"Living aboard, like you planned?"

"Not so much now as before. I got an apartment with Honduras. It's easier that way, with two of us. It gets a little crowded aboard, and whenever I hadda take her out, I hadda move Honduras out first, or else she'd hafta come along as mate, and that's not really her idea of a good time, going fishing with a bunch of fat, half-drunk, middle-aged salesmen from Cleveland."

"No, I suppose not."

"You like that boat, don't you, Bob."

"Belinda Blue? Jesus, yeah. Man, I still lie back some nights and rerun whole days I spent on that boat, out beyond the Isles of Shoals, down around Newburyport and Plum Island, that time I took her all the way through the canal to the south side of the Cape and cruised back around Hyannis and Truro and Provincetown home across the bay to Portsmouth. . . . I guess that's about as happy as I've ever been, days and nights I spent on that

boat. It's hard to say why, but that boat gave me a feeling that I owned myself. You know? I'd get a few miles out, and all of a sudden, my whole world was that boat. And I had it under control. I could take care of it, and it could take care of me. It's hard to explain. You probably understand.''

"Yeah, sure I do," Avery says. "It's that, having complete control of your whole world. Trouble is, my whole world has expanded a little since then. I mean, I've got me a condo now, and this van, and I'm thinking of buying another boat, one real different from *Belinda Blue,* though, a sport fisherman that can go out after big game and get back before dark. Ol' *Blue*'s good for taking parties out in the bay and out along the Pine Islands and so on, you know, for small stuff and maybe for some bonefishing, but it can't handle the really heavy stuff, marlin, swordfish, the tournament fishing, where for a guy like me the big money is.''

Bob glances at his watch and curses, opens the van door and jumps down to the pavement. "We're late," he says. "Visiting hours was over half an hour ago! Elaine's gonna be pissed!''

Avery follows him across the parking lot, assuring him as they trot along that she'll understand, Elaine always understands how when the two of them get together they forget all about time, and she'll especially understand now, since they haven't seen each other in over three years and all. "We'll just talk the nurse into letting us by," he says, but Bob does not hear him. He's suddenly flooded with his knowledge of Avery's having made love to Elaine, and coupled to that knowledge, piercing it, is his realization that Avery doesn't know about Elaine's confession, which means that they can never talk about it, he and Avery, and so can never get it behind them. The way it is now, Avery himself would have to confess having fucked Bob's wife, and then Bob would have to pretend to be surprised, enraged, hurt, all over again.

As they enter the hospital lobby, half-lit and nearly deserted, Bob finds himself unexpectedly wishing that

Elaine had never told him about her having slept with Avery. But then, he thinks, he would never have known who she was. It's a terrible thing, to know someone else's secrets, but it's the only way you can know someone. It's hard to say beforehand which is more to be avoided, knowing another person's secrets or knowing no one at all.

The nurse at the information desk by the elevators says no. They cannot go up to the maternity ward at this hour. And no, they cannot go to the nursery and see Mr. Dubois's son. Avery smiles at the gray-faced woman, lightly touches her shoulder, which she retrieves swiftly. He tells her how far he's come, that he's the baby's godfather, but no, it's still no.

"Forget it, Ave," Bob says, and turns away. "We'll come over first thing in the morning. I'm not ready tonight to tell her about the job anyhow. You know, about quitting Eddie and all. I hafta figure out how to tell her the bad news," he says, scuffling along, head down, hands in pockets.

Avery comes up behind him and drapes one long arm over his friend's shoulders. "Look, Bob," he says, "why don't we come in together tomorrow morning real early, and we'll go take a look at your new son and make sure he looks like you and not the milkman, right?"

"Yeah, right."

"Okay. And then we'll go visit your lovely young wife, and instead of giving her some bad news, let's give her some good news."

"Yeah, sure. Like what?"

"Okay. Here's the deal. Tell her you're gonna work with me, down in the Keys. Tell her you're gonna run *Belinda Blue* for me."

They stop walking and face each other. "You serious?" Bob says, too surprised by the idea to know if it's a good one.

"Sure, I'm serious. I didn't think of it till a minute ago, but that doesn't mean I'm not serious. I'll go ahead and buy this Tiara 2700 I've been looking at all summer, and I'll run that, while you run ol' *Blue*. Actually, if you want, you can buy into her, and we'll split whatever profits she makes. That's probably the best way to go. You buy into her, and we split according to how much you own. Fifty fifty, seventy-five twenty-five, or whatever you can afford. Deal?"

"Oh, God," Bob says, "I got to think about this. I got to think about it. It's really a sudden development, you know. I mean, it's a hell of a long ways from where I was a year ago, you know. I got to think on it."

They walk slowly across the parking lot toward Avery's van, passing in and out of pale circles of light, two tall young men, dear friends, as close as brothers, as close as lovers, and neither. Avery's arm is flung over Bob's shoulder, and as they walk he explains exactly how Bob's moving to Moray Key and running the *Belinda Blue* will not only save his life and the lives of his wife and three children, but will turn out to be the best time the two of them, he and Bob, will have had since they were kids.

"Yeah," Bob says.

"And not only that," Avery says. "We'll get rich."

"Yeah."

Grand Chemin

IMMAMOU

1

THE CAPTAIN WAS ROAN-COLORED, BALD AND HEAVY-LIDDED, almost Japanese-looking, and he wasn't so much fat as round, round-headed, thick-necked, with a wide, hard chest and belly, powerful arms, large, cruel hands and feet. He stood on the foredeck in a dark green tee shirt and floppy, stained chinos and bare feet, staring at Vanise and the boy and baby as if they were merely three unexpected, additional bits of cargo. They had stepped from behind a batch of empty oil barrels on the pier and had quickly come aboard with the man named Robbie, who had brought them across from McKissick's farm on North Caicos. Robbie's price for his service was easily paid. In exchange for negotiating with the captain of the *Kattina,* a patched and leaking prewar island freighter, and bringing Vanise, Charles and Claude Dorsinville over from North Caicos in an open fishing dinghy borrowed from his cousin, Robbie wanted only the Haitians' absence from George McKissick's farm. He wanted his old job back, and he wanted McKissick angry. The absence of the Haitians obtained both.

Vanise did not ask Robbie how she would pay the captain of the *Kattina,* nor did either man bring the subject up. All Robbie had said was, *Doan you worry none, gal, me take care of everyt'ing. Dis mon, him a fren of mine an' long time now him owe me a payback.* Then one sun-baked afternoon in October, Robbie had simply appeared at McKissick's farm, had told her to pack her clothes in a bag and come along with him, and Vanise, with the baby in her arms, and Claude, who carried in a bundle their few clothes and some food stolen from McKissick's kitchen, had followed Robbie across the corn fields through the palmettos and sea grapes down to the beach, where they saw the dinghy. They climbed into the boat, Robbie pushed it out, jumped in and started the motor, and in minutes they were beyond the reef and headed across the channel toward South Caicos, which they reached by nightfall, tying up in the slip next to the *Kattina* in Cockburn Harbour.

The fat man said nothing to her when she and the children came aboard, looked at them as if measuring how much salt they'd displace in the hold, turned and walked to the stern, where he leaned back against the rail, crossed his meaty arms over his chest and stared down at the engine and a man who was bent over, working with a wrench. The man looked up, and Vanise saw that he was a white man, shirtless and oil-stained, with long brown hair that he flipped away from his face with a toss of his head. Then a slender young brown man emerged from the cabin near the bow and strolled by her to the others in the stern, and the three men talked for a few seconds in English.

Abruptly, the white man swung himself onto the deck and closed the hatch on the engine, and the captain came forward to Vanise, steered her toward a hatch, opened it and waved her down the ladder that led into the darkness below. *G'wan now, get down dere,* he growled. He pushed them with one hand and held the hatch open with the other until they had descended and got their footing and saw that the hold was nearly filled with sacks of salt stacked on pallets, with water sloshing below the pallets. Then he closed the hatch, and they were surrounded by darkness, as if buried.

She heard the engine turn over and catch, heard the men walk and talk abovedecks, and suddenly the boat was moving, drifting languidly. The engine chunked into gear, and the motion of the boat shifted and became purposeful, and she knew they were moving away from the pier and the village, away from the Turks and Caicos islands, away from George McKissick and his farm, his drunken belligerence and his threats to turn them over to the police, away from his sudden visits to her mat in the tiny shack behind his house, away from the long, lonely months of hard work in the sun planting and tending McKissick's corn fields and garden, cleaning his house, cooking his food, listening to his rambling, drunken speeches in English that she could understand only by ignoring the words and listening to the sounds as if they were of the wind and water, watching his face as if it were clouds on the horizon.

THE BOY SAID, WE HAVE TO STAY DOWN HERE SO THE police won't see us. He rarely asked questions now; it seemed to him that the baby Charles would soon be the one to ask questions. Claude knew that he was a boy rapidly becoming a man and so must learn to provide answers. Also, since coming to North Caicos, he had learned to see his aunt in a different light, for though she was, to him, clearly a *serviteur* and possessed a surprising knowledge of the loas and had on several occasions in his presence been mounted by Agwé, her *mait'-tête,* so that he suspected she had become under his mother's tutelage a *hounci canzo,* an initiate, he nevertheless saw her sadness now and knew that when she was silent and seemed to be looking inside herself, as she did with increasing frequency, she was not thinking of anything. She was like an animal resting. And so, instead of asking questions, he had recently taken to making statements about the world, to which her habit was to nod agreement, as if she herself knew nothing of the world.

Claude groped his way over the bags and found a spot

toward the bow where, after shoving several of the heavy sacks aside, he made a space for them to lie together. Come! he called to Vanise. Here's a more comfortable place. He returned to where he had left her and the baby, reached out in the darkness until he felt her shoulder, took her hand and led her forward. He placed the bundle against the wooden hull and patted it with his hand. Lie down with your head here. It's nice, he said, to listen to the water against the boat and be safe and dry inside. He moved his long legs over, made room for Vanise and the baby on his left, and stretched out in the darkness, his hands behind his head, as if waiting cheerfully for sleep.

He did not want to think about where they were going, as he had no name for the place, nor did Vanise. They knew it was not America, not Florida, not Miami, and they knew it was not back to Haiti, where, no doubt, Victor was still rounding up people desperate and frightened enough to ignore the rumors that he seldom took people all the way to America and instead dropped them off on the deserted beaches of small islands in the Bahamas. Sometimes Victor did take people all the way to America, however, and sometimes the people he dropped off in the Turks and Caicos or Inagua Islands managed after a year or two somehow to get to Florida on their own. Then one day a letter would come from America to a hill town in the north of Haiti, and Victor's reputation as a savior would be renewed, so that often he'd find among his passengers a man he'd carried from Le Môle and dropped off in North Caicos the year before. It was never seen as Victor's fault that the man had not got farther from Haiti than a beach fifty miles to the north. It was the fault of a *baka,* an evil spirit, or the fault of the passenger himself, who had not made his *engagement* a strong one or had failed to feed the loas adequately or had not obtained a proper *garde* or *wanga* from a proper *houngan* before coming down to Victor in Le Môle to arrange for the journey over the sea to America.

Claude had heard the name of the place they were

going to, had heard the man Robbie promise it several times, but it was difficult to separate that word from the other words Robbie spoke and a struggle for Vanise and Claude just to understand that Robbie was going to help them escape from George McKissick, so they had come to concentrate on that, escaping, and to put the nature and name of the place they were going to, its distance from here, out of their minds. Wherever they went, they knew, the loas would be there, *en bas de l'eau*. Wherever they went, there would be the island below the sea.

THE CHUG OF THE ENGINE FROM THE STERN, THE SLAP OF the water against the bow, the steady lift and fall of the boat and the quiet slosh of bilge water below the pallets lulled the boy, and he soon slept. Perhaps the baby Charles slept, perhaps Vanise slept, perhaps Claude slept for only a second or two, he could not say, for he woke suddenly and totally without having dreamed, when he heard far to the stern the squeak of the hatch cover being lifted, then heard it clunk shut again, and saw moving sheets and circles of light coming forward, heard a man grunt with the effort of climbing over the cargo, finally saw the man, the captain, heave himself forward, until he was kneeling next to them on their couch, his shadow large and wobbly against the dark planking of the hold, his face somber, disinterested, his small eyes looking only at Vanise. She had sat up and held her son in her arms and now looked down at the top of the baby's head, as if searching for a place to send her spirit into his.

The fat man reached forward with his flashlight and nudged Claude, pushing him on the arm with the light. He spoke rapidly in a harsh whisper. *Get now, bwoy, dis no place for you. Take dat pickney and get aft.*

Claude did as he was told, gently took the baby from Vanise's arms and moved quickly away, sliding over the wall of cargo into the shadows beyond, where he sat down and waited and listened to the sound of the man as he struggled with his trousers, listened to the man's coarse breath as he yanked Vanise's clothing away and his grunts as he pushed himself into her.

A few moments later, circles of light flashed against the hull and cargo, and the huge shadow of the fat man hove into view, and as the man passed Claude, he stopped a second and said to him, *Don't make no trouble for yourself now, bwoy.* His voice was almost pleasant, advisory. Claude did not know what the words meant, however, and stared at the man's large, bare feet.

Bwoy! he shouted. *Cyan unnerstan' me, fuckin' Haitians. Bwoy, just you don't make no trouble, dat's all. You can be whore too, y' unnerstan'.* He reached forward and grabbed Claude's skinny shoulder. *G'wan forward dere wid sister,* he snarled, and lumbered away, his flashlight beam spreading white light ahead of him in circular waves.

Claude hurried forward, the baby clinging to his hip with its legs, and once behind the wall of bags of sea salt, in darkness again, heard the fat man lift the hatch from below, heave his bulk up the ladder, then close it with a bang. The boy reached out until he felt one of Vanise's ankles. He could hear her heavy, rasping breath, as if she had been chased by a huge, fierce animal and had barely escaped to this cavelike hiding place.

You'll be all right again soon, he told her.

She asked for her baby, and he passed the child over. Then she asked him to find her headcloth, which she had lost.

He groped between the sacks and finally came to it and handed it to her. A few seconds later, she passed the crumpled cloth back and told him to soak it in the bilge water for her, which he did. In a few moments, he could hear the baby sucking, and Vanise's breath had slowed and disappeared beneath the sound of the water against the hull and the engine aft, and the boy leaned back again, stretched out his legs and rested.

Sometime later, as in a dream, though it was not a dream, the slender, brown-skinned man and the white man with the long brown hair appeared in the hold together, the white man sending Claude and the baby aft with a gesture, then holding the flashlight on Vanise while the other man silently raped her. When it was the white man's turn, he gave over the light, pulled down his trousers, said a few words in English that Claude overheard, *Cunt,* and, with irritation, *Bloody Christ, just relax now, I ain't gonna hurt ya,* and after a while it was over, and the men had gone, once again dropping the Haitians into their pit of darkness, their cave, their black nest where the only sounds they heard were their own thoughts and the hammering of the engine and the slap of the low waves against the bow of the boat as it drove steadily west toward Great Inagua.

BACK IN COCKBURN HARBOUR, WHEN VANISE AND CHARLES and Claude had first descended into the hold, day had gone clean away, and night now went away too, for there was only blackness, broken unpredictably, swiftly and absolutely by the men from above with their flashlight and few words and quick, violent moves that seemed to relax the men for a while, as if they were injecting themselves with a drug—the fat man, who, after the first time, came with a flask of clear rum in one hand and drank from it and gave it to Vanise to sip from when he was done with her, and the slender brown man, who came to the hold alone now and tried talking to Vanise and then got angry because she would not respond, so he slapped her, and the young white man, not much older than a boy, but hairy across his chest and shoulders, his stringy long arms and legs casting wild shadows when he took the woman, as if he were beating her. When the men were down in the hold, their flashlight shattering the darkness, the place seemed tiny, cramped, closed in upon the human beings, as if they were under a huge house; but when the men had gone and had taken their light away with them, the place seemed to open up and grow enormous, like a black tent. And with both day and night gone, all of time was gone, too, except for the scratchy, mechanical time that passed through whenever the men appeared, abrasive interruptions that Claude had begun to accept like a shift in dreams, his mind returning gratefully, as soon as the men were gone, to the sweet-flowing timeless dream of perpetual darkness— when suddenly the throb of the motor ceased, and the sound of the sea smacking the planks near his head diminished, and the steady lift and drop of the boat changed to a gentle, rocking motion.

He heard a thud against the side of the boat, and voices, the captain's and the Englishman's, and then, astonished, Claude heard a Haitian voice, a man shouting in Creole.

Resté arresté la! Pa wé ou, messieurs! Moin la!

Claude sat upright, and hearing now a mumbling mix of English and Creole as several people came aboard, understanding more of the English words than the Haitians seemed to and more of the Creole than did the captain and his crewmen, he decided that this was a prearranged stop, that the *Kattina* was picking up marooned Haitians and the captain was being paid in American dollars for it.

Haitian people, Claude said to Vanise.

How many?

I don't know. More than two. Listen.

Police.

No. People from Haiti, going to America. The *gros neg* is taking money from them.

Vanise grunted. What food have we? They'll want our food.

Maybe they have their own. We have only biscuits and cheese and some tinned beef.

I'm thirsty, Vanise said in a low voice cut with resignation, as if she expected never to drink again.

Maybe the Haitians will have water with them. Listen, he said. I believe one of them speaks English.

The men were standing almost directly overhead now, and indeed, one of the Haitians was speaking in broken English to the captain, arguing that they should be allowed to stay abovedecks, promising to go below if another boat came in sight and assuring him they'd stay out of the way of the captain and his crew. *We pay money, plenty money. We have got wet from the open sea, now we must dry, or a cold will enter us, Captain. No problems for you.*

All right den, mon. Stay above if dat what you want.

Ah.

Got sumpin down dere better'n up here, mon.

Yes?

Got a gal. Haiti gal down dere, jus' waitin' for a big ol' black Haiti mon to come down an' chat wid her.

Yes?

Haiti gal an' her pickney an' a pretty bwoy down dere wid her.

Yes? A pretty boy, eh? Massisi?

The fat man laughed. *Yas, mon, him a pretty bwoy, all right, but de gal, dat de real beef. Make de journey sweet.*

Yes. So we dry and warm ourself in the morning sun, eh? Then we go chat up the Haiti gal and pretty boy, eh?

Eh-eh-eh, the captain said, laughing, walking aft toward the wheelhouse. *Eh-eh-eh. Dem Haitians-dem, all over de fuckin' ocean, worse'n Cubans-dem.*

THE ENGINE TURNED OVER SLOWLY, CAUGHT, AND RESUMED its steady, familiar rhythm, and the bow of the boat lifted slightly, and once again Claude and his aunt and her child adjusted their balance and body weights to fit the lapping of the waves and the slow rise and fall of the boat.

We will get to America now, Claude said. Because of the Haitians.

In a short time, it got very hot, still and close, and soon they were taking short, shallow, quick breaths, like dogs sleeping in the noonday sun. Claude stripped off his shirt, rolled it into a ball and stuffed it into the bundle behind his head. He was very thirsty, thirstier than he had ever been before, and he knew Vanise was also, and after a while he pulled himself slowly to his feet and made his way aft, climbed the ladder and pushed the hatch cover up.

The glare of the light hit him in the eyes like a hard

slap. All he saw was white, a pure, sourceless field of white. Staggered by the blow, he looked back down into the hold. Then, shading his eyes with one hand, holding up the cover with the other, he squinted and saw through a white cloud that three Haitian men were lounging on the deck a few feet away. They were young men, under thirty, thin and wearing farmers' clothes, short-sleeved shirts and faded cotton pants and sockless leather shoes. One of them, who looked the oldest of the three, smoked a pipe. He turned slowly and saw Claude.

Hello, boy, he said, speaking Creole. You decide to come up for some air?

The others turned and looked at him with idle curiosity.

This the *massisi?* one asked.

The man with the pipe laughed.

Will you ask the man for water for us? Claude said. The breeze on his face cooled him and smelled clean and fresh, and he pulled himself halfway out of the hold.

What de hell you doin' up here! the captain called. He was at the wheel in the aft cabin. *Too many fuckin' Haitians up here already!*

Him want water, the man with the pipe said.

The captain nodded and sent the young white man forward to the hatch with an old rum bottle full of water. When the Englishman handed Claude the bottle he smiled, and Claude saw that he was missing most of his front teeth and was very ugly.

Now get yer arse back down there, the white man said. *These boys here are travelin' first class. You an' yer sis are steerage.* He laughed, and he shoved Claude back down the ladder and closed the cover over him again.

The hold stank of seawater and burlap and body sweat and got worse as the temperature rose. They urinated and defecated into bilge water between the slats of a pallet as far from their place in the bow as they could, and the soft, hot odor of their own wastes drifted slowly back to them. There were rats now, emboldened by the stillness of the people in their nest in the bow. Twice Claude reached to adjust the bundle at his head and heard a rat scuttle away in the darkness, until he took his shirt and the biscuits and cheese out of the bundle, gave half the food to Vanise, ate half himself, and threw the bundle toward the stern, where he soon heard the rats foraging for crumbs.

They suffered silently, even little Charles, although now and then Vanise, in a weak, low voice, sang a line or two from a baby's song and then left off, as if the effort were too much for her. And much later, when the heat lessened somewhat, the men came back down again, the brown Inaguan and the Englishman, laughing and drinking clear rum, sending Claude with the baby aft while they raped his aunt.

When the Haitian men came down, Claude was surprised, for they behaved like the others, even the man with the pipe, who tried to grab Claude when he stepped away from them, grasping at the boy's trousers and yanking on them, and when Claude fought and squirmed free, the man hit the boy in the face with his fist and cursed at him and moved forward to where the others were holding Vanise against the sacks of sea salt.

They did not sleep, but, like small animals in shock after being hit by an automobile, they were not awake, either. It was cool for a measureless period of time, and then it grew hot again, like the inside of an oven, and when it was hot, the men did not come down into the hold, so that Claude almost felt grateful for the stifling, stinking heat. But soon it began to cool, and he knew they would come again, and they did, sometimes one at a time, sometimes two or even three, and eventually one of the Haitians, not the one with the pipe, grabbed Claude by his arms from behind so that he could not get away. The man threw the boy down, and when he had yanked his trousers down, the man jammed his knee between Claude's legs and spread them and entered him—a savage tearing, a rip in both his body and his mind that made the boy scream and left him crumpled, burning with rage and shame and holding inside himself a dark star of pain. When the man was through with him, the boy cried, and when he could stop himself from

crying, he picked his body up with pathetic care, as if it
were not his own, and carried it forward to where Vanise
lay with her child.

THEN ONE TIME, AFTER IT HAD BEEN COOL FOR A LONG WHILE,
it did not get hot again as it usually did, and the boat
began to surge and dip, and the waves began to smack
harder against the bow, until soon the boat was lifting in
the water at a steep angle, as if climbing a mountain,
then tipping, sliding swiftly down into a hole. The bilge
water sloshed wildly, and sacks of salt shifted and fell.

Claude and Vanise and the baby scrambled about in
the hold, struggling to find someplace safe, where they
could curl up against one another and not get tossed
about, until at last they ended clinging to the ladder
below the hatch cover. Vanise held her baby with one
arm, the ladder with the other. Claude, wrapping himself
around both woman and child, clutched the rails of the
ladder and clamped them to it, as the boat tipped and
fell, then rose again and tipped and fell again.

They could hear a wind roaring abovedecks and heard
waves slam against the boat with furious force and weight.
Pray for us! Claude ordered. Pray to *les Mystères* the
way you know how. Pray to Agwé, your *mait'tête*, he
pleaded, so the boat will not sink and drown us. Pray to
the Virgin and to the saints and to Jesus Christ, to Papa
Legba and Damballah and all the others. Pray! he shouted
into her ear, and Vanise began to murmur incoherently,
mixing half-remembered songs and prayers and chants
together as best she knew how: *Coté ou yé, metté
hounsi-yo deyors, gan malice oh, cé passé'l t'ap passè.
Dou quand Bon Dieu rêle ou. Je vous prends pour me
rendre les services que je veux, au nom de Mait' Carrefour et de Legba, generation paternelle et maternelle,
ancêtre et ancêtere, Afrique et Afrique, au nom de
Legba, Baltaza, Agwé, Erzulie, Ghede, Ogoun, Damballah* . . . and on and on, as the storm raged against
them.

After a long time, Vanise grew weary and confused
and too ashamed to go on, for she knew only scraps and

bits of the proper prayers and calls to the loas, and she said to her nephew, I can't! I must not! We must let *le Bon Dieu* take us over now.

No, he said. Go on, pray for us!

And so she resumed, throughout the storm, until, at last, the roar of the wind lowered somewhat, and the boat ceased to tip and thrash about as wildly as before, and gradually, after many hours, they came to believe that the storm had passed by and that it could not have been a hurricane or even a northwester, but a squall, perhaps, for now they heard rain falling on the deck above their heads, steadily and heavily, without wind, and the sea seemed almost calm.

First Claude loosened his grip on the ladder, and then Vanise let go of it, and they slid slowly to the pallet below, where they lay collapsed around one another, like lovers, their child between them, about to fall peacefully asleep together. Yet even as they lay, they still clung to the base of the ladder, as if manacled to it.

THE CAPTAIN LIFTED THE HATCH COVER AND WAVED CLAUDE, Vanise and the child up. It was night, and the rain had stopped. In the northwest, a crescent moon floated behind strips of silver-blue cloud, and the sea glittered with phosphorus.

The boat had rounded the western tip of New Providence Island, and when Claude and Vanise had pulled themselves up the ladder to the deck, it was as if they had returned from their own drownings: There was air here, fresh, cool air, and endless space that seemed tangible, and though it was night, the air was filled with light and the smells of what it was not—the sea, land, trees, fruit, human beings. They inhaled and looked at their hands and each other's faces and rediscovered their own battered bodies. They looked off the starboard side and saw the headlights of automobiles beading the north coast of the island. Off the bow, they saw the first lights of the city, Nassau, casting a dull, whitish glow against the bruise-colored sky. They had come over three hundred miles as if chained in darkness, a middle passage, and the sight of so many of humanity's lights at once was a sharp, confusing blow to them that left them stunned, for they had come to believe that, except for the six men on the boat, there was no one else left in the world. Now they looked out and saw high, rectangular hotels on Cable Beach a half mile away, glittery casinos, crowded restaurants, strings of streetlights, beacons blinking off North Cay at the entrance to the harbor, a jet plane taking off from the airport inland, banking southwest and disappearing, small boats and yachts passing slowly out of the harbor, and there ahead of them, the city itself, with tall pink buildings, a green and white Holiday Inn and a half-dozen more hotels, with spotlights hidden among hibiscus and casuarina trees playing against the terrace windows while shadows of royal palms fluttered against brightly painted pink, yellow, white and blue walls.

They passed the large wharf and two Scandinavian cruise ships tied up there, sleek, white and huge, with strings of lights running up the masts and stacks like Christmas tree decorations, and slowly moved farther down the harbor, with Paradise Island off the portside, downtown Nassau off the starboard, where taxis cruised through Rawson Square, turned and headed out to the casinos or cross-island to the airport for late-night arrivals from London, New York and Miami.

It was as if Claude and Vanise had been carried to another planet than the one they had known, and they stood silent and awestruck, crowded with the other Haitians into the aft cabin, where the captain had told them to stay. The three Haitian men ignored Claude and Vanise now, treated them as if they had never seen the boy and the woman before and were not in the slightest interested in or even curious about them.

The captain had instructed the Haitian with the pipe to explain to the others that they should all stay low inside the cabin until the boat was tied up, and then, when it was clear that no one was watching, they were simply to walk off the boat one by one, to move down the pier and away. No one would stop them, he said, not at this hour, if they walked quickly and seemed to know where they were going. Every one of them, including Claude and Vanise, had been listed as crew members, he said. The harbormaster wouldn't check for them until morning, if he checked at all. *Dese Bahamians, mon, him don't care where you go, long's you not standin' next to him when him look for you.* The captain laughed and walked forward, while the white man steered from the bridge and brought the boat safely around and put her with silent ease into a slip on the dark side of a small pier next to a pair of low turtle boats.

There was a moment of confusion and some heat, while the three Haitian men argued over who would leave the boat first, but the man with the pipe, called Jules by the others, prevailed. The youngest of the three would go first, then the next youngest, and finally Jules himself. They would meet on the street, he said, and he would lead them on the journey across the island to his cousin in Elizabeth Town. He glanced at a hand-drawn map, apparently sent to him by the cousin, and said he was sure Elizabeth Town was on the outskirts of Nassau and they would be able to arrive there before sunrise. He carefully folded the map and put it in his shirt pocket.

We will follow you, Claude announced.

The men turned and looked at him with mild surprise. No, you can't do that, Jules said evenly. There would be five of us then and a baby, he said, and the police will want to know right away who we are. It's bad enough we have three to travel together. And until we are outside the city, he instructed the other men, we should walk separately. That way, if one of us is captured, it will be too bad, but it will only be one of us. But you two, Jules said to Claude and Vanise, you and the infant, you're on your own now. We don't know you.

Claude said nothing. The boat bumped softly against a pair of old truck tires tied to the pier, and the Inaguan leaped out at the bow and tied the boat to a bollard there, then ran to the stern and tied her to another. The first Haitian stepped from the cabin and in seconds had strolled nonchalantly down the length of the low pier, passed through a chain-link gate at the end and down an alley beyond, until he disappeared behind a squat gray cinderblock storage building. They saw a car splash by on the street where he had disappeared, and a second later, the second Haitian left the boat. When he, too, had disappeared, Jules left.

What should we do? Vanise asked.

Follow them.

But you heard . . .

No matter. We'll follow them. We can't stay here, he said.

Our clothes, Vanise said, looking suddenly confused. Our bundle, it's down there. We left it down there.

No matter. It's better not to carry anything. Like them. Come, he said, grabbing her hand. Come! and he pulled her from the cabin, over the rail to the pier and quickly away from the boat, where the captain stood in the bow, hands on hips, watching.

The white man came forward and joined him. *It's pathetic, ain't it?* He flipped his long hair away from his face and lit a cigarette.

The captain nodded. *Dem Haitians, mon, dem worse'n Jamaicans. Live like dogs, mon. You cyan deal wid 'em like dey was normal people.*

The white man smiled as if the captain had told a joke. *Ain't that the fuckin' truth, though.*

2

IT WAS LATE, AFTER MIDNIGHT, AND THE AREA AROUND BAY Street and Rawson Square, downtown Nassau, was nearly deserted. Across the harbor on Paradise Island, however, and out along Cable Beach and east on Montague Bay, hotels and casinos were bustling with noise and bright lights as cars and blatting motorcycles pulled up and departed and sunburned white people laughed and danced, drank and gambled happily through the night.

The three Haitian men, Jules leading them by about a half block now, turned right at Bay Street and headed for the quiet, locked-up center of the city, past exclusive shops that hid behind iron grilles to Rawson Square, where the darkened straw market and Prince George Wharf were located. Taxis, like seabirds, swept in along Bay Street to the square, looped toward the harbor and discharged half-drunk ladies and gentlemen beside the Scandinavian cruise ships, then hurried back out to the hotels and casinos for more.

Claude, as he and Vanise came off the pier onto Bay Street, caught sight of the last of the three men. There! he said, and he started walking quickly, pulling Vanise along behind. At the square, Jules turned left down a quiet side street and walked casually, as if heading home from a long day's work at the straw market, past the post office and courthouse. Palm trees shuddered overhead in the light offshore breeze, and the narrow, wet street below, shiny as polished ebony from the recent rain, reflected back streetlights and lamplit second-story windows.

Then Jules was leading them uphill, away from the harbor and the downtown area, around Shirley to East Street, with the top of the hill and a water tower in the east silhouetted against a pale, peach-colored glow from Montague Bay and the Fort Montague Hotel beyond, past old pink limestone houses shuttered against the night, until at last, beyond the city, Claude and Vanise were sweating from the effort of keeping up, out of breath, and then—as the street became a darkened road leading south from Nassau and as one by one the Haitian men ahead of them disappeared into the gloom. —they grew frightened again, alone in darkness, lost.

They stopped. Behind them were the lights and streets of Nassau, the hill outlined sharply against the sky, the water tower, the harbor, boats moving in and out; ahead of them, a soft, enveloping darkness that had swallowed the three Haitian men whole and was now about to swallow Claude, Vanise and Charles as well. They could feel the rough limestone road beneath their feet, but did it narrow to a pathway, did it suddenly loop to the left or right, was there a cliff at the edge of the road, a wall, a prickly hedgerow? The sky was clouded over here, remnants of the squall that had passed over them at sea; there was no moonlight, no stars.

Charles squirmed in his mother's arms and whimpered.

Shut up, Claude whispered, and Vanise stroked the baby's face and soothed him.

Claude could hear the men now, could hear their hard shoes crunch against the roadway and their low, melodious voices as they spoke to one another and now and then lightly laughed. He took hold of his aunt's sleeve and led her as if she were a stubborn child. Don't be scared, Vanise, he said in a low voice. *Les Invisibles* are with us, always, everywhere. Even here.

Up ahead, Jules suddenly stopped the others. *Silence*, he commanded, and they listened carefully. It's someone walking behind us, he whispered. Come, stand off the road a ways and wait for them to pass by. Moving with care, the three felt their way to the side of the road and into the stony ditch beyond, where they crouched down to wait.

Shortly, Claude and Vanise drew abreast of them, and then, when they had passed a few steps beyond, stopped.

What is the matter? Vanise asked.

Shhh. I can't hear them now.

They have flown away, she said.

Suddenly, the men were beside them. Boy, Jules said, you are like a dog who won't stay home.

Claude said nothing. The baby started to cry.

We'll go back, Vanise said.

No, Claude said.

Go back to the city, one of the other men said. Someone there will take care of you.

The police, Jules said, and laughed.

The baby was crying loudly now, squirming in his mother's arms. Claude reached over and took the child, hitched him against his hip, and the child automatically clung to the boy and quieted down.

Go now, go on back, the man said again.

No, Claude repeated.

Yes, we'll go, Vanise said, her voice tight and high with fear.

No, Claude said. He took a step away from the man, and Vanise followed.

What shall we do with them? one of the men asked.

Jules sighed heavily. When we come onto houses or a village, he said, or if an automobile comes, we must separate as we did back in the city, so that no more than one of us can get caught by the police.

Fine, the man said. But what about them?

Where we are going, Jules said to Claude, there is no place for you. We cannot help you. Do you understand me?

Yes, Claude said.

Then go back now. You will do better in the city, where there are many strangers. No one will know you are Haitian.

No, Claude said firmly.

I'll make him go back, the other man said, and he stepped toward Claude and reached for the boy's shirt.

Never mind, Jules said. He drew the other man back. I thought you liked the pretty boy, he said.

Ha. Only at sea, he said, laughing. He's white man's meat now. We have all those Bahamian women to choose from. We don't need to fuck a pretty little boy or a Haitian whore.

Jules turned away and started walking. Don't be so sure, he called back. Those Bahamian girls get one look at you and they'll run in the opposite direction. He laughed and walked on.

The others ran to catch up, joking and teasing, talking eagerly now about women. Claude, with Charles on his hip, followed. Come along, he said to Vanise.

Slowly, in silence, she came up behind him and walked there the rest of the way.

In a few hours, they reached Elizabeth Town, a village on the south coast with one street, a half-dozen sandy lanes and a cluster of pink, cut-limestone cottages roofed with thatch. Spreading from the north side of the village, like a junk-strewn backyard, was a shantytown, corrugated tin shacks and buildings that were little more than huts made of scrap lumber and cast-off sheets of iron. The narrow lanes were deserted, and except for the dim glow of a kerosene lamp behind a window here and there, the town was dark. The sky had cleared, however, and now Claude and Vanise could let themselves hang back a ways from the other Haitians and still see to follow them as they cut through the sleeping village to the shantytown beyond.

They saw Jules walk boldly up to one of the shacks facing the lane, where he knocked against the door once, then a few seconds later, again, and a third time, until at last the door opened a crack. Jules exchanged words with the person behind the door, and then the person closed the door, while the three men waited in silence outside. A few moments passed, and the door opened again, and the men passed into the house.

Claude could smell the sea, just over the low hill south of the village. A dog barked in the distance, then went suddenly silent. The wind shifted to the west, and Claude smelled oranges.

I'll go and speak to them, Claude said. He passed Charles across to Vanise, led her out of the street to an alleyway between a pair of closed-up shops. Sit down here, he said, and rest.

She obeyed and sat down, tenderly arranging the sleeping child on her lap, while Claude crossed the street and walked to the cabin that the Haitians had entered.

He knocked, as Jules had done, and waited. After a moment, he knocked again. He heard movement inside, a chair scraping the floor, low male voices. He knocked again, sharply.

Who dat? a man called from the other side. Claude recognized the voice, Jules's, even though it spoke English.

C'est moi, he said.

Boy, you are a pest! Jules shouted in Creole. If you don't go away now, I am going to come out there and beat you!

Got a machete here, boy! Claude heard the other man call. Chop you up!

A woman spoke rapidly and in a hushed voice to the men, and they answered, explaining, and then the woman groaned.

I am going to chop that little *massisi* to pieces, the man said, and Claude heard more chairs moving, feet clumping, men and women arguing. No, no, Raymond, he will leave soon. He will leave, or the police will catch him before morning. He is only a poor country boy, and the police will catch him and send him back, if we just ignore him.

They were silent then. Claude stood before the closed door, tried the latch and pushed, but it was bolted or barred from inside. Suddenly, he smelled oranges again, they were eating them inside the house, and the boy realized that he was very hungry.

He turned and crossed the lane and walked past the shacks and huts to where he'd left Vanise. When he came around the corner of the building next to the alley, one of the few two-story structures in the village, he saw that Vanise, sitting cross-legged on the sandy ground with the child sprawled in her lap, had fallen fast asleep. Her head lay back against the side of the cinder-block building, and she looked beautiful and familiar to the boy, and for the first time in many days, he thought of his mother in Allanche and his sisters and their cabin on the ridge above the sea. Even when he and Vanise and Charles had been suffering on the boat, with the men coming down into the hold to rape them, with the rats and filth and terrible stench and heat, he had not thought of his mother and sisters and the place where he had lived his whole life, for he had been ashamed and afraid and did not want to think of his mother's face when he felt that way. Now, however, he had gone beyond shame and fear, which he did not understand, but he knew that he would never be ashamed again, nor would he ever be afraid again. And so he thought freely about his mother, imagined her dark brown face, her large, wet eyes, her smell, the smooth skin of her hands. He heard her voice, heard her sing his sisters to sleep, *Bon jour, mes infants, bon jour . . .* and he thought he heard her say to him, Oh, my poor son, how you have suffered, and how hungry you must be. Here, let me feed you, let me prepare a meal for you, my poor son. Let me comfort you.

3

IN THE VILLAGES OF THE ENGLISH-SPEAKING CARIBBEAN, the businesses called shops are often owned and operated by middle-aged men who are entrepreneurial dreamers, men who, with a great deal of energy, diligence, gregariousness, and with a little financial acumen, combine under the roof of one small house several different business ventures—a neighborhood grocery store, pub, dry goods establishment, hardware store, taxi service, tourist guide service, restaurant, juke joint, and so on. They also sometimes venture into backroom gambling and upstairs prostitution and have been known to invest, in a small, safe way, in locally controlled real estate development, smuggling and drugs.

It was such a man as this, Jimmy Grabow, and not the local constabulary, who caught Claude and Vanise and her baby Charles asleep in the alley next to his shop, and when he discovered they were Haitians, which he did when, by poking them with his foot, he woke them and heard them speak, he did not turn them over to the town's one police officer, who had nothing to do that day anyhow and would have welcomed the opportunity to drive to Nassau to turn the illegal aliens over to the immigration office. Instead, Grabow smiled broadly, warmly, even, and took the Haitians into his shop and out back to the tiny kitchen, where he fed them leftover jerked pork and rice and beans, gave them Coca-Colas from the cooler, imported biscuits and jam, and even offered them a fresh pack of Craven A cigarettes from the rack behind the bar, which Vanise declined and Claude accepted.

Grabow was a short, compact man with light brown skin. He had excellent teeth, large as a horse's and white, of which he was justifiably proud, and when he smiled, he pulled his lips back and showed his teeth off. He smiled often, talked rapidly and volubly and enjoyed touching people while he rattled away at them, enjoyed putting his hands on whomever he talked to, his arms around shoulders, his hands on cheeks, arms, chests, so that most people, when they left the shop, reached for their wallet, and finding it, wondered what Grabow had taken from them, for always, after talking with Grabow, one felt that somehow he'd managed to take away something that wasn't rightfully his.

When Grabow had led Claude and Vanise and the baby to a small room upstairs and had left them there, Claude felt this way too, felt it more strongly, perhaps, than others might, because he did not understand more than a few words of what Grabow had said to him and his aunt and therefore had paid particularly close attention to the man's inflection and his facial gestures and physical mannerisms. And when the boy asked himself what the Bahamian had taken away from them, he concluded that he had taken what little freedom remained in their possession, that scrap of freedom they'd obtained when they stepped off the *Kattina* in Nassau. In exchange, they had been given a meal and a pack of cigarettes, Claude knew that much, and now, apparently, they had been given shelter also.

We should leave here now, Claude said. He stood by the curtainless window and looked down on the backyard of the place, where he saw a battered old white Toyota van, odd piles of sand and cinder blocks, an outhouse, several chickens scratching in the packed dirt, and a large sleeping pig like a long gray boulder in the shade of a scrawny breadfruit tree. Beyond the yard was the ramshackle backside of the shantytown, where Jules and his friends were now, and beyond that a field of rough, dry, slowly rising ground, pocked and rocky, with small patches here and there of withered corn stalks and pole beans.

Vanise sat on the narrow bed in the corner of the room and placed the baby on the floor, where he crawled eagerly around the foot of the bed and stood, one hand clinging to the rail at the end, the other reaching for the dresser just beyond. He seemed happy for the first time since they had left North Caicos, free, finally, of his mother's and his cousin's arms, to move about a room, to touch and measure things with his fat hands, to test his recently discovered ability to stand.

They argued, Claude and Vanise. She would not leave. You go if you want to, she said, but Charles and I will not.

No. We should be together, but we must leave now. This man is bad, a *gros neg*.

Claude walked to the door, turned the knob and pulled. It wouldn't open. The bastard locked the door, he whispered. You *see?*

No, she said. Now *you* see.

He returned to the window and looked down again. I can jump to the ground, it's not far. Then you can drop Charles to me, and I'll catch him, and then you can jump down too.

No.

He won't catch us. He's busy in the bar now. I can hear him. Come, he said.

No.

Come!

No, she repeated, crossing her arms over her breasts.

Tempérament d'esclave, he cursed, and he swung himself over the windowsill and turned his long, skinny body against the side of the building, where he let himself hang by his hands, then let go. In seconds, he was gone.

GRABOW WAS NOT ANGRY OR EVEN DISAPPOINTED THAT THE boy had fled; he was relieved and only wished he'd taken the baby with him. But the baby kept the girl happy and busy, when she wasn't fucking the men he sent upstairs to her room. The men, a few from the town but most of them from the fishing boats and yachts that tied up at the marina in Coral Harbour, just beyond the hook, paid Grabow for the girl's services, and Grabow in return housed and fed and clothed the girl and her baby from his own stock and did not turn her over to the police, for which she seemed grateful. At least she did not resist or try to leave, which she easily could have done, just as the boy had. In fact, she could have left even more easily than Claude, for after a few weeks Grabow found it inconvenient to keep the door locked and have to let her out himself whenever she needed to go to the privy or had to wash herself or clean the baby. He soon allowed her to come down to the kitchen and feed herself and the child, allowed her to cook chickens and jerked pork and fish, Haitian style, with hot peppers and onions, for him and the bar customers, though he would not let her come out front or leave the building, except to go to the privy or to wash at the standpipe by the back door.

The room she lived in was bare and small, but not unpleasant, especially in the mornings, when sunlight streamed through the window and splashed across the painted gray floor and over the bed. She made up a bed for the baby in one of the dresser drawers and placed it in the corner of the room farthest from the window. Generally, when the men who visited her saw the baby asleep in the corner of the room, they lowered their voices and tried not to wake him, but sometimes they were drunk and noisy and even angry at the sight of the child in the room and complained of it afterwards downstairs to Grabow, so he took the dresser drawer out of the room and put it in a windowless storage room next door and made it clear to Vanise that she would have to keep the child there at night from now on.

The men who came to her, rarely more than one or two a night, were mostly seamen. They were fishermen and turtlers from the small open boats in Coral Harbour and sometimes Bahamian crewmen from the big charter boats, sometimes a Cuban or a Jamaican, and sometimes even a white man, an American, who came up the narrow stairs from the bar and spent an hour with her, fucking her and then trying to talk with her, which of course always failed, so they would often simply ramble on as if she understood.

A few of the men she liked, a short, round, chocolate-brown man who affected huge, winglike sideburns and operated the only taxi in town other than Grabow's, and a Cuban, tall, skinny and black, who always brought Vanise a cold Heineken and seemed disappointed when the baby Charles got moved out to the storage room, and she liked a young Jamaican man who wore a carefully trimmed, very thick beard and finger-length dreadlocks, a man named Tyrone, who spoke some Creole and always rolled and smoked a cigarlike spliff of ganja before making love to her. She liked the smell of the ganja, perfumy and dry, and when he offered it to her, she accepted. It seemed to make the time with Tyrone a respite from the painful silence of her mind. For her mind, an utterly silent, burned-out charnel house by now, was filled with images of *les Morts* from the dark side, Ghede and Baron Cimitière, whose evil presence no longer frightened her, whose presence, in fact, she had begun to encourage and make welcome. She lay back in the dimly lit room over the shop and opened herself to these dark, malevolent spirits the same way she opened herself to the men she did not like, men who were dirty and quick and stunk of fish and rum and sweat, men who were drunk and half impotent, which made them irritable, men who fucked her in unusual ways, and now and then the man who slapped her until she wept and only then would he fuck her.

This last was Jimmy Grabow himself. It would be three or four in the morning, and the domino game downstairs would have broken up, the metal screen pulled down on the front of the shop, the lights turned off, and he would come trudging upstairs half-drunk and bumping against the sides of the walls in a way she recognized immediately. Then he'd come into her room and light the kerosene lantern on the small table next to the bed and stand over her, while she pretended to sleep.

Wake up, gal. It was always the same on nights like

this. He reached down and yanked the sheet off her and examined her as if angry at what he saw, a young woman in bra and panties, sitting up and drawing herself away from him, covering her breasts and crotch with her hands, her eyes watching his so that the first time he swung his heavy hand at her face she'd know before he swung it that it was coming and could move her head slightly so as to catch the blow at an angle instead of directly.

That oughta wake you up. He unbuckled his pants and stripped them off, took off his shoes and shirt, and stood there a second, again as if angry with her. His penis hung limply between his legs. Then he hit her a second time, and her eyes filled with water from the force of the blow. A third time he hit her, and a fourth and fifth, back and forth, until at last she began to weep, and suddenly his penis was erect and Grabow was panting with excitement and from the effort of slapping the girl, and then he would come forward onto her and force his way into her.

Afterwards, in silence, he left the room, and she heard him lunging back down the stairs to the room next to the kitchen, where he slept. The next morning, he whistled cheerfully downstairs and throughout the day was kindly toward her, smiling that horsetoothed smile, chucking the baby under the chin with approval as she passed through the kitchen to the privy in the backyard.

Someday, gal, he said to her when she returned to the kitchen and started to prepare breakfast for the three of them, *someday you gonna hafta get shipped back to Haiti. Bound to come. Everybody know you here, gal. So you better enjoy yourself while you can, get yourself fattened up now, while you can.*

SHIRTLESS, BAREFOOT, A MACHETE IN ONE HAND, A PLAS-tic water jug in the other, Claude peered into the low thatch lean-to where the old man lay at the back, sleeping on a rumpled blanket. They were deep in the Barrens, west of the airport and east of the golf course at Simms Point. The old man wore a dirty undershirt, shiny black gabardine trousers, and was barefoot. His empty rum bottle lay at his side, the cap scattered and lost somewhere in the lean-to among cook pots, a transistor radio, an old *Playboy* and the various hoes and rakes they used to plant and tend the marijuana plants and the plastic garbage bags they used to package it.

As Claude ducked and entered the shady lean-to, the old man stirred, groped automatically for his bottle, and lifting it, realized it was empty and woke. Bastard, he said. You finished my rum.

Claude sat down cross-legged in a corner of the hut and laid the machete carefully from knee to knee. He was growing weary of these attacks by the old man, but in the end, despite their both being Haitian, they had little else to talk about. They couldn't talk about the Chinaman's marijuana crop—Claude was a farmboy, young, sober and intelligent, and knew how to tend, harvest and guard the plants; the old man, an assistant tailor, drunk all the time and stupid, knew nothing of farming. And they couldn't talk about Haiti, because the old man had come twelve years ago from where Claude had never been, a small town outside Port-au-Prince, and Claude, from Allanche in the north, had come from where the old man had never been. And they couldn't talk about Nassau and the island of New Providence, for everything about the place that interested him—its geography, people, economics—Claude had learned in a matter of weeks, and the old man in twelve years had not learned one-half as much. As for the Chinaman, upon whose special needs and goodwill and trust Claude now depended, and the Haitian community, which Claude had penetrated the morning he fled from Grabow's shop and returned to the door that Jules and the others had entered before him, and the Bahamian police, who, Claude now believed, would not bother him if nothing drew their attention to him, and the Bahamians in general, who seemed to have a fondness for Haitians, whom they saw as childlike in their honesty and exploitable in their need—about these, the old man had nothing to say that was of use to Claude. It does happen that sometimes the old have nothing to teach the young, except by sad example. The old man could not even tell Claude anything useful about how to get to America. He himself did not want to go to America. It's all white people there, he had said, and they hate the blacks, and their own blacks hate all the other blacks. Their police will arrest you and put you in jail until they send you back to jail in Haiti. The Americans have an arrangement with Papa Doc . . .

Bébé, Claude corrected.

No. With Papa. And they send you back so he can put you in jail in Port-au-Prince forever. Better to stay here in the Bahamas, the old man said. Forget America.

Claude could never forget America. Not now, not after all he'd suffered, all the pain and humiliation and fear he'd faced and overcome for it. There was an exchange that had taken place, and he'd come out with a vision, and he clung to it, like a sailor off a sunken ship clinging to the wreckage of the ship. There was a big difference now between him and Vanise, he thought, and also between the boy he had been, as recently even as when he had been locked down in the stinking hold of the *Kattina,* and the boy he was now, raising marijuana for the Chinaman in the Barrens on New Providence, and the difference was that while Vanise still looked to *les Invisibles* for definitions she could not provide herself, he was beginning to look to America for that. The loas had moved around from in front of him to the back, and in their place *America* had come forward, insisting, like the loas, on service and strategy, promising luxury and power, scolding, instructing and seducing him all at once, and in that way, as the loas had done before, creating him.

I know you drank off my rum, the old man said, holding the empty bottle upside down before the boy's face, as if that were proof.

I don't drink rum, Claude said wearily. It makes your brain mushy. Like yours. He smiled.

The old man grunted, farted loudly, and mumbling curses at the boy, *Zobop . . . diab . . . ,* turned away from him.

Claude looked out from the shade of the lean-to at the marijuana plants, large, thick-stalked, mature plants cultivated in clots among small patches of corn so as to be indistinguishable from the corn if seen from the air. François, the boy said in a low voice. Tell me this, François. How come I work all day weeding and watering and tending the plants, while you sleep all day, and yet the Chinaman pays us the same? And how come I sit up all night guarding the plants alone, while you go into town and get drunk, and yet the Chinaman pays us the same? What's your secret, *Loupgarou?*

François sat up and rubbed his eyes. He stroked his grizzled chin and said, If he paid either one of us less than he does now, then he'd be paying one of us nothing. Zero.

True.

So if you want to make more money than I do, you must ask the Chinaman for a raise.

Claude smiled. You're not as stupid as you look, he said. No, I don't need to make more money than you do. What I want is for you to do your half of the work.

Someone has to go into town for food and report to the Chinaman about his crop, right? He told *me* to do that, every day, or he'd think we stole his crop ourselves or maybe got chopped up by someone else stealing the crop or maybe got arrested by the police and were locked up over in Nassau. Unless he hears from us once a day. This is serious business, boy. We're not out here raising yams, you know. The old man lay back on his filthy blanket and eyed the boy. Give me the water, he ordered.

Claude passed the jug of tepid water over to him. Tonight, Claude said, I'll be the one to go into town. You can sit up and watch over the plants.

No. You don't know where to go or what to say. I'll have to be the one to do it.

I'll bring you back your rum.

No, I'll go. You stay. I know where to go. No one bothers with me. They'll stop you.

Claude said, I know where to find the Chinaman.

He'll be with his woman, the *mambo,* his *placée,* taking all the Haitians' money by cheating them at dominoes. I'll just go in the back way and tell him his crop is fine, and I'll buy you your bottle of *clairin* and some sardines and tinned beef and come back. I won't stay all night and come back drunk in the morning like you and then have to sleep all day.

Like hell you won't, the old man grumbled. You'll get drunk, you'll find yourself a *jeunesse* and get caught by the police or beat up by the Bahamian boys. They'll find you dead on the beach in the morning. I know what happens to young boys like you. All you want is a *bousin,* a whore. You have to go to Nassau for that anyhow. They don't have any whores in Elizabeth Town.

They don't, eh?

No.

There's one.

Which?

The one above the shop. Grabow's whore, Claude said. You've heard about her, the Haitian girl he keeps there.

Yes, certainly. But that's not for you, boy. She's not for Haitians. Grabow, he keeps that girl for his friends and for the fishermen. If you walked in there and asked for the girl, he'd throw you out, if he didn't feel like turning you over to the police. Or beating on you. He's bad, that one.

Well, Claude said, no matter. I'm not going to town for a whore.

You're not going to town at all, François said.

Claude stood up and stepped out of the lean-to into the bright sunlight. Of course I am, he said. Give me the water, he said, pointing with the machete at the jug.

Slowly, the old man reached over and handed up the plastic container. Claude took it and tipped it up and drank, spilling water in glistening sheets down his bare chest and shoulders.

VANISE DID NOT HEAR HIM ENTER THE ROOM, AND WHEN SHE saw him she did not at first recognize him, for somehow in the intervening weeks his face had changed. His chin line was sharper, his features had lost a boy's softness around the cheeks and brow, and his hair had bushed out, so that he looked older, stronger, more dangerous, and for a second she thought he was a man sent up from the bar by Grabow.

As soon as she recognized him, however, she was afraid. Go away, Claude! she said. You must not be here.

He smiled. The man didn't hear me. He's drunk, out front at a table on the street, playing dominoes with friends. I came in the back way. Besides, he said, I'm not afraid of him. Claude was wearing his short-sleeved shirt and thin, tattered trousers and was barefoot. He carried his machete loosely at his side, as if it were a plaything.

They sat down on the bed and talked in whispers, Vanise asking questions, Claude telling her about the Chinaman and the marijuana fields and old François, and also telling her about the Haitians he had found living right here in Elizabeth Town and in the bush nearby, whole communities of them, he said, many of them working in the kitchens of the hotels and in private homes as gardeners and maids.

She did not seem impressed or even surprised, which disappointed him. There was even a *société* here, he told her, a *hounfor* with many *houncis* performing all the services for the loas, and although he himself had not yet been to any of the services, he said, as if apologizing, he soon would go. He wished to make an *engagement* with the loas, he explained somberly, so as to get them over to America, which he now knew was not very far from here. Every day there were boats going across to Florida with Haitians on board, boats operated by Americans who knew how to carry you over to Miami itself, where there was a whole city of Haitians living in their own houses just like Americans, with automobiles and plenty of food to eat and nice clothes to wear.

She knew about the boats, she said, and how close America was. She told him about the Jamaican, Tyrone, who worked on a boat for a white American, a fishing boat they used for carrying over Haitians, as many as ten and twenty at a time, Tyrone had told her. Tyrone's job was to round up the Haitians. The white man just drove the boat.

But it costs lots of money, she sighed. Too much.

How much?

She wasn't sure. Hundreds of dollars, however.

Claude asked her about the baby. Where was Charles?

She explained that Grabow made her sleep the boy in the storage room next door.

Claude asked her to bring him so he could visit with him.

No, no, she said. He'll wake up and maybe cry, and then Grabow will hear from downstairs and will come up and find you.

That's all right, Claude said. Are you his slave? He looked down at her carefully. She, too, had changed. It was as if the dark, hard thing, like a piece of coal, that had always been at the center of her mind had been heated with too hot a flame and had become a cinder that finally had crumbled to ash. He noticed the slight swelling and discoloration around her eyes and cheeks that he knew came from beatings, and her mouth, which used to be firm and tautly held against her teeth, seemed loose and slack, with all the old, familiar, irritated tension gone out of it, and all the force as well.

They both heard it at the same time, the clank of metal as Grabow drew down the shutters and closed the shop for the night.

Go now! Vanise whispered, her eyes suddenly wide with fear.

Claude stood and made for the door, but she stopped him with her hand. No, you can't! He sleeps in a room downstairs, he'll hear you.

Claude turned to her. Why do you stay? You can leave too, he said. Come with me.

No. I can't.

Why? What can he do? Just leave with me now, you and Charles.

He'll beat me. Or he'll do something bad to Charles,

give him over to the police so I'll never see him again. Something bad will happen! I know it!

Won't the loas protect you?

The loas are angry with me, she said. So I must stay here.

Claude grabbed her by the arm and wrenched her toward the door. Come! Wake Charles and bring him. We'll leave here together. I know a *mambo,* the Chinaman's woman. She'll help you feed the loas and make a new *engagement.* I have some money, enough for a *service.* I can pay for it.

When he pulled open the door and stepped into the dim, narrow hallway, Grabow was almost at the top of the stairs. Their eyes met for an instant. Grabow took one more step, and Claude swung the machete, slicing the man across the midsection, opening him up like a piece of fruit. The man's eyes, suddenly wild with horror, bulged and rolled, as he realized what had happened. As if he had a bellyache, he clasped his hands to his stomach, and they filled and overflowed at once with blood. He flung himself back against the wall of the corridor and stared open-mouthed at Claude, who swung again, an overhand chop across Grabow's shoulder, slicing muscle and tendon all the way through to the joint. The man's lungs instantly filled, and blood poured from his mouthful of scarlet teeth, and he went down.

Claude stared at the man's body, and with both hands raised the machete over his head, held it there, then slowly brought it down to his side. He sucked in his breath, a loud, chugging intake of air, snapped his head to the right, and almost falling, turned away from the corpse and stumbled back through the open door to Vanise's room.

She had hidden herself in the far corner behind the dresser, crouched down near the floor, and she had not seen, but she knew what had happened, and she moaned quietly.

Stop that! Claude hissed. Stop!

Slowly, she rose and faced him. He was shuddering, as if a cold wind had blown over him, and he looked like a little boy again, about to cry. Beyond him she could see Grabow's feet, like two chunks of wood. She took a step toward the door and stopped. Is he dead? she asked.

Claude could make no words. He nodded his head up and down.

Vanise took the boy's hand in hers, and still watching Grabow's feet, as if she expected them to move, she said, He's dead? You know that?

He's meat! Dead meat! he cried, and he yanked his hand away. Now, he croaked, now you can leave here!

No! No, they will find us and kill us for this! Where can we go now?

His arms at his sides, the machete still in his right hand, dripping blood onto the floor, Claude moved away from the door, as if offering it to Vanise and inviting her to step through. *America,* he said.

She placed her hands over her eyes like a blindfold, shook her head slightly and took her hands away. Then, without looking at the boy, she said, Do you know how to find this *hounfor?*

Yes.

You know the *mambo?* And you have money?

Yes. Some, a little.

We must go there, then, to the *mambo.* Wipe the machete on the bed, she instructed him calmly. I'll make up a bundle for our clothes and Charles's blanket, and I'll wake Charles. We can leave by the back door downstairs, and no one will see us, she said.

Claude nodded and obeyed.

Vanise tied some clothing in a towel and left the room for the baby. Look in his pockets, she called back. He always has plenty of money late at night. Be careful not to get any of his blood on you, she warned.

Claude stepped back to the hallway, and without looking at the man's face or his huge wounds, carefully searched Grabow's trouser pockets and came away with a fat roll of bills, which he showed to his aunt as she came out of the storage room, her half-awake child slung against her hip and her bundle grasped firmly in her other hand. She looked over coolly at the money and said, He must have won at dominoes tonight.

She dropped the bundle at Claude's feet and took the money from him and stuffed it into the front of her blouse. Carry that, she said, and she stepped with care over Grabow's legs and moved quickly into the darkness of the stairway and down. Claude picked up the bundle with his free hand and followed her.

4

A FEW MILES WEST OF ELIZABETH TOWN, THE ROAD DIPS and slants toward the sea before it makes the bend at Clifton Point and curves back along the north side of the island to Nassau, and from the road, the land on both sides seems empty, save for the dense brush that grows to the edge of the pavement. The bougainvillea, cassia trees, mahoe and annatto, a tangled weave of flower, thorn and hardwood, rise up like a hedgerow and block the human life and cultivation that go on there from the sight of passersby—tourists in rented cars, teenagers on motorbikes, policemen from Nassau in their Toyotas, air-conditioned tour buses filled with peering, pink-skinned ladies and gentlemen from the continent.

North of the road and beyond the dense underbrush, the land rises, the topsoil thins out and short, reddish pine trees take over, with occasional bayberry and myrtle oak interspersed among the pine. This area is called the Barrens, and except for the sight and roar of the jets coming in and taking off from the airport a few miles north, one could be in the wilderness. The air is usually still here, no land breeze, no sea breeze, and the sun beats down with belligerent intensity on the heads of solitary men and boys who cultivate secret marijuana patches throughout the Barrens, hauling water in barrels and buckets long distances by hand and pickup truck over rocky paths and narrow trails from as far away as Lake Killarney beyond the airport and the ponds and marshes east of Elizabeth Town.

Also here among the pine trees are small vegetable gardens planted and tended by whole families, people from the outskirts of the towns, squatters and shack people, whose lives are official secrets. They are off-islanders, most of them, illegal immigrants from Haiti, wandering foreigners whose presence on the island is officially forbidden and unofficially tolerated, for they provide a considerable part of the huge, underpaid, un-protected labor force that is required by the tourist in-dustry on New Providence. They wash the dishes, scrub the pots, clean the toilets, clip the grass and haul the trash for the managers of the enormous glass, steel and concrete hotels and casinos in Nassau and along Cable Beach and Paradise Island, working twelve-hour days and nights six and seven days a week for wages accept-able only to someone who would otherwise starve. They perform these tasks with gratitude, good cheer and alac-rity, for in Haiti, they would have no choice but to starve.

South of the road beyond Elizabeth Town and behind the thicket of small, thorny trees and bushes, the land slopes down to the sea, and set in sandy soil among the thatch palms, invisible from the road and accessible only by means of winding, overgrown trails, are crowded settlements of shacks and shanties built of driftwood and cast-off iron and plastic from the villages and towns nearby. Pigs, chickens and goats wander the sandy path-ways, skinny yellow dogs sleep in the shade and naked children play in doorways or in the yards, while idle, hungry men and women lean on the sills of open win-dows and stare out at the sea.

Usually, no more than one person in a large family, as often a woman as a man, a child as an adult, has been able to find work in the hotels, and this person with his few dollars a week supports the rest and bears their envy and their constant, malicious attempts to rob and cheat him. Often, if the person is a man, he drinks too much *clairin,* that cheap, clear, hundred-fifty-proof rum sold in bottles without labels in the village shops and kitchens, and he smokes too much marijuana, and he broods day and night on his fate, contemplating the hopelessness of his situation, until, finding himself provoked by a trivial affront, he either cuts someone with a knife or machete or is himself cut and ends up in the hospital and then in jail or ends up dead. Or else he turns to voudon and the loas, *les Invisibles* and *les Morts*, the universal spirit world from which he can draw solace and the strength of powerful allies and the sense to continue with his life.

If the person is a woman, she may not drink as much rum or smoke as much marijuana, but she, too, will brood fatalistically day and night on the difficulties of her life, its stunted, thwarted shape, and she, too, will often fall helplessly into an explosive kind of depression that can be detonated into crazed violence by an idle, careless spark, by gossip, petty thievery, a misbehaving child, a wayward man. And so she, too, in order to save herself, turns to voudon, spends her nights at the *hounfor* in prayer and song, gives herself over to the guidance of ritual and the superior, trained knowledge of a *mambo* or *houngan*, feeds the loas and lets herself be mounted by Papa Legba, Agwé, Ogoun and Erzulie, dances the congo dance and the *yanvalon dos-bas* and connects her sad, suffering moment on earth to universal time, ties the stingy ground she stands on to the huge, fecund continent of Africa, makes an impoverished, illiterate black woman's troubles the pressing concerns of the gods.

EVEN BEFORE THEY LEFT THE ROAD FOR THE ROCKY PATHway that led into the Barrens, Claude and Vanise, with Charles on her hip, heard the drums, a rapid, high-pitched, rattling sound undercut by the throb of the *assator*, the huge bass drum with the righteous voice of an ancient father. It was dark, very late now, and Claude, brushing back low branches and thorny macca bushes with his machete, led his aunt by the hand over the limestone outcroppings and roots that crossed the path.

The sound of the drums excited and comforted them, and they quickened their pace uphill through the brush to the pinewoods, where the sound traveled more easily and where they could make out the clang of the metal *ogan* and then the high, chanting voice of a *houngenikon*, the woman who leads the singing. A moon was on their left, full and snow white, the velvety, deep blue sky splashed with stars, and they could see their shadows on the ground, small, hunched-over companions running alongside them toward the sound of the drums and the singing, as urgent and thrilled and deeply lonely as they. When they rounded the top of the low, scrubby hill where the land fell away to a dark, brush-filled gorge below, they heard the hoot of a conch shell, long, trembling calls as old as the human species' desire to signal its presence to itself, as old as solitude and fear, and their chests filled with light.

Claude hurried on, scrambling down toward the darkness of the gorge; Vanise halted for a second a ways behind him. Listen, she said, and Claude stood still. The conch cried out, stopped, fluttered and cried again, a musical instrument making private speech public. It's a *service* for Agwé, Vanise whispered.

Your *mait'-tête,* Claude said.

Yes. How far now?

Not far. In the trees there, he said, pointing toward the dark end of the gorge, where two moonlit ridges came together as if clasping hands above the leafless, yellow-blossomed branches of a tall wildcotton tree surrounded by darker, denser, lower trees, almond and mahogany, that hid the ground from view. The *hounfor* is there, for the *société,* he said.

It's all right, then?

Yes. We are all from Haiti. And we have money for the *mambo* to make a *service*.

You know them, Claude?

A few . . . some. I work for the Chinaman, who knows them all. But I have not been here to the *hounfor* before. The old man told me it was here. François, who works for the Chinaman also, so, he said. He turned away and resumed descending to the gorge.

Vanise shifted her child to her other hip and followed.

There was a broad footpath at the bottom that snaked in darkness through the dense brush, and the drums and singing and the steady, warbling cries of the conch shell grew louder and sharper as they made their way over roots and stones, drawing them forward and out of themselves, until soon they were walking faster, almost running, and then suddenly they were free of the darkness and stood at the edge of a large crowd of people in a clearing, men and women and a few children, most of them dressed in white, their black faces large and open and sweating cheerfully as they chatted, danced, watched and argued and sometimes moved in and out of the dense center of the crowd, where the woodpole-and-thatch peristyle itself, the temple for Agwé, could be seen.

Several Coleman lanterns glowed phosphorus white beneath the roof of the peristyle, casting long shadows over the crowd, while the *mambo*, in a scarlet satin dress, and her assistants, young women wearing simple white dresses, passed back and forth with baskets and bowls of flowers, cakes, pigeons, bananas, yams, oranges, rice, many kinds of food and bottles of liquor, which they placed gently before the center altar, a long, canopied table covered with white cloth. Off to one side, three lean men, like athletes, worked their drums, while the *houngenikon*, a gaunt, tall, aged woman, sang and chanted, and the crowd around her picked up the songs and chants and enlarged, elaborated and amplified them, as more and more men and women emerged from the darkness and underbrush that surrounded the peristyle and joined in.

Between the centerpost of the peristyle and the altar table, a large straw mat had been laid out on the ground, and clean, white, embroidered sheets and pillows had been placed so as to make a wide bed for Agwé and his mistress Erzulie, with roses at the foot, perfume near the pillows and a pink, curling conch shell at the center. Tied to the centerpost stood a ram goat, its long, silky hair dyed indigo blue, its yellow eyes gently tranquil. At the right, beyond the altar table, where the *mambo* and her assistants brought forth the offerings to Agwé, was a large, square, boxlike structure with flat, wide-railed sides, Agwé's *barque,* a raft the size of a small room, made of wood and painted bright blue with elaborate floral decorations and *vevers* covering the sides and rails—the mermaid that signified the presence of Erzulie la Sirène, the snakes and stars for Damballah, Ogoun's crossed banners, the scarlet heart of la Maîtresse, the crab for Agassou, the fish for St. Ulrique. Set among these designs, in holes in the rail, were vases filled with cut flowers, liquors and perfumes. And arranged carefully around the edge of the *barque* itself were eight men standing two to a side, as if waiting for a signal from the *mambo,* who ignored them, passing them by as she and the young *houncis* bustled back and forth with their loaded baskets, pots and bowls.

At last they had made a huge heap of offerings before the altar, and they stopped, as if to catch their breath before commencing the next stage of the rite, while the drums kept up the steady, deep pounding and the singing went on independently, rising in pitch, tempo and volume like a tide, slowly, almost imperceptibly and quite as if it could go on rising forever, until the entire earth were covered by the sea.

The *mambo,* a full-breasted woman with high cheekbones and deep-set eyes, an attractive but fierce-looking middle-aged woman, shook her calabash rattle, the *asson,* and suddenly she was rushing about the peristyle, darting in and out of the crowd, giving orders, ringing a tiny brass bell in people's faces, moving them, organizing them, shaping the mixed, affable, passive crowd of men and women into a coherent force. The eight men by the *barque,* as one, lifted the raft from the ground to their shoulders. A number of women hefted the baskets and bowls at the foot of the altar, passed them back until they had all been taken away, and a slender, attractive woman in white untied the blue ram and led him away from the centerpole. The drummers rose, and still beating on their large instruments, began to leave the peristyle, followed by the *houngenikon,* who sang now with great joy.

The crowd parted, and the procession began, with people joining in as it passed, until the crowd had become the procession, a river of people singing and dancing, waving banners, carrying baskets of food and flowers, and the huge, brightly decorated *barque* as if it were a raft floating downstream toward the sea. Vanise and Charles and the boy Claude merged with the crowd and floated with it, as the people made their way along the pathway through the trees, down the length of the gorge between the ridges to where the ground leveled.

Soon they had departed from the Barrens, had crossed the road and were passing through a village of huts on the other side, where still more people came out and joined them. The sky had grayed slightly in the east, and a breeze off the sea drifted toward them. As the sky lightened, the palm trees went from black silhouettes against it to gray to green, when finally the crowd rounded a turn in the broad, sandy trail beyond the village and came to the sea, silvery and smooth in the dawn light. The waves lapped placidly at the spit of sand that ran out from the point, and fifty yards beyond the spit, anchored in shallow water, was the boat, a low turtler, broad-beamed, with a short, dark red, single sail.

The people sang and danced as they marched, clanging on the steel *ogan,* blowing the conch shell, the *lambi,* as if it were Gabriel's horn, beating the *assator* and the *tambour* drums with joyous fury, and when they reached the water, as if it were not there, as if there were no firmament between the firmaments, they strode on, moving directly into the sea, a black river foaming and churning down from a mountaintop to the shore and merging with the sea. Soon they were wading in chest-high water, the offerings, drums, goat, *asson* and *barque* held high as they neared the boat, and when they reached the boat, the men carrying the *barque* of Agwé steadied themselves a second and then slid it up and over the rail into the boat and clambered aboard, with the rest following helter-skelter, grabbing at rails on all sides, clinging and swinging themselves up and over, scrambling into the boat, even climbing the masts, until it seemed the boat would capsize from the load. And still there were stragglers trying to come aboard, among them Claude and Vanise and Charles. Vanise held her baby up above her head, as if he were an offering to Agwé, and a man took him from her. She reached out her hand, and another man grabbed it and hauled her aboard. Claude grabbed at the gunwale, and at that moment, someone on the other side hauled up the anchor and the boat shifted to starboard, and Claude lost his hold and fell back into the sea. Gasping, his mouth filling with salty water, flailing wildly, Claude cried out in terror, *Vanise! Oh, Vanise, moin la! Moin la!* for he could not swim, and he knew that he was supposed to drown now, because of Grabow. It was Grabow himself pulling him down and shoving the crowded boat away from his grasp, Grabow's blood-soaked hands yanking at Claude's legs, Grabow and all the Petro loas in dark concert working this poor, frightened boy down, when suddenly his hand felt human fingers, and he tightened his hand around another and looked up into the bland, calm face of the *mambo,* a sweetly organized, mother's face.

The woman pulled, and Claude came free of Grabow's grasp and scrambled over the rail of the boat and fell into a mass of arms, legs, bowls of food, drums, goat, flowers, the huge, awkward *barque*. He ended in a crouched position facing the woman who had pulled him aboard, the *mambo* in the scarlet dress. She shook her *asson* at him and demanded in a fierce voice to know who he was, where did he come from, who was his family. I do not know you, she said coldly.

Claude Dorsinville, he said. I am Claude Dorsinville. His breath came in harsh patches and grabs, and he stammered that he had come in search of her, the *mambo,* had come with his aunt and her infant. He nodded in their direction, and the woman glanced over, quickly returning her gaze to the dripping, frightened boy before her!

You want a *service,* she said, you got to pay me, boy.

Mézi lagen ou, mézi wanga ou! Your money is your charm.

I . . . I have money, Claude said, and he looked across at Vanise, who had retrieved her child and sat comfortably on the broad rail of the boat, which dipped and caught the morning wind, despite its great load, and was headed smartly across the spreading bay toward the open sea. The starboard rail, where Vanise sat with a dozen others, flashed along near the surface of the sea, sending a silvery spray into the air, blue-green jewels in the new sunlight.

Vanise! the boy called. Talk to her, and he nodded at the *mambo*. Tell her what you want! he pleaded.

Vanise looked at him as if she did not know him.

He understood. He possessed the money for the *service,* and he had promised it to her, and she was holding him to his promise. Grabow's money, the fat roll of dollars that had come from his corpse, had come from the loas. It was blood money. The money he had earned from the Chinaman, the dozen wet dollars in his pocket, was to be given back to the loas. An even exchange. It was only fair.

He reached into his pocket and drew out the crumpled, sopped bills and passed them into the woman's outstretched hand. She took the money, shoved it swiftly into her clothing, so fast he could not say where it had gone, it had simply disappeared, and she said to him, The Lord of the Sea will protect you.

No, her, he said, pointing at Vanise.

Her, then, the *mambo* said, and she moved away from Claude toward Vanise and began there to shake her *asson* over Vanise's bowed head and to pray for her. *Moin la avec asson. Asson c'est Bon Dieu qui baille li avec la foi. . . .*

The boat was now a half mile or more from land. Down in its broad-beamed belly, the *houncis* were busily loading the *barque* with offerings, arranging the food, flowers, liquors and perfumes with respectful precision, sweating under the morning sun, which had risen into a cloudless sky. The *houngenikon* sang as loudly as ever, with the energy of someone discovering her voice anew, and the drummers beat on as if they had found lost drums only a moment before, and the *mambo*, apparently finished with Vanise, stood at the mast and waved about her head a pair of white chickens held by their feet and chanted and prayed to Agwé and his mistress Erzulie la Sirène. The passengers, awash with sweat from the heat, their bodies stilled by it, nevertheless sang along with the *houngenikon*, keeping up the joyous pilgrimage despite the heat, the work and discomfort, the long hours it was taking.

Suddenly, one of the *houncis* assisting the *mambo* delicately plucked the white chickens from the upraised hand of the *mambo* and slit their throats and laid them on the *barque* below her, and at that moment, several women in the boat, one of them Vanise, were mounted by Agwé. She stiffened, her head snapped back on her spine and came as quickly forward and then slowly rose again, with her features changed, gone, replaced by the features of the Lord of the Sea, a powerful loa, dark and masculine, somber and even sad, a god who has watched too long the troubles of men and women on earth, who has seen too many bad times come back again. It was the very face of history that Agwé wore, skin tightened back to ears, lips grim and taut, eyes filled with watery understanding. There was no look of impatience and no look of patience, either: he was beyond the notion. Agwé in Vanise looked around the jammed, noisy, busy boat from one sweating black face to another, from the *mambo* to the *houncis* to the men arranging the *barque* to the sailors at the tiller and the boom, at these men and women and children from the hills of Haiti, even at the face of young Claude and his cousin Charles, and Agwé viewed them all with infinite compassion, as if for a moment a whale with a whale's understanding of life had risen from the deep to view human life and had seen humanity's busy terror, its complicated affections, its nostalgia and longing, its shame and pain and pride. Tears flowed down the face of Agwé. The people nearby said, Don't cry, oh, no, don't cry, please don't cry.

* * *

THE GOAT, BLUE AS SAPPHIRE, IS LIFTED OVERHEAD BY A PAIR of young, muscular men, and the *mambo* shakes her *asson* in the animal's yellow-eyed face, empties a vial over its indigo horns and chants, Agwé, Agwé, Lord of the Sea, protect your children. And taking a slender knife from her *hounci,* she slices open the animal's throat. Blood billows over its silky chest, and the young men extend the goat, its eyes glazing over, beyond the gunwale. Blood splashes in sheaves into the sea, and the body of the blue ram-goat follows, drawn instantly to *le zilet en bas de l'eau,* the island beneath the sea. Agwé mounts a man, several women, the drums rise in tempo and timbre, the conch shell bleats, the *houngenikon's* voice takes on strength and fairly shouts its affection and awe, and when the *mambo* signals with her bell, the young men lift to the gunwale the loaded *barque.* The boat dips, and the *barque* slides into the sea. It floats for a moment on the waters and then, as if clutched from below by a gigantic hand, is gone.

IT IS MIDDAY. THE GODS ARE PROPERLY FED. THE WIND dies, then it shifts. The boat turns, and the Haitians silently resume their separate journeys.

Selling Out

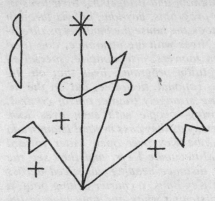

1

*Casual observers on the causeway, people in loaded
vans and station wagons with out-of-state number plates
driving the tail end of Interstate 95 south from Miami to
where the turnpike dwindles to Route 1 and stutter-steps
across the Keys to Key West, American families looking
out open car windows toward Florida Bay, suede gray
above the mud flats, greenish-blue where channels cut
intricate pathways in and around the tiny, mangrove-
covered keys that dot the bay from the causeway to the
Everglades, observers who are kids wearing Disney World
tee shirts and quarreling in back over who gets to use
the Walkman, dads and moms in Bermuda shorts, tank
tops and rubber thong sandals, sunburnt Dad, his
Budweiser hat pushed back on his head, wishing he
could take time to stop by the side of the road and fish
from the shore till dark, and Mom, with her new Ray-
Ban sunglasses on, catching her reflection in the side
mirror and turning quickly away from the aging, worried
face she sees trying to hide behind the movie-star glasses,
these people in an expensive hurry to have fun before*

heading back to their sad, workaday, clock-driven lives in Cleveland, Birmingham and Bridgeport, their lives of high-tech retraining programs, day-long prowls through suburban malls to stock the house the bank keeps threatening to take away, lives with life insurance, dog food and kitty litter, lawn mowers, orthodonture, special-ed and school-desegregation programs, lives that on the outside seem stable, rational, desirable, but on the inside persist in feeling strangely fragile, out of control, compulsive and boring—people with such lives look north from the causeway as they pass beyond Islamorada and Upper Matecumbe Key over open water toward Moray and Lower Matecumbe Keys, and they see the Belinda Blue *in the distance heading full speed across the basin from Twin Key Bank, a charter fishing boat, a converted trawler glistening white and pale blue in the midday sun, her stubby bow breaking the still water of the flats into crystalline spray, men in bill caps holding beer cans and fishing rods and chatting animatedly on the afterdeck, a tall, suntanned man in white tee shirt and captain's hat up on the bridge at the wheel bringing the boat smoothly off the basin into Indian Key Channel, and the people in the car, kids and Dad and Mom, all think the same thing: That man up there on the bridge of the fine white and blue boat should be me. I should feel the sea breeze in my hair, the sun on my arms, the flow of the boat through the soft Florida waters beneath me. I should have the rich Northern fishermen on the deck below grateful to me for my knowledge and experience and the reliability of my craft. I should be that man, who is free, who owns his own life simply because he knows whether to use live or dead shrimp for bait, jigs or flies, and where the bonefish feed, he knows where the basin narrows to a channel deep enough to bring his boat lunging in without touching its deepwater keel against the mudded bottom, he knows at sunup whether a squall will blow in from the northwest before noon, and he's been able to trade his knowledge for power and control over his own life. His knowledge is worth something. Not like the knowledge*

*we own, we who look enviously out the windows of our
cars. To us, our knowledge is worth nothing, is merely
private information, the names and histories of our family relations, our secret fears and fantasies, our person-
alities observed obliquely from the inside. We exchange
our knowledge for mere survival, while that suntanned
man in the captain's hat up on the bridge of the* Belinda
Blue—*out of Moray Key, Florida, it says on the tran-
som—that man rises above mere survival like a gull
lifting from the sea, like the thought of a poet soaring
toward the sun. Oh, Lord, wouldn't that be a wonderful
life! we think. But we do not say it, not exactly. Mom
says, "I read where all those fishermen now are smuggling drugs. Because of the recession and all." And Dad
says, "When I was a kid up in Saginaw, all I wanted was
one of those boats. Not like that one, more a cabin cruiser
type. You can buy a damned house, what one of those
things costs these days." And the kids say, "Why are we
going to Key West anyway? What's there? What'll we do
there? Why can't we go out on a fishing boat instead?"*

2

MORAY KEY, A SLENDER, HALF-MILE TUFT OF TREE-TOPPED
coral cut from the tail of Upper Matecumbe Key in 1955
by Hurricane Janet, is located on the northwest side of
where three narrow channels converge. Shell Key Channel leads northeasterly into the trout and redfish grounds
at the Everglades end of Florida Bay; the second, Race
Channel, loops off to the western end of Florida Bay,
where the bonefish and snook cruise the shallows and
huge jewfish hide in the rocky deeps; the third, Teatable
Key Channel, leads southwesterly under a Route 1 bridge
with a twenty-foot clearance at high tide to the open sea,
across Hawk's Channel to the reef and beyond, where
the bottom drops off to depths of four and six hundred
feet and rises again ten and a half nautical miles away at
the Hump, where the blue marlin lie waiting, where
tarpon, blackfin tuna and swordfish feed.

Moray Key, then, is a judicious place for Avery Boone to have begun his career as a fisherman. He studied the charts, talked long into the nights in bars in Islamorada and Marathon with the old hands, hired an experienced mate and explored the waters on his own, until he had memorized the channels, lights, reefs, currents and fishing grounds. His boat, the *Belinda Blue,* though slow and with a four-foot draft, was large and simple enough for him to take parties of four and six north into the bay, where he could fish either from the channels or, with the dinghy, on the flats; and she was enough of a deepwater boat that, once fitted with outriggers, depth sounder and fifty-channel receiver, she could be pushed as far out as the Hump and beyond. The *Belinda Blue,* however, compared to the flashy, fast, sports-fishing thorough-breds that galloped to the Hump in less than an hour and returned before noon with record-breaking marlin and swordfish aboard, was a slow mule of a boat, so Ave had quickly specialized in taking amateurs, weekend fishermen from the North, families on daily outings, into the bay, leaving the deepwater fishing, the tournaments, leaving the big money, to the men whose boats were designed for nothing else.

He didn't care. Ave was making a living now doing what he had always regarded as recreation, and he was doing it in year-round sunshine among people he liked and admired, fishermen, bartenders, small-time drug dealers, young women whose entire wardrobes consisted of string bikinis, designer jeans and men's dress shirts, people who'd never worked more than part-time or not at all but who managed to keep a little cocaine or grass around and always had enough money and time to sit up late drinking tequila sunrises and listening to Jimmy Buffet tapes.

When some Miami-based developers built a forty-unit condominium complex overlooking the marina, Ave bought a unit on the second floor, above the pool and with a view of the Clam Shack below and the boats bobbing in their slips beyond. The directors of the Marathon branch of the Florida National Bank thought he

was a good risk, and the *Belinda Blue,* appraised gener-
ously at $75,000, served as collateral. Then, one night a
few months later, he met the girl named Honduras at a
party aboard a sixty-foot sailing yacht owned by a Philadelphia dentist who spent his winters cruising the Caribbean with attractively tanned young male and female
companions he picked up in ports like Montego Bay,
Negril, Freeport and Nassau. The second Honduras saw
Ave's lean, handsome face and sandy hair, she knew his
sign was Sagittarius, and ended up staying at his new
condominium for several days, until the dentist in a
pique left for Grand Cayman without her.

She stayed on with Ave, and a week later he bought
the van, with which, as he told the directors of the bank
in Marathon, he expected to supply fresh fish from the
bay to restaurants up on Key Largo and Islamorada and
south in Marathon. At Honduras's urging, however, he
had the van carpeted and upholstered throughout and
installed a water bed and a quadraphonic stereo system,
and never carried any fish anywhere, although he and
Honduras started taking off for weekends in Miami and
out to Key West, where Honduras had a number of
friends with no visible source of income, ex-lovers and
acquaintances who hung around glossy waterfront bars
and lived in furnished apartments. Many of them played
musical instruments and had more than a passing ac-
quaintance with the technical vocabulary of the film and
recording industries, which impressed Avery Boone from
New Hampshire. He decided he was circulating on the
fringes of show business.

His life had got expensive. But soon he was learning
from his new friends how, with the *Belinda Blue* and his
knowledge of the intricate maze of channels crisscrossing Florida Bay, he could afford that life. He risked
several nighttime runs from Moray Key across to Fla-
mingo City, loaded to the gunwales with bales of Colombia marijuana taken off a Panamanian freighter a few
miles off Alligator Light, and cleared enough cash to
start thinking about buying another boat, a high-speed
31-foot Tiara 3100, maybe, with twin 205-horsepower

OMC Sea Drive engines, fitted with outriggers, a flying bridge and fighting chairs, a Loran C navigational unit and an extra fuel tank for occasional long-distance runs to places like Grand Cayman, the Bahamas, West Palm Beach, a boat that would let him fish the big tournaments from Pensacola to Nassau while someone else chugged in and out of Florida Bay in the *Belinda Blue*, lugging day-trippers and kids and dads with Christmas-present rods and reels to fish the flats, providing the business with a small but steady income and, when Ave came back in the Tiara from Grand Cayman, Nassau and West Palm Beach with plenty of cash but no fish to show for his efforts, providing a cover.

THE SECOND THE *BELINDA BLUE* TOUCHES THE PIER AT THE Moray Key Marina, Bob Dubois jumps ashore, leaving the fishermen behind him. They look up from the afterdeck, and he's gone. "Where'd the sucker go? Hey, Cap, where're you off to so fast?" They look around in confusion. What now? They've caught twenty-six fish, sea trout and redfish, had one hell of a fine morning out there on the bay, got exactly what they paid for, but they're not sure what comes next. And the fact that just as they docked at the marina the captain of the boat took off, just jumped ashore and disappeared, leaves them confused and slightly irritated.

The Jamaican mate says, "You wan' keep dese fish, mon?" He wraps the last of the rods and reels in oilcloth and lays it in the locker atop the others. "Can filet dem if you want."

There are four fishermen, friends and relations from Columbia, Missouri, partners in an insurance company. Two are sons-in-law, the older two are brothers, all four are red-faced, with fat pink bodies, loud voices. They've finished their three-day convention stay in Miami and have come out to the Keys in a rented car for a few days of "R and R," which means drinking and fishing and calculating their combined financial conquests made during the convention—a couple of real estate packages in Louisville and a chemical manufacturing company trying to get started in Arkansas. They laugh and plan and count, and they remind Bob Dubois of his brother Eddie. The ease with which they hurtle through financial abstractions brings back to Bob Eddie's hectoring lectures, his impatience and condescension, and Bob has found himself treating his clients the same way he usually ended up treating his brother, with sullenness, feigned inattention, partial deafness—as if he were out on the bay this morning for his own private amusement and the fat men in shorts, Hawaiian shirts and bill caps were keeping him from it. Naturally, since the men have hired him, his mate and the *Belinda Blue,* not vice versa, they condescend to him from an even greater height than they might otherwise, calling him "Cap" and referring to the *Belinda Blue* as "the tub," and when their lines snarl on the reels or tangle with one another, simply handing Bob or his mate the rod and reaching into the cooler for another cold Budweiser.

It's been a hard morning for Bob Dubois, then. Hard, too, for his mate, Tyrone, a knotty, dark brown Jamaican with a dense beard and finger-length dreadlocks. Tyrone is in his late thirties, has spent his entire adult life crewing for charter fishing boats on the Keys, the last three years working for Avery Boone, and it's he more than anyone else who taught Ave, and now Ave's old friend from the North, Bob Dubois, how and where to fish these waters. As a teenager, Tyrone fled a migrant work camp in the cane fields west of Miami and drifted across the Everglades and down the Keys, putting to good use everything he'd learned as a boy working for white American yachtsmen back in Port Antonio. Ave's dependence on Tyrone's knowledge, and now Bob's, is like that of the Americans back in Jamaica; it gives Tyrone power in a world in which he is otherwise powerless.

One of the sons-in-law laughs and slaps Tyrone on his bare back. "You betcha goddamn ass we want them fish, boy! We earned them suckers."

"Paid for 'em too," the other son-in-law adds.

The older men, brothers, fathers of the brides, have

stepped free of the boat and are waiting on the pier. One of them announces, "I'm gonna get me a real drink. An al-co-hol-ic beverage. See you boys over there at the restaurant," he says, and he and his brother head down the pier toward the Clam Shack.

When they reach the wobbly screened door of the place, they notice Bob a few feet away about to get into his car, and the older of the two, who wears mirror sunglasses which he no doubt fancies make him look like a state trooper, stops and hails Bob. "Hey, good buddy, you runnin' out on us?" The younger brother, eager for his drink, has continued into the restaurant.

"No," Bob says.

"Well, then, whyn't you sit down and have a drink with us. Tell us some fish stories." His glasses glint in the noonday sun. The man is portly and soft-fleshed, but he moves and makes faces like a man who thinks he is lean, hard-muscled and a little mean-tempered. Everything he says and does has a trace of sarcasm to it. " 'Course, you don't have to sit down with us if you don't want to. That ain't part of the deal."

"No. I just . . . I got to get on." Bob opens the door of his green station wagon. Four hours earlier, up on the bridge of the *Belinda Blue*, alone, bringing the boat out of the marina at dawn and breaking the still, milky waters of the bay, he was at peace, a rock of a man, smooth-grained, balanced, centered. He was in charge, he was the captain, and for a few moments he knew he'd earned that right, which only added to his pleasure at finding himself up on the bridge, the waters spread before him newly familiar, the boat an old, trusted ally and the smell of the sea in the morning breeze filling him like a particularly cheering childhood dream, a dream of flying over the cold, gray surface of the Catamount River, of leaping from the hill above the mills, the brick smokestacks and tenements, gliding across the river to the high, ancient glacial moraine on the other side, and once on the other side, still soaring, over pine trees now, toward the mountains. He'd come down here to Moray Key and after three months of hard work under

Ave's and Tyrone's tutelage, he'd made himself into a fisherman, not the best, not even as good as Ave, but good enough, which was something to admire, he knew, and every morning when he had occasion to take the *Belinda Blue* out of her slip and gunned her into the bay, he enjoyed a few moments of admiring himself. He felt like granite then, warmed by the rising sun.

Now, however, he feels crumpled and torn, papery, subject to puffs and gusts from any direction. It's no one's fault. He can't blame the man in front of him or the man's brother or the sons-in-law. They're nobody and everybody, the kind of people every man has to deal with to get through his day, just four more insensitive men, self-centered and arrogant and carrying wallets stuffed with credit cards and traveler's checks that they use to buy themselves their own kind of pleasure, a few hours at a time.

"Up to you, Cap," the man says. "You want any of them fish for yourself? My son-in-law's got your nigger gutting and filleting 'em right now. Too many for us."

"Well . . . thanks, no. You keep 'em." Now, that was stupid, he thinks, and he's grateful Elaine is not here to hear him say it. There's fifty dollars' worth of fish that's going to be tossed out, she'd say, while we buy hamburger at the A & P for two dollars a pound.

"You sure? We can't cook 'em in our motel rooms, Cap."

"No, thanks," Bob says. "I'm sick of fish."

"Are you, now? I'd say you're in the wrong business, then, Cap. What would you say?" The man swings open the door of the restaurant and takes a step inside.

"I'd say you're right," Bob answers, and he slides into his car and slams the door shut. Now, he thinks, let's hope this sonofabitch starts. He turns the key in the ignition, and the engine kicks over easily and catches. Thank Christ for something.

THE CHEVY WAGON SHUDDERS AND RATTLES SLOWLY AWAY from the marina, passes out of the parking lot and cuts behind the blond, three-story apartment building and pool, and Bob looks automatically up and sees Ave Boone standing on his tiny terrace overhead, shirtless in cut-off jeans, a cigarette in one hand, a drink in the other. Champagne-colored fiberglass drapes swell through the sliding glass doors behind Ave, and behind those drapes, Bob knows, the girl Honduras lies naked or nearly naked on the king-sized bed, her wet belly cooling under the slow-turning overhead fan. It's a little past noon, Ave and his girlfriend have been awake for maybe an hour, and they've probably fucked twice, made each other gin and tonics, smoked a couple of cigarettes and listened to a new Willie Nelson tape, and now Ave has come out for a bit of air and sunshine before he showers, shaves, dresses, has lunch at the Clam Shack and strolls down the pier to his Tiara, which he's named *Angel Blue*, after a famous movie star, he explained to Bob.

He'll hose down the decks, check the fuel tanks, and when Tyrone has finished filleting the two dozen fish caught by the insurance men from Missouri and has cleaned up the *Belinda Blue*, he and Ave will leave Moray Key, heading south by Teatable Key Channel under the bridge, southeasterly to the reef and then west, across open sea toward the Bahamas, Andros Island, Nassau. Bob has asked him why he makes these trips with only Tyrone aboard, and Ave has explained that he is "getting into gambling a little lately." He wrapped his arm around Bob's shoulder and added, "Also, pardner, I'm getting to know a lot of the big-time fishermen over there. I'm trying to get a shot on *American Sportsman*, that TV show. Maybe take Jerry Lewis or Kenny Rogers out for marlin. You got to know the right people for a shot like that. Publicity like that, pal, you're set for life."

It makes sense, as do most of Ave's easy, confident explanations of behavior that, to Bob, is often puzzling. What he, Bob Dubois, does every day of the week—take out in the *Belinda Blue* whoever will pay him for it, and when there's no one to pay him for it, hang around the marina waiting for customers, putter around the boat, clean and oil tackle, study and memorize charts, drink beer and gossip with the other idle fishermen— that makes sense. But what Avery Boone does every day of the week—sleep till noon, play with Honduras and her friends, disappear on the *Angel Blue* with Tyrone every few days for a day and a night and sometimes more—that frequently does not make sense. Not to Bob. A man likes to be able to explain the things in his life that puzzle him, because if he can't, he may have to accept his wife's explanations for them, which in this case means that Bob would have to accept Elaine's often-voiced, worried explanation of Ave's behavior. "He's in the drug business, Bob, don't you realize that? Can't you see the obvious, for heaven's sake?"

Bob lifts one hand from the steering wheel and flips a wave at Ave on the terrace above. Ave makes a signal for him to stop, and Bob brakes the car and gets out. The sun is behind Ave's head, and Bob visors his eyes with the flat of his hand. "What's up?"

"You have a party this morning?"

"Yeah. Four guys."

"How was it?"

"Okay. Buncha trout and redfish from out by Twin Key Bank."

"No bonefish?"

"They wanted stuff they could land. You know."

"Assholes."

"Yeah."

Ave takes a sip from his drink. "We gotta talk soon, Bob," he says.

"Yeah?"

"Yeah. You've been going out—what—three, four half days a week, maybe a full day now and then?"

"Yeah. Now and then."

"This time of year, we should be booked solid three weeks in advance, seven days a week."

"Yeah, I know. It's the recession, I guess," Bob says in a low voice. "The fucking Arabs."

"How're you making it, buddy?"

"What do you mean?"

"You know. Dollar-wise."

"Oh, okay," Bob says. "Fine, actually. Listen, I gotta get home. Ruthie's been sick."

"Okay, sure. We'll talk, though, right?"

"Yeah, sure. We'll talk," Bob says, and he slides back into the car, closes the door and slowly drives away, out the sandy, unpaved lane toward the highway, past the piles of steel rods and mesh, cinder blocks, sand and building materials stacked for the second condominium building. The developers from Miami have plans for a half-dozen buildings, forty apartments to a building, and a shopping center, a much improved and enlarged marina and restaurant, a nightclub, a nine-hole golf course, until the entire island has been stripped and laid out, covered over from the bay to the gulf with buildings, pavement and small plots of cropped grass kept fresh and minty green by slowly turning sprinklers.

BOB TURNS LEFT ONTO ROUTE 1, CROSSES THE BRIDGE ONTO Upper Matecumbe, and a few miles down the road, just south of Islamorada, turns right onto a bumpy dirt road not much wider than a path. He drives through clumps of shrubby saw palmetto trees and bitterbrush for a quarter mile, to a clearing near the water, where he parks his car in front of one of three rusting, flaking house trailers situated on cinder blocks in no discernible relation to one another or the landscape. All three trailers have tall, wobbly-looking rooftop television antennas with guy wires staked to the ground. Scattered around the trailers are several rusted car chassis, old tires, tossed-out kitchen appliances, children's toys and bicycles, a broken picnic table, a dinghy on sawhorses with a huge, ragged hole in it, a baby carriage with three wheels.

When Bob gets out of his car, a mangy German shepherd tied on a short rope to a cinder block under one corner of the trailer across the road stands and barks ferociously. Leaning down, Bob picks up a small chunk of coral rock and tosses it feebly in the direction of the dog, and the animal slinks back to the trailer and crawls underneath it.

A paunchy, middle-aged woman sitting on the stoop of the third trailer drawls, "Don't let ol' Horace catch you doin' like that, Bob. He'd as soon you tossed rocks at his wife instead of his dog." She's wearing a wavy ash-blond wig, a pink cotton halter, and aqua shorts that cut into the flesh of her thighs. She's smoking a cigarette and sits spread-legged, her elbows on her knees, a king-sized can of Colt 45 on the step next to her. "Hot," she says. "Ain't it."

"Yeah, for January."

"Inside, I mean. Wait'll you go in. Elaine and the girls, all of 'em, they went swimming up the beach early, so your place's been closed up all morning."

Bob thinks, That's good; he'll be alone. He can drink a cold beer, maybe make himself a sandwich and take a nap. The trailer is small, thirty-three by ten feet, with one bedroom in the back and a closet-sized cubicle off it for Bob junior, or Robbie, as they've started calling him. Bob and Elaine sleep in the living room on a convertible sofa, and from the foot of the sofa, when it's pulled into a bed, Bob can reach over the kitchen counter and open the refrigerator, turn on the propane stove, run water in the sink.

"She say when they was coming back?" Bob asks the woman, whose name is Allie Hubbell. She's divorced, makes her living selling beadwork and shell jewelry to tourist shops along the Keys, lives alone and sometimes reminds Bob of his old New Hampshire girlfriend, Doris Cleeve, although Allie is about ten years older and, according to Elaine, may be a lesbian. "Why else would a nice, attractive woman her age live like that, all alone?" Elaine said impatiently, as if offering him a self-evident truth. Lots of reasons, Bob wanted to answer, but he didn't say anything, because he was thinking of Doris Cleeve.

Bob doesn't know why Allie brings back to his mind the image of Doris, sharp memories of those brief, heated visits to her dingy, small flat above Irwin's bar in Catamount, unless it's because, to him, both women seem to be waiting for another kind of life to come to them. Their good-natured passivity pleases Bob, and he almost envies them for it, as if it were a kind of wisdom they possess. This mixture in him of pleasure and near-envy was what lay behind his sexual attraction to Doris, and it works on him as well with Allie. It's an easy attraction to resist (though he's never resisted it), for there's almost no erotic power to it, none of the deep, frightening curiosity that fed his hunger for Marguerite, none of the wonderful fear that the woman might expose him to depths and sides of himself that he does not know exist.

"No, she didn't say when she'd be back, but probably not till late, what with the heat and all. Horace give 'em a ride up," Allie says.

"Hah," Bob says. "Nice of him."

Allie smiles knowingly. "You don't hafta worry none about Horace. He talks big and makes lotsa noise when it comes to women, but that's all. Besides," she says, "you and Horace ain't in the same league. You got class, he's . . . well, you know."

"Yeah. He's the kinda guy who calls this junkyard of his a trailer park," Bob says, sweeping his hand in a half circle around him. "Some park."

Allie has removed her wig and placed it on the step next to her can of beer, where it looks like a sleeping, long-haired pet. "Thing's hot, like wearing one of them ski hats." Her hair is cut short, is straight and black, streaked with gray.

"You got good hair, Allie. You oughta let people see it."

"Think so?" She brushes the nape of her neck with one hand, reaches for the beer with the other. "Makes me look older'n I already am, is what I think."

"Naw. Makes you look more sophisticated."

"Think so, eh? Sophisticated."

"Oh, yeah," Bob says, backing away from his door and stepping to the ground. "Horace and his wife around?" he asks, peering over at the battered, junk-crowded trailer across the lane. The dog has crawled out from under the trailer again, and with his snout between his front paws, watches Bob carefully. The air is still, and the saw palmetto trees droop in the heat. Beyond Allie's trailer, the pale limestone ledge of the key drops off directly into the water, where, from the shore to nearly a quarter mile out, coral heads emerge at low tide, dripping and alive with sea urchins and hermit crabs. The tide is coming in now, but the water rises slowly, without waves, like a bathtub being filled, and one by one the dark clumps of coral get swallowed by a tepid, dark green sea. In the distance along the southern horizon, gray-topped cumulus clouds heap up against the sky and promise rain by nightfall.

Allie flicks her cigarette butt onto the sand in front of her, then runs her fingers through her short hair, loosening and lifting it. "No, they both went out this morning, when Horace give your wife and kids a ride to the beach. Ain't nobody here but us chick-ens."

Bob has crossed the lane from his trailer and has approached to within a few feet of Allie, when he stops short, crosses his arms over his chest and says, "You remind me of an old girlfriend of mine. A real nice woman, she was. Probably still is."

"That so? From up north?"

"Yeah. New Hampshire."

"Your wife know about her, this woman you're comparing me to, this old girlfriend of yours?"

"No, she never knew. It wasn't a real big thing anyhow."

"But you're telling me about her now. Because I remind you of her." Allie has large, sad, dark blue eyes that turn down at the corners, a narrow-browed Irish face with tight mouth, longjaw, pale skin. "Did she look like me, or what?"

"No, nothing like you at all. I don't know, it's just something about the way you talk, how you're so relaxed and easy, maybe. Actually, you're both kind of sexy in the same way," he blurts. "It's hard to describe," he adds, almost as an apology, wondering suddenly if she is in fact, as Elaine wants to believe she is, a lesbian, wondering if therefore she finds his compliments offensive, because after all, he tells himself, he's not propositioning her or anything, he's not asking her to fuck him, he's just complimenting her, that's all, which he is sure doesn't happen to her every day, since she's not what most men would ordinarily think of as attractive or sexy. Still, to him, she is sexy. So why not tell her so? Even if she *is* a lesbian. Hell, it's better that way; it's *better* if she's a lesbian.

Allie's eyes are wide open now, her breathing is tight and quick, and leaning forward toward Bob, her hands clasped to her knees, she says, "Well, I think you're pretty sexy yourself, mister. If you want to know the truth."

"You do?" Bob smiles.

Allie stands up and looks around the yard with care, at the faded gray trailer next to hers, over at Bob's salt-pitted, lemon-yellow trailer, into the trees and shrubs and out along the sandy lane. A pair of egrets with gray bodies and rust-colored heads and serpentine necks, eyes like agates, legs like bamboo stalks, stroll watchfully along the shore. Allie says, "You want to come inside, Bob?"

"What?"

"You want to come inside awhile? With me?"

Suddenly he understands what he's done, and at first he's ashamed of himself. He's not surprised, however, by anything that's happened, by anything he's said or she's said, and he's not surprised that now she's inviting him inside so he can fuck her. But he feels the way he did an hour ago, when he brought in the *Belinda Blue* and ran for his car, though he cannot fully explain to himself why he feels that way—like a liar and a fool, a man who has ruined his own life and has no one to blame but himself.

A moment before, talking to Allie about Doris Cleeve, flirting a little, sure, and curious, he'd felt good, a normal man chatting up the woman across the way, nothing serious, nothing dangerous to either of them, certainly nothing cruel. But now he's got to say no to her, and he's never said no to a woman before. He asked for something, and now he's received it, and it's turned out to be undesirable to him. The problem lies in asking in the first place, he suddenly realizes. Not that he can't imagine fucking Allie Hubbell; he could do it if he had to. But he knows, perhaps for the first time in his life, that he's supposed to *want* to fuck her, and her in particular. Jesus, he thinks, if you can control what a man wants, you can control everything he does. "Listen, Allie, I . . . I'm really sorry. I better go on home, okay?" He turns and steps away, looking back over his shoulder, as if a little afraid of her.

"Yeah," she says. "See you later." She sits back down on the stoop, places her elbows on her knees again and watches Bob make his retreat.

3

IT'S HOT AND STUFFY INSIDE THE TRAILER, AND IN BOB'S dream he's aboard an airplane, a long, narrow commercial jet. He's seated alone, somewhere near the middle, with seats on both sides, and the interior of the plane is hot and moist, almost as if he were underwater. He struggles with the overhead controls, trying to turn on the fan, but nothing happens, and he gives up. There's no evidence of a crew, no attendants and no other passengers. He's waiting for takeoff, he knows, though there's no reason he should know this, no particular indications of it. He looks out the rain-obscured window along the wing to the engines, which are silent, cold. Suddenly it comes to him—everyone's abandoned this plane for another, the crew, the attendants, all the other passengers. This plane has mechanical problems, faulty wiring, a fuel leak, trouble with the hydraulic systems, and in fact it may blow up any second. No wonder they swapped it for another. He smells smoke. Sweating, terrified, he struggles to get out of his seat, to flee the plane and join the others. But he can't get out of his seat. It holds him down, hugs him around the waist, where he's clamped by a seat belt. He laughs at his own stupidity and unhooks the seat belt, tries to rise, but as before, he can't move. The smell of smoke is stronger now, almost like burned wiring. He knows the plane is about to explode. He wrestles the belt loose a second time and lurches away from his seat, but he still can't get free of it. He calls out for help, *Help! Help!* He fiddles with the belt buckle, twists and yanks at it, zips down his fly, feels his penis, a prick, erect, large, and a flash of pride and relief passes through him, when he remembers that he's got to forget his prick, he's got to get out of this plane before it explodes and tears him into a thousand bits of flesh and bone. He lets go of his penis, pats it back into his underpants and zips up his fly. Calmly, rationally, he unlocks the seat belt, and it comes free. The smoke and heat are now dense, heavy, dark, and he gropes his way forward, feeling his way along the aisle between the seats, when he is aware that, as he passes each row of seats, he's patting people on the shoulder, a man, a woman, another man, all of them dressed in Sunday suits and dresses, the men with neckties, the women with hats. He's in church, St. Peter's in Catamount, and it's a funeral service. He sees the white coffin in front of the altar, the lid raised, and as he nears, he knows that he will look in, and he'll see his mother's face, her dead face. He can't imagine what she will look like. He did not look into the coffin when they had the funeral in Catamount, though he pretended to. He just dipped his head and kept his eyes closed. But this time he will look, as he's very curious now, and also he knows that everyone wants him to look—his brother Eddie, who wasn't afraid of looking, and his father, who died the year before his mother did but was given a closed-casket service, closed because of his wife's wishes, for she insisted she did not want her memory of the man alive tainted by the sight of him dead. Elaine wants him to look into the coffin too. She's right behind him in line, prodding him, nudging him on, saying, Go on, Bob, you can do it. You *should* do it. He smells smoke again, a foul, acidic smell, an electrical fire somewhere, he knows, probably in the coffin, in the wiring of his mother's body, put there by the undertakers, the Webb Brothers that Eddie insisted on hiring for the job. *Fire!* he shouts, and he grabs at the font to the right of the coffin, lifts it and empties the water into the coffin, pours holy water over the maze of smoldering wires and wheels, cables, shafts and belts, putting out the fire and saving everyone on the plane. His father comes forward and pats him on the shoulder. Good work, Bob, he says in his gruff voice. Eddie comes up behind him and catches him by the elbow. Way to go, kid. Way to go. Elaine and the girls and little Robbie look up at him from their seats, their eyes wide with love and gratitude, their small, delicate bodies strapped tightly into their seats. There's still a foul, wet, smoky smell coming from the coffin, and Bob reaches out and brings down the top of the coffin with a bang.

Elaine is home, and the screened door slaps shut behind her, opens again and slams as each of the girls follows her inside. "Oh, Jesus, Bob!" Elaine cries. "You left the stove on!" She rushes to the stove, grabs at a smoking pan, yelps in pain, snatches a potholder and takes the pan off the stove. She tosses it into the sink and turns on the water, shouting to the girls, "Open the windows! Get the windows open!" The pan hisses and smolders in the sink, while Emma and Ruthie race through the trailer opening windows. Elaine turns off the stove, shifts the baby around from her hip, where he's been riding, terrified and silent, and begins to comfort him. "There, there, honey, everything's okay now, everything's okay."

Then the girls are back, Ruthie sucking intently on her thumb, her younger sister prowling through the refrigerator. "I'm hungry, Mama. I want somethin' t' eat," she whines. Ruthie stands off to one side of Bob, works her thumb and drifts into a dreamy-eyed state that in recent weeks has come to be characteristic, though Bob has not seen that yet. To him, her thumb-sucking and dazed expression and silence are merely embarrassing and somewhat irritating, and he treats her behavior as if she were doing these things on purpose, just to antagonize him.

Elaine says quietly, "Ruthie, please, take your thumb out." Then, to Bob, who has swung his legs off the couch, planted his feet on the linoleum-covered floor and squared to face her: "You could die that way, Bob, falling asleep with a pan on the stove. Asphyxiated in your sleep. It's lucky I came home when I did. . . ."

"I forgot. I was warming up some hash, you know? And I was tired, so I just lay down for a minute, and then, pop, I was gone."

"You got up early," she says, wiping off the baby's mouth with her fingertips.

"I get up early every day. I don't know why I'm so tired lately, though." He stretches and yawns, as if to back his claim.

"It's not like you're overworked," she says, adjusting Robbie's diaper.

"What the fuck's that supposed to mean?"

"Nothing."

"No, what the fuck's that supposed to mean?"

"Nothing, nothing."

"Sure."

"It's just that the 'fishing business' is not exactly booming these days." She always says it that way, with quotes around the phrase, and Bob cringes when she utters the words, as if she were drawing her fingernails across a blackboard. He knows what she means, knows that she fully intends for him to cringe and feel guilty, she desires it, because she's angry at him, she's angry for his having quit the job at Eddie's liquor store and joining up with Ave, for having sold their mobile home and put the money into the *Belinda Blue,* buying 25 percent of the boat and splitting profits and costs with Ave, three parts to Ave, one part to Bob, though, as Ave says, anytime Bob wants, he can buy the whole thing and keep all the profits, which, Elaine knows, would not get them out of this ramshackle trailer at the end of a dirt road at the edge of a tiny town filled with tourists and fishermen. She is angry, and she has long days and nights when she is depressed. She is lonely, overworked, without money, she hasn't lost the weight she gained during the pregnancy, and both she and Bob know that everything, all of it, is Bob's fault.

His tee shirt is sopping wet, and his hair is plastered against his head. "We all oughta go out on the boat," he announces. "You know? Just go out for the rest of the day and fish a little and cool off, like we used to, the whole family. Remember those trips we used to take up to Sunapee in the whaler? What do you say, honey?"

"Not interested." She gets up, walks past him with Robbie and disappears behind him, returning a few seconds later without the baby. "He should sleep till supper now. He took a lot of sun," she says to no one in particular, as she begins trying to clean out the burned pan. "I don't think I can save this. . . ."

"How come you're not interested in us going out on the boat for the afternoon? This is more fun?" Bob asks. He spreads his arms and peers around at the dim interior of the tiny trailer. In a corner of the crowded living room, Ruthie and Emma are seated on plastic mesh folding chairs in front of the television set that Eddie gave them a year ago, watching a soap opera, *General Hospital*.

"Tell you what," Elaine says, not looking up. "You take the kids out for the afternoon."

"What?"

"Yeah, you go out on the boat. Leave me here for the afternoon, alone."

"Wha . . . ?"

"You watch out Emma doesn't fall overboard and drown, though," she goes on. "And keep Ruthie from getting too much sunburn, and change Robbie's diapers and make sure he gets his bottle on time. You be the one to make sure the kids don't stick themselves with fishhooks. You do that, and I'll take a cool shower, read a magazine, sit out by the water and watch the seagulls. How's that sound?"

"C'mon, Elaine. I mean, I got to run the boat, you know that. I mean, I can't run the boat and watch the

kids at the same time. We should all go out together,"
he says. Why does she always have to make these things
complicated? Why can't she just say, "Fine, let's go,"
or "No, thanks, I'm too tired," or something? It should
be that simple. Instead, she's coming on all sarcastic,
suggesting absurd, impossible alternatives, and Bob is
feeling guilty.

He stands and walks to the screened door and looks
out at the yard, sand with bits and patches of witchgrass
scattered through it. Across the road, Allie is still seated
on her stoop, smoking cigarettes and drinking beer. She's
got her wig on again, and it makes her look younger, just
as she said. Bob thinks, I should have gone ahead and
fucked her. Then he thinks, It's a good thing I didn't. I
could've, but I didn't, and he walks to the refrigerator
for a beer.

"I'm just trying to come up with something to make
you and the kids happy," he says. "That's all I'm doing.
It's not like I'm trying to think of ways to make you
more miserable than you already are. So for Christ's
sake, please stop acting like I'm some kind of bastard,
will you?"

She scrubs furiously at the blackened pan, her face
twisted and red and sweating from the effort. "God
damn. You really ruined this pan."

"The hell with it. Throw it out." He pops the top of
the can of Schlitz and takes a long gulp.

"Sure, I'll throw it out. Just like everything else when
it breaks or won't work anymore. Only we can't afford
to replace anything now when we throw them out, so
after a while there won't be anything to throw out," she
says. Frantically, she scrubs at the pan in the sink.
"Just toss it out with the garbage! Easy! Except that
next time I want a saucepan to cook supper in or maybe
just to heat up the baby's bottle, I won't have any!"

Bob moves away from her, backs to the door, pushes
it open with one hand and steps outside. "I'll be back in
a while," he says softly.

"Fine."

"Anything you want in Islamorada?"

"Nope. Nothing."

"Thought I'd buy me a dip net for shrimp. The shrimp're running out by the bridge. All you got to do is stand there and scoop 'em up. Maybe I'll get nets for all of us, you know? So we can go out there on the bridge below Moray Key after dark tonight."

"Fine."

"You kids want to come up to Islamorada with me?" he calls.

They don't answer. Ruthie leans forward and turns up the volume on the television.

"Hey, I'll buy you a new pan," Bob says to Elaine. "Ave's got a charge at the tackle shop up there, and they got pots and pans and stuff like that."

She stops scrubbing for a second and stares at him outside in the yard a few feet beyond the door. He's still a large man to her, muscular and brown and kindly-looking, a bearish man. His face is open and sad and confused. "Bob," she says in a low, even voice. "You still have to pay for it. You can charge your shrimp nets and your pots and pans or anything you want, but you still have to pay for it."

"Yeah, I know, I know. Things'll pick up soon," he says. "I promise." He turns abruptly, walks to his car and gets in, finishes off the beer and tosses the empty can onto the floor. Starting the engine, he looks over at Allie Hubbell and raises his hand in a short wave.

Allie grabs her can of beer, takes a sip, replaces it at her side. She doesn't wave back.

Bob drops the car into gear and moves slowly away from the trailer, turns around in Horace's driveway, causing the German shepherd to come barking out from under the trailer, and leaves.

4

THE DREAM BOTHERS BOB. IT FEELS LIKE A RASH ACROSS his belly beneath his shirt, so that he rubs against it when he least expects to, in the car idling at a stop sign as he emerges from the road and prepares to turn north on Route 1, at the roadside grocery store where he stops to pick up another can of Schlitz, out on the highway again, when he looks to his right and sees rain clouds rolling up in the southeast.

He remembers not so much the dream as the emotions it carried, conflicting emotions that Bob can't imagine resolved: shame and pride; solitude, desertion, being left behind—a child's horrified view of these conditions—and social acceptance, the security of rite and family affection; fear of death, pure terror of it, and an uncontrollable longing to confront it, an obsessive curiosity, almost. The images come and go—his mother's hands crossed on her chest in the coffin, his father's glad hand clapped on his suited shoulder, Elaine nudging him from behind, saying, Go on, Bob, you can do it, you *should* do it, and the abandoned, sweltering airplane, the smoke, the holy water from the font splashing into the coffin. But somehow the images from the dream are mixed with his memories of the actual people and events they shadow. He remembers the spring night his father came home after work at the tannery and sat in his easy chair and picked up the *Catamount Patriot* and saw a picture of his son and discovered that Bob had been selected to the all-state high school hockey team, just as Eddie had been the year before. The local sportswriter had coined the phrase "The Granite Skates" for Bob and Eddie when they had played together that year, and the headline read: SECOND GRANITE SKATE ALL-STATE ICEMAN. His father said nothing to commemorate the event, Bob now recalls. He ignored it completely, until finally at supper Bob asked him if he'd seen the paper yet, and the man nodded and smiled across the table, and Bob smiled back. That was all. Eddie was gone by then—had been working ten months at Thom McAn's, had his own apartment on Depot Street above Irwin's bar and in a year would leave for Florida—or there might have been an animated, prideful discussion of the award, back-slapping and jokes, fantasies and teasing, which would have left Bob feeling sated instead of somehow disappointed and then embarrassed by his disappointment, even ashamed of it.

In everything his father did and said, there seemed to be one lesson: life is grudging in what it gives, so take whatever it gives as if that's all you're ever going to get. A dog finding a tossed-out bone doesn't celebrate; it simply sets to gnawing, before the bone gets yanked away. Bob knew his father had a secret, fantasied version of things that was different, that often, after everyone had gone to bed, he'd sit in the living room half-drunk, playing "Destiny's Darling" on the phonograph, but that was the man's weakness, not his strength. Bob understood his father's weakness; it was his strength that left him confused.

His mother he viewed as all weakness, all fantasy and delusion, a vessel filled with a resigned optimism that she used to make her passivity and helplessness coherent to herself. There was, of course, God's will, and, too, there was a blessedness, a magical election, that she believed her sons possessed—at least until incontrovertible evidence proved otherwise, and even then, there was always the possibility that God had long-range plans that just hadn't been revealed yet. She knew her boys were destined to be rich and famous, and she suspected that one of the reasons (there were doubtless many) God had made her poor and obscure was to help make her sons rich and famous, a kind of trade-off. In the end, she treated Bob's and Eddie's few accomplishments and honors exactly as her husband treated them, as if they were to be expected. She would smile and nod approvingly, as if to say, See, God's looking after you, just like I said He would.

Neither parent, then, treated the boys' futures as something the boys themselves had any control over. And when you come right down to it, Bob thinks, as he drives north on Route 1 into Islamorada, they were both right. That's what Eddie's finding out, and because it's coming late, it's coming hard. He's been lucky, that's all, which is the basic difference between his life so far and mine, Bob decides. It's not intelligence or hard work or courage. It's luck. And luck can't last a lifetime, unless you die young.

ON THE NORTH SIDE OF ISLAMORADA, A HALF MILE BEFORE the bridge that crosses to Windley Key, Bob turns off at the Whale Harbor Tackle Shop, a long, low building on the bay that's more a general store than a tackle shop, with a marina and boatyard behind it. There are only a few cars in the lot, and Bob parks deliberately behind a white Chrysler convertible with the top down. He gets out of his car and strolls around it and for a few seconds admires the Chrysler, standing next to it while he finishes off the can of Schlitz, rubbing his tee-shirted belly and examining the rolled and pleated red leather upholstery, which smells like nothing but itself and reminds Bob of polished wood, Irish tweed, gleaming brass. Glancing at his own face in the tear-shaped outside mirror, Bob suddenly sees himself as he must look from inside the store, a man in work clothes guzzling beer and drooling over someone else's luck. Abruptly, he turns and heads inside, pitching the empty can into the trash barrel by the door as he enters.

He wishes he'd taken his captain's hat with him when he left home, as he believes he's treated with more respect here with the properly crumpled captain's hat on his head than he is without it. The hat ordinarily embarrasses him, especially when he's not running the *Belinda Blue,* and off the boat he usually bends it and stuffs it into his back pocket. The hat had been sort of a joke anyhow, a present given to him by Ave one night over beers at the Clam Shack after Bob had gotten his commercial license. He sensed that somehow Ave was mocking him with the hat, or maybe Honduras was, he couldn't be sure, so he accepted it with mixed feelings and wore it reluctantly after that, as if it were merely and strictly part of the uniform that men with his job were supposed to wear.

Inside, beyond the high rows of canned goods, picnic supplies, beachware, past the racks of suntan lotion, the beer and soft drink coolers and the bins and shelves of household goods, Bob passes over into the serious side of the store, the tackle shop, where on both sides of a long glass counter there are pyramids and cones of fishing rods, shelves and tall displays of hand-tied flies, plugs, jiggers and lures, line, weights, knives and reels, with repair equipment and worktables behind the counter and huge color photographs on the walls of record-breaking marlin, tuna and bonefish, game fish held up dead to the camera by their captors.

Behind the cash register at the far end of the counter, a tall, thick-bodied man, taller and thicker than Bob, is talking with great force to the balding man who runs the place, a wiry, pale-faced man in his forties nicknamed Tippy, as if he were a Keys "character," an old conch, which does not suit him at all, for he is an essentially humorless, shrewd businessman who by his looks and manner could as easily be running a lumberyard in Toledo as this place. The tall man talking to Tippy, lecturing him, it seems, looks familiar to Bob, though all he can see of him is the back of his sandy-gray head, his broad back, tanned neck and arms. Tippy is listening intently, nodding in agreement, while the man plows on, gesturing with his hands, his low, slightly nasal voice rising and falling rhythmically with his hands. The man is wearing a white bill cap and aviator sunglasses, a white polo shirt that's old and baggy enough to surround his ample stomach without pointing to it, floppy GI-style work pants with huge pockets, and smudged white tennis shoes.

Instantly, Bob decides that this is the man who owns the Chrysler convertible outside. Though there are a half-dozen others in the store who also might be said to own the car, it's only this man, at least as far as Bob Dubois is concerned, who is capable of owning it, who deserves to own it. If that white car in the lot is Bob's idea of a proper grownup's car, then this man in front of him is his idea of a proper grownup.

For years, Bob was one of those people who believe that there are two kinds of people, children and adults, and that they are like two different species. Then, when he himself became an adult and learned that the child in him had not only refused to die or disappear, but in fact seemed to be refusing to let the adult have his way, and when he saw that was true not only of him but of everyone else he knew as well—his wife, his brother, his friends, even his own mother and father—Bob reluctantly, sadly, with increasing loneliness, came to believe that there are no such things as adults after all, only children who try and usually fail to imitate adults. People are more or less adult-like, that's all.

Except, that is, for the man in front of him. For the first time since he himself was a child, Bob Dubois believes that he is looking at a full-fledged adult, and it's as if he has stumbled onto a saint or an angel right here in the Whale Harbor Tackle Shop in Islamorada, Florida, a saint having an animated discussion with sober, businesslike Tippy—no, not really a discussion, because the saint's doing all the talking. Tippy just nods and listens and nods again, and it's as if the saint is telling Tippy how the world looks from his miraculously elevated position.

The saint swings his arms in tandem, clearly explaining a particular kind of cast, low, close to the water, snaking the line in under mangrove roots for bonefish. His large, gray-haired head and deeply tanned face seem to have an aura swirling around them as he speaks, as if he were either not really present or were more profoundly present than anyone else. His size, larger than a large man's, and the swiftness of his gestures, the pure, muscular clarity of his motions and his crisp, good-humored, rapid-fire speech—everything about him that Bob can see and hear manifests the kind of superiority and self-assurance that only saints, or what Bob used to think of as adults, possess.

Bob moves a few feet closer along the counter, so he can hear what Tippy is privileged to hear. The saint glances to his left, sees Bob and goes on talking as if he has not seen Bob at all. Filled with wonder, afraid he will cry out, Bob says to himself, hopes he says it only to himself, for he cannot be sure, My God, it's Ted Williams!

Ted Williams turns to him. Bob *has* said it aloud. "I'm . . . I'm didn't mean interrupt . . ." Bob stumbles. His tongue feels like a hand, his hands like tongues.

Tippy looks at Bob as if he's just discovered a counterfeit bill in the cash register. "Want help, mister?" he asks, folding his arms over his chest to make it clear that his question is only a question, not an offer.

Ted Williams peers down through the glass counter at the black and silver reels on the shelf and seems to be examining them for flaws rather than for possible purchase. He purses his lips and falls to whistling a tuneless tune.

Bob says, "I'm sorry . . . I mean, excuse me, but you're Ted Williams, and . . . I didn't mean to interrupt . . ."

Ted Williams looks up from the reels, casts a quick glance at Bob and nods, just a swift, impersonal dip and tug of his massive head, and returns to the reels, waiting, obviously, for Bob to get his business done and move away.

But Bob takes a step closer. "Mr. Williams, I'm from New Hampshire. The Red Sox . . . I'm a Red Sox . . . I mean, I love the Red Sox, Mr. Williams, since I'm a boy. And my father, him too, he loved the Red Sox, we all did. My father, he . . . he saw you play, down in Fenway, he's dead now, he told me about it, and I saw you on television, when I was a kid, you know. . . ." Bob's mouth is dry, and he's gulping for air. What's the matter with me? This is crazy, he thinks. He's only a man, just a human being like the rest of us. Visions of his father flood Bob's mind, and he feels his eyes fill, and suddenly he's afraid that he's going to start weeping right here in front of Ted Williams. What's happening to me? He clamps both hands onto the counter and steadies himself. He asks it again, What's happening to me? And he sees his father's face, sad and pinched, a cigarette held between his teeth, his lips pulled back as if in a snarl, while the man tightens the nuts on the front wheel of Bob's bicycle. Bob says to Ted Williams, "My father wanted me to see you play, but he couldn't. I couldn't, I mean. I miss my father a lot, you know? I . . . I know it sounds foolish, but . . . well, that's all," he says, stopping himself. "I'm sorry, Mr. Williams."

Ted Williams, without looking up, says, "No problem."

Suddenly, Bob is running from the store in flight, bumping customers and knocking over displays, as if he's stolen something. Outside, the sky is dark and low, and rain is pouring down. Bob splashes through puddles to his car, and when he gets in, discovers that he left the windows open. The seats are soaked. When he leans over and cranks up the window on the passenger's side, he sees a small, white-haired woman inside the Chrysler convertible, her face angry and impatient as she draws the top down against the windshield bar and wrenches it closed.

Slowly, Bob closes the window next to him. He lays his head against the wet seat back and shuts his eyes. "Oh, Jesus," he says. "Why, why, why? What's the answer?" He watches his breath cloud over the windshield and window glass, while the rain pours down outside. When he can no longer see the world outside the car, he closes his eyes again and rests, like an animal momentarily hidden from its pursuers.

5

ELAINE ASKS OVER HER SHOULDER FROM THE STOVE, "YOU get what you wanted?"

The girls, still posted in front of the television set, are watching a puppet who lives in a garbage can holler at a man in a bird suit. Bob takes up a position at the kitchen counter on the living room side and leans over it as if it were a fence. "I just saw Ted Williams," he announces.

"Oh. Did you get what you wanted? You know, the nets for the shrimp. I managed to save the pan. Shrimp would be nice. A change."

"Yeah. I mean, no, I . . . I guess I got so excited and

all, seeing Ted Williams like that, alive. You know? Ted Williams! I mean, I knew he was alive, and I knew he had a place around here, in Islamorada, but I never expected to actually walk up on him like that. It's really amazing to me. You probably can't understand that.''

"No," she says in a flat voice, and it's clear to Bob that she doesn't want to, either.

But he goes on. "Ted Williams is like a god to me, ever since I was a kid. My father took me once to Fenway Park down in Boston, and it was really to see Ted Williams play. He was old then, Ted Williams, I mean, not my father, and about to retire. Old for a ballplayer. Anyhow, we got there and got seats out behind the third baseline so we could see him better. He played left field. And then it turned out he didn't play that day, I think they put Yastrzemski in, who was only a kid then, just come up from Pawtucket or someplace. Williams was sick or something. My father, he was more pissed off than I was, I think, and he bitched and moaned about it all the way home, and that was the only time we ever went to a ball game together. Whenever I asked to go again, he'd say, 'Remember last time we drove all the way down to Boston and Williams didn't even play.' And then, the next year, I think it was, Williams retired, and from then on left field belonged to Yaz. I really should've gotten Yaz's autograph last spring up in Winter Haven. Actually, I should've gotten Ted Williams' autograph today. . . .''

"Bob," Elaine says, interrupting him. "We have to talk." She turns and faces him, holding a wooden spoon in her hand as if about to wave it at him to make her point.

"Yeah?" He whips out his cigarettes and lights one, and his hands are trembling. "Everybody seems to want to have a fucking talk with me these days." Then, without his knowing how or why, his voice has changed pitch and tone, and he's shouting at her. "Ave wants to talk to me! You want to talk to me! Anybody else around here wants to talk to me?" he barks, turning to the children, who look up startled, confused.

"Bob, for heaven's sake . . ."

"I can't even come in here and get a little excited about seeing my goddamned childhood hero, a man who's a fucking god to me, without you bringing me down for it!"

"All I said was . . ."

"All you said was, 'I want to have a talk with you,' in that damned accusing way of yours, as if I was a fucking little kid, like you're going to tell me what's what and how it's all my fault! I *know* already what you got to say to me."

She folds her arms over her breasts. "What, then? You tell me."

"I know. I know."

"What?"

He spins and walks toward the door, stops, and without looking at her, says, "You want to tell me what I already know. You want to tell me what shit this all is. *Shit*. This . . . this whole damned life."

"Is it? You feel that way about it?"

He remains silent for a second. "Yeah. It's shit. All of it, shit, shit, shit. And now you want to tell me how it's all my fault," he says in a low, cold voice. "You like doing that, telling me how it's all my fault."

"Is it?"

"No! No, goddamn it! It's *not* all my fault!" He's bellowing again, glaring at her from the door. "It's shit, all right, but it's not my fault!"

"Bob, the girls! Please! You'll wake the baby."

"Send 'em outside. We'll get this settled now, once and for all, dammit!"

"Send them outside yourself," she answers. "They're your children too, remember."

"Ruthie, Emma! Get outside for a while and play in the yard or something. Me and Mommy got to talk about something private."

The girls whine and argue that the show's not over yet, they don't want to go outside, it's raining. They turn back to the screen, and Ruthie slides her thumb into her mouth.

"Take your damned thumb out of your mouth!" Bob shouts. "And get the hell outside when I tell you to! It's not raining now."

Quickly, they obey, careful not to touch him as they pass him at the door.

Elaine turns down the burner on the stove and sits heavily at the kitchen table. She crosses her legs and lights a cigarette, waiting. "Well?"

"Well what?"

"Whose fault is it?"

"How the fuck should I know? I'm not a genius. You think you know, though. You're the fucking genius. You think it's all *my* fault because we're broke all the time and living like niggers in a shack in the middle of no-where, eating goddamned macaroni and cheese out of a goddamned no-name box." He looks scornfully over at the saucepan on the stove. "You could use a little more imagination, you know. You didn't show much interest when I brought up getting some shrimp tonight. I could've gotten ten or fifteen pounds of shrimp easy, the way they're running, and we could freeze what we didn't eat right off, or we could sell some. The catwalks along the bridges are crowded these nights with people using a little imagination."

"You forgot to get the nets," she says, "because you saw an old retired baseball player."

"Well, you didn't want me to go out shrimping any-how. All you do is bring me down about things I get excited about. You, you never get excited about any-thing anymore. All you do is mope around here with a long face." He crosses to the television set and snaps it off. "I hate that fucking thing!"

"Bob, you can't hear yourself, or you'd shut up. Can you listen to me for a minute?"

"Gimme a beer."

Elaine gets up and opens the refrigerator and passes a can of Schlitz over the counter, as if she were a waitress and he a customer. Then she stands at the counter, both hands grasping the edge of it, and says to him, "Now, you listen to me for a few minutes. I know you're working hard, as hard as anyone can. And I know you're worried and scared. Like I am. And you're right, it's true, this life is *shit*," she says, and the word "shit," because he's never heard her say it before, sounds to Bob so powerfully derogatory in her mouth that he shudders. To Bob, Elaine has made the term suddenly so strong that he instinctively wants to defend this life, his life, against it. But he's too late. He has said it himself, and now, with her saying it, he sees the word and his life as one thing, as waste, excrement, offal, as a secret, dirty thing that should be hidden or buried, as a thing to be ashamed of.

His mind is flitting wildly about, a maddened bird in a cage, pursued by a word that repels him but that cannot be denied, and he hears only bits of what Elaine is telling him, for, having no sense of the impact of her use of the word, believing she was merely quoting him, reassuring him, she thought, Elaine goes on to tell him what she knows he does not want to hear. She tells him that their daughter Ruthie is ill, "emotionally disturbed," the counselor at school said, and that she's going to have to start getting twice weekly treatment at the mental health clinic in Marathon, which will cost money, not a lot of money, but because they're poor, more money than they have, which is no money at all, so she, Elaine, has decided to take a job in Islamorada. In fact, she accepted the job this morning, waiting on tables at the Rusty Scupper five nights a week. "I know," she says rapidly, trying to stave off the explosion, "I know I should've talked it out with you first, but it had to be done, Bob, and I just saw the sign this morning when I took the girls to the beach. . . . No, that's not true. I asked Horace next door if he knew of any jobs, when he took us up to the beach, and he told me about it, and I just went in and asked about the job and got it offered to me, so I took it. And I know I should've told you about Ruthie when the school called, but it was only yesterday, and it seemed so hard a thing to tell you, Bob, because of all you have to worry about, and the way you've been lately, kind of distant and lost in your own thoughts and depressed and all. I just wanted to wait till I had a way to pay for it before I told you about it, so it wouldn't seem so bad.''

"Sonofabitch! There's not any goddamn thing wrong with Ruthie that some steady discipline wouldn't cure!'' Bob smacks the flat of his hand against the counter, and his face tightens and reddens. "You never tell her to cut out that damned thumb-sucking. You just sit around whispering with her about how rotten everything is, and then I come home, and I have to be the bad guy. You tell that fancy counselor down to the school that? It's no fucking wonder she's acting retarded!''

"Emotionally disturbed.''

"Emotionally disturbed, then!'' He bats the words back. "I can tell you about 'emotionally disturbed'! *I'm* 'emotionally disturbed'! I'm goddamned disturbed that you go around my back the way you do. The way you always have, too. And you know what the hell I'm talking about, so don't give me that look. And now with this job business. Jesus H. Christ! And Horace! Horace, that fat pig, that slimy, woman-sniffing pig. I know what that guy's interested in, don't worry. And you do too.''

"You sound crazy. I don't even know you anymore. I don't know what's important to you anymore, like I used to,'' Elaine says sadly. "And I don't know what you mean, going around behind your back. I've never gone around behind your back. I was just waiting until I could tell you, and we don't talk much any . . .''

"Like hell!'' he shouts into her face. "You know what I'm talking about. You know. You got a memory. You know.''

"No, I don't.'' She backs away from him toward the stove.

He raises and slowly extends his fist toward her. He howls. He howls like a trapped beast, and with both hands he clears the counter of bowls, dishes, kitchen implements, clock.

Elaine's face has gone all to white, her eyes are wide with fear, and she can't speak. From the rear of the trailer, the cries of her son start up and rise, and suddenly Elaine finds words and says, "Bob, the baby! The baby!"

But it doesn't matter what she says, for he can no longer hear her or the baby. He lurches around the tiny, cluttered room like a blindfolded deaf man, sweeping tables and shelves clear, knocking over chairs, sending the television set crashing to the floor, the clock-radio and pole lamp beside the sofa, the floor lamp next to the easy chair, kicking at magazines, jars, ashtrays as they fall.

"Stop! Stop this!" Elaine shrieks at him. "You son of a bitch! You're wrecking my house!"

For a split second, Bob looks over at his wife, and then, as if what he's seen has compounded his rage, he turns on the chairs and tables, and grunting, tips onto its stiff, flat back the tattered green sofa. Elaine grabs his sleeve with both hands, and when he swings away from her grasp, her face stiffens, for suddenly she is afraid of him, of his size and force, as if he were of an utterly different species than she and her children, a huge, coarse-bodied beast with a thick hide, like a buffalo or rhinoceros, and berserk, rampaging, maddened, as if by the stings of a thousand bees.

Eyes widened, mouth open and dry, hands in tight little fists against her belly, Elaine slips by him and darts down the hall to the back of the trailer, where her baby is, while Bob continues smashing through the trailer, moving like a storm from the living room into the kitchen, then back along the narrow hallway to the bathroom, where he rips the tin medicine cabinet from the wall and kicks over the rubbish can, yanks the contents of the linen closet to the floor, and then moves on to the bedroom at the end, and when he lurches through the door, he stops, panting, enormous in the small doorframe, a giant looking down on tiny beds, dolls, stuffed animals and picture puzzles, building blocks, books and pictures, articles of clothing. He hears sniffling and looks up and sees his wife in the corner of the alcove beyond, behind the crib, with the baby in her arms. And he sees that she expects him to keep on coming, and then he sees what she sees, and he stops.

Bob hears Emma at the screened door off the living room asking in a high, scared voice if she can come inside, and the sounds of Ruthie, poor Ruthie, crying quietly behind her younger sister.

Turning, Bob shuffles slowly back through the wreckage to the front door and lets Emma come inside and then Ruthie, who, as she passes, removes her thumb from her mouth. Neither girl looks at her father.

"Mama?" Emma cries, and Bob hears Elaine call from the back room, "Here! I'm back here with Robbie!" and the two girls run toward her.

He steps outside. The trees are still dripping from the afternoon rain, and shallow puddles glisten white as milk in the yard and roadway ruts. The clouds have passed over the Keys toward the mainland, and the eastern sky, deepening into dark blue as night comes on, pulls from the horizon a large, dark orange half-moon, as if delivering it from old smoke and volcanic ash.

As soon as Bob has driven away, his red-dotted tail-lights disappearing around the far bend in the road, a man emerges from the trailer across the road. He's a middle-aged man with a beer belly tightly encased in a sleeveless undershirt, barefoot with skinny legs sticking out below khaki trousers cut off at the knees. He stands in the middle of the road, snaps his fingers for his dog, which emerges obediently from under the trailer, and looks cautiously in the direction taken by Bob's car and then over toward Bob's darkened, now silent trailer.

Allie Hubbell, too, has come outside and stands in her yard, peering into the darkness of the road where Bob has gone. "Horace? That you?" she calls to the man.

"Yeah."

"Some kinda ruckus."

"I'd say so."

"She all right, do y' know?"

"Sonofabitch can do what he wants to his own stuff, but he better not ruin anything of mine, I'll tell ya," he says.

"You think we better check on Elaine?"

"Elaine?"

"Yeah. Maybe just to check, you know?"

"Naw," he says, rubbing his grizzled chin. "You don't wanta go buttin' into other people's fights. Sonofabitch better not've banged up any of my stuff, though, I'll tell ya. I had some kids there once that punched a buncha holes in the walls one night when they was drunk."

"Maybe we better just go on over and check on Elaine, make sure she's okay." Allie takes a step off the grass onto the road.

"Naw. She can always call the cops on the bastard if she's scared of him. Besides, he ain't the type to shoot or cut anybody. He might knock her around a little, but he ain't the violent type."

"You think so?"

"Oh, yeah," Horace says, and he turns and starts heading back to his own trailer. "Men can tell these things about each other," he says. "He's harmless. Just screwed up is all. See you later," he says, and goes inside.

Allie stands by the road for several moments, arms crossed below her breasts, hands cupping her elbows. Then she turns and slowly walks back to her trailer, where she sits down on the stoop and smokes a cigarette and watches Bob's trailer until the lights come on inside it. Then she stands, opens the door and goes in.

6

BY THE TIME BOB CROSSES FROM UPPER MATECUMBE TO Moray Key, it's dark, and the shrimpers are already out, dozens of them leaning over the rail of the catwalk along the bridge, men, women and children with lanterns hung from the catwalk and long-handled dip nets stuck down into the channel. Bob drives by barely noticing them and does not remember that a few hours earlier he was planning to join the shrimpers tonight. Without intending it, without particularly desiring it, almost without being aware of it, he has momentarily severed the connection between his past and his future. During this moment and the several that will immediately follow, Bob is floating free of time, a man without memories and without plans, like an infant, conscious only of the immediate present. If you stop him and ask where he is going on this tropical winter's eve, he'll blink and look down the hood of his car at the piles of sand, cinder block and steel, and recognizing the marina and the apartment building beside it and the Clam Shack, he'll say, "To Moray Key." If, when he parks the car in the lot behind the apartment building, you ask him where on the key he's going, he'll blink again, and noting that his car is next to Avery Boone's van, he'll say, "To Ave's." And if, as he climbs the narrow iron stairs to the second floor and pauses on the terrace before Ave's door and raises his hand to knock, you ask him what business he has with his old friend and new partner Avery Boone on this lovely, breezy, moonlit evening, he'll blink a third time, hold his hand in the air and say, "Why, no business at all."

Honduras answers the door. She swings it open and stands there on one foot, like a stork resting, except that she's not resting, she's been painting her toenails and has hopped on her right foot from the low, blond sofa over to the door, afraid the shag rug will mess the wet paint on the toes of the left. She's got a cigarette clamped between her lips and a tiny maroon-tipped brush in one hand.

"Oh, hi, Bob," she says, her lips not moving, the cigarette bobbing up and down as she speaks. "C'mon in." She turns and hops back to the couch and puts the cigarette into a conch shell and resumes painting toenails. She's wearing a man's pale blue dress shirt, Ave's, and tight cut-off jeans with raggedy Daisy Mae cuffs. The gold hoops on her wrists clank against one another as she lovingly lays down the paint. "Jesus, I hate doing this," she says, but she does it with delicate, slow, affectionate swishes, licking her lips each time she completes a swirl on one toe and moves on to the next. "What brings you out on a night like this?"

Bob doesn't answer. He's entered the room, closed the door behind him and is looking around him, as if it's the first time he's been here, though he's been here many times, has sat at the table in the dining area off the kitchen drinking beer and talking into the night with Ave, has peered out all the windows, even bedroom windows, and admired the view of the marina, the boats tied up there, the channel and the bay beyond, has listened to the thump of the jukebox in the bar below, has used the bathroom at two in the morning before leaving to drive home to Elaine, asleep alone on the sofa in the dilapidated yellow trailer five miles away on Upper Matecumbe Key. He has said to himself, though he does not now remember it, that he would be content with an apartment like this, larger, of course, with bedrooms for the kids, and maybe two baths instead of one, but no fancier.

Honduras looks up, peers at Bob through frizzy red hair, her hand poised over the little toe of her right foot. "Ave's not here," she says. "Left with Tyrone this afternoon, for the Caymans, I think. Won't be back till . . . Thursday? Yeah, Thursday, I think."

Bob sits down slowly, like an old man, in the low easy chair opposite the sofa. "Got a cigarette? I left mine in the car. Or home."

"Sure." She tosses him a pack of Marlboro Lights. "You okay? You're looking kind of strung out. Want a joint?"

"A joint? Okay, sure."

"Right there, in the box on the table next to you," she says, going back to her painting.

Bob lifts the cover of the small brass box, takes out a joint and lights it up, inhaling deeply. "Nice."

"Sure."

They are silent for a few moments while Bob smokes and Honduras paints, until finally she sticks her bare legs out in front of her and admires the maroon nails from a distance.

Bob says, "Want some?" and he extends the butt end of the joint to her.

"Thanks." She plucks it from his fingertips and finishes it off. "Good shit, right?"

"Good shit."

"So, big man, what's up? You are a big man, you know that?"

"Yeah." He's silent for a second, and then says, "Well, I'm kinda curious. How do you get this stuff? I might like some for myself. You know?"

Honduras tosses her head back and laughs, and here things start happening too fast for Bob later to recall clearly and in order. It's not that he's not paying attention (if anything, he's paying too much attention). It's that he has no conscious plan, no intent—which is to say that he's got no connection between his past and his future, none in mind, that is. When one gives oneself over to forces larger than one's self, like history, say, or God, or the unconscious, it's easy to lose track of the sequence of events. One's narrative life disappears.

Here's what he will recall later of this evening's events, in a sequence obtained by logic rather than memory. First, Bob and Honduras smoked another joint together. Then she told him, again, the story of how she got her name, which led to a brief discussion of Ave's travels in the *Angel Blue* with Tyrone James, who is a Jamaican, like the man who gave Honduras her name, though not a full-blooded Arawak Indian, as that man was. Bob said, "What the fuck's a Arawak Indian? I never heard of them. I know Abenaki, I know Apache. And then you got your Comanches, your Iroquois, your Algonquins, and so on. But I never heard of Arawak." She explained that they were the descendants of the Indians who were in the Caribbean when Columbus discovered America, and they were tall, good-looking, fierce Indians who smoked a lot of grass and lived up in the hills of the bigger islands like Jamaica, Cuba and Haiti. And they practiced voodoo, she told Bob. "Wow," Bob said. "That's really far out." Her lover, the Arawak from Jamaica, had taken her to some voodoo ceremonies in the hills. "It was really amazing," she said. Bob believed her. "That's how I first got into herb," she said.

"Moving it, I mean." She explained that the Arawaks in the hills of Jamaica grew the strongest, heaviest ganja on the island, and she got top dollar for it from rich Americans in Montego Bay, which is where and how she met the dentist from Philadelphia with the sailboat who brought her over to the Keys. And then she met Ave. "And you know the rest," she said brightly. "No," Bob said, "not really." But by then he'd forgotten what he had asked her in the first place, something to do with Ave and the *Angel Blue,* something to do with Tyrone. He remembers deciding that it couldn't have been very important, when suddenly Honduras asked him if he wanted to do a little coke. He said, "Sure, why not?" and she jumped up, drew the curtains closed, went into the bedroom and returned with a small vial. Bob remembers being excited and a little frightened, and he was relieved when he realized that he wasn't going to have to inject the cocaine into his arm, that he could kneel down next to the glass coffee table opposite Honduras and imitate her as she rolled a fifty-dollar bill into a tube and sucked a two-inch line of the white powder into her nostril. He didn't want to admit he hadn't done this before, so he was glad that the procedure was simple enough that he could appear to be a practiced user. He waited for her to finish and sit back onto the sofa, and then he reached for her fifty. "You realize," he said as he picked it up and tightened the roll, "I'm flat broke." She smiled benevolently, and he went to work. Then, when he had sat back on the floor with his legs crossed under him, she said, "Broke is bad, big man," and he said, "Baa-a-ad." She laughed. It appears that at this point Bob started quizzing Honduras about voodoo, because he remembers challenging her to prove she knew how to perform a voodoo ceremony. "C'mon, prove it. And don't just stick some pins in a doll and say some mumbo jumbo and tell me it's over. I know there's more to it than that, or else people wouldn't be so uptight about it, and it wouldn't be such a big secret and all. It's something black people know about, Haitians and stuff. Comes from Africa," he said, smiling. "You ain't black," he said. "You white as rice. I bet *I* know more about voodoo than you," he teased, and she got up and started dancing around the room, a combination of hula dance and bunny hop, which, to Bob, was very sexy. "Bum-diddy-bum, bum-diddy-bum!" she chanted as she danced, her lips pouty and full, eyes half-closed, hands stroking her belly and thighs. The next thing Bob remembers saying is, "Let's fuck," and the next thing he remembers doing is fucking. It was in the bed, he knows, with the lights on, he thinks, and both of them stark naked. He swears he did it three times in quick succession and that she giggled throughout the third. When it was over, at least for him it was over, she prodded and poked at him, trying for a fourth, and he rolled away from her, saying, "Oh, Jesus, Honduras, you're crazy. Enough is enough." She laughed, like a spoiled, defiant child, and said, "C'mon, let's see you get it up again. I bet you can't." He said, "You're right, I can't. You'd hafta do voodoo to get me up again. Otherwise you just gotta let nature take its course." She jumped out of the bed and yanked on her shorts and shirt, and grabbing up his clothes, bunching them into a bundle, made for the door. "I'll show you some voodoo! I need your clothes, that's all," she said, laughing. "What?" Bob cried. "Gimme my stuff!" "Nope. Gonna do some hex work with 'em. Gonna get your peter up." "Aw, c'mon," he begged. "Gimme my clothes." He got out of bed and started toward her, his limp penis swinging heavily between his legs. "I got to get outa here anyhow." She slammed the door in his face. "Hey," he said. He caught sight of himself in the dresser mirror, a stranger's body, a pale trunk and legs with red arms, neck and face. There were pimples on his shoulders, a dark mole under his right arm, hairy thighs and knobby knees. He wanted to cover himself, grab a blanket off the bed, tear down a curtain, anything, just get that pathetic naked pink and white thing covered and out of sight. "Hey, let's have the clothes," he said sternly, and he pulled on the doorknob, which came off in his hand, the door still closed. "What the fuck?" he said, examining the doorknob, and he heard Honduras laughing on the other side. "Ha ha ha! You see? Voodoo!" "Shit," Bob said. He hollered this time. "C,mon, open the fucking door and gimme my clothes!" He slid the doorknob back onto the stem, and bearing down and twisting it at the same time, managed to turn the knob and open the door, and he saw Honduras slipping out the farther door to the terrace, closing it behind her. He searched the living room, found no clothes, went to the front door, opened it an inch and peeked out, but she was gone. "Sonofabitch," he whispered, and closed the door. He crossed the room and looked out the window on the far side. When he saw her down there on the pier, he cranked open the window and called, "Hey, Honduras!" He remembers her face in the dim light from the Clam Shack as she looked up at him, a joyful, young face, childlike almost, but frightening to him, as if, in her, curiosity were stronger than fear. He turned away and raced back through the bedroom to the bathroom and wrenched a towel off the rack. Tying it around his waist, he stepped out the door to the terrace and quickly walked to the stairs and down. By the time he had rounded the building and could see the boats tied up in their slips, like horses in their stalls, Honduras had started the engine of the *Belinda Blue*. He recognized the cough and chug and the steady, slow throb of the old Chrysler, and he started running. When he reached the slip, the boat was ten feet out. Honduras waved down at him from the bridge. "You sonofabitch! Pull that boat back in!" Bob snapped at her. "No way. Gonna put a spell on you! Gonna do some voodoo on you! Gonna put you in my pow-wah!" she said. Bob hissed at her, "Give me back my clothes, goddammit!" She threw back her head and laughed. "Try an' get 'em!" Bob stepped swiftly to his right and ran the length of the neighboring slip, a narrow walkway off the central pier between the slip of the *Belinda Blue* and the slip for the *Angel Blue*. He reached the end of the walkway, and when he jumped, Honduras gunned the engine, and the boat churned water, lurched away, leaving open space instead of deck for Bob to come down in. He came up sputtering, slapping at the water with fury, and then lay back and treaded water and watched the *Belinda Blue,* her running lights on, cut south and head toward the bridge. He saw the shrimpers in the glow of their lanterns scramble to yank up their dip nets as the boat approached them, then it passed under and charged beyond, heading down the channel in deep water toward the open sea. He remembers that, and he remembers swimming slowly back to the pier, climbing up, naked, then climbing back down for the towel, wringing it out and wrapping it around himself again and padding along the pier toward the Clam Shack. He returned to the apartment and took a pair of Ave's designer jeans and a Mexican shirt from his closet and left. He closed the door behind him and started praying that he had been stupid and distracted enough to have left the keys in the car ignition. The keys are there. He says, "Thank God for something," starts the motor, backs out of the lot and eases away from Moray Key, heading home.

7

WHEN BOB ARRIVES HOME, ELAINE IS SLEEPING. HE STEPS barefoot through the door, wearing Ave's clothes, which are too tight on him and pinch at the crotch, waist and shoulders, and his hair is still wet. He has prepared an explanation: he and Ave got to drinking and wrestling out on the pier, and he fell in. But Elaine asks no questions. She stirs as he enters, opens her eyes when he snaps on the kitchen light, turns away from him and says nothing.

Bob goes to the bathroom, returns and notices suddenly that all the signs of his earlier rampage have been eliminated, as if it never happened. If anything, the house looks neater, less cluttered and more ordered than it did before, and for a second he allows himself to think of his fury as if it were a rational and deliberate thing, a painful but necessary kind of housecleaning. He checks, and he notes with approval that the pole lamp, which he always hated, has been thrown out. The television set looks unbroken. Stripping off Ave's shirt and jeans, he flicks off the light in the kitchen and slides naked into bed, his back to his wife's back.

"You see the message by the phone?" she asks in a low, cold voice.

"No."

She says nothing, just lifts and drops her heavy hips to make herself more comfortable in the lumpy bed.

"What's it say?"

She's silent.

"Oh, for Christ's sake, Elaine, what's the message?"

She yanks on the covers and draws them over her bare shoulder.

Bob sighs heavily, gets out of bed and crosses to the counter where the telephone is located. Reaching out in the dark to the wall, he switches on the light again and plucks from under the telephone the sheet of lined paper and reads, *Call Eddie. He says whenever you come in and it's urgent.* As easily as if he heard her speaking aloud, Bob can read and hear in Elaine's swift, tiny handwriting the woman's anger and detachment. She just wants to be left alone now. She doesn't care what he does, whom he sees, what he feels, as long as he leaves her alone. If, in return, she has to leave her husband to his own dreamy devices and illusions, leave him to his own messy life, if that's the price of her survival, then she will pay it. Her priorities are both clear and powerful, as if determined not so much by her mind as by the chemistry of her body. Bob, she has said to herself over and over tonight, can go fuck himself. And she means it.

The phone rings a long time before Eddie answers, and when Bob hears his slurry voice, he thinks he's wakened his brother and cringes in anticipation of Eddie's grumpiness and sarcasm. "Sorry I woke you up, but Elaine said to call no matter when I got in. . . ."

"No problem, no problem. I was just . . . sitting around anyhow," Eddie says.

Bob looks over at the kitchen clock. Three-forty. Maybe

Eddie's drunk, he thinks. "That's good. So . . . what's up?"

"Well, how you doing down there? Everything okay?"

"Okay, I guess. You know, it's . . . risky."

Eddie blats a hard, single laugh. *"Risky!* Yeah, but that's the only way to go, right? Right?"

"I guess. So, listen, what's up? How's Sarah and Jessica? Everyone okay?"

"Oh, sure, sure, great, just great. Everyone's fine."

"That's good."

"Yeah, things're okay here, not great, you know, not like I was hoping . . . but you win some, you lose some, right?"

"Right."

"Well, you know, I haven't heard anything from you guys in a while, not since you left, except for the Christmas card, which was nice. Thanks. But, you know, I was just sitting around here wondering how you guys're doing down there. You know what I mean?"

"Yeah, we're doing okay. Not as much business as I'd like, not as many customers as I'd kinda hoped for, but we're surviving. Barely. But we're doing it."

Eddie laughs again, that same sharp, flat laugh of disbelief. "I bet!"

"No, it's nice here. Real pretty, you know, and the fishing's real good. Hey, I saw Ted Williams today. Can you believe that? He lives around here, in Islamorada."

"No shit. The Kid, eh?"

"Yeah. In real life. He looks real good, too."

"Yeah." Eddie pauses. "Well, listen, Bob, the reason I called you, I got to ask you something."

Bob is silent a second, and he realizes that he hasn't been listening to his brother at all and that the man is speaking in a way that's almost unrecognizable to him—no foul language, no bragging, no fast talk, no sarcasm. Something's wrong. "What's the matter, Eddie?"

"Well, I got a problem up here. A problem I thought maybe you could help me out with, you know?"

"Sure. Anything."

"Yeah, well, I'm in a little trouble here. I told you

about it a little last October, when you and me talked and you decided to quit the store and so on. You remember.''

"Oh, Jesus, Eddie. What's happening?"

"Nothing. Nothing yet. Don't worry none about it. I still got everything under control. You know me, kid. I don't give a rat's ass about a little trouble now and then. You expect it, the game I play. But I got to deal with some people here I owe money to. I really do have to come up with the bucks now . . . well, yeah, let's just say I got to come up with the bucks. You understand? I'm not the kinda guy who asks for help when he doesn't need it. Right? Especially from my kid brother. Right?''

"Sure, Eddie. But Jesus . . .''

"Anyhow, I figured maybe since now you're in business for yourself . . . you know what I mean . . . well, I figured you could come up with enough fast cash to help me out a little. We can work a deal, keep it off the books, maybe cut you in on the business up here as part of the payback. It's okay to talk, isn't it? I mean, your phone is okay, isn't it?''

"Oh, yeah, yeah. Sure. My phone . . . oh, sure."

"Good. I'm not so sure about mine, you understand, so be cool. Right?''

"Right. Cool. Who . . . ah . . . who'd be listening in?''

"Doesn't matter. Interested parties, okay? You got me?''

"Yeah.''

"So, whaddaya think? Can you help me out, like you said?''

"God, Eddie. I . . . I'm fucking broke, you know that.''

There is a silence on the other end. Bob hears his brother light a cigarette and inhale deeply.

"I mean, I'd do anything I could, I *will*, I will do anything I can, but Jesus, Eddie, I'm even more broke than ever. Even worse than up there. I don't have a pot to piss in, like they say," he says, forcing a laugh.

Eddie says nothing, so Bob goes on. "I suppose you've tried everything else. . . .''

"Everything."

"God, Eddie, I'm really sorry. I mean, maybe I can dig up a couple hundred someplace," he says, thinking of Ave's return from the Caymans on Thursday.

"A couple hundred bucks! Whew! That's really something, kid. Look, let's talk straight, Bob. Okay? I know what you and your pal Boone are doing down there. Okay? You understand what I'm saying? I mean, I *know*. I've known Boone since he was a kid, and I know you too. So I know, okay?"

"Well, yeah, but you're wrong. I'm not . . . I'm pretty much on my own, and I only get a quarter of what we make with the boat, you know? Which is almost a quarter of nothing, the way it's been going."

"Bullshit," Eddie says in a low voice.

"Aw, c'mon, Eddie. I'm fucking broke!"

"Yeah. You and the Pope. Look, kid, we gotta talk. I think I get the picture, we can't talk on the phone, right? So we gotta talk in person. What do you say I drive down to Miami, we meet there for a drink and lunch tomorrow, say, and we talk. In private. I understand how it is right now, on the phone, I mean. I can call you tomorrow from a pay phone, and we can arrange to meet in Miami around one."

"No, Eddie. No big meetings in Miami. I'm telling you the truth. No bullshit, I'm really broke. Busted. Flat. You don't understand that; you never did understand that. I'll do anything I can to help you, you're my brother, for Christ's sake, but I'm fucking broke!" he shouts.

"Yeah. Sure. I hear you."

"No. No, you don't, you bastard. You never did hear me. You don't hear me now, and you never heard me in your life."

Eddie is silent a second, then, in a hoarse voice, "I heard you a lot more'n you got any idea. Maybe I didn't show it much, but I heard you. I know it's been tough on you, but it's tough for me. I got real problems, Bob. Even my epilepsy, it's been coming back lately, like when I was a kid."

"Jesus, Eddie. You see a doctor?"

"Yeah, sure. He give me some fucking pills and said go take a vacation. But that's not important, the epilepsy. Not compared to the other stuff." He is silent for a second. Then, "For Christ's sake, Bob, I'm asking. You got that? I'm *asking*."

"Eddie, goddammit, you're always asking. You've been asking since the beginning. You make it look like you're giving, but all you're doing is asking. I'm sorry about the epilepsy and all your problems. But I got lots of problems too, and you're one of the fucking reasons why. You say you're giving me a big job, a chance of a lifetime, you say you're gonna make me rich, but really all you're doing is asking, you're using me to work for nothing, to be your loyal clerk, your fucking nigger, while you add up all the profits and take 'em home to buy another fucking boat with. Listen, man, I learned something that year up in Oleander Park. I'm a little slow, I know, but eventually I learn, and I learned not to listen to you when you say you're giving. I tune out now when you start saying you got just what I need, because it's going to turn out instead to be just what *you* need."

"Bob, listen. For Christ's sake, Bob. You got burnt, I know, and I'm sorry. I . . . I thought things would be better for you. And that stupid stuff about the gun and all, I didn't understand that stuff, I admit it. Shit, I still don't understand. But it don't matter. Things like that don't matter anymore."

"Fuck they don't matter. They mattered then, they matter now. You think I'm a bozo."

"No, Bob. Aw, shit . . . listen . . . I'm . . ." he stammers, and then his voice breaks, and he's weeping. "I . . . I'm really gone now, Bob. This is no shit, this is how it comes out. Lemme give it to you straight, okay?" He stops weeping and gathers himself together. "Sarah and Jessie . . . she left me, just took the kid and left. She went back up north to her parents in Connecticut. It's all gone now, Bob. All of it. The boat, that's a fucking laugh! Gone. The store, the new store over in Lakeland? Forget it. All I got is what I got in my pockets, Bob. And the house. But I only got that for a few more days is all. Then it's gone too. And then *I'm* gone, right along behind. You understand me? If I can't come up with the money, I'll be gone too. Repossessed, just like the fucking house and the boat and the store and everything. You didn't know that, probably. There's people can repossess people.''

Bob hears the man, he understands what he's saying and feels a great wave of pity and fear for him, but he also feels a counterwave of anger that keeps on sweeping in from the opposite side, neutralizing his pity and fear, making him cold, quiet, withdrawn, as if he were idly watching a TV soap opera. "How much money you talking about?"

"A lot. A fucking lot."

"How much?"

"I thought you said you was broke."

"I did, I am. Dead stone broke. How much?"

"Hundred and thirty thousand."

"A hundred and thirty thousand bucks you need! And you think maybe I can help you out!"

"I hoped, that's all. I just figured you and Ave were into some big bucks now, with the boat and all. I hear things. I figured you'd be able to put a hand on some large cash, that's all. You know?"

Bob is laughing, a high-pitched, rolling, derisive laugh that goes on and on, like a train whistle.

Then Eddie clicks off, and all Bob hears now is the dial tone and his own subsiding laughter.

Elaine watches him from the sofa bed, her upper body propped on one elbow. She's been watching him throughout. When Bob sees her, he stops laughing altogether and realizes that he's naked, standing at the kitchen counter with the telephone receiver in his hand.

"What's happened?" she asks calmly.

Bob scratches his head and puts the receiver back on the hook. "I guess . . . well, I guess the bottom's dropped out. For Eddie."

"He thinks you can help him?"

"He thinks I'm smuggling dope."

"Ave is. Why not you?"

"You want me to? That what you're telling me now?"

"No. I mean, why shouldn't Eddie think you're doing it too? He's right to think Ave's doing it. That's all," she says in a thin, watery voice, as if deeply tired and a little bored, and she lays her head on the pillow, rolls over and leaves her back to him. "Shut off the light soon," she says. "I have to get up early in the morning. You obviously don't."

"Yeah. Sure." He reaches over and flicks off the light. But he doesn't come to bed. He stands at the counter as before, thinking about his brother Eddie. His anger has left him now, like a storm blown out to sea. The horizon is dark and turbulent, but here, directly overhead, it's clear skies and sweet breezes.

"He's alone now," Bob says in a quiet voice, almost a whisper. "Sarah and Jessica left him. And he's got the epilepsy again." He reaches over in the dark and grabs Elaine's foot and shakes it. "It's really bad for him, Elaine. He's scared."

"Talk about this tomorrow. I'm exhausted. Now let me sleep. This has not been an easy night for me, you know."

He lets go of her foot and walks over to the chair next to the TV and sits down, the plastic netting cold against his naked buttocks and back. Eddie the man deserves everything he gets, Bob thinks, but Eddie the boy, the boy that's still in him, doesn't deserve to be alone, to lose everything he ever wanted and worked for, to be deserted by his only brother. It's hard for Bob, though, to see the boy in his older brother; he has to struggle to see him. He knows he's there, but Bob has to will himself to remember Eddie as a boy and to look back and down on him from where he stands now, a grown man looking down on a nervous, wildly energetic, tow-headed boy, and ruffling the kid's hair, give him an easy pat on the shoulder and say, "Go on, kid, try it anyhow. If you screw it up, you can always try again, until you finally get it. Don't worry, kid, you got all the time in the world."

Elaine doesn't understand that. All she can see is Eddie the man, and the man she sees is childish, selfish, cruel, manipulative and shallow, a man who mistreats his wife and daughter and doesn't deserve their love, a man who manipulated and deceived his younger brother and therefore doesn't deserve his loyalty and support now, a man who made big money fast and easy and shouldn't complain when he loses it just as fast and just as easy.

Bob gets up from the chair, and his back sticks to it as he rises. He reaches out in the dark for the phone, realizes he can't see to dial, and switches on the kitchen light, then dials his brother's number. He lets it ring a half-dozen times, ten, twelve. No answer.

8

IT'S RAINING WHEN BOB ARRIVES IN OLEANDER PARK, a steady, heavy rain from low clouds, and it's cold. He's got the heater of the old Chevy on, and the dry smell of it reminds him of driving in New Hampshire on cold, wet spring mornings along slick highways, stomach growling from too many cigarettes, too much Dunkin' Donuts coffee in paper cups, heading out from Catamount alone like this, early in the morning like this, to fix somebody's oil burner. In those days, he knows now, he was constantly depressed and, to avoid the fact, had gone to some secret place deep inside himself, where he went over again and again the trivial details of his life, as if fingering the beads on a rosary, rehearsing, always rehearsing, how he'll fix the porch steps, how he'll clean out the cellar this weekend, how he'll stop tonight on the way home for a few beers at Irwin's, how he'll clean his fishing gear this week so he can go out the first day of trout season—filling his mind with scrupulous visions of the actions that most people do automatically and without anticipation, living his life as a constant, slow-motion preview of coming attractions in which the boring, linking, low points are in fact the crucial scenes of the movie.

For a second, as Bob turns off Highway 27 a few miles south of Oleander Park, he forgets why he's done this, why he's left his home and family at four in the morning and driven north across Florida for five hours. He knows where he is and recognizes the roads, marshy lakes, trailer parks, palmettos, orange groves, recognizes the acrid smell of the citrus-processing plants, the signs pointing with excitement to Cypress Gardens, the Water Skiing Hall of Fame, Disney World, recognizes on his left the Lake Grassey trailer park and back on Tangelo Lane the blue trailer he owned for close to a year, and recognizes the white cinder-block building out on Route 7 where he worked and where he shot one black man and chased after the other. The windows are covered with sheets of plywood now, the store blinded and abandoned by the side of the road. He sees the road to Auburndale, where Marguerite Dill and her father live, and his chest suddenly fills with a mixture of shame, nostalgia and longing that momentarily frightens and confuses him. Then he recognizes the turnoff to the country club, and he remembers Eddie's birthday party, the way he saw himself then, poor, stupid, clumsy and inept.

Finally, as he approaches Eddie's house, low and dark, with an acre of lime-green lawn in front, a plain of slate-gray lake behind it, he remembers why he has come here. He's come to provide aid and comfort to his elder brother, simply to be present in the man's time of troubles. He knows there's little he can do or say, but he believes that his presence will be helpful, that together they will be able to remember who they are and will in that way be able to withstand the awful pressures of the moment. He believes, too, that Eddie will help him as much as he will help Eddie.

Bob is not angry anymore, and he's not worried. He knows Eddie will be all right as soon as he sees his younger brother's face, sees that Bob has raced through the Florida night and cold, gray, rainy morning to be at his side, to be family, the Granite Skates, the two of them against the rest of the world. They'll hug each

other, Eddie will gruffly welcome him in, and they'll sit
down, maybe at the huge dining room table, where they'll
drink coffee, smoke cigarettes and discuss possible solutions to these problems, both their problems, and now
and then they'll remember something amusing or touching from their childhood, and they'll laugh a little.

Bob will tell Eddie about Ave and about Honduras,
and maybe he'll tell him about what happened years ago
between Ave and Elaine and how it still bothers him.
He'll tell him about his money problems and about
Ruthie's emotional problems, and he'll let his brother
know what a fool he was last night. He'll tell about
Marguerite, too, at last, and what she meant to him and
how confused loving her became for him because she
was black. Everything will be made clear in the telling.

He'll admit that Ave fooled him, though not deliberately, into thinking he could make good money by selling his trailer in Oleander Park and buying into the
Belinda Blue. They'll curse the Republicans and the
Democrats, Reagan and Carter, and blame the recession
and the Arabs for the falloff in the tourist trade. Bob will
even tell his brother about Doris Cleeve back in Catamount and the night he saw his life there for what it was
and decided to trade it for another. And he'll tell Eddie
how his feelings toward Elaine have changed, how, even
though she does nothing wrong that he can point to, she
still manages to make him feel guilty all the time, which
he never used to feel, even when he was now and then
sleeping with Doris Cleeve, an act no better or worse
than fucking Honduras last night or falling for Marguerite last summer. He's no different from the way he's
always been, he'll say to Eddie, and yet now he goes
around feeling guilty all the time, especially toward Elaine
and the kids.

Eddie will understand, and there's probably a lot of it
that Eddie will be able to explain away. And by the
same token, there's probably a lot in Eddie's life that's
just as confusing to him, things that Bob will be able to
explain for him. Bob will know what to say when Eddie
tells him how he got himself into debt to people he never

should have borrowed money from. He'll know how to reassure his brother that he did everything a man could to make Sarah happy and that her desertion of him now is an act that should never be forgiven. Bob will tell him not to worry about losing his daughter, you never lose your children, no matter what. They eventually discover the truth about you, and they come back, he'll say. Bob will tell Eddie he can start over. He's only thirty-three years old, a young man, and he's smart and energetic. His epilepsy will get better as soon as the pressure on his daily life has eased.

They'll come up with a plan, two plans, one for Eddie and one for Bob, and by God, then they'll crack open a bottle of Scotch or maybe Canadian Club, and they'll drink the sonofabitch dry, talking about the old days, remembering their parents, growing up in Catamount, the house they were raised in, the winter days they skipped school together and played hockey with the American Legion guys down on the river, the way their father used to snore, the way their mother constantly nagged them to go to church early with her and then, when they did, told them to go to late mass on their own because they made her so nervous with their fooling around and whispering that she was too distracted to pray. They'll remember everything together!

Parking the car before the closed garage door, Bob gets out and runs under the rain across the lawn to the front entrance and pushes the doorbell. A new pink Lincoln driven by a woman wearing a pink pillbox hat and veil sloshes past and turns into the driveway of the pink stucco house next door. The garage door lifts automatically, and the pale car slides into the darkness, and the door descends.

Bob pushes the brass button again. Maybe he's asleep, Bob thinks, and he holds the button in until it sounds angry to him, or worried.

He pushes the doorbell a third time, with no response from beyond the thick oak door, and it occurs to Bob that Eddie may have driven into town or gone to his office early, though he's not sure Eddie even has an office anymore, or a car. The liquor store is closed, the store in Lakeland never even opened, his birthday boat is gone, either sold or repossessed, and Eddie said that the house was about to go too.

Stepping from the doorway into the rain again, Bob jogs across the lawn and around his car to the garage. He tries the door, and discovering that it's locked, hunches his shoulders against the downpour, steps to the side of the building and peers through the small, dark window there. The first bay, where Sarah used to park her Celica, is empty, but in the gloom beyond it, Bob sees Eddie's white Eldorado, which looks unexpectedly huge and vulgar to him. He recalls the white Chrysler he thought Ted Williams owned. Eddie, he thinks, doesn't really have much class. Then he sees his brother inside the car, his curly blond head laid back on the headrest as if he were sleeping. The windows are all up, the doors closed, and rags have been jammed along the bottom of the garage door. Putting his ear close to the pane of glass, blocking his other ear against the sound of the spattering rain, Bob hears the motor running, and only then does he see the hose that leads from the tailpipe over the fender and through the rear corner window, and the tape sealing the opening around it, and he knows that he's come too late, his brother is dead.

BOB'S HAND IS BLEEDING; HE CUT IT WHEN HE SMASHED THE window with his fist. Eddie's body is lying on the cement floor of the garage, the wide, two-bay door is open, and Bob stands beside it, sucking in the fresh, moist air, while the rain splashes down on the driveway before him, on the dark green roof and hood of his old Chevy wagon, on the thick, freshly cropped lawn and, beyond the lawn, the road and the fenced-in meadow and, in the distance, the scattered, silver-gray shapes of Brahma cattle grazing beneath tall, spreading live oak trees. Bob squints and makes out strips of Spanish moss dangling from the branches of the trees, and he thinks, What a stupid place to die. So far from home, so far from ice and snow, dark blue spruce trees, maple and birch trees and granite hills, so far from small, redbrick milltowns huddled in narrow river valleys and old white colonial houses and triple-decker wooden tenement houses, and churches with tall spires—so far from what's *real*. And for the first time since he left New Hampshire, Bob believes that he will never return there, that somehow, as much for him as for Eddie, it's too late.

With fastidious care, as if writing out a shopping list, Bob itemizes what he must do now. He must, of course, call the police, who will rule Eddie's death a suicide and will have the body placed with a local mortician. Then Bob will call Sarah in Connecticut and tell her what has happened and place himself at her service for the next few days. Her parents' address must be inside the house somewhere. He will give her the note that he found on the car seat next to Eddie's body, still apparently unopened, as if Bob had not read it, since, after all, though it was unsealed, it did have Sarah's name written on the envelope, and he should not have read it. The note, back inside the envelope, is in Bob's shirt pocket, and no doubt the police will want to read Eddie's last words, neatly typed, to his wife: *I'm a failure.* Three short words that must have taken Eddie an hour to compose, and when he had them down on the white sheet of paper, they must have made the rest easy, Bob thought when he first read them. That was when Bob started making his list of things to do, for he thought, I'm *not* a failure.

After he has talked with Sarah and knows how long he'll have to stay here in Winter Haven and how much of the funeral he has to arrange himself, he will call Elaine. He'll apologize for everything and tell her she's right about everything, and she won't have to take the job at the Rusty Scupper, because he's going to take an evening job himself, pumping gas, maybe, or tending bar, anything to bring in the money they will need to pay for Ruthie's doctors and the rent and food and maybe some new clothes for spring, and who knows, they might be able to put a few bucks away and save enough for a down payment on a new trailer or possibly even one of

those three-bedroom condominium apartments going up
at the marina, though of course that probably will be a
little too steep for them, as the price, he's heard, is over
a hundred thousand dollars for the large places, ninety-
five for the smaller units. He'll tell her what he plans to
tell Ave: if Ave, who has plenty of cash, will loan him
the money to buy the rest of the *Belinda Blue,* he will
then be able to keep all the profits, instead of the one-
fourth he keeps now, and will be able to pay Ave back
in a couple of years, maybe even sooner. The way it is
now, he'll never be able to buy more of the boat than
the one-quarter share of it he bought with the money
they realized last October from the sale of the trailer in
Oleander Park. Ave will be grateful for the idea. He
probably never expected that Bob would not be able to
make enough from his share of the boat to buy more
than that share. Right from the start, the night Robbie
was born, Ave said that what he wanted was for Bob to
own and operate the *Belinda Blue* while he owned and
operated a second boat. Bob will admit to Elaine that
yes, he knows Ave owns and operates that second boat
to smuggle marijuana and cocaine, but that's no concern
of his. He himself would certainly never do such a thing,
nor would Ave want him to. It's safer for Ave anyhow if
Bob keeps straight and the *Belinda Blue* never carries
anything but fat, half-drunk fishermen out into the bay
for bonefish. If Ave wants to sneak drugs into Florida
from the Bahamas or the Caymans or off freighters from
Colombia, that's his business. Those risks are his, not
Bob's.

After he has talked about this plan with Elaine, then
Bob will call Ave himself, and he is sure Ave will like
the plan and will want to draw up the papers immediately. Bob is amazed that he didn't think of this before,
back when he and Ave first talked about going into
business together. Bob has decided that he and Ave will
also have to talk about Elaine, and he knows that during
that particular discussion, which will concern Elaine's
confession to Bob and will therefore oblige Bob to confess to Ave his somewhat complicated and delayed reac-

tions to it, he will reveal that, as one aspect of those complications, he made love to Ave's girlfriend Honduras. This will clear the air, Bob believes, at last, and then they will stand on an equal footing once again, just like they did years ago, for Ave will own one boat, Bob will own the other, they will split the profits of the fishing business, and both of them will have slept with the other man's woman once, a thing done in the past and completely forgiven now. Bob knows he'll never make love to Honduras again, especially after the way she treated him the one time he did make love to her. He'll be friendly with her, all right, but cool.

Then, finally, when he has finished talking with Ave, Bob will go through his brother's papers and will try to put the poor man's affairs in order as best he can. He'll approach all the problems and tasks, meet everyone's needs, in a perfectly rational way, be the man everyone can count on, Sarah, Jessica, the police, even Eddie's creditors. He'll leave the weeping to the others, let them be sad, frightened, angry, hurt or relieved; he will be calm, logical, competent. At times like this, he thinks, a man has to know how to take charge.

Of course, nothing works out as Bob planned. He finds himself weeping in front of the police, for the sight of his brother's body as they lift it onto a wheeled stretcher suddenly fills him with a strange, overwhelming pity that he has never felt before. In a flash, he realizes that Eddie is totally powerless now; a glowing red bed of coals has become a bag of waters. A spirit that shouted at Bob, that beat on him and prodded and directed him, scolded and shamed him for thirty-one years, has been miraculously transformed into a typed note that claims only absence for itself.

It's a terrible thing, Bob thinks. To go from being something to being nothing! A terrible thing for a man to endure—to be nothing after having been something. And for the first time, Bob pities his older brother, and his pity instantly releases him, so that when he weeps aloud for Eddie, in sorrow, of course, like any brother, but, more crucially, with pity as well, he weeps for himself, in joy. And as he weeps, he trembles, torn by the contending emotions that are called grief—pity and sudden potency, sorrow and joy, the horrified, abandoned child, bereft and frightened, and the exhilarated man, powerful and self-admiring.

He has trouble speaking to the police officer in charge, and as a result instantly forgets the name of the funeral home the officer recommends to him and to which Bob agrees they should send the body, so that, a few minutes later, when he is speaking on the telephone to Sarah, his brother's widow, he is unable to tell her where they have taken Eddie's body.

"You asshole," she says, and she quickly apologizes but then begins to speak to him as if he were an adolescent boy. She tells him that she'll fly down this afternoon and for him not to bother picking her up at Orlando, she can get out to the house on her own. "Just leave everything the way it is," she instructs him. "And don't let anybody inside the house. No lawyers, no bankers, no accountants, no nothing," she says. "You stay there and watch TV or whatever you want, but don't touch anything and don't let anyone into the house. Jesus, what a fucking mess, excuse my French. Did he leave a letter or a note or anything around?"

Bob says yes, there was a note.

"What's it say?"

He pulls out the envelope and reads the note to her, slowly, as if reading it for the first time.

Sarah laughs. "I guess the hell he *was* a failure. Took him long enough to admit it, though."

"Sarah, for God's sake! How can you say stuff like that? The man's dead now. You've *changed*, Sarah."

She is silent for a second, then says, "No, I haven't changed. You just never paid attention in the first place. Just like him. I'm sorry he's dead, of *course* I'm sorry he's dead, but our marriage went down the tubes years and years ago, whether you wanted to see it or not. So I can't pretend to be the grieving widow. Frankly, I'm pissed. I'd feel a lot sorrier for him if it had been a car

accident and he was drunk and hit a pole or something.
But Eddie was a bastard. You know that as well as
anyone. And he was a sad bastard, a pathetic little boy
of a man, and I always knew that. And you did too. No,
I feel sorrier for Jessie than anyone else, because now
she has to live with the fact that her daddy killed himself
because he felt sorry for himself. Because he thought he
was a goddamned failure."

"Shit, Sarah, let's not talk like this, not right now.
Okay? He's my brother. I've lost my brother. Let me
. . . let me just be . . ."

"I've lost a husband," she cuts in. "And Jessie's lost
a father. I've got a right."

"Yeah, I know. I know. But let's not argue about
what kind of man he was, or how we ought to be feeling.
Plenty of time for that later. It doesn't matter right now
what kind of man Eddie was. He's a dead man is what
matters. You know?"

"Yes. Fine."

"I'll . . . I'll get the name of the funeral home they took
him to. I'm sorry about that, it was just that I was kind
of upset right at that moment and all and wasn't paying
the right kind of attention. I'll take care of things here,
till you get here, I mean."

"No," she says. "Just stay in the house, and don't do
anything, you hear? Don't let anyone in, either. Things
are more complicated than you know. Eddie got everything screwed up, so it's not gonna be easy to untangle
things. The bastard."

"Sarah, he *tried*. Eddie tried. For Christ's sake, I
know a *little* bit."

"Bob," she says sweetly, "you only know a little. I
know a *lot*."

Bob tries to argue with her, not to prove her wrong, just
to soften her feelings somewhat, but he can't get over
the wall of authority she's put up between them: she
knows the truth, has always known the truth, and he
knows almost nothing.

He does know, however, that his wife Elaine, unlike
his brother's wife Sarah, will not treat him and Eddie in

such a hard, self-centered way, and he's right, for when he calls her and tells her about Eddie's death, she is indeed properly dismayed and feels deep pity for both Bob and Eddie, which pleases him and fills his heart with renewed affection for her. But not for long. When he tells her what he planned to tell her, that he will take an evening job himself, as soon as he gets back down from Oleander Park, which may be a few days, since he has to run things up here, she responds coldly and says only that she can make more money as a waitress in one night than he can pumping gas part time for a week. And when he unfolds to her his plan to borrow enough money from Ave to buy the remaining three-quarters of the *Belinda Blue* from Ave, she laughs outright. "For God's sake, Bob, now you sound just like Eddie," she says, as if she were talking to a child and the consequences of his acts could in no serious way affect her life, only his.

When Bob Dubois is confused, he often responds by becoming angry, and now both his sister-in-law and his wife have confused him, so he slams down the phone and stalks out of Eddie's kitchen, a large, shadowy room cluttered with dirty dishes, glasses, pots and pans, piles of dirty laundry, unread mail and newspapers, the room smelling of old garbage and burned cooking, and heads for Eddie's liquor cabinet below the wet bar in the living room. The shades are drawn here, and the room is dim and sedately gray. Bob pours himself a double shot of Canadian Club and tosses it back in two gulps.

Refilling the glass, he eases himself down into the large, L-shaped, wine-colored sofa, picks up the phone from the table next to it and dials his old friend Avery Boone.

It's Honduras who answers. Bob does not want to talk to any more women. He speaks to her as if she were a receptionist. "Ave, please." She recognizes his voice and laughs, that same, high-pitched, mocking laugh she threw at him from the boat last night. "Let me speak to Ave, please," he repeats.

"I got some stuff of yours here, Bob. Pair of pants, tee shirt, shoes and socks. Even a pair of underpants.

All nice and clean, freshly washed and dried and pressed. Got your wallet here too. You were right, honey, you are broke.''

Bob says, "Just put my stuff on the boat." The wallet he needs only because his driver's license is inside it; the money in his pocket now is what's left of a twenty-dollar bill he took from Elaine's purse before leaving this morning. He's suddenly afraid he won't have enough money to get home on. Maybe he can borrow some money from Sarah when she gets in from Connecticut this afternoon. Oh, Christ, he thinks, I don't have enough money to buy a damned newspaper when I want to. I have to live like a goddamned kid, begging and borrowing money I can't pay back from the grownups, who all happen to be women now.

"Where's Ave?" he asks.

"You know, honey. Still out on the boat with Tyrone."

"Tell him when he gets in that I have to talk with him, so he should call me right away."

"Now, don't you go carrying any tales back to him. You were just as bad as me, you know."

"Yeah, don't worry, I won't say anything. But last night was it, girl. Never again. You understand?"

She laughs and says, "Of course," as if she does not believe him, though it's not clear to Bob if that's because she thinks she's irresistible or he is. He decides it's because she thinks she's irresistible, which means he'll have to be on his guard from now on. Bob understands men; it's women who confuse him and make him angry, which he is, once again, and so once again he slams down the receiver and knocks back the Canadian Club.

The room is gray and damp and smells to Bob of the death of men and of their debts. Everywhere he looks he sees something that reminds him of male helplessness and ineptitude—the framed pictures of Jessica on horseback, on water skis, in her Holy Communion dress, pictures of a girl gone north to Connecticut with her mother because her father, the fool who snapped the pictures, was too loud, too selfishly obsessed with becoming rich, too insensitive to anyone's pain but his own. And the room itself, with its department store decorations, huge, ornately framed pictures of New England villages and covered bridges in autumn hung above the long, low sofas and marble-topped tables, the pale green wall-to-wall carpeting, the neo-colonial wet bar with thirty different kinds of liqueurs underneath, everything in the room expensive, ready-made, impersonal—Bob sees it clearly now, all for show.

All for nothing, Bob thinks. His brother's strut and brag were empty from the start, and in a deep, barely conscious way, Bob knew that all along and forgave him his strut and brag simply because they *were* empty. But he never believed that it would all come to this, to nothing. Actually, he had envied his brother's show, had thought that the appearance of confidence, knowledge, wealth and power would somehow over the years demand or create the reality, and Eddie would in fact *be* confident, knowledgeable, powerful and wealthy. Bob thought that was how you became those things. You created an outer man you could admire, and then after a time, over years, the inner man gave in to the pressure of the outer and fell into line, and from then on, the two marched in step together, like brothers. And when one died, the other died with him.

But here is Bob, living on alone, and if he feels more like a child than a man, it's the women who make him feel that way, he thinks, his wife, his sister-in-law, his friend's girlfriend. What he believes he needs to induce these women to make him feel like the grown man he's become is money, and he has none, or sex, and after last night with Honduras, he hasn't much of that, either. Since the birth of Robbie last fall, a shadow has fallen between Bob and Elaine, so that they rarely make love now, and when they do, it's perfunctory and routine, a polite form of exchange. Elaine grew fat during the pregnancy and stayed thick in the hips and belly afterwards and started to speak of her body as if it were not hers but belonged instead to a pathetic, neglected, insecure friend. Anything that pointed to its existence distressed her, and sex most emphatically pointed to the existence of her body. And for Bob, the birth of his son has resulted, oddly, in his feeling outnumbered and alienated from his entire family—the three children and mother became one unit, and he became a solitary, outriding, secondary unit, like a comet passing accidentally through their solar system and moving on into deep space alone. That is not the kind of man who strolls through his house feeling sexy.

Bob remembers that the last time he felt truly sexy, which is to say, the last time he felt like an adult male instead of a boy inside an outsized body, was with Marguerite, before he went out there with the gun, of course. If only he could see her now, tall and mocha-colored, with her soft, Southern voice licking him all over, if only he could lie with her in a darkened room and tell her about Eddie and how strange the idea of going on alone without him makes him feel, then he would be able to understand it all, Eddie's death and life and the suicide that's made one the expression of the other. He would be able in the telling to learn how he is different from Eddie, as one man is different from another and not as a child is different from an adult.

But it's too late now for him to talk to Marguerite. He ruined that possibility the last time he saw her, that afternoon in October when he nearly went crazy with a gun in his hand. She hates him now, Bob is sure. She probably hates all white men now, he thinks, and then he winces, for he is once again thinking of them both in terms of color, which he cannot seem to avoid doing, even though every time he does it, he loses sight of her face and voice and almost forgets her name. It's not that he believes there is anything morally wrong with this; it's that he's genuinely frustrated, feels deprived, experiences a loss when it happens.

Maybe if he called her on the telephone and chatted for a few minutes about trivial things, for old time's sake, say, just to catch up, say, he would be able to read her voice well enough to know whether, if he asked her to meet him, she would say yes, sure, why not? He will not ask her to meet him if she is going to say no. Then it would be like talking to all the other women he's talked to this morning, and it's specifically to counter the effect of those conversations that he is deciding now to call Marguerite Dill.

He can't remember her number and has to look it up in the telephone book in the kitchen, which he finally locates under a stack of old newspapers on the table. It's almost twelve-thirty, he notices, and a weekday. She won't be home. He says this to himself with relief, which surprises him. But then she answers the phone, says, "Hello?" and he's so glad to hear her voice, so thrilled by its familiar, buttery tone, that he cannot speak.

She repeats, "Hello?"

He opens his mouth, wets his lips with his tongue, but says nothing.

"Who's there? Hello?"

"Marguerite, it's me, Bob. I . . ."

She's warm and quick, a kind, friendly, intelligent woman who takes the initiative in the conversation, as if she knows that to do otherwise would threaten Bob and make the conversation difficult. She asks him questions, where has he been living since he left the store, what kind of work has he been doing, how is his family, and she succeeds in conveying with the form and tone of her questions the clear impression that she now regards him as a dear, old friend.

Bob responds as he must, as a dear, old friend. "Well, I was in town . . . and I wanted to say hello. My brother . . . Eddie, he died."

Marguerite is shocked, saddened, full of pity for everyone. "You must feel awful!" she exclaims. "Daddy's going to be sad to hear this. He was right fond of your brother, you know. He hated leaving him when the store closed up," she says, adding, "That's how come you managed to catch me now. I come home at lunchtime to check on Daddy, 'cause he's here alone now. He's fine," she says, as if Bob has asked after the old man.

"Good, that's good. Give him my regards. Listen, Marguerite, I really wanted to talk to you . . . to apologize for . . . well, for the way I acted there, back in October, you know. I . . . I was under a lot of pressure, a hell of a lot of pressure, and, well, I guess I kinda lost it for a while, you know?'

She is sweet and forgiving. He needn't apologize, she understands, though maybe she didn't really understand it all as well then. But what with the new baby coming, and what with his troubles with Eddie and the store, after that robbery . . . which reminds her, she says, her voice brightening. "You remember that man, husband of my cousin, the one you chased over here?"

"Yeah, listen, that's what I'm talking about, that's what I want to apologize to you about, that more than anything else. I mean . . ."

"No, no, no! You were right about him! That one, he's a bad man, all right. He got himself arrested by the police up in North Carolina about a month ago. My cousin told me all about it. Robbing a liquor store, just like he was robbing yours, and turned out he told the police up there everything."

Bob is dumbfounded. "What? What do you mean?"

"Leon, that's his name, Leon Stokes, he admitted robbing a whole bunch of liquor stores, including yours, most of them in Florida and Georgia. They found some drugs in his car, and I guess they made some kinda deal with him on who sold him the stuff or something, because he's in jail now. But only for a couple years for robbing the liquor store in North Carolina, because he had to witness at a couple other big drug trials up there and in New York. So you were right."

"I was right?"

"Sure were, honey. Right as rain. It's me who ought to be apologizing."

"I was right? That doesn't make sense. I was *wrong*."

"Nope. You had the man, all right. Leon Stokes. I had no idea, you understand. I was just giving him a lift over to Auburndale, where he said he had some friends who were putting him up a while. If I'd have known, well . . ."

"No, no, you don't understand," Bob says. "I was

wrong! It doesn't matter that I was right about the guy; I was acting crazy. I didn't know what I was doing, you know? I mean, Jesus, Marguerite, I could've *shot* the guy, and I didn't even know it *was* the guy."

"Yeah, and you would've done a lot of people a favor, probably, if you had shot him."

"No, listen, you don't understand. Listen, I really do need to talk with you. Can we get together, can we meet someplace? After you get off from work?"

There is a long silence, and finally Marguerite says in a quiet, steady voice, "I don't think we should meet, Bob."

"What? Why?"

"Bob, it's over now between us. Right?"

"Well, yeah, sure."

"There's no sense firing it all up again. It was nice and . . . and interesting for a while, and we're friends now and all. But we shouldn't see each other anymore. Besides, I got a man now, and he wouldn't like it. . . ."

"Aw, Christ!" Bob bawls. "Jesus H. Christ! You got a *man* now. I suppose a black man."

"Well, yes, as a matter of fact. But I don't see what that's got to do with anything." Her voice has gone cold.

"Nothing, nothing, nothing at all. Look, I'm just . . . I'm disappointed, that's all. I'm sorry. I wanted to talk with you, see, about stuff. Eddie and all, I guess, and oh, Jesus, what the hell does it matter? I'm really sorry for everything. You . . . you're fine, you're wonderful. Don't worry, I won't come around or call you anymore or anything. Don't worry, I understand. Well, look," he says, changing gears, "I got to go now, I gotta arrange Eddie's funeral and all, and his wife is flying down from Connecticut. . . ."

"I'm real sorry about your brother, Bob."

"Yeah, well, I guess he was a lot worse off than anybody thought. Look, I got to go. It's been good talking to you."

"I'm real sorry, Bob."

"Yeah. Me too."

"Goodbye," she says, and quickly hangs up. He holds the dead receiver in his hand for several minutes, then places it slowly back in its cradle. The blood on his hands has dried to a dark brown map.

He stands, studies the wreckage that surrounds him, and walks slowly through the living room to the front door, opens it and walks outside, leaving the door wide open behind him. It's still raining, a dense, straight, windless rain from a low, overhanging sky. Bob wants to keep going, but he doesn't know where to go. He wants to get into his car and back it slowly down the driveway to the road, turn and head out of here, light out of Florida altogether. But to where? He can't go back to New Hampshire, and there are no new places anymore, none that he can imagine, and if he heads south again, back to Miami and the Keys, it'll be as if he's gone in a circle. He turns and returns to Eddie's house and slowly, methodically, starts cleaning up the mess his brother has left behind.

9

BOB IS SEATED AFT IN THE *ANGEL BLUE* IN ONE OF THE fighting chairs, swiveling it idly from side to side. Ave emerges from the galley carrying two king-sized cans of Schlitz. "Here you go," he says, handing one of the cans to Bob.

It's dark, the boat is tied up in her slip in the marina next to the *Belinda Blue*, and there's a three-quarter moon in the eastern sky, scraps of silver cloud drifting across its face. A pair of pelicans perched on a piling near the bow of the *Belinda Blue* seem to watch the two men. The boats rock gently in the still water, and along the pier here and there a man and a woman or sometimes several men and several women sit aboard their boats and talk and drink. Behind them, at the end of the pier, the jukebox in the Clam Shack is playing a Kenny Rogers song about a gambler.

"Sorry I couldn't see you yesterday or sooner today," Ave says as he eases into the other fighting chair. He's barefoot, wearing shorts and a zippered nylon jacket. His long reddish hair fluffs out from his head like an aureole, and the pale hairs on his tanned legs and the backs of his hands shine in the moonlight like straw. He puts his feet out and rests them on the gunwale and lights a cigarette, offering the pack to Bob.

"No, thanks." Bob is dressed, as usual, in chinos and white tee shirt, and tonight he's got his captain's hat on. He takes a sip of beer. "No, that's okay. I had a lot to do anyhow the last couple of days, with the funeral and all. And then I had a party of six this morning to take out. This's the first chance I've had to sit still for more'n ten minutes."

"Yeah, well, I didn't get back till real late last night. And then I had some business to take care of today, so, yeah, me too," Ave says. He studies the pelicans a second, as if aiming a weapon at their long, drooping heads. "You know how I feel about Eddie, Bob. I'm real sorry. Whew! Incredible, isn't it? Who'd have figured it? You know?"

"Yeah."

"I mean, who'd have figured ol' Fast Eddie would take the fucking pipe?"

"Yeah."

"There's . . . ah, there's no way it was accidental or something, is there? I mean, he was epileptic, I remember, and funny things happen sometimes."

Bob snorts. "No way. I found the body, his body. He was having them, seizures, quite a lot lately, but no, this was his own doing, his decision."

"Jesus. I just can't believe it. You know? There's no way it coulda been fixed up? You know, arranged. He was playing with some pretty heavy dudes up there, and maybe . . ."

"No. They did an autopsy."

"Incredible, man. Just fucking incredible. Ol' Fast Eddie, always running around yakking and laughing his head off, a million theories. Good hockey player, though."

"Yeah."

"Incredible, though. I just can't figure it."

"Well, Eddie wasn't what he seemed, that's all. And it took something like this, I guess, to let us know that."

"Yeah." Ave takes another slug from his Schlitz. "A lot of people aren't what they seem. You know?"

"Yeah."

The men are silent for a moment, and then Ave says, "Honduras told me you fucked her the other night."

Bob says nothing, looks down at the top of the can of Schlitz as if lowering his head to pray. "Honduras told you that?"

"Yeah. True?"

Bob is silent, and then he says, "Well, Ave, what if I said no? What if I said I drove over here the other night looking for you, and you weren't here, so she gave me some grass and some coke and then came on to me, only I turned her down? What if I said that?"

"You saying that's what happened?"

"Jesus H. Christ, Ave. If I *did* fuck her, why would she turn around and tell you? It only makes sense for her to claim I fucked her if instead what I did was turn her down. She'd hafta be pretty pissed at me, wouldn't she?"

Ave scratches his pointed chin. "She's a strange girl, lots of weirdness there. But she doesn't fuck my friends. Not while she's fucking me, anyhow. She knows that. And my friends, they don't fuck her, either. They're supposed to know that. Did you fuck her, Bob?"

Bob says, "I'm going to tell you the truth. And then I'm going to ask you a hard question that I expect you to answer with the truth. Fair?"

Ave looks over at his friend, who is staring upward, the fighting chair tilted back, at the night sky, a wash of stars overhead. "Yeah. Fair."

"No. I didn't fuck Honduras," Bob says, still looking at the dark blue sky. "Did you fuck Elaine?"

"What?"

"I said, 'Did you fuck Elaine?' "

"Jesus Christ, Bob! Why do you ask a thing like that?"

"She told me you fucked her. That's why. Four years ago, back in Catamount. But as far as I'm concerned, it's like it was last night, you know?"

"Women are crazy, man," Ave says. He exhales noisily. "Crazy."

Bob sips slowly from his beer and watches Ave over the top of the can. "Did you?"

Ave says, "Listen, I like Elaine a lot. A whole lot. But if she says I fucked her, she's lying."

"That so?"

"Yeah. We . . . okay, we talked about it once, you know, kind of flirting with the idea. I guess I'd had a few too many, and maybe she had too, I don't know, it was a long time ago. I don't know where you were."

"Out on the boat. Fishing. I remember where I was. I was a couple miles off the Isles of Shoals outside Portsmouth. It was summer, late July, early August, the bluefish were running, and you had some kinda excuse for staying home."

"Okay, okay, I don't remember what it was. But anyhow, she didn't exactly come on to me, but it was sort of clear that if I made a move . . . well, she'd respond in kind. But honest to God, Bob, I said no. Hey, she's a good-looking woman, but no way I was going to fuck my buddy's wife."

"So why'd she tell me you did?"

"Beats the shit out of me! Women are crazy, man! Like Honduras. I mean why'd she tell me you fucked her?"

"I didn't," Bob says quietly.

"I *know* you didn't, man! But why'd she say you did?"

"She was pissed at me for turning her down, I guess."

"Well," Ave says, "there you go."

"I guess so," Bob says, and he sighs. "I guess so."

For a while, the men say nothing. Fireflies dart past them and go out, and the pelicans shift their weight, turn and watch a boat on the opposite side of the pier. Bob says, "Ave, I have got to make more money than I'm making."

"No shit. I'm glad you noticed." Ave gets up from his chair. " 'Nother beer?"

"Yeah." He collapses the empty can and hands it to Ave, who heads forward to the galley. When he returns and passes Bob a fresh can, cold and solid as ice, Bob says, "I'm stuck in a fucking rut, Ave. My wheels are spinning. I can't make enough from my share of the *Belinda Blue* to live on, let alone save up a few bucks every month so I can buy a larger share so I *can* make enough money to live on. It's what you call a vicious circle. And it's making me crazy, it's making Elaine crazy—for Christ's sake, she's gone and taken a job working nights at the Rusty Scupper up in Islamorada. I just dropped her off there a while ago. Hafta pick her up at one."

"Jesus. What about the kids?"

"Baby-sitter. Tonight. Woman across the way. Otherwise, me."

"Jesus."

"It's worse. Ruthie, she's got . . . she's got some problems, emotional problems, and now the school says she's got to get some kinda special treatments at the mental health clinic down in Marathon, and who the fuck can afford Blue Cross these days? I used to have a great health insurance plan when I was fixing oil burners, but working for yourself like this, you know, you just say forget it, I'll take my chances."

"Yeah. I don't have any health insurance."

"You don't have any kids, either. That's really what I'm talking about. I got to make more money."

Ave says, "Well, Bob, there's ways."

"Yeah, I know. But I got kids and a wife, like I said. I can't take the kinda chances you take. Anyhow, what I've been thinking is, there's a way I can get a bigger share of the boat, which would let me keep a bigger share of the profits. But I need you to help me."

Ave listens carefully, like a bank director, as Bob unfolds his plan: Ave will loan Bob forty-five thousand dollars, which Bob will then pay over to Ave for the rest of the boat, and then, with Bob's increased share of the profits, he will pay Ave back, say, a minimum of five thousand a year, or whatever Ave thinks is right, with interest, which should also be whatever Ave thinks is right. Bob will pay for all repairs and maintenance, operating costs and so on, everything associated with the *Belinda Blue,* just as if she were his own boat.

"It would be your own boat," Ave points out. "That's the trouble."

"What do you mean?"

Ave sighs heavily. "I owe a lotta money, Bob. A shitload. And the *Belinda Blue*'s my collateral. I can't sell her without paying off the bank what I owe. They got the title. For the apartment they got it. If I hadda come up with that kinda money, to buy the title back, plus loan you forty-five more, I'd be talking close to a hundred grand. More, maybe. I haven't checked lately what I owe on the apartment. And even if I could come up with that kinda money, look where I'd come out. You'd own the *Belinda Blue* for a total of sixty grand, and I'd be out fifty grand minimum plus my three-quarters of the profits she turns, which ain't much, I know, but it makes a difference."

"Well, there'd be five thousand a year, plus interest . . ."

"You don't call that money, do you?"

Bob sinks lower into his chair. "Shit," he says. "I thought you owned the boat outright. I didn't know . . ."

"No, man! The bank's got me by the nuts. Just like everyone else around here. Why the hell do you think everyone with a boat is running dope, for Christ's sake? It's not to live good, pal. It's just to live. It all ends up going back to the banks. I couldn't run anything with the *Belinda Blue,* she's too fucking slow, so I hadda borrow money to buy a boat fast enough to make enough money to pay back the money I borrowed in the first place. That fifteen grand you gave me for your share of the *Belinda Blue,* man, that gave me the down payment for the *Angel Blue.* You talk about vicious circles. We're all in one. Circles inside of circles."

Bob lights a cigarette, inhales deeply and slouches

further down in his chair. "How come the bank let you sell off one-fourth of the boat, if you'd gone and borrowed against it? I never dealt with any bank, I just dealt with you. I got that bill of sale you wrote out, that's all."

Ave gets up from his chair and stands at the stern, looking over at the broad bow of the *Belinda Blue* rocking lightly in the water. Then, his back to Bob, he says, "I suppose you could get me into a heap of trouble with that bill of sale."

"Jesus." Bob feels himself falling backwards and down, as if down a well. In front of him and inside a small circle of blue light is Avery Boone's back, getting smaller and more distant, while he himself descends faster and faster and waits for the crash when he hits the bottom, for that's all that's left to him now, a backwards plummet and then a crash, and then nothing. It's over. He's ruined everything, he's lost everything, he's given away everything. There was the house in Catamount and the Boston whaler, their furniture, shabby and mostly secondhand, but theirs, and his job at Abenaki Oil and promises of an eventual office job there—there was a life, and because it was under his control, it was his life; and then he traded a big part of that life for one with more promises and less control, but even so, it felt much of the time like his life, for there was still a part of it that he controlled; and then he made another trade, giving away control for promises again, property for dreams, each step of the way, until he's ended up tonight with nothing but promises, dreams and fantasies left to trade with. And no takers.

He's run his life backwards, from what should have been the end to what should have been the beginning. He's reached the end too soon, at thirty-one, and has nowhere else to go. You could say he shouldn't have listened to Eddie, he shouldn't have listened to Avery Boone, he shouldn't have trusted these men, his brother and his best friend, men whose lives, though slightly more complicated than Bob's, were no more in control than his, and you'd be right. You wouldn't get any argument from Bob Dubois, not now, not tonight aboard the *Angel Blue* in Moray Key. He knows, however, that even if he hadn't followed his older brother to Oleander Park and hadn't followed Ave on down to the Keys, if instead he'd struck out for Arizona or California, where he knew no one, a stranger in a new world, he'd still end up one night just as he is now, his life a useless, valueless jumble of broken plans, frustrated ambitions, empty dreams. He'd end up with nothing to trade on.

It's not bad luck, Bob knows, life's not that irrational an arrangement of forces; and though he's no genius, it's not plain stupidity, either, for too many stupid people get on in the world. It's dreams. And especially the dream of the new life, the dream of starting over. The more a man trades off his known life, the one in front of him that came to him by birth and the accidents and happenstance of youth, the more of that he trades for dreams of a new life, the less power he has. Bob Dubois believes this now. But he's fallen to a dark, cold place where the walls are sheer and slick, and all the exits have been sealed. He's alone. He's going to have to live here, if he's going to live at all. This is how a good man loses his goodness.

Ave turns and faces him. Someone aboard a ketch a few slips down is running a blender, making margaritas. "I can get you some quick money," he says. "Not a shitload, but enough. Enough to pay for Ruthie's shrink or whatever."

Bob speaks in a low, thick voice. "Not drugs. No. I still got kids. I can't afford to lose. Like you can."

"Who can afford to lose? Nobody can. Anyhow, no, not dope. Haitians."

"Haitians?"

"From the Bahamas. Five, six hundred a head, whatever the market bears. It's easy. You just drop them off along the beach someplace—Key Largo, North Miami, they don't give a shit. You can load up with ten or twenty of them over at New Providence, drop them off before daylight and be home by breakfast. Tyrone knows the lingo. He can set it up for you. All you do is drive the boat. And what you make is yours, less the twenty-five percent or whatever you work out with Tyrone. Look, I owe you, Bob.''

"Yeah. Yeah, you do. A lotta people owe me. I'm starting to see that."

"You can always do dope, you know. The money's bigger, and the work's steadier. I mean, you run outa Haitians after a couple trips and have to wait till some more come over or save up the money for the ticket. Same with the Cubans from Mariel. But there's always a market for coke and grass, and there's always somebody looking for a boat to take it to the marketplace. It's riskier, of course. They got a lot more guys out there from Customs than they do from Immigration."

Bob cracks open his can of Schlitz and takes a long swallow from it. "I dunno, it's not the risk. Though that's part of it. I just don't like dealing with drugs somehow. I'm still a country boy at heart, I guess."

Ave steps forward and slaps his old friend on the shoulder and grins. "You sure are, you ol' sonofabitch. A goddamn New Hampshire country boy!" Then he starts to laugh, and Bob joins him, lightly at first, then merely smiling, as if Ave has told a filthy joke he doesn't quite get.

After a few seconds, Ave stops laughing and takes a swig from his beer, wipes his chin with the back of his hand and says, "Whew! It really is funny, though, when you think about it."

"Yeah? What, exactly?"

"Oh, shit, man, you know. The two of us, a coupla hicks outa the hills of New Hampshire, ending up like this. Running coke from Colombia and niggers from Haiti. It's fucking incredible."

"Yeah. Incredible."

"I mean, who'd have thought it?"

"Yeah. Who'd have thought it."

"I mean, you," Ave says, pointing a finger at Bob, and he starts to laugh again. "The Granite Skate! You!"

Action de Grâce

1

A FEW MILES WEST OF CORAL HARBOUR AND ELIZABETH Town on the southwest shore of New Providence Island, the beach hooks into the sea and offers a shallow, sandy-bottomed shelter. Inside the bay and about two hundred yards off the silvery, moonlit beach, the *Belinda Blue* cuts her engine and drops anchor. It's close to midnight, under a nearly full moon in a cloudless sky, and the boat, even without running lights, is easily visible from shore, a low, wide trawler fitted for sport fishing with outriggers and, according to the antennae atop the bridge, with navigational equipment.

She rocks lightly in the quiet waters for a few moments, then there's a splash from the starboard side. A motor-powered dinghy curves at low throttle around the stern of the trawler and heads toward shore. A black man is alone in the dinghy, half standing, one hand on the tiller, while aboard the *Belinda Blue* a white man can be seen making his way to the bow, where he gives several sharp tugs on the anchor line and, evidently satisfied, returns and disappears into the darkened cabin.

327

It's a warm, balmy night splashed silver-blue with moonlight, and the low waves and swells in the bay are streaked with phosphorus. Along the beach, tall, gracefully arched palms lay dark blue shadows against the white sand at their feet, and a short ways up the beach, a freshwater stream down from the inland hills emerges from the brush, broadens and empties discreetly into the bay.

The black man in the dinghy nears the shore, then cuts to his left and cruises along the beach just beyond the breaking waves, until he passes the shallow gulley in the beach where the stream enters the bay and the waves are calmed, neutralized by the counterflow of the stream, and here he's able to bring the boat in to shore easily and step from it directly onto the gravel. He draws the boat to shore and drags it a short distance into the brush.

Walking quickly inland along the east bank of the stream, he's soon beyond sight of the trawler anchored in the bay and, moments later, of the bay itself. His eyes adjust to the darkness, and he starts to see what he expected to see, a small village set among palm trees and scrubby undergrowth, a settlement of huts and shanties. He smells old woodsmoke from cold cookfires, and he smells garbage also, and human excrement and urine, poultry, pigs and goats.

A dog starts to bark nearby, probably from underneath one of the several huts set on cinder-block posts, and then another picks it up, and then a third and fourth in the distance. The man leans down to the pathway, gropes around for a second and picks up three small stones, rough bits of limestone. He hefts them in his right hand and walks hurriedly on.

Except for the several dogs, whose harsh cries pick up and join each other and erratically leave off, the village seems deserted. The cabins—sad, tiny, patched-together shelters against rain—are closed up and dark, with no cracks of light under doors, no orange glow from kerosene lanterns or candlelight flickering through windows. The man knows country villages well, and even as late at night as this, there are usually plenty of signs of life—men on stoops talking quietly, a child bawling, a boy chatting up a pretty girl at her door. This particular village is known to him, though he's only been here in daylight, and it was crowded then, Haitians, whole families of them and separate bits and pieces of families, too, people from all over Haiti. He did his business with them, got their names down, set the price, and said he'd return soon with the boat. Now he's back again, and he has the boat; but all the Haitians are gone.

Moonlight falls in swatches on the tin roofs of the cabins and shacks, and thick shadows gather and shift, as if turning in sleep, as the man passes along the lane that threads through the village. He remembers a settlement in the hills behind Port Antonio in Jamaica, a place he came home to as a boy after working all week in the Port loading bananas on freighters bound for New York and Liverpool, coming home to a sleeping village, his pockets full of money, his head full of dreams of someday going to America and becoming a millionaire, like those white people on their yachts he saw every day from the United Fruit pier, where he'd stop work for a moment and stare out from under the high, corrugated iron roof of the packing house across the pier to the blue water of the bay, the sparkling, slender boats, the peach-colored people in white shorts and shirts holding frosty drinks in their hands, their pretty mouths opening and closing toward one another like the mouths of elegant birds. Six days of it, and he'd ride back up to the hills on a wheezing, top-heavy, scarred and dented bus full of exhausted, sleeping workers from the piers, and he'd get off at the stop at the unpaved lane that led down to the village where he had been raised and where his mother and his younger brothers and sisters lived, and he'd begin the two-mile walk in through darkness, sudden splash of moonlight, dense shadow, between palms and impenetrable bush. Every noise from the bush made him jump, made him think, *Duppy!* and run a step or two, until he thought better of it, remembered he was supposed to be a man now and walk bravely through the night like one. But even so, he'd walk trembling and terrified of ghosts the whole way, until at last he reached the hamlet on the side of the ridge in the shadow of the Blue Mountains where his mother and family lived, where everyone he knew lived, and there would be a few men still playing dominoes and sipping rum by the shop who'd nod at him as he passed by, who would call, "Evenin', Tyrone. Back from de Port fe' good dis time, eh?" He would laugh and say, "No, mon, me home fe' check de fambly an' den me gone lak bird, mon."

AT THE FAR END OF THE VILLAGE, WHERE THE LANE CURVES into the bush, Tyrone turns and looks back. Where have all the people gone? He expected simply to walk into the settlement, ask for one or two of the Haitians whose names he'd taken down, go to them, have them round up the others, and then leave, all within an hour. He's done it that way before—he assured Boone and now Boone's friend Dubois he could do it that way again—and there's never been a hitch. The Haitians always wait for him diligently night after night, until he finally shows up with the boat, and within minutes, he's got their money in his pocket and has got them aboard, and by morning the Haitians are in Florida, and he and the white man who owns the boat are back on the Keys counting their money.

Of course, you can never rely on Haitians the way you can rely on other people. They're different somehow, almost another species, it sometimes seems, with their large, innocent eyes, their careful movements, their strange way of speaking. Creole. He learned it from the Haitians he worked with in the cane fields in Florida as a youth, when he was housed with them for months at a time in sweltering, filthy, crowded trailers. They drank the white rum they call *clairin* and played dominoes and listened to their music on the radio, and he, alone among the Jamaican workers, would join in, and before long he learned to talk with them, not well but enough to enjoy their company. The Jamaicans, most of whom were older than he, seemed to him morose, bitter, angry, in ways he was not. The Haitians, no matter what their age, seemed innocent in ways he was still trying to hold on to. If he had been a few years older, if he had known then what he learned about the world after he fled the work camp, he might never have dealt with the Haitians, but in those days he was still a boy, and like the Haitians, he felt lucky to be where he was, doing what he was doing, suffering as he was suffering.

He sees a shadow, a man, step forward from between two cabins and then step quickly back again, a tall, thin figure with a machete or big stick in his hand. Tyrone jumps off the lane into shadows of his own.

"Moin dit, monsieur!" Tyrone calls to the figure. *"M'apé mandé qui moune. . . ."*

No answer.

Tyrone takes a few tentative steps toward where the figure disappeared. *"Ça nous dit?"* he tries. *"Ma p' mandé coumen nou' yè, monsieur."*

Suddenly the watery voice of an old man comes out of the darkness. *"Bon soir, monsieur. Rajé gain' zoreille, monsieur."* The shadow has become an old man wearing an undershirt, baggy pants, barefoot, hobbling on a stick.

Tyrone approaches him, then draws back. The man's eyes are wild, red-rimmed, and he's grinning. A madman, Tyrone thinks. *"Bon soir, Papa,"* he says quietly.

"Comment nous yé, monsieur?"

"Bien, merci," Tyrone says.

The old man hobbles into the lane, where Tyrone can see him clearly in the moonlight. He's still grinning, broken-toothed, red-eyed, scrawny. *"Ça nous dit? Bel Français, pas lesprit pou' ça, monsieur."*

"Non. Mais . . . où est le peuple?"

"Eh?"

The people, the people who live here, Tyrone says. Crazy old man, he thinks, rum-drunk, telling Tyrone his good French doesn't make him smart, when he doesn't understand simple words like *peuple* himself.

"La famille semblé, monsieur."

"Coté yo, Papa?" Tyrone asks. Where are they?

"Eh?"

"Coté yo, le peuple? Les gens, Papa. Les Haitians."

The old man comes closer, his rum-sopped breath driving Tyrone backwards. His movements are abrupt, angry, a little confusing to Tyrone, who's starting to worry about time. They don't have much time to waste; none, in fact. It's a long trip back to the Keys in the *Belinda Blue*, especially loaded with passengers.

The old man is rambling in a singsong fashion, rattling out sentences Tyrone barely catches, about how he hurt his foot, why he's here alone, who's to blame for all his troubles. His name is François, Tyrone gathers that much, and evidently he hurt his foot because he was left unattended by the boy who was supposed to be his aide. *"Gain yun grand moune qui va facher!"* he says of himself. *"Li retou'né pied cassé!"* The old man who came home with a broken foot is going to be angry, he promises, which leads him to a litany of complaints: *"Depuis moin sorti la ville, moin apé cassé piéd moin. Ça qui fait petit moun fronté."*

Tyrone stops him, draws out his list of names, says the first name on the list, and the old man explodes with wrath, bangs his stick against the ground as if to wake the dead, for the very boy who deserted him and caused him to break his foot is nephew to that woman, who is herself a *jeunesse*, he claims, though Tyrone, of course, knows this about her, for he met her first of this group, met her almost a month ago, when she was in the room upstairs in the shop of the man who was murdered, Grabow, and in fact was thought by some to be the murderer, for she disappeared the same night Grabow was killed. Then, a week later, in the company of a boy who spoke some English, her nephew, probably, she came one night to Coral Harbour while Boone was over in Nassau doing his cocaine business. She had the boy call Tyrone out of a bar where he was playing dominoes and asked him to carry her over to Florida with her nephew and baby. He agreed to take them for the three hundred dollars they had, but only if she could find them ten or more additional passengers, who could pay five hundred a head, and she led him to the Haitians in the settlement west of Elizabeth Town. He hadn't asked her about Grabow; he figured that was between them, and if she did chop the man with a machete, he probably deserved it. Tyrone knew the man beat her and kept all the money she earned with her body in that tiny room above the shop. Pathetically, one night she told him, the only time she ever complained, *"M' pas 'ti bête, m' pas 'ti cochon, pou' on cové, pou' on marré moin,"* repeating in a sad, whimpering voice that she was not a little pig, a little animal that a man can keep tied up like this. Tyrone patted her tenderly on her naked shoulder, and then he walked downstairs and quickly departed, unable to look Grabow in the face. When he learned later that Grabow was dead, cut almost in half by a machete, probably by the whore he kept over his shop, Tyrone was glad.

The old man goes on complaining about *"le peuple, les gens, les Haitians . . . dipis temps y'ap pa'lé sou moin! Pilé pied'm ou mandé'm pardon. Ça pardon-là, wa fait pou' moin?"* and Tyrone finally interrupts him and asks to know where they've gone tonight.

The old man sputters, *"Le moin vlé pa'lé ou pas vlé moin pa'lé!"* When I want to talk, you won't let me.

Tyrone slaps his hands against his thighs, spins around and takes a step away. *"Non mélé kilé oudé, Nèg', non mélé-jodi-à."* We're all mixed up today.

"Non, monsieur," the old man calls, and scrambles after him. Then he asks for his gift, for money. *"Coté ça ou ba moin pou'm allé?"*

Tyrone digs into his pocket and comes up with some change, which he passes into the old man's outstretched paw.

"Merci, monsieur. Jé wè bouche pé," he warns—see but don't say. *"La famille semblé . . ."* he whispers, and he looks warily over his bent shoulder, like a dog warning off other dogs as he's about to eat. *"Soso na pé tué, soso, jodi-à!"* A pig is to be killed today. *"Pour Erzulie, 'Ti Kita, Gé Rouge, Pié Sèche. Pour les loas, les Invisibles, monsieur!"*

"Oui, Papa?"

"Oui, monsieur." Then he warns Tyrone to get himself gone, for this is not his country. This is Africa, he hisses. *"Poussé allé. Ça lan Guinée."*

Tyrone shakes his head no and asks where they've gone to kill the pig. He has to see some people now, tonight, for he has important business with them.

The old man jerks and turns himself around, wobbling on the pivot of one leg, a twitching, sudden kind of dance, almost a seizure. Then, his back to Tyrone, facing through the cluster of huts toward the sea, he speaks. His words seem jumbled at first, incoherent, uttered as chant, prayer or prophecy, Tyrone can't tell which, but the old man's voice and words frighten him.

"Nèg' nwè, conça ou yé, y'ap coupé lavie ou débor!" A black man like you, the old man warns, will eat with you, will drink with you, will cut the life out of you. *"Santa Marie la Madeleine, sonné une sonne pou' moin, pour m'allé."* Ring a bell for me, Mary Magdalene, so I may go. *"Sonné une sonne pou' les petites nagé."* Ring a bell for the drowned children.

Reaching forward with both hands, Tyrone grabs the old man's shoulders, and calling him by name, "François!" as if to break the spell, demands to know where the *hounfor* is located. Now, he must go there now, or it will be too late in the night to do his business.

François stops his dance, and he laughs, a long, loud, sardonic laugh. *"Bien,"* he says. *"C'est bien bon."* He will take him to the *hounfor*, he says, giggling. Now. But first there must be more money passed between them.

Tyrone unfolds a dollar bill and gives it to the old man, who limps past, mumbling and grumbling, one minute complaining about having to do this dirty business, the next promising Tyrone that he will love what he will soon see. *"Ou malhonnête, compé, compé à moin,"* he says. You are dishonest, my friend. And a second later, *"Nan Guinée plaisi-à belle! Oh, a n'allé wé yo!"* In Africa, pleasure is beautiful, as we shall see.

François heads into the darkness, taking an invisible path off the moonlit lane at the edge of the village. Tyrone hurries to catch up to the old man's bent form and follows him, a few feet behind, through the brush a ways, until he hears a stream nearby, where they turn right and walk upstream along the rocky bank. The old man walks quickly, more easily, it seems in rock and brush than back in the village, as if, once he stepped into the bush, his broken foot were miraculously healed.

2

FOR THE JAMAICAN, THE NEXT FIVE HOURS ARE DIFFICULT. He and Dubois had arrived at the Haitian settlement on New Providence later than they planned, which gave them little enough time as it was to anchor, come ashore, round up the Haitians and get out to sea again. Dubois was too cautious coming across from the Keys, afraid, perhaps, of the open sea, though he claimed he'd fished in the North Atlantic off New England in rough waters many times and this, to him, was a pleasure, easy sailing, a two-hundred-mile run due east across the Florida Straits and the Gulf Stream, south of the Biminis and north of Andros, with a mate, the Jamaican, who's made the trip a hundred times. Even so, he held the *Belinda Blue* back to half-speed, not much more than fifteen knots, and when they arrived at Coral Harbour, it was already ten o'clock at night, and though they didn't really need gas, Dubois insisted on filling the tanks. Then, because of the time, they had trouble getting anyone at the marina to sell them gas, which delayed them yet another hour.

"Better safe than sorry," Dubois told his mate, who nodded and said nothing, although he was already a little worried about how much time they were taking. This whole journey, once they had the Haitians aboard, ought to be made under the cover of darkness, or they were likely to be spotted in the Florida Straits by plane or helicopter and boarded minutes later by the coast guard. The surest way to get away with this was to come back across from the Bahamas in the nighttime, do the whole thing in darkness, which meant that you had to leave

New Providence before midnight, and even then you risked being seen at dawn off the crowded coast of south Florida.

Tyrone did not particularly like Boone's idea of bringing Dubois into their smuggling operations in the first place. Dubois is a good-natured man and a good fisherman, and he handles the boat well; he is not a hard man, however, not like Boone or most of the others in the trade. And something about Dubois puts Tyrone off, makes him mistrust him. He's too fretful, too unsure of himself, maybe too innocent, for this kind of work. And now, just as the Jamaican feared, here they are on their first job together, and they're already taking chances they should not take.

With the Haitians off in the bush for one of their African voodoo ceremonies, Tyrone thinks, they might as well postpone the crossing to Florida until tomorrow morning anyhow, and he hopes Dubois doesn't panic when the mate does not return quickly to the boat, that Dubois will simply wait for him all night anchored in the bay, even if it takes Tyrone till daylight to get back, as, with these crazy Haitians, it might. Haitians aren't like other people; everything is both more complicated for them and simpler, in ways you can't predict. Tyrone hopes that Dubois somehow knows this and that he won't be afraid or confused and pull anchor and run. Dubois himself, Tyrone thinks as he makes his way through the tangled bushes and scrambles over limestone rocks behind the mumbling old man, is a little like the Haitians. You never know what he might do. He seems to have his own peculiar way of seeing things, and that worries Tyrone. This kind of operation ought to be simple, he thinks, but with a man like Dubois, it can get complicated in a minute.

The Haitians' voodoo ceremony interests Tyrone only slightly. As a child in rural Jamaica, with his mother and aunts and uncles he attended many dances and ceremonies that he remembers now with no real pleasure and little understanding. Though the forms and content of these ceremonies are indeed the half-retained remnants of ancient African rites, they're not much more than scraps and rags torn off the intricately woven cloth of old Dahomeyan worship, and in rural Jamaica, these worn and faded bits of song, dance and drumbeat have been patched together with no conscious model or pattern for guidance, so that what was once a gorgeous, intricately coherent robe is now an ill-fitting smock that serves as a kind of peculiarly anachronistic invitation to sing and dance oneself into a frenzy and, for many, ecstatic possession.

That particular aspect of the Haitians' voudon, possession, is also ordinary, common, to Tyrone, something for old women and drunken men—he's seen it in church, on dance floors, at feasts in the maroon towns in the Cockpit Country of west Jamaica, and because he's never wanted it for himself, he has no interest in watching it in someone else.

As the Jamaican follows the old man up the long, gradually narrowing gorge in the Barrens and hears the drums grow louder and more insistent and the singing and chanting more coherent, as he glimpses through the bush flashes of light from candles and kerosene lanterns, he believes that, when he finally arrives at the *hounfor,* he will be able simply to move through the crowd as if he were at a camp meeting or revival back in West Kingston and tap each of his passengers on the shoulder and draw him or her away from the crowd and down the hill to the settlement, where they will quickly pack their bundles, take their money out of hiding and follow him down to the beach, where he will run them out to the *Belinda Blue* in the dinghy six or eight at a time. While he sweats and gasps for breath from the effort of keeping up with the old man, Tyrone busily speculates and worries about how he and Dubois might hide the Haitians once they are aboard, cover them with a tarpaulin, maybe, so the boat will look empty to a plane crossing overhead in daylight. Then they might be able to get across the straits and enter crowded waters by nightfall tomorrow, drop the Haitians south of Miami and be in Moray Key by midnight, drinking beer in the Clam Shack.

Tyrone is an eminently practical man; he believes that someday he will own his own boat. This Haitian mumbo-jumbo is country nonsense to him, an embarrassment of sorts, because they are black West Indians and he is a black West Indian also, and white people can't easily tell the difference between them. He'll be glad when this part of the journey is over.

Dubois will be glad too, Tyrone thinks. The man's nervous, worried that his wife will find out he's dealing in Haitians. As if it matters what she knows. Dubois told Tyrone his wife believes they're taking a party of Canadians out of Nassau and will be gone for no longer than a day and a night and the next day. Now, if they're ten or twelve hours late getting back to Moray Key, the woman will fret. And she may do something stupid, like call out the coast guard. This Dubois is trouble. Men like him should stick to fishing.

Suddenly, the old man leading Tyrone has entered a clearing, and Tyrone has automatically followed and has found himself in a crowd of men, women and children, their faces raptly attentive to what's going on beyond them. They are looking into a cleared space the size of a large room, covered with thatch, where a *service* is being conducted. The drums have ceased, and the people have been stilled, and the *action de grâce,* the formal invocation, has begun.

An elderly man with spectacles and dressed in white, the *prêt' savanne,* stands by the centerpost and reads from a prayerbook. In the dust at the base of the centerpole, an elaborately geometrical *vever* has been drawn in flour and ash, and a short ways behind the post, an altar has been set up, a long table covered with white cloth over which have been carefully arranged lithographs of the saints, a plastic crucifix and vials of holy water, lighted candles, bowls of food—rice, cassava, chicken, bananas, corn—and glasses of coffee, orange soda, Coca-Cola.

A short way to the right of the *prêt' savanne,* a woman in a red satin dress, the *mambo,* is seated on a kitchen chair. She's rocking slowly back and forth in the chair, her eyes tightly closed, her right hand rhythmically shaking the *asson* in time to the drone of the old man with the book, who chants on and on, occasionally rising to song and then falling back to chant again. Every now and then, as if to punctuate a particular phrase or prayer, the *mambo* calls out, *"Grâce mise' corde!"* and the audience repeats her call, *"Grâce mise' corde,"* and the *prêt' savanne* drones on,".*. au nom de Dieu, au nom de Sainte Vierge de Cièl, au nom de Saints de Tè', au nom de Saints de la Lune . . ."*

The Jamaican scans the crowd for familiar faces, but is momentarily distracted by the sight of a group of animals tethered to a small mahoe tree off to his right and attended by a trio of young women wearing white, full-skirted dresses and scarlet headbands. The animals are various and peaceful together, several ruffle-feathered chickens, a pair of doves, a black, yellow-eyed goat, a small gray pig and a large black boar. Beyond the animals is a cookfire and next to it a second altar table covered in white and loaded with bowls and bottles of food and drink. Tied to the top branches of a tall cottonwood tree are several white and red banners, hanging limply in the windless moonlight.

The people all suddenly kneel, and Tyrone, the only person left standing, quickly kneels with them, as the *prêt' savanne* intones the prayers, a Pater Noster, the Credo, the Ave Maria. During the prayers, Tyrone lifts his head slightly and sees that the *mambo* is staring directly at him, a hard, hot look that alarms him. He peers around at the crowd on his left, recognizes, despite their bowed heads, one or two of the Haitians he signed up, scans the group to his right and sights Vanise and the boy, her nephew. Vanise is praying fervently, crossing herself over and over, but the boy is watching the *mambo*. His gaze follows hers across the clearing of the peristyle and into the audience, and when he sees Tyrone, he smiles broadly and nods.

Tyrone smiles back.

There is a benediction offered by the old man in spectacles, and everyone rises, and the man shifts into a chanting, hymnlike song, accompanied now by the drums, slowly, seriously, bringing the people's voices into it one by one, until soon everyone is singing together, and all three drums are throbbing in unison. The *mambo,* who has not once taken her powerful eyes off Tyrone, begins to move in time to the song, shouting as she stamps and whirls across the smooth ground:

> *Poussé allé,*
> *Poussé allé,*
> *Icit pas pays ou!*
> *Ça lan Guinée,*
> *Icit pas pays ou!*

Gradually, her dance circles her toward the audience, which parts for her as she spirals near, making a path that leads straight to Tyrone. Coming toward him from the other side, pushing and pulling at people's shoulders, squirming between them, is the boy Claude. Both the *mambo* and the boy reach Tyrone at the same instant.

The woman glares into Tyrone's face, studies it sharply, bit by bit, his eyes, nose, mouth, his beard and dreadlocked hair, as if expropriating each piece of him and making it her own.

"Icit pas pays ou!" she hisses. This is not your country. *"Ça lan Guinée!"* This land is Africa. *"Poussé allé!"* she shrieks at him. Get you gone!

Over on his left, Tyrone sees the old man with the stick, the man who brought him here, laughing and joining in with the chant, *"Poussé allé! Poussé allé!"* In seconds, the entire mass of people, sixty or seventy of them, has taken up the cry, and their faces have turned ugly and threatening, even that of the old man, François. There are young men and old, mothers, grandmothers and maidens, people in tattered clothes and people dressed meticulously in white, drunk men and sober, people who look sane to Tyrone and people who look insane, and all of them are raging at him, Get you gone! Get you gone! Get you gone!

Except one, the boy, Claude Dorsinville, who grabs

Tyrone by the arm and yanks him away, pulls him back into the trees and away from the crowd. The *mambo* wheels around and heads for the peristyle, where she takes up her dance again, and a woman is mounted by a loa, and a cheer goes up. The drums rise in intensity and pace and are joined by the clanging beat of the *ogan*. Another woman is mounted by the loa Damballah and throws herself face forward on the ground, where she writhes like a snake.

Back in the bushes, in darkness and shadow, Tyrone and the boy begin to speak to one another. The boy speaks almost as much English now as the Jamaican speaks Creole, and soon they have worked out a plan. Tyrone will wait down in the gorge a short ways, and the boy will bring the passengers to him, one by one. Some of them he already knows; others Tyrone will have to read out to him, for the boy cannot read. When they have all assembled in the gorge, the boy will join them, and together the group will go down from the Barrens to the village, where they will gather their few possessions, pay Tyrone and be transported to the boat, which is waiting for them in the bay. "Den we go to America, mon," Tyrone says. "Yout'-man, bring dem Haitians forward now," he tells the boy, who grins and ducks back into the bushes and heads for the *hounfor*.

Moments later, the boy returns with a scrawny, nearly bald man in tow, a man half-drunk, who turns obsequious as soon as he sees Tyrone. The boy disappears again, reappearing a moment later with two young men, tall, stringy twenty-year-olds who formally shake Tyrone's hand and cross their arms over their chests and wait in shy silence. Then a middle-aged woman with two small children, and an old, half-blind woman whom Claude leads by the hand and passes over to the woman with the children as if handing her a third child. This goes on rapidly, until at last Claude has brought out of the *hounfor* fourteen people, all the people on Tyrone's list but two, Claude himself and his aunt, Vanise.

The drums have reached a frantic yet still organized and coherent pace. The voices of the singers, however, as Claude has removed them one by one from the crowd, have diminished in volume and intensity way out of proportion to the numbers of the missing members of the chorus. It's as if every time Claude removes one singer, four others fall into silence. The Haitians surrounding Tyrone down in the dark confines of the gorge have begun to grow restless and agitated; they move about nervously, looking back toward the *hounfor* one minute and at each other the next, as if for corroboration or denial of the truth of what they have seen there.

Tyrone puts his list before the boy's sweating face and points out the boy's own name and that of his aunt. He himself doesn't really care if she comes or not, especially since he promised her a bargain rate, but he knows that she holds the boy's fare and there is now no way he will be able to leave without taking the boy. "Where Auntie, yout'-man?" he asks the boy. "Cyan forget Auntie."

"Him cyan come . . ." the boy says, looking at the ground. "Him . . . him got loa *en tête* . . . ," he stumbles.

Tyrone puts his arm around the boy's bony shoulders and steps him away from the others. "You got de money?"

Claude shakes his head no.

Tyrone shrugs his shoulders. "Got to get Auntie, den."

The boy turns and walks back toward the *hounfor*, which suddenly—or so it seems to Tyrone—has gone silent. He hasn't been paying attention to the noise and flickering lights from the *hounfor;* he's been concentrating on his passenger list. The Haitians in his group have grown extremely restive now, shifting their feet and looking at one another, then peering back up along the gorge to the trees that surround the *hounfor* and the red and white banners in the cottonwood tree, which have begun to flutter in an offshore breeze.

The group is made up half of men, half of women, with three small children. Tyrone goes back to counting them and adding up their fares in his head, calculating his share of the profits, one-fourth plus whatever he's able to skim off the top, when he hears someone breaking noisily through the brush behind him. He turns and sees the boy Claude, a small child slung against one side and the woman Vanise being dragged along behind. The boy is out of breath and grunting from the effort of pulling the woman through the short macca bushes and over the rough limestone, for the woman seems dead drunk or drugged, in a stupefied state with her eyes rolled back, her mouth slack, her legs and arms loose and wobbly. Her white dress has come undone almost to her waist, exposing her brassiere and dark belly, and is torn and spotted with mud; her hair is matted and awry, and her face is splotched with dirt.

Before Tyrone can respond, however, he's grabbed from behind. Hands like manacles clamp onto his upper arms, and he turns his head and faces a pair of large men, both carrying upraised machetes. Then the *mambo* herself steps free of the bushes and strides through the crowd, passes Claude and the baby Charles and Vanise without a glance. The woman in the red dress is smiling, but it's a calculated smile. She's carrying her rattle, the *asson,* in one hand, a small brass bell in the other, and as she passes, the Haitians back away in fear of her, as if her heat could burn.

Tyrone yanks against the men gripping his arms, but he can't move—their hands are like tightened vises that simply take another turn and hold him even more firmly than before. They aren't controlling him with their machetes; they don't have to: instead, they hold the huge, razor-sharp blades over his head in a ceremonial way, as if awaiting a signal to bring them down and slice the Jamaican in half.

The *mambo,* her coffee-colored face sweating furiously, her hair and dress disheveled, shakes the *asson* in the face of the Jamaican and spits her words at him. *"Moin vé ou malhonnet!"* I see that you are a dishonest man. *"Lan Guinée gangin dent','"* she says. In Africa there are teeth.

Tyrone answers in a low, careful voice: I am just passing through. *"C'est passé n'ap passé là."*

Yes, indeed—she nods and smiles—he *is* just passing

through. She makes a gesture with her rattle for the men with the machetes to release him, and then she turns to her flock. She separates Claude from the group with a push and says he, too, must pass through. Take the infant and pass along with the hairy one.

Vanise staggers when the boy lets go of her hand, and seems to be coming to, for she takes a step to follow him and Charles. But the *mambo* stops her with her bell. No, *hounci,* you stay.

Tyrone has backed off one careful step at a time, with Claude and the baby beside him, until they have moved out of the group and are standing in the gorge a ways below the others. He sees the red-eyed face of old François in the bushes next to him. The old man sneers at the *mambo* and shouts at her. *"Nen point mambo ou houngan passé Bondieu nan pays-yà!"* There is no *mambo* or *houngan* in this country greater than God.

The woman shrieks at him. *"Enhé, enhé, enhé!"* she curses. *"Papa Ogoun qui gain' yun mangé, tout moune pas mange, li!"* Now, she says, where are my children? *"Coté petits moin yo?"* She turns and looks across the faces of the crowd.

Signaling to the pair of men with the machetes, she starts back up the rocky path toward the *hounfor,* and they follow. The others mill about for a second, cease their movement and watch her go. Then they turn, Vanise included, and begin filing down the path after Tyrone.

As one by one they pass the old man, he cackles and taps them on the shoulder with his stick. Then at last they are gone, and the old man is standing alone in the narrow gorge, mumbling and every now and then breaking into a dry laugh, as if he knows what no one else knows.

"C'est pas faute moin!" It's not my fault, the old man sings. *"C'est pas faute moin! C'est pas faute moin!"*

3

WHERE THE STREAM ENTERS THE SEA, THE HAITIANS COME alone and in twos and threes from their huts to meet the Jamaican. In the bay, a half mile away, the trawler rocks lightly in the soft lavender predawn light, and beyond the hook of beach that protects the bay, open sea stretches straight to Africa, where the eastern sky is born, cream-colored near the horizon, fading to zinc gray overhead. In the west, above Florida, the sky deepens to purple, with glints of stars. A pair of gulls cruise hungrily along the beach toward the sandy hook, while overhead, its huge, motionless black wings extended like shadows, a frigate bird floats, watches, prepares to dive.

The Haitians are wearing their best clothes: for most of the men, clean white shirts, dark trousers, black shoes; for the women, brightly colored cotton dresses, sandals, headscarves. They carry cardboard suitcases, woven bags and baskets into which they've packed a change or two of clothing, if they own that much, a few personal items, maybe a small bottle of perfume or cologne, a family photograph in a gilt frame, a Bible or prayerbook, their *gardes* and *wangas,* and food for the journey—fruit, cassava, chicken, a bottle of *clairin,* some tinned milk. They may own more than these pitiful few possessions, a pot and a pan, some dishes, gourds, tools, bedding, a bicycle, but they don't hesitate to leave these things behind, for they are starting over, and soon, they know, they will own all the things that Americans own—houses, cars, motorcycles, TV sets, Polaroid cameras, stereos, blue jeans, electric stoves. Their lives will soon be transformed from one kind of reality, practically a nonreality, into a new and, because superior, an ultimate reality. To trade one life for another at this level is to exchange an absence for a presence, a condition for a destiny. These people are not trying merely to improve their lot; they're trying to obtain one.

Tyrone, the Jamaican, greets them as they arrive at the beach, and he takes each of them off a few steps from the others to complete his business with them privately, for he has agreed with them separately on the cost of the journey. When he has obtained all the money, he divides it into two packets, one thicker than the other. The thicker packet he will turn over to Dubois, telling him that's all he was able to extract from them.

The other, smaller packet he will keep in a separate pocket for himself. He feels no guilt for this; without him, Dubois would have nothing to show for his trip from the Keys but a sunburn and a gasoline bill at the marina in Coral Harbour.

When the Haitians have assembled on the beach, Tyrone drags the dinghy out of the bushes and across the gray sand to the water. He jumps in, seats himself at the stern and points out the first six and waves them over toward the bow of the boat.

He hollers to the boy, Dorsinville, and instructs him to hold the bow and help the others into the boat, and the boy jumps to the task. First the old lady and the young woman with her two children come aboard, then an old man going to Florida to be with his son and daughter, and a woman whose husband went over four years ago, and a young man whose older brother is in New York.

Tyrone signals the boy to push the boat out, which he does, and then he starts the motor, brings the boat around toward the sandbar, and in seconds he has the boat slicing through the still, velvety-gray water of the bay toward the *Belinda Blue*.

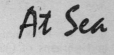

At Sea

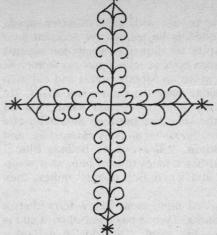

IT'S THEIR FACES THAT AGITATE HIM, BOB DECIDES, AND then he changes his mind: No, it's the way they move, silent as sheep and careful not to touch what the act of climbing aboard does not require them to touch. They bunch together like gazelles, nervous but apparently not frightened, and too shy to reveal their curiosity, so that their eyes seem glazed slightly, as if they've been stunned by the sight of the *Belinda Blue,* the tall, bulky white man standing on the deck reaching out his hand to help them board from the dinghy, the spaciousness of the boat, its long afterdeck and the cabin forward, which they glance at but do not examine, and over the cabin, the bridge, where the wheel and other controls are located, a radio squawking static and a red scanner light dancing back and forth along a band of numbers.

They seem so fragile to Bob, so delicate and sensitive, that he's suddenly frightened for them. Even the young men, with their hair cut close to the skull, seem fragile. He wants to reassure them somehow, to say that nothing will hurt them as long as they are under his care, nothing, not man or beast or act of God. But he knows he can't even tell them where they are going, what time it is, what his name is, not with the half-dozen words and phrases of Québécois he learned by accident as a child, learned, despite his father's prohibition against speaking French, from boys at school and old women at LeGrand's grocery store on Moody Street and old men fishing from the bridge over the Catamount River. He suddenly pictures the huge green and white sign on Route 93 north at the state line between Massachusetts and New Hampshire, *Bienvenu au New Hampshire,* and he says to the Haitians, *"Bienvenu au* Belinda Blue!" They turn their coal-black faces toward him, as if wanting to hear more, and when Bob merely smiles, they look down.

The boat is crowded now, more like a ferry than a fishing boat, Bob thinks. Tyrone has come aboard and is tying the dinghy to the stern. "We got to get up a cover," he says. He says it without looking at Bob, as if he thinks the two of them are alone on the boat.

"A cover?"

Tyrone stands, shakes out his stubby dreadlocks and comes forward to Bob, who's poised at the foot of the ladder, about to climb to the bridge and start the engine. The sun will be up, it will soon be daylight, the Jamaican explains slowly, as if talking to a child. More worrisome than the sun and heat, if they don't cover their cargo, they'll be spotted by a plane or helicopter, especially later in the straits. The Bahamians won't bother us; they're relieved to see the Haitians go. It's the Americans we have to worry about.

Bob nods somberly, though he resents the way the Jamaican speaks to him. In fact, he's found it difficult to like Tyrone since he discovered the man's connection with smuggling, first drugs with Ave and now Haitians with him. He's not sure why this should be so, for after all, he and Ave are even more directly involved with the trade than he is, but he thinks it has something to do with Tyrone's being black. It's not natural, somehow. He felt the same odd judgment come over him one morning out on Florida Bay a few weeks ago, when Bob asked Tyrone about the dreadlocks, asked him why the

Rastafarians grew their hair into tubes, something he'd been wondering about since the first day he saw them.

Tyrone smiled slyly and said that white girls liked it that way.

"Oh," Bob said. "I thought it was . . . you know, religious."

"For some, sure, mon. All dat Marcus Garvey song 'n' dance. But de white gals, mon, dem don't want to deal wid no skinhead, dem want to deal wid Natty Dread, mon. Got to have locks, got to have plenty spliff, got to say, 'I and I,' sometimes. Dat way dem know you a Jamaican black mon, not de udder kind. Den you got plenty beef," he said, laughing. "Too much beef! Oh, too much beef, mon!"

Together, Bob and Tyrone rig a tarpaulin cover over the deck, stretching it taut aft from the cabin and tying it at the corners, so that it's head-high at the cabin and waist-high at the stern. When they're satisfied with the job, Tyrone herds the Haitians under the tarp, forcing most of them to squat below the low end, warning them that if they don't huddle together back there, they'll be caught by the police and thrown in jail. They understand and follow his orders quickly and efficiently.

Tyrone scrambles forward to pull up the anchor, and Bob climbs up to the bridge and starts the engine. It gurgles and chuckles and then smooths out, and when Tyrone waves up to him, Bob hits the throttle, and the aft end of the loaded boat dips, the bow rises, and the *Belinda Blue* moves out of the bay, cuts northwest along the shore of New Providence past Clifton Point, where she edges back slightly to the west and heads into open sea. The sun is two hands above the horizon now, and the blue-green water glitters like a field of crinkled steel. Gulls dart across the wake, frigate birds drift past far overhead and a school of flying fish loops by on the starboard side.

It's a beautiful day, Bob thinks, and he says it, calls it out to Tyrone, who's perched out on the foredeck coiling the anchor line. "It's a beautiful day!"

The Jamaican looks up at him, cups his ear and says, "What?"

"It's a beautiful day!"

The Jamaican nods and goes back to work.

WITH THE EXTRA WEIGHT OF THE HAITIANS ABOARD, THE *Belinda Blue* wallows a bit and sits somewhat low in the water, but the day is calm, and she rides the swells and small waves with ease. Far to the south, the northern tip of Andros Island lifts like a whale, passes slowly to the east and drops again. The sun is higher now, and Bob is hot up on the bridge. He calls down to Tyrone, who's in the cabin stretched out on a bunk, and asks him to bring him a beer. A few seconds later, Tyrone, shirtless, hands up a can of Schlitz, frosty and wet from the ice.

"Whaddaya think, the Haitians, they thirsty?"

Tyrone looks back toward the tarpaulin, steps down to the deck and peers underneath. He'll give them a bucket of water and a dipper, he says to Bob. They'll share it out themselves.

"Fine, fine. Poor fuckin' bastards," he murmurs, as Tyrone disappears below. From the moment he first saw them ride out from the beach at New Providence in the dinghy, saw how astonishingly black they were, *African*, he thought, and saw how silent and obedient, how passive they were, he's been struck by the Haitians. There's a mixture of passivity and will that he does not understand. They risk everything to get away from their island, give up everything, their homes, their families, forsake all they know, and then strike out across open sea for a place they've only heard about.

Why do they do that? he wonders. Why do they throw away everything they know and trust, no matter how bad it is, for something they know nothing about and can never trust? He's in awe of the will it takes, the stubborn, conscious determination to get to America that each of them, from the eldest to the youngest, must own. But he can't put that willfulness together with what he sees before him—a quiescent, silent, shy people who seem fatalistic almost, who seem ready and even willing to accept whatever is given them.

He almost envies it. The way he sees himself—a man equally willful, but only with regard to the small things, to his appetites and momentary desires, and equally passive and accepting too, but only with regard to the big things, to where he lives and how he makes his living—he is their opposite. It's too easy to explain away the Haitians' fatalism by pointing to their desperation, by saying that life in Haiti is so awful that anything they get, even death, is an improvement. Bob has more imagination than that. And it's too easy to explain away their willfulness the same way. Besides, it's not logical to ascribe two different kinds of behavior to the same cause. There's a wisdom they possess that he doesn't, a knowledge. The Haitians know something, about themselves, about history, about human life, that he doesn't know. What to call it, Bob can't say. It's so outside his knowledge that he can't even name it yet.

He's intelligent and worldly enough now, however, not to confuse it with sex. That is, even though black people are still sexier to Bob than white people, it's only because they look better to Bob, for to him, a white man, black is presence and white is absence, which means that he can see them in ways that he can't see white people. Which also means, of course, that he can see white people in ways he's utterly blind to in blacks, as he learned by trying to love Marguerite. Bob has become one of those fortunate few men and women who have learned, before it's too late to enjoy it, that sex is just sex and it's all of that as well. He can take it *and* leave it, which is a much happier condition than having to do one or the other. He's not sure how this has happened to him, but he knows it has happened and that it has something important to do with Marguerite. There was no exact moment when his conscious understanding of his own sexuality changed; there simply came a time when he behaved differently—that is, without fantasy. As with Allie Hubbell in the trailer across the lane. As with Honduras. As with Elaine.

By the same token—his intelligence and worldliness—
Bob is unable to attribute to the Haitians' poverty what
he perceives as their wisdom. In the past, certainly, he
sometimes regarded poor people through the cracked
lens of liberal guilt, but that was before he discovered
that he was a poor person himself and stopped envying
the rich and started hating them. That was before he
learned that what was wrong with the rich was not that
they had something he wanted, but that they were unconscious, often deliberately so, of the power they wielded
over the lives of others. His brother Eddie was rich for a
while, and Bob envied him, until he himself suffered
sufficiently from his brother's unconsciousness to begin
at last to hate him, so that when Eddie lost everything,
Bob discovered he could love him again. If Bob had
gone on envying his brother, if he'd never learned to
hate the rich man he'd become, he would have been glad
when the man lost his wealth.

Bob remembers the night he shot the black man in the
liquor store, and the kid with the cornrows shitting his
pants in the back room, and he shudders. The sun overhead is warm on his shoulders, and the tropical sea
sparkles like the laughter of children at play, while up on
the bridge, his hands clamped to the wheel of the *Belinda
Blue,* Bob Dubois shudders as if an arctic wind has
blown over him. He remembers the night he came close
to shooting a man simply because the man had a haircut
like that of one of the pair who tried to rob him, the
night he turned the gun over to Eddie and walked out of
Eddie's house waiting to hear the sound of Eddie using
the gun on himself, half of him wanting Eddie to use it
on himself, the other half struggling to erase the thought
altogether. I didn't hate Eddie then, he thinks. I envied
him. It was only later, on Moray Key, when it seemed
to Bob that he was now truly poor, that he could begin
to give up clinging to fantasies of becoming rich. Then,
when it became clear to him that he had as much chance
of becoming rich as he had of becoming Ted Williams,
he gave up envying those he saw as rich. That's what
freed him, he believes, to love Eddie again the night he

called in such fear and pain, a lost brother returned to him for only a few moments, but returned nonetheless, and for that Bob is grateful. What Eddie did to himself he did himself, but how much sadder for Bob it would have been if, when Eddie died, Bob had been glad of it.

To say that Bob Dubois is intelligent is to say that he is able to organize his experience into a coherent narrative; to say that he's worldly is to say that he is in the world, that he does not devour it with his fantasies. Not anymore. These are relative qualities, of course, both of them depending on the breadth and depth of Bob's experience, and depending, then, on accident, since Bob has no particular interest in, or need for, broadening or deepening his experience per se. He's not an especially *curious* man. Mere psychological and moral survival will be enough for him to feel able to say, in the end, if he's given a chance to say anything at all, that he's lived his life well. He does not need, therefore, to poke into the mystery these Haitians present to him. What are they to him or he to them, except quick means to ends? They need him to carry them to where starvation and degradation are unlikely; he needs them to help him stay there.

He can't stop himself, however, from believing that these silent, black-skinned, utterly foreign people know something that, if he learns it himself, will make his mere survival more than possible. They cannot tell him what it is, naturally, but even if they spoke English or he spoke Creole, it could not be told. He shouts down to Tyrone, waking him this time. The Jamaican stumbles out of the cabin and blinks up at Bob.

"Want to take the wheel awhile? I need a break," Bob says.

The Jamaican nods and climbs the ladder to the bridge. Bob descends, ducks into the cabin, pulls a cold beer from the locker in the galley and eases himself back on deck. Squatting, he peers into the darkness under the tarpaulin, a sudden, hot, densely aromatic darkness that makes the can of Schlitz in his hand look luminous.

The Haitians are mostly lying down, a few seated on their heels and eating, one or two talking in low voices, several evidently asleep. But as one person, when Bob appears at the open end of their lean-to, they look up and, it seems to Bob, stare at him. He looks quickly away, sees the empty bucket and draws it toward him.

"More water?" he asks, his voice unnaturally high.

No one answers. They go on looking at him, their eyes large and dark brown, not curious or demanding, not hostile or friendly, either, just waiting.

"Water? Want more water?" he repeats. He picks up the bucket and turns it upside down, as if to demonstrate its emptiness.

A skinny teenaged boy squirms his way out of the clot of people and comes forward on his hands and knees and extends the metal dipper to Bob, then quickly retreats.

"Merci beaucoup," Bob says. He stands up and takes the bucket back down to the galley, refills it and returns to the Haitians, sliding it over the deck toward them.

Again, it's the boy who separates himself from the others by retrieving the bucket and dipper. Then, turning his narrow back to Bob, he proceeds to fill the dipper and hand it to the others, one by one—first the women, who let their children drink before they themselves drink, and then the old man and the other men—and finally he drinks. It's hot under the tarp, but not uncomfortably so, for there's a light breeze that sneaks across the rails at the sides. It's dark, however, and despite the breeze, it's close, moist with bodies crammed this tightly against one another, and Bob wonders if he should allow them to come out from under the tarp and stretch and walk about.

He calls up to Tyrone. "Whaddaya think, be okay to let them stretch their legs a bit? Seems kinda crowded and stuffy under there."

The Jamaican looks down at the white man, shakes his head no and goes back to scanning the western horizon.

Bob is sitting flat on the deck now, his legs stretched out in front of him, his can of Schlitz in one hand, a lighted cigarette in the other. He's got himself far enough under the tarp to be wholly in the shade, so he takes off his cap and drops it onto the deck next to him. The motion of the boat is choppier than it was, and Bob can tell from the sound of the engine that it's working harder, lugging a little. There's been an east wind behind them all morning, and now they've changed course a few degrees west-southwest, and consequently the wind is hitting them slightly to port. He knocks his pack of Marlboros against his knee, extending several cigarettes from the pack, and holds the pack out to the Haitians, who still have not taken their eyes off his face.

"Cigarette?"

The Haitians look from his face to the pack of cigarettes, back to his face again, their expressions unchanged.

Bob puts down his can of Schlitz and digs into his pocket for his butane lighter and again holds out the Marlboros. "C'mon, have a cigarette if you want."

It's the teenaged boy who finally comes forward and takes the cigarettes from Bob's hand. Bob passes him the lighter, and the boy draws out a cigarette for himself and passes the package around among the others, several of whom take out a single cigarette and put it between their lips. The boy lights his up and one by one lights the others. Then he turns back to Bob, passes the lighter and what's left of the Marlboros to him, and while they smoke, resumes watching him.

They aren't afraid of me, Bob thinks. They can't be—they must know I'm their friend. Quickly he corrects himself: No, I'm not their friend, and they're not foolish enough to think it. But I'm not their boss, either, and I'm not their jailer. Who *am* I to these people, he wonders, and why are they treating me this way? What do they know about me that I don't know myself?

The question, once he's phrased it to himself, locks into his mind and puts every other question instantly into a dependent relation, like a primary gear that drives every other lever, wheel and gear in the machine. That must be their mystery, he thinks—they all know something about me, and it's something I don't know myself, something crucial, something that basically defines me. And they all know it, every one of them, young and old.

It's almost as if they were born knowing it. He stares back into the eyes of the Haitians, and he can see that it's not just knowledge of white men, and it's not just knowledge of Americans; it's knowledge of him, Robert Raymond Dubois, of his very center, which he imagines as a ball of red-hot liquid, like the molten core of the earth.

For an instant, he breaks contact with the Haitians, and he thinks, This is crazy, they don't know anything about me that isn't obvious to anyone willing to take a quick look at me. He insists to himself that he's making it all up. It's only because they're so black, so African-looking, and because they don't speak English and he doesn't speak Creole, that he's attributing awesome and mysterious powers to them. It's their silence and passivity that frighten him and seem to create a vacuum that he feels compelled to fill, and what he's filling it with is his own confusion about who he is and why he's here at all, here on this boat in the middle of the ocean, carting sixteen Haitians illegally to Florida, when he should by all rights be someone else someplace else, should be old Bob Dubois, say, of Catamount, New Hampshire, a nice, easygoing guy who fixes people's broken oil burners, and on a late afternoon in winter like this, he should be heading back to the shop at Abenaki Oil Company to punch his time card, walk across the already dark parking lot, get into his cold car, listen to the motor labor against the cold and finally turn over and start, and drive down Main Street to Depot, turn left and park across from Irwin's and go in for a couple of beers with the boys and maybe a flirt or at least a beer with his girlfriend Doris, before he gets back into his car and drives home to his wife and children and eats supper around a table with them in the warm kitchen, and later a little TV in the living room while the snow falls outside and the children sleep peacefully upstairs, until finally he and his wife grow weary of watching TV and climb the stairs to their own bedroom, where they quietly, sweetly, even, make love to one another and afterwards fall into a deep sleep.

But that's all gone from him now, as far away as childhood. There's a difference, though, for childhood was taken from him, simply ripped away and devoured by time, whereas the rest, the life he believes he should be living now, Bob has given away. And he didn't give it away bit by bit; he gave it away in chunks. What's worse, he gave away Elaine's life too—or at last he believes he did. She might say it differently, for she is, after all, a kind woman who, despite everything, loves him. Regardless, Bob believes that he gave away everything in exchange for nothing, for a fantasy, a dream, a wish, that he allowed to get embellished and manipulated by his brother, by his friend, by magazine articles and advertisements, by rumor, by images of men with graying hair in red sports cars driving under moonlight to meet a beautiful woman.

He looks into the darkness at the Haitians again, and he smiles. It's a light, sympathetic smile.

The teenaged boy smiles back, startling Bob.

"How're ya doing, kid?"

The boy looks shyly down at his lap and remains silent, but to Bob, it's an answer, a response, and suddenly, through this boy, at least, the vacuum that the Haitians created for Bob to fill has been broken into and filled by them, for to Bob, one of them is all of them.

Bob says, "'Nother cigarette?" and holds out the package.

The boy shakes his head no. He's seated cross-legged next to a pretty young woman with a small child in her lap, both of whom, she and the child, continue to stare at Bob, as do all the other Haitians. But their stares no longer threaten him.

"You understand English, kid?" Bob asks. "Comprendez English?"

The boy smiles, shrugs, nods yes, then no, then yes again.

"C'mon, kid, you want to ride up on the bridge?" Bob stands and puts his cap on and waves for the boy to follow. Claude slides forward and stands next to him, and when Bob climbs up to the bridge, he climbs up also.

Tyrone studies the pair for a second, shrugs and hands the wheel over to Bob and descends without a word. At the bottom, he turns and calls, "Gulf Stream coming up! Got to keep track or you'll move north wid it!"

"I know, I know," Bob says, and he peers out ahead, searching for the Stream, the green river that flows from Mexico to Newfoundland and east to Europe with the force and clarity of a great river draining half a continent. As you enter it, the color of the water changes abruptly from dark blue to deep green, and the current drags you north at up to ten knots an hour if you do not compensate for it.

Claude stands next to Bob, and pointing out across the bow, says, "America?"

Bob nods. He's spotted the rich green streak ahead near the horizon, and he cuts the boat a few degrees to port so that she'll enter the Stream at more of an angle, bringing them out, he expects, a half-dozen miles south of Key Biscayne sometime before midnight. "Yep, just over the next hill. Land of the free and home of the brave. You probably think the streets are paved with gold, right?"

The boy looks up, not understanding. "Monsieur?"

Bob says nothing but smiles down at the boy, who has gone quickly back to searching for America. Like me, Bob thinks. Like my father and Eddie too, and like my kids, even poor little Robbie, who'll be as big as this kid is before I know it—like all of us up in our crow's nests keeping our eyes peeled for the Statue of Liberty or the first glint off those gold-paved streets. *America! Land, ho!* Only, like Columbus and all those guys looking for the Fountain of Youth, when you finally get to America, you get something else. You get Disney World and land deals and fast-moving high-interest bank loans, and if you don't get the hell out of the way, they'll knock you down, cut you up with a harrow and plow you under, so they can throw some condos up on top of you or maybe a parking lot or maybe an orange grove.

Bob looks down at the boy's black profile, and he thinks, You'll get to America, all right, kid, and maybe, just like me, you'll get what you want. Whatever that is. But you'll have to give something away for it, if you haven't already. And when you get what you want, it'll turn out to be not what you wanted after all, because it'll always be worth less than what you gave away for it. In the land of the free, nothing's free.

The sun has yellowed and is nearing the horizon. Flattened like a waxy smear, it descends through scraps of clouds to the sea. The breeze off the portside is cool now, and the waves have grown to a high chop that causes the boat to pitch and yaw slightly as she plows on toward the west. Up on the bridge, Bob wonders what this Haitian boy will have to give away in order to get what he wants, what he may have already given away. It's never a fair exchange, he thinks, never an even swap. When I was this kid's age, all I wanted was to be right where I am now, running a boat from the Bahamas into the Gulf Stream as the sun sets in the west, just like the magazine picture Ave carried around in his wallet. So here I am. Only it's not me anymore.

"You want to take the wheel?" he asks the boy. Bob stands away and waves the boy over. Shyly, the lad moves up and places his hands on the wheel, and Bob smiles. "You look good, son! A real captain." The boy lets a smile creep over his lips. "Here," Bob says. "You need a captain's hat," and he removes his hat and sets it on the boy's head, much smaller than Bob's, so that the hat droops over his ears and makes him look like a child, pathetic and sad.

"Steady as she goes, son," Bob says. The boy nods, as if following orders. The sky in the west flows toward the horizon in streaks of orange and plum, and the sea below has turned purple and gray, with a great, long puddle of rose from the setting sun spilling over the waves toward them. Behind them, the eastern sky has deepened to a silvery blue, and stacks of cumulus clouds rise from the sea, signaling tomorrow's weather.

*   *   *

THEIR FIRST SIGHT OF LAND IS THE FLASH OF THE LIGHT-house below Boca Raton, which tells them that the *Belinda Blue* has come out of the Gulf Stream farther to the north than they intended, miles from where they planned to drop off the Haitians and so far from Moray Key that they can't hope to get home before dawn. Tyrone grumbles and blames Bob, who blames the south-east-wind and his not being used to running the *Belinda Blue* with so much weight aboard.

It's dark, thickly overcast this close to shore, and the sea is high. The boat rides the swells, and when she crests, they can see the beach stretching unbroken from the pink glow of Miami in the south to the lights of Fort Lauderdale in the north. Then, when the boat slides down into the belly between the huge waves, they see nothing but a dark wall of water and a thin strip of sky overhead.

Frightened, the Haitians have crawled aft from their lean-to, and peer wide-eyed at the sea. The pitch and roll of the boat tosses them against one another, and several of them begin to cross themselves and pray. The old woman, hiding behind the others, has started to sing, a high-pitched chanting song that repeats itself over and over. The boy Claude is still up on the bridge with Bob, where Tyrone has joined them. Claude, too, is frightened, but he watches the white man's face closely, as if using it to guide his own emotions. Right now, the white man, who is at the wheel, seems angry with his mate, and the mate seems angry also, for they are scowling and shouting at one another in the wind.

"For Christ's sake, we drop them off at Hollywood or Lauderdale now, they won't know where the hell they are! They'll get busted in an hour. They'll stick out like sore thumbs, for Christ's sake! If we take them down to Coral Gables, like we said we'd do, they'll get to cover in Little Haiti right away."

"Too far, Bob! Dem too heavy in dis sea, mon! Got to leave 'em up here, let 'em find dere own way!"

Bob argues a little longer, but he knows the man is

right. "All right. Hollywood, then. Be midnight by then, we can drop them by the A-One-A bridge at Bal Harbour. The water's calm there once you get around the point. Christ only knows how they'll get down to Miami from there, though."

"Not your problem, Bob."

"Go down and talk to them," Bob says to Tyrone. "Tell them what's happening, you know? Maybe one of 'em's got family or something can come out with a car. Who knows? At least let 'em know where they're going to get dropped off. Draw a map or something for 'em."

Tyrone shrugs his shoulders and turns away. "Don't make no never mind to dem, mon. Long's dem in America."

"Yeah, sure, but do it anyway." Bob brings the boat around to port, facing her into the waves, and moves the throttle forward. The boat dips and slides down and hits the gully, yaws into the sea and starts to climb again. Tyrone motions for Claude to follow, and the two of them start down from the bridge. When the boat reaches the crest and hangs there for a second before beginning the descent again, Bob looks off to his starboard side and sees the beach like a taut, thin white ribbon and believes that he can hear the waves crashing not a half mile distant. Beyond the beach he can see the lights of houses between the sea and the road to Palm Beach, where here and there cars move slowly north and south—ordinary people going about their ordinary business.

Again, the boat rolls a second and starts the drop, pitches across the smooth trough, yaws between waves and rises, and this time, when it reaches the crest of the wave, Bob looks out over the dripping bow and sees the lights of another boat. It's less than two hundred yards off the portside and headed north, and it's a large boat, twice the size of the *Belinda Blue*—that's all Bob can see of her, before the boat disappears from sight, and Bob realizes that they have pitched again and are descending. He yells for Tyrone, who's under the tarpaulin talking to the Haitians, and frantically waves him up to the bridge. "Boat!" he shouts. "Boat!"

Tyrone scrambles up the ladder to the bridge, and when the *Belinda Blue* crests again, Bob points out the lights of the stranger.

"Coast guard," Tyrone says. "Cut de lights."

Bob obeys at once. "Oh, Jesus H. Christ!" he says. "The fucking coast guard." He can hear the twin diesels that power her and can see that, yes, it is a cutter, ninety or a hundred feet long, with the high conning tower and the fifty- and sixty-caliber machine guns bristling at the stern and bow. "I don't think they spotted us," Bob says. But then he realizes that the cutter is turning slowly to port. "Oh, fuck, here they come!"

Tyrone reaches out and cuts the throttle back.

"What the fuck you doing?"

"Bring 'er around, gwan get dem Haitians off," Tyrone says.

"What? What're you saying?" Bob grabs Tyrone's shoulder and flips the man around to face him.

"Dem can get to shore from here, mon!" Tyrone shouts into the wind. "It not far!"

"Not in this sea, for Christ's sake! We can't *do* that! We can't!"

"Got to, Bob!" The Jamaican turns away and starts to leave.

"Wait, goddammit! *I'm* the fucking captain, you're not!"

Tyrone looks at Bob with cold disgust. "We cut dem fuckin' Haitians loose, den *maybe* we get home tonight. Captain."

"Otherwise?"

Tyrone does not answer.

Bob shouts, "They've got us anyhow, the coast guard! We're caught anyhow!"

"No, dem got to stop to pick up de Haitians. Wid dem gone, de boat fast enough to get us out of here first maybe!"

"Or else we end up in jail, and they go back to Haiti! Right? Right, Tyrone?"

Again, Tyrone says nothing.

Bob says, "All right. Go ahead." Tyrone leaps away and down the ladder.

Bob looks over the rail to the deck below, where the Jamaican frantically, roughly, yanks the Haitians out from under the tarpaulin. He's shouting at them in Creole and Jamaican patois, making it very clear that they must jump into the water, and they must do it now. Every few seconds he points out to where they spotted the coast guard cutter, though Bob can no longer see her, for they're down in the trough between waves again, and Tyrone pulls at their arms, shoving the Haitians toward the starboard rail, but they shake their heads no, and a few start to cry and wail, no, no, they will not go. They cling to one another and to the chocks and cleats and gunwales and look wild-eyed about them, at the towering sea, at Bob up on the bridge, at Tyrone jumping angrily about, at each other, and they weep and beg, No, no, please don't make us leave the boat for the terrible sea.

The *Belinda Blue* rises to the ridge of water, and Bob sees the cutter again, now clearly turning back toward them, and they've got searchlights whipping wands of light across the water. "They're turning, they're gonna try to board us!" he yells down, and he sees Tyrone step from the cabin with a rifle in his hand, the shark gun, a 30-06 with a scope, and Bob says quietly, "Tyrone, for Christ's sake."

The Haitians back swiftly away from Tyrone, horrified. With the barrel of the gun, he waves them toward the rail and tells them once again to jump, but they won't move. The babies are screaming now, and the women and several of the men are openly weeping. Claude's face is frozen in a look of amazed grief.

Tyrone pulls the trigger and fires into the air, and one of the Haitians, the boy Claude, leaps into the water and is swept away. A second follows, and then a woman. Tyrone screams at the rest to jump, and he fires again.

Bob bellows from the bridge, "Tyrone! For Christ's sake, stop! They're drowning!" But the Jamaican is now bodily hurling the Haitians into the sea, one after the other, the old man, the woman with the two small children, Vanise and her child, the old woman. He's clearing the deck of them. They weep and cry out for help from God, from the loas, from Bob, who looks on in horror, and then they are gone, lifted up by the dark waves and carried away toward the shore.

Tyrone scrambles back up to the bridge, the rifle still in his hand, and he wrenches the wheel away from Bob and hits the throttle hard, bringing the boat swiftly around to port and away. Off to the north a few hundred yards, its searchlights sweeping over the water, the cutter has slowed and stopped, for they have apparently spotted the Haitians bobbing in the water. Bob sees that they are dropping a lifeboat from the stern. He follows one of the beams of light out to where it has fixed on a head in the water, one of the young men, and then he sees the man go down. The light switches back and forth, searching for him, then seems to give up and move on, looking for others. "They're drowning!" he cries. "They're drowning!"

Tyrone doesn't answer. He shoves the rifle at Bob and takes the wheel with both hands, bucking the *Belinda Blue* into the waves, driving her against mountains of water and quickly away from shore, heading her straight out to sea.

Bob holds the gun for a moment, looks at it as if it were a bloody ax. Then he lifts it over his head with two hands and hurls it into the sea.

Tyrone looks over his shoulder at Bob and says, "Good idea, mon. Dem prob'ly heard de shootin'. Nobody can say we de ones doin' de shootin' now. Got no gun, got no Haitians," he says, smiling. Then he says, "Better clear de deck of anyt'ing dem lef' behind, mon."

Slowly Bob descends to the deck, and kneeling down, he crawls under the tarpaulin, reaching around in the dark, until he comes up with several battered suitcases, a cloth bundle, a woven bag, and he tosses them overboard one by one, watches them bob on the water a second, then swiftly sink.

*   *   *

IT'S A PINK DAWN, THE EASTERN SKY STRETCHED TIGHT AS silk on a frame. Overhead, blue-gray rags of cloud ride in erratic rows, while in the west, over southern Florida, the sky is dark and overcast. A man with white hair leads a nosy, head-diving dog, a blue-black Labrador, from his house and down the sandy walkway to the beach.

The man and the dog stroll easily south, and now and then the man stops and picks up a piece of weathered beach glass for his collection. The dog turns and waits, and when the man stands and moves on, the dog bounds happily ahead.

A quarter mile from where they started, the dog suddenly darts into the water, and the man stops and stares, as a body, a black woman's body, passes by the dog and with the next wave is tossed onto the beach. A few yards beyond, a child's body has been shoved up onto the beach, and beyond that, a pair of men lie dead on the sand.

The man counts five bodies in all, and then he turns and runs back up the beach, his dog following, to his home, where he calls the local police. "Haitians, I'm sure of it. Washing up on the sand, just like last time. Women and children this time, though. It's just awful," he says. "Just awful."

A MILE SOUTH OF WHERE THE OTHER BODIES CAME TO SHORE at Golden Beach, and five miles south of Hollywood, while ambulance crews are lugging the bodies away from the water and up the beach to the ambulances, a woman struggles through the last few waves to the shore. She is alone, a young black woman with close-cropped hair, her dress yanked away from her by the force of the water, her limbs hanging down like anchors, as she staggers, stumbles, drags herself out of the water and falls forward onto the sand. Her name is Vanise Dorsinville; she is the only Haitian to survive the journey from New Providence Island to Florida on the *Belinda Blue*.

*   *   *

AT THE SAME TIME, POSSIBLY AT THE SAME MOMENT, FOR these events have a curious way of coordinating themselves, Bob Dubois brings the *Belinda Blue* in from the open sea, passes under the bridge at Lower Matecumbe Key and heads for the Moray Key Marina. He cuts back the throttle as he enters the marina, letting the boat drift around to starboard so he can reverse her into the slip next to the *Angel Blue,* and he notices that Ave's boat is gone from the slip.

He puts the boat into reverse, and his Jamaican mate jumps onto the deck in the bow, ready to tie her up. Bob is backing the boat skillfully into the slip, when he sees, standing on the pier, apparently waiting for them, two Florida state troopers.

The Jamaican looks up at Bob on the bridge. "Get out, Bob! Reverse de fuckin' boat, mon, and get 'er out of here!"

Bob simply shakes his head no and calmly backs the boat into the slip.

Gan Malice O!

Two nights after the night the Haitians drowned in the waves off the beach at Sunny Isles, a man and two women lead Vanise Dorsinville from a small white bungalow in northeast Miami, out a door at the back of the house into the packed dirt yard, the ground speckled in beige and dark brown in new moonlight and shade, palm fronds beyond the rickety fence chattering in the cool breeze, cars whizzing past overhead on the throughway. They step with care through an opening in the fence, replace the loose board that hides it, and soon they are walking directly beneath the highway, Interstate 95, which swoops over them from north to south, eight lanes of steel and concrete rushing as if downhill toward the tip of the continent, with garbage, broken bottles, rusting tin cans, old tires, rats and the carcasses of cats and dogs scattered below in the tufts of long yellow grass.

Vanise leans heavily on the arm of the man, her brother and father of the boy Claude Dorsinville, who had liked and admired the white captain of the boat and had been the first of the Haitians to leap into the water, as if to show them how easy it was, and, though he could not swim at all, must have believed that he was close enough to America to walk ashore, for he made no attempt to swim, did not struggle, did not even call out, but simply went to the bottom, as if thrown surprised from a great height.

His body and the body of Vanise's baby will eventually be found, like most of the others, bloated, purplish-gray, half eaten by sharks and birds, in the sands along the stretch of fine white beach south of Bal Harbour, by horrified joggers, beachcombers, early morning surfers and fishermen. No one will be able to identify them, although everyone will know they are the Haitians the newspapers said were cast off an American boat when the coast guard threatened to board it, a boat that slipped away while the coast guard tried to save the drowning Haitians and raced away to the south without giving up its identity or the names of the man who was the captain and the man who was his mate.

Vanise alone survived, which she believes is due to the particular intervention of Ghede, dark and malicious loa of death and regeneration, who needed one of them to survive the drownings, any one of them at all, so why not Vanise, a strong young woman with firm, warm loins, which Ghede, in his gluttony for flesh, is known to relish? Ghede, Vanise believes, wanted one of them to survive so as to feed him the others, to act as his agent, for he is a devourer of human flesh, insatiable, jackal-like, a loa who schemes endlessly to obtain what he endlessly needs. There is no other explanation for her not having drowned in the storm with the others, for she cannot swim any more than her nephew or child could, and the waters were as fierce for her as for them, the waves as heavy, the sharks as hungry, hard and swift.

People who have no power, or believe they have none, also believe that everything that happens is caused by a particular, powerful agent; people who have power, people who can rest easily saying this or that event happened "somehow," call the others superstitious, irrational and ignorant, even stupid. The truly powerless are none of these, however, for they and perhaps they alone know that luck, bad luck as much as good, is a luxurious explanation for events. When you have even partial control over your destiny, you're inclined to deny that you do, because you're afraid the control will go away. *That's* superstition. But when, like Vanise, you have no control over your destiny, it's reasonable to assume that someone or something else does, which is why it's reasonable, not irrational, for Vanise to believe that the bizarre fact of her survival, her destiny now, is due to a loa's intervention, and because of the particulars, it's reasonable for her to assume that the loa is Ghede.

After God, we are in your hands, Ghede Nimbo, the *hounsis canzos* sing to the loa who stands at the entrance to the underworld, the loa who leans wickedly on the jambs of the gate before the abyss, smokes his cigar, peers through sunglasses and in his reedy, nasal voice says, *You,* and *Not you,* and *You,* and *Not you.* He waves and pokes and even shoves you through the gate and over the abyss with his thick, stiff hickory stick, then holds back with his stick you who are to stay on this side, lifting your skirt above your hips, if you are a woman, smacking his lips voraciously and poking the men and boys on their crotches and butts, turning his back and flipping up the tails of his long black coat in a shameless prance.

Ghede is the cynical trickster, the glutton, he who foments not death but dying, not salvation but consumption, not fucking but orgasm. He celebrates the passage over from one state to another. Whether physical or metaphysical, Ghede could not care less; it's all the same to him. Morality he scorns altogether, for he knows he is the last recourse; sentimentality he mocks in song, in his high, childish voice singing, *I wuv, you wuv, she wuvs! And what does that make? L'amour!* he cries, and strokes his erect penis beneath his trousers. With his motley, his costumes and beggar's bowl, he derides worldly ambition; with his complaints about the exorbitant costs of keeping up his Dynaflow, he parodies materialism. He dresses women as men, men as women, and asserts the insipidity of biology's brief distinctions. As clown and trickster, he's called Mr. Entretoute. As erotic lord, he's Brav Ghede. As cannibal, he's Criminelle, devourer of living flesh. And when he stands before the open grave, he's Baron Cimetière, the trickster become transformer, the clown become magician, he who has the power to animate the dead and slay the living, master of the zombis, he who can change men into beasts and who, properly placated, can bring the sick and dying back to life. And as the loa of regeneration and death, the loa of soullessness, Ghede it is whom you must please if you have lost a child and the child, in its leaving, because it has no soul yet, has stolen yours.

Such a one is Vanise Dorsinville. When her brother was taken to her by the Haitian man who found her wandering dazed along the side of the highway a few hundred yards south of the town of Sunny Isles, the man who found her, a groundskeeper walking early to work at the Haulover Beach Park Golf Course, said, The woman is gone, Émile. She says she's gone off to be with Baron Cimetière. She knows her name and yours, but not much else.

They have worked together for several years, Émile Dorsinville and the man who found his sister, and like most Haitians in south Florida, live close to one another in Little Haiti, that section of northeast Miami between I-95 and Second Avenue where the narrow streets and alleys and the low bungalows, cinder-block warehouses, garages, shanties and boarded-up storefronts house thousands of recently arrived Haitians; where the air is thick with the smells of their food—baked yams, cassava, plantains, goat and roast pig cooked in yards on charcoal fires or in crowded, makeshift kitchens on hot plates and kerosene burners; where the quick, sexy Haitian music blasts onto the street from record shops and drifts from car radios and all day and night long from transistors set up on windowsills; where women walk barefoot along the dusty sidewalks in ankle-length dresses of gorgeously colored cloth and the men wear white shirts and dark trousers and fedoras and put one foot up on the bumper of a parked car and talk Haitian politics or sit around with a piece of Masonite on their laps and play dominoes until dawn, slamming the large ivory pieces down one upon the other in a long, superbly intelligent run, followed by a round of drinks and yet another game.

Émile took his sister home on the bus that morning, left her in the room with the women who share it with him and returned to work, scolded and docked a half day's pay by the head groundskeeper. That night, when he arrived back at his home, he learned his sister's story. She was asleep now, washed and put to bed by Marie and Thérèse, second cousins to Émile, fat women in their middle fifties, legal residents of America, Catholic churchgoers, kindly and without family, except for the skinny man they hide in their room and who, in return, supports them when they cannot find work cleaning the houses of white or Cuban people.

The women had succeeded during the day in getting the girl to talk, or at least to nod yes and no to their questions while they washed and soothed her. They did not learn about Vanise's child, and they did not learn about Émile's son Claude. Instead, they concluded that Vanise had come over from Haiti alone, as they themselves had done years before and as Émile had done.

She was on a boat, they told Émile, and there was a great storm, and the Haitians on the boat had to jump into the sea when the boat began to sink. She was saved from drowning by Brav Ghede, no other. That's all she can say, Thérèse reported. Ghede, Ghede, Ghede.

Émile shook his head no, frowned and looked down on the face of his sister as she slept. Not that one, he said. Not Ghede. She'll tell us more when she's rested and has eaten.

But she did not tell them anything more. She woke and wept and murmured the name of Ghede, Brav Ghede, Baron Cimetière, moaning and turning in the wide bed, her face wet with sweat, her arms and legs tangling in the sheets. Émile and the two women washed her head with rags soaked with herbs—*trois paroles, gaté sang* and *trompette*—and to warm her heart and liver, made her sip a tea brewed from citronella grass.

But Vanise spoke no more words, and soon she seemed not to recognize where she was or whom she was with. She stared at the worried dark faces above her as if they were cat faces or cow faces. Émile went to work the next day, and when he returned that evening and saw that his sister was the same, learned that she had called all day long for Ghede in all his names, he went out and made the arrangements to take her to Ghede.

AT THE REAR OF A FLAKING WHITE WINDOWLESS TWO-STORY building with a flat roof, an abandoned warehouse located at the eastern end of Little Haiti several blocks off Miami Avenue, Émile stops and hands his sister to Thérèse and walks slowly up the rotting stairs to a loading dock, faces a door with a small square of plywood where there was once a pane of glass, and knocks. Rusting railroad tracks pass down the alley between the warehouses; from Miami Avenue in the distance comes the bustle of cars cruising late, windows open, radios blaring. A siren howls for a few seconds, then goes silent. Émile glances down the steps to his sister, held in the thick arms of Thérèse and Marie like a rag doll, limp and tiny, head lolling forward, arms hanging down, hands open as if to reveal stigmata. They have dressed her in a white frock, and she is barefoot.

The door opens a crack, and Émile steps quickly away so he can be seen. Come in, Dorsinville, a man's voice says. Émile turns and waves the others up.

The two women hesitate, then Thérèse shakes her head no. You take her now, she says to Émile. I cannot go in there. I am Catholic. She checks Marie, who approves.

Quickly, Émile descends the stairs and takes his sister from the women's arms. I am Catholic also! he hisses, and he turns away and hitches the girl up the steps to the platform and takes her inside. The man closes the door and drops a bar to lock it.

The man is carrying a flashlight, but aims it down, so

Émile cannot see his face. They are inside a huge open space, he can feel that, despite the total darkness, and he can smell old paper and cloth, dry ticking and straw, as if the place had once been used to store mattresses.

This is your sister, eh? the man says, and he shines his light on Vanise's face, gray now and closed to everything. Ah, he says in a low voice. Poor thing. Poor little thing.

Where . . . ? Émile begins.

You wish to pay me now? the man interrupts. The Baron has already arrived. He's eager to see you. Both of you, he adds.

Émile reaches into his pocket and draws out the bills, two crinkled twenties, and passes them into the man's outstretched palm.

Come now, the man says, and he leads them into darkness, playing the beam of his light on the floor as they walk. They cross the broad expanse of the warehouse, stepping over pieces of snake-like electrical conduit, around piles of old cardboard boxes and tipped and scattered stacks of newsprint, to a set of narrow wooden stairs in the far corner. The man mounts the stairs ahead of him, and Émile sees that he is a round and not young man and is wearing white shoes, socks, trousers and shirt, with a band of red, glossy cloth tied around his thick waist. Tucked into the waistband on one side is a machete, on the other a long, narrow knife. When, at the landing at the top of the stairs, Émile gets a glimpse of the man's face, he realizes that he has seen the man probably a hundred times on the streets of Little Haiti, a most ordinary-looking, brown-faced man, a clerk or deliveryman or barber, with round, smooth cheeks, thin mustache, high, shiny forehead with short hair graying at the temples.

The man smiles, knocks three times loudly on the door before them, then twice. The door opens, as if by itself, Émile steps inside and brings his sister with him, and the man in white closes and locks the door behind them. They are inside *la chambre de Ghede*.

The room, evidently at one time an office, is large,

separated into two sections by plexiglass dividers and counters, with fly-spotted asbestos panels and old, tubeless, fluorescent light fixtures hanging half-attached from the ceiling, sheets of water-stained wallboard broken through to the lathing behind, several large desks pushed to the side to clear an open space in the front half of the room, where there is a gathering of animals—speckled hens, a black duck and a large black goat. The animals are hobbled by strings held in the hand of a teenaged boy in jeans, shirtless and barefoot, squatting on the floor. A crowd of people is clustered in the further space, but Émile can't make out what they are doing, for the entire room is illuminated by a dozen or so candles in bottles placed erratically on the counters and desks and along the walls at the floor. Émile hears a woman weeping, sobbing loudly, as if grieving for the loss of a husband, though no one in the crowd seems to pay particular attention to anyone else. It's as if they are in the dim, brown waiting room of a provincial train station, strangers all of them and bound for different destinations. A few people murmur a song, low, dirgelike, and a thin, high-pitched drum, a *dun-dun* or *bébé*, is being played someplace near the middle of the crowd.

The man who brought them in tells Émile to wait by the door and disappears into the further antechamber. Émile breathes in and peers around him, first at the animals, who look half asleep, then at the boy, who is smoking a cigarette and seems bored, as if wishing he were down on Miami Avenue with his friends. All of Vanise's weight has fallen onto Émile's side now, and he has to work to hold her in a standing position, grabbing her under one arm and slinging the other over his shoulder.

The air of the room is hot and ripe with the smell of sweating bodies, as if people have been dancing energetically for hours. There is also the sweet smell of white rum, cut by the smell of herbs, sharp and dry, and overripe bananas and the greasy smell of recently cooked chicken. Now Émile sees on top of one of the old desks a row of green jars and small baskets, *govis,* that hold the spirits of the dead, and midway along each wall, a grinning human skull set on the floor, and over his head, nailed to the doorframe, what appears to be the gleaming white skull of a horse. He spins on his heels, dragging his sister's body in a circle with him, and sees in a dim far corner of the room, beyond the animals and the boy tending them, a grave-sized mound of dirt half-covered with pale green tiles, a short cross planted at the head of the mound. In the corner opposite, three picks, three shovels and three hoes, gravedigger's tools, lean against the wall, and on the floor before them is a balancing scale. Émile turns again, counterclockwise, and faces in the near corner a long military sword, its point up, and next to it the scabbard, lying flat on the floor. In the fourth corner of the chamber is a batch of sticks—canes and walking sticks and a furled black umbrella—leaned against the walls, as if parked there by Ghede on previous visits and forgotten afterwards.

Suddenly, the drum is beating furiously, like the wings of a hummingbird, high, tight, too fast to separate the beats, and the crowd of people in the further section of the room is falling over itself trying to get out of the way and open a path from out of its center, when a figure nearly seven feet tall seems to rise up out of the crowd of people, as if he has been kneeling in prayer among them and has stood up. He pushes them roughly aside with a thick, gnarled stick and leaves them and passes into the section of the room where Émile-amazed, frightened, grateful—stands waiting.

This is surely, truly, he, Brav Ghede, Baron Cimetière. This is the loa himself, with his awesome, intricate powers over death that can bring Vanise back to the world of the living. No other loa is at once so powerful and so tricky, so strong and so scheming, so kind and so cruel. And it's a very good Ghede, too. Convincing. Émile stares up at the loa, and his breath goes away, and he is afraid that he will fall. Ghede is just as Émile hoped— taller than a man, made even taller by the battered top hat on his head, and cadaverous, with a head and face like a skull, his eyes hidden behind black, wire-rimmed glasses, his teeth large and glittering with gold. He's wearing a mourning coat with no shirt beneath it, and his bony brown chest is slick with sweat. His striped gray trousers are held up by a thickly braided gold rope knotted over his crotch, and on his feet he wears white shoes with pointed toes. He's a magnificent figure— awesome, frightening and delightful.

As if she's turned magically into a light, airy bush, Vanise no longer feels heavy to Émile, and he turns to see if she has taken her own weight onto herself, but she still leans all her weight against him, her head still hanging loosely down, eyes closed, mouth open, as if drugged. Ghede, Vanise! Émile whispers. It's Ghede!

Ghede smiles and pokes Vanise in the belly with his stick. In his high, whining, nasal voice, he says, *Mine?* Oh, monsieur, how *thoughtful* of you!

No, no, Brav! Émile says. I want . . .

I want, I want, I want! *Everyone* wants, wants, wants!

Forgive me, Ghede. She's just come from Haiti, my sister, and the boat sank, and we found her like this, only she grows worse, and she's called for you. . . .

No!

No?

No, no, no! Not true. Her *mait'-tête* is Agwé, or she'd be *en bas de l'eau* this moment, with all the others. Several people from the group who have gathered behind the Baron nod sagely as he speaks.

Oh, Émile says. Agwé.

Ghede scratches his chin and leans close to Vanise and studies her face a moment. He points at her nose, her chin, her forehead, with a long, extended forefinger, then reaches into her mouth and draws out her tongue and examines it with thumb and forefinger, rubbing it lightly, before putting it back into her mouth. Lifting up one eyelid at a time, he examines her yellow eyes. The pupils have rolled up and she looks all but dead to Émile.

Agwé is gone now. Gone far away. Took her from the waters, then left her, the Baron says. He seems puzzled and begins mumbling in no language Émile can understand, not Creole, not French, certainly not English. *Kala, kala, diman kon, lé ké dja, lé ké dja.* . . . His mumble becomes a chant, *Kala kala, diman kon,* and he starts shuffling his feet side to side and turning in a slow circle, counterclockwise. Behind him, a wizened old man with a stringy beard picks up the rhythm of Ghede's dance with the tiny, high-pitched drum, and several people in the knot surrounding the drummer join in the chant and commence shuffling their feet in the same odd, crablike, side-to-side step. Ghede's face has turned to black stone, obsidian, shiny and opaque, and he dances faster and faster, over and back, from side to side, like a pendulum increasing its velocity with each new arc, and then, suddenly, he wrenches Vanise out of Émile's arms, lurches across the room with her and tosses her onto the grave. Freed of his sister's weight, Émile, without thinking it, has joined the dance, as if grabbed at the arms from behind by a pair of *les Invisibles* and thrust forward toward the other dancers and then shoved back and forth in time to their movements, until he has caught the movement on his own—then a blur, whirling motion, light creeping forward from the back of his skull, until he has been mounted, taken over, displaced by Agwé, who is immediately confronted by Ghede to learn the truth:

Ghede: Agwé Ge-Rouge, you've gone off with this woman's soul, this nice young African woman here, and she's sad, Agwé, sad and empty, a shell, Papa. A shell.

Agwé [in a dark, low, bubbling voice, as if from under water]: Not I, Brav. [Looks down at Vanise, examines her face carefully.] But she's gone, all right. Too bad.

Ghede [angry]: You're the woman's *mait'-tête!* If she's gone, you're gone too!

Agwé: No.

Ghede: No?

Agwé: It's her infant son, unbaptized, who's gone off with her soul. The child's *en bas de l'eau,* that's where, and I'm with *him* now, Papa. Not her. It happens that way, Ghede. This one, the mother, she's yours, if you want her, if you want to install yourself in her head.

Ghede: Her son's dead, eh? And how do you account for that?

Agwé: Lots more dead, too.

Ghede: True? [Smacks his lips, leers.]

Agwé: True. This woman's son, the infant. And also her nephew, a boy, Claude Dorsinville, the only son of my very own *cheval* here. A nice boy, too. All dead in the water, all of them, sad to say. But it was time.

Ghede: Time! They drowned, then, these children?

Agwé: Yes.

Ghede: The boat sank, and they drowned, except for this young woman?

Agwé: No. It was evildoing. Evil. A sad thing. An evil thing.

Ghede: Tell me!

Agwé: The man who owns the boat sent them all over the side in a storm, fired his gun and sent them over. Evil.

Ghede: And you went off with the infant?

Agwé: He was not baptized. It was better for me to do that than to stay with her and let him roam, a *lutin*. But you can have her, if you want. You want her, Ghede?

Ghede [Looks Vanise over with salacious precision.]: Well, yes, she's a good meal, whether you're hungry or not.

Agwé: Take her, then. I'm with the child now. As for the others, they're baptized, they're all fine, *en bas de l'eau*. Even the boy, Claude, son of my *cheval*, he's fine.

Ghede: No other came out of the waters but this woman?

Agwé: No other, and she came without me. She's yours. You brought her out this far, Ghede. Bring her the rest of the way now.

Ghede [with impatience]: Leave now, go on, leave! I know what I need to know! You go now, get out of here, you'll get fed plenty in good time. You've got a good horse there, he'll feed you. [Waves his assistant over to take care of Émile, and the man escorts Émile away from the crowd, calming him and talking him back out of his possession.]

The drum and the dancing resume, with Ghede swiftly working himself into a practiced frenzy over Vanise's inert body on the grave, until he signals for the animals to be brought forward, and his assistant, the man in white with the machete and the knife, obeys. First the speckled chickens are cut at the throat, their blood dribbled over Vanise's bare legs. Then the duck. Same thing. And finally the black goat, lifted by two men in the air and throat cut over Vanise, blood allowed to spurt down first on Ghede with his huge mouth open and looking up as if into rain and then on Vanise, who is now awake and alert to the proceedings. Songs, initiated by Ghede, are picked up by the rest, until Ghede leaves off singing and spins, caught by the rite. He bites at his arm, wildly chewing, until controlled by his assistant, and then he bites at the carcass of the black goat. Vanise joins him, possessed now clearly by Ghede himself, in a crab-walk dance, the two facing each other, eye to eye, as equals. Song. Smell of chicken cooking. Goat carcass dragged away to be butchered and cooked. Song.

Feeding the Laos

TAKE A SINGLE SIDESTEP, AND GO BACK THREE OR FOUR IN time, over and back to the moment when Bob Dubois and Tyrone James brought the *Belinda Blue* into the marina at Moray Key. It's dawn, a silver sky bleeding pink in the east. Putty-colored pelicans rise on wobbly legs and drop from their perches atop the bollards and piles of the pier, catch the damp air with ponderous wings and cruise low over the still water toward Florida Bay.

From the bridge of the *Belinda Blue,* Bob gazes down at two Florida state policemen standing on the pier at the end of the slip. Tyrone scrambles up to the bridge, grabs Bob's shoulder and says in a harsh whisper, "We got to hide de money!"

"Well, where is it?" Bob spins the wheel to port and brings the bow of the boat alongside the slip and lets the engine idle noisily. One of the troopers walks forward and catches hold of the gunwale, reaches for a line and ties the bow to a low chock on the slip. The other moves toward the stern.

Tyrone hesitates. "I got it . . . I got it here," he

blurts, and he pulls a wad of bills from his pocket and shoves it at Bob.

"How much is it?"

"Maybe one, two thousand, maybe more."

"You don't know exactly?"

"No, mon! Me take what dem Haitians give me!"

"I thought you made a price." Bob is as calm as a gravestone. "Five hundred a head."

"You take what you get!" Tyrone says, and he pushes the bills at Bob.

"You take your cut?" Bob folds the bills into his wallet, swelling and stiffening it, and squeezes the wallet into his back pocket. It's too tight, so he takes the money out of the wallet and shoves it into the left front pocket of his baggy chinos.

Tyrone says, "No, mon . . . me didn't take de cut yet." He glances nervously over his shoulder at the policemen below. "Just say we was fishing, Bob," he whispers. "Dem cyan prove we wasn't. Okay, mon?"

"Yeah." Bob studies Tyrone's eyes for a second and knows the Jamaican is lying to him about the money.

"Me get m' gear from below now," Tyrone says, and moves toward the ladder. "Just walk off like everyt'ing normal, Bob. Dem cyan prove nothing. Okay?"

"Yeah."

"Tarpon," he whispers. "We was lookin' fe tarpon off New Providence. Tell 'em dat. De same fe me," he says, heading for the cabin below.

Then one of the state troopers on the slip, the larger of the pair, hollers, "Robert Dubois?"

Bob answers, "Yeah. Be right down!" and cuts the engine.

The other trooper steps aboard, but the first reaches out and draws him back to the slip. Behind them, in the distance, a second pair of troopers jog heavily toward them from the parking lot, while from around the corner of the apartment building, three or four more, two of them carrying shotguns, and two burly, crew-cut men in loose, short-sleeved shirts and chinos, walk with alert haste past the Clam Shack and out along the pier to the

Belinda Blue and what seems to be a crowd gathered at the slip, where they join the crowd, which now includes both Bob and Tyrone.

The two young plainclothes officers show their badges and swiftly shape the group and give a sudden, hard focus to it. "Both of you, hands on your heads, turn around, spread your legs." And while one man reads from a card that tells Bob and Tyrone they have the right to remain silent, another gropes his way down their bodies, finding no weapons, except for Tyrone's filleting knife, and missing Bob's slab of money altogether. A third man flashes in front of Bob what he claims is a search warrant, and two or three, or maybe more—Bob can't see to count them, for he stands facing the channel and the bridge beyond, where cars cross over to Matecumbe, their headlights glowing uselessly white in the gray, early morning light—board the *Belinda Blue* and begin searching her aft from the bow and inboard from the bridge down to the keel.

Bob thinks, I'm glad. It's over and done with now, and no matter what happens, I'm glad. He fights a sudden impulse to drop his hands to his sides, to turn and face the silent men behind him and say, "Thank you," but he knows he must not move, he must stand here on the edge of the pier, a prisoner with his hands crossed over the top of his head, or he will be shot dead. He must act the part of a man who, if given the chance, would flee, even though he feels half in love with these grim, dough-faced men, deeply grateful to them, as if they are members of a search party that, long after he gave up hope of ever being found again, has located him at last. It's as if, by holding guns on him and arresting him and searching his boat, they have brought him back into the community of man, and he is so profoundly grateful to them for it that if he did drop his hands and turned and stepped forward, hands extended, to thank them, and if, to stop him, they fired their shotguns into his chest, it would not be a terrible thing.

But this is not to be. For no sooner have the policemen welcomed Bob Dubois back into the community than they have rejected him again, sent him home in his car, with his awful secret undetected, leaving him his stinging visions of black children and women and old and young men, helpless, history-weakened people battered and driven down to death by the waves, human faces with mouths begging for what's an absolute right, pleading for help, eyes bulging in horror as they realize what has happened to them and suddenly discover their terrible fate, to be drowned at sea, to be cast into deep, storm-torn waters at night by a white man claiming to act as their friend and savior and a black man claiming to help him at it. This is an ordinary variation of an ancient story on this part of the planet, so ordinary that even Bob Dubois knows it, and now it's his story as well, and he knows that too.

The police finally conclude that, because of the half ounce of grass wrapped in brown paper and the unexplained thirty-two hundred dollars in cash at the bottom of Tyrone's blue Eastern Airlines flight bag, they can charge Tyrone with possession of a controlled substance and make arrangements to charge him with intent to sell it. But shortly afterwards, in Marathon, while booking him, they discover that he is a Jamaican national with no visa, so they simply take away his money and turn him over to Immigration and Naturalization in Miami for deportation.

As for Bob, they do not believe that he is as his friend and business partner Avery Boone insists, that is, innocent of the charges they have placed against Boone himself, which charges result from Ave's attempt the night before to deliver three-quarters of a pound of uncut cocaine to a man employed by the Federal Narcotics Commission. They do not believe that anyone, especially a man with a boat, can rub as closely to Ave's business as Bob has and not also be profiting from it. There is no clean evidence that links Bob to Ave's drug smuggling and sales, however, just as there is nothing and no one to tie the girl who calls herself Honduras to the trade, so both Bob and Honduras are let go. With Ave's van, like both his boats, now impounded and his condominium instantly repossessed by the bank, Honduras packs her duffel and hitches down Route 1 to Key West, where by the following sunset she has moved into a beach house owned by a screenwriter who spends his winters on the Keys bonefishing and phoning his wife up in Michigan every few days to report on his loneliness. Unable to make bail, Ave mopes in jail in Marathon. Bob, reluctantly, goes home.

BOB LAYS THE NEWSPAPER DOWN ON THE KITCHEN TABLE. There is a photograph above the article, and he studies it for a moment as if trying to memorize every element of the picture, as if preparing to draw a copy for himself. With his fingertip he traces the dark line between the white beach and the gray sea, from the upper right corner diagonally across to the lower left. Then he traces the outline of the black body lying face down on the beach, a woman, her arms folded under her chest, the soles of her bare feet facing the camera.

"Awful, isn't it?" Elaine says, looking over his shoulder from the sink, where she stands, eggy plate in hand, cleaning the breakfast dishes while Robbie takes his morning nap. The girls have left for school. Bob has been home for a day and a night now, since being released by the police, but he has not slept. He's reading this morning's newspaper for the fifth or sixth time, smoking his third pack of cigarettes since walking in the door yesterday at ten, bleary-eyed, limp-limbed and, for the most part, silent.

He didn't have to tell her about Ave. She'd already been informed by the police the previous evening, when, after arresting him in a bar in Key Largo, they'd raided Ave's apartment, detained Honduras, impounded the *Angel Blue* and gone looking for Bob, Tyrone and the *Belinda Blue*. Confident that Bob was in no way involved in Ave's smuggling and drug selling, Elaine nonetheless was terrified for him. She repeated to the police what Bob had told her, that he'd gone to New Providence in the Bahamas to take a large party of French Canadians out tarpon fishing and would return the next morning. When the police had finally seemed to believe her and had driven off, she got down on her knees right there in the living room and prayed straight out that Bob had not unknowingly allowed the *Belinda Blue* to carry drugs for Ave. Bob was capable of that, she knew. He's not stupid, she thought, and he's not naive about Ave's business, not anymore, but even so, she knew that his capacity to behave as if he were both was great. His arrival home, then, relieved her, as if a terrible and likely disaster had been barely but wholly avoided.

His behavior afterwards confused her, however, and then it began to frighten her. He went out around noon and bought copies of all the newspapers he could find, the *Miami Herald*, the *Marathon Keynoter*, the *Key West Citizen,* examined each one carefully, and apparently not finding what he was searching for, tossed them all into the trash can under the sink. Elaine assumed he was looking for accounts of Ave's arrest.

"It won't be in the papers till tomorrow," she told him. "Or tonight at the earliest. If then. They don't write about those things anymore, they're so common."

"What things?" he snapped. He had turned on the radio and was spinning the dial rapidly past music, stopping for a few seconds whenever he found a news broadcast, then, when it turned out to be a weather or sports report, moving impatiently on.

"You know. Drugs. Except when it's millions of dollars' worth. Ave's not one of those big-time drug dealers, I'm sure. Which means he'll probably have to go to jail. It's always the big guys who get off, isn't it?"

"Yeah."

"It's awful, though," she said, her voice going tender. "I know how you must feel. I feel it too."

"About what?"

"Ave. Him going to jail."

"Yeah. He'll do okay, though. A couple years, maybe."

"But then he'll have to start all over again," she said. "With nothing." She stood behind him, her hands lightly kneading his taut shoulders, while he went on fiddling with the radio. "Why don't you try to sleep? You must be exhausted after all this. Otherwise, you won't be able to stay awake tonight when I'm at work. . . ."

"I'll stay awake," he said, cutting her off.

And, indeed, he did stay awake. He lay down in the kids' room and tried to nap while Elaine ironed in the living room, but in five minutes he was back in the kitchen, flipping the dial of the radio back and forth, then drinking beer and smoking cigarettes, pacing from room to room in the trailer and outside in the cluttered yard, walking to the sea, where, lost in a reverie, he'd stand a moment, then quickly step away, as if discovering he'd walked to the edge of a cliff.

He was shuffling back toward the trailer when he saw his daughters coming toward him along the sandy lane from the school bus stop. Emma waved and walked faster toward him, but Ruthie showed no sign of recognition and fell behind her younger sister.

Bob scooped Emma into his arms, lifted her up and leaned his weight against the front fender of the car. "Hi, baby. How'd it go? Good day at school? You like kindergarten?"

"Yeah," she said, and shoving a fistful of crumpled paper in his face, she said, "Look! I got a star for drawing." Then she wrinkled up her face and pulled away. "Yuck, Daddy! Whiskers!"

Bob put her down, spread out the sheet of paper and studied her drawing for a moment, lollipop people in front of a rectangle that, despite the absence of windows and doors, was clearly meant to represent their trailer. The broad crayon strokes against tan, pulpy paper had caught with precision the faded shade of flaking yellow. In the foreground, there were five stick figures of various sizes with large, disk-like heads, all but one of the five, the tiniest, wearing grim faces, mouths that were straight lines, eyebrows pointing down in scowls.

"Who's the happy one here?" Bob asked. "The little guy."

"Robbie. That's Robbie."

"How come he's the only one who's happy?" Ruthie had come up to them and stood silently behind Emma and peered anxiously back over her shoulder at the trailer, as if expecting someone to come out the door and scold her.

"Hi, Roots," Bob said. "How's it going?"

She turned and faced him, her dark head a heavy blossom on a thin stalk.

"You okay?" Bob said too quickly.

She nodded.

"Good day?"

Emma looked at the ground, as if embarrassed by her older sister, who nodded again, silent and withdrawn.

"Did you see Emma's drawing?" Bob asked. "Isn't it terrific? Look, here's Robbie, smiling to beat the band." He held the sheet of paper out before her and pointed with his finger at the figure that was Robbie. Ruthie raised her eyes and glanced at the drawing.

"Which one's Ruthie?" Bob asked, turning to Emma. "It's hard to tell." Indeed, of the five figures, the three in the center were as alike as triplets, all with sour expressions and masses of dark curls on their heads. The tiny, bald, grinning figure on the left was the baby, of course, and the large, bald, frowning figure on the right, though the same size as the triplets, was clearly Bob. The three females in the center, as grim and harsh-looking as Furies, were drawn exactly alike.

"That's Mama," Emma said, pointing at the Fury standing next to Bob. "And that's Ruthie. I'm next."

Ruthie's interest in the picture suddenly flared, and she edged closer and seemed about to smile.

"How come only Robbie's little? All the rest of us are the same size," Bob said. He could see them now, all five of them, exactly as Emma had. The Dubois Family —an angry male out on the right and, despite his proximity to the others, a solitary, who's either in command of the others or their surly slave; then three angry females at the center; and last, as solitary as the first, a male, but half the size of the others and wearing a silly grin on his face.

"Well . . . Robbie's a baby," Emma said.

"He doesn't know anything yet," Ruthie added in a low voice.

To Bob, the three females seemed to be glancing toward the man, as if angry at him, whereas the man, like the baby, seemed to be looking straight out at the world. "Who're you guys mad at?" Bob asked. "You all look so mad."

"I don't know," Emma said slowly. "I think . . . I think everybody's worried. That's why Robbie's smiling. He's not worried yet. He's only a baby."

"Well, what're we worried about?" Bob asked. "The way all you guys are looking at me, you must think *I'm* the one who made you worry or something." He laughed, but it was thin.

"No. We're just worried, that's all. About things. School and stuff, and supper. Stuff like that . . ."

"You're not mad at *me*, then?"

"No," Ruthie pronounced.

"I'll make another picture later," Emma said, and grabbing the sheet of paper, she started for the trailer. "One that shows us happy. Like Robbie." Ruthie turned and followed, her sweater, held by one sleeve, dragging the ground behind her.

"That's all right," Bob said. "This one's fine. I like this one fine."

Then he, too, entered the trailer. He told Elaine he was going up to Islamorada for the evening papers, grabbed a beer from the refrigerator and went out again.

"Take the girls with you!" Elaine called through the screened door.

"They don't want to go," he said, and kept moving.

Elaine turned to her daughters, both already in front of the TV, watching a soap opera. "Don't you want to go to the store with Daddy?"

"No," Ruthie said without turning.

"Emma?"

"Nope."

Robbie was crying loudly now from the bedroom. "Ruthie, go change your brother's diapers and bring him out here."

Ruthie didn't respond.

"Ruth! You heard me!"

In silence, the girl got up, her eyes fixed on the TV screen, and edged backwards from the room.

"For God's sake, *move!* The baby's crying and wet!" She slammed the iron back and forth over the wrinkled blouse, muttering to herself as she worked, "This family . . . this damned family. The way we ignore everyone around here . . ."

Ruthie returned carrying Robbie and deposited him like a teddy bear in the plastic playpen in the center of the room. Unable to sit yet, he immediately collapsed into a reddening heap. By the time Ruthie had returned to her seat on the floor in front of the TV, the baby was howling.

Elaine stood at the ironing board and watched him. Ruthie sucked her thumb and stared at the doctor and nurse making love on leather upholstered furniture in the doctor's paneled, book-lined office. Emma leaned forward and turned up the volume.

AT THE WHALE HARBOR TACKLE SHOP, BOB WENT DOWN the row of newspaper-dispensing racks and bought the two Miami papers and the Marathon paper, and standing outside the store, leafed quickly through all three. There was nothing about the Haitians in any of them.

Maybe it never happened, he let himself think. Maybe it was a nightmare, some kind of hallucination, a craziness worse than anything I've ever experienced before. Is that possible? he wondered. Nothing else seemed real to him now. And for a moment at least, the split made it easy for him to believe that the part of his life which now seemed most vivid and clear to him—the trip over to New Providence, the long wait in the bay and then the arrival of the Haitians in the dinghy with Tyrone, the trip back across the straits, the sudden storm off Sunny Isles, the arrival of the coast guard cutter, and finally that awful moment when the Haitians leaped into the sea—all that might well have been experienced by Bob on a different plane of reality than the plane where everything else was taking place: Elaine and the children, home, groceries, laundry, television, a can of Schlitz from the refrigerator, work, the *Belinda Blue,* Ave, Ave's arrest, Tyrone's arrest, Honduras's disappearance, the seizure of the boats. These things made sense. They weren't all happy things, but they could be lived with somehow. Even the particular terrible consequences of Ave's arrest, that is, Bob's sudden unemployment, seemed likely, bland, vague and conditional to him, of a piece somehow with Elaine's familiar complaints about money, his irritation and embarrassment at his wife's having to work nights as a waitress, his anxiety over Ruthie's deepening strangeness, his ongoing disappointment and bewildered surprise at his own inadequacy.

Could it be? Could the strong part of his life be dream and the weak part real? If so, then he was just crazy, that's all. Crazy. A quiet kind of madman who lived his dreams and dreamed his life. Most people were a little like that anyhow, especially people whose lives, like Bob's, were ordinary and, despite the ordinariness, gave them constant trouble. Maybe, just possibly, the awful pressures that Bob's ordinary life had placed on him, the difficulty, for him, of living an ordinary life well, had finally made him crazy. Most men, he was sure, lived such a life easily: they worked and saved, they took care of their wives and children, who were grateful and respectful for it, and their days and nights passed cheerfully by, until finally they were gray-haired and a little fat and semiretired and spent the winters in Florida with the wife, fishing, watching baseball on TV, waiting for the kids and grandkids to come down for the holidays. But a few men, like Bob, despite their being just as intelligent, dutiful and orderly as the others, turned their ordinary lives into early disasters and never knew why. That can make a man crazy, Bob thought.

For a second, he thought of going inside the store, just in case Ted Williams was there again. He peered across the parking lot, looking for Ted's white Chrysler, then remembered his mistake regarding the Chrysler and said to himself, See, I *am* crazy! What I imagine, what I remember and what I actually experience get all mixed together, and I can't tell the difference. He was now sure that he had dreamed the death of the Haitians.

The relief and pleasure he took from the conviction lasted only a few seconds, however. As he started toward his car, he put the folded newspapers under his left arm and shoved both hands deep into his pants pockets and with his left hand instantly felt the money, a packet of bills a half-inch thick. There it was, blood money, uncounted, forgotten, invisible for whole hours at a time, then suddenly reappearing, linking everything back together again, closing and welding fast the split in his life, so that his dreams and his daily life were one thing again. It's horrible, *horrible!* he thought, and he almost cried out, and he withdrew his hand as if he had touched a cold, dry serpent there.

He wandered in and out of the trailer all the rest of the afternoon, unable to leave the place, unable to sit down and make his home there, a ghostly figure who repeatedly appeared in the yard and then stood at the threshold outside the screened door for a few moments, until finally the woman and children inside felt his presence and looked up at him, and he turned away and went back to the road again. Up the lane to the highway he walked, then back, past the trailers to the water, where gulls and terns poked between chunks of coral and blond, almost translucent crabs scrambled in the shallows for shelter. A car driven by Horace came and went, and all the while Bob kept his back to the man. Around five-thirty, Allie Hubbell came home from the crafts shops in Key Largo, walking in from the bus stop on the highway, and Bob kept his back to her too. She stood a moment on her stoop, watching him, and not until she had lit a cigarette and gone inside did he turn slowly back toward his own trailer. He stopped next to his car, got in, sat behind the wheel awhile, got out, walked to the water again, resumed peering at the horizon. The sky was low, zinc gray and smooth, like sheet metal. A steady southeast wind blew, keeping the water choppy and dark as old, cold coffee.

Finally, Elaine came out on the steps and called his name. He turned and faced her.

"You want supper?" she shouted into the wind.

He shook his head no and turned away from her, and she went quickly inside, closing both doors against the wind.

A little later, when it was nearly dark, Elaine came out again, this time wearing a pink cardigan sweater buttoned to the throat to cover her bare shoulders and the low neckline of the short black dress she wore for work. Wobbling on high heels in the sand, she came up to Bob and asked him for the car keys.

"I'm sick of taking the bus," she said. "I hate being seen like this five nights a week, and you don't like anybody from up there giving me a ride home, remember?"

"What'd you do last night?" he said. As if he'd asked an idle question, he pursed his lips and watched a crab at his feet scuttle to the water.

She studied his profile for a second, then said, "Sunday and Monday I'm off, Bob. Remember? I spent the evening at home, talking to the police."

"This Tuesday?"

"Yes, this is Tuesday. What did *you* do last night?"

He didn't answer.

"I said, 'What did *you* do last night?' "

"You know what I did. Where I was," he said in a thick, sullen voice.

"No. As a matter of fact, I don't. All I know is you left here early Sunday in the car and you drove back into the yard this morning, and that's all I know. That's it. Oh, yes, I know the police met you this morning at Moray Key as you came off the boat. Because they said they would, and if you hadn't been there, they would have been back here. And I know they thought for a while you were involved with Ave's drug business, because they said they did. Maybe they still think it. But really, in the end, that's everything I know about you lately. You, though, you know everything about *me*. What I do every minute of my life. No surprises. Nothing to sneak up and hit you on the head when you're not looking. If you told me right now this minute that for the last two days you were smuggling heroin or cocaine or whatever, guns, anything, I'd just say, 'Oh, so *that's* the kind of man he is.' You could tell me you had a girlfriend in Miami or someplace and spent the last two days in bed with her, and I'd say the same thing. Because I don't know anymore. I don't know what kind of man you are, Bob. That's the truth. You understand that? Somehow it wouldn't seem so awful to me, so hard to take, if you didn't know what kind of woman I am. But you do. You know me. And it's not fair. And it's hard. Hard. This is not like it used to be with us. And I don't know where it went from being fair to being unfair. Because I never knew that's what it was between us, fair. I only knew it after it was gone, after it had been unfair a long time. A long time now. And you know it. Don't you?''

He didn't answer. He couldn't look at her eyes, so he turned away from her altogether and faced the darkening sea.

Finally, he said, "You can quit that job. Tonight, if you want. You don't have to go in. Just call and say you quit. I made . . . I made good money this trip.''

"Running drugs.''

"No, no. Fishing. A big party. Big spenders.''

"Bob,'' she said, and she sighed. "I just don't . . . I don't believe you, Bob.'' She looked at his broad back, a wall, and shook her head slowly.

"Well . . . what if I did, what if I did do something that was illegal . . . and got away with it? What the hell difference, what would that make different, to you, I mean?''

"I'd think you were stupid,'' she said. "And lucky. For once in your life. No, I don't know what difference it'd make, really.''

"Well, let's say I did, okay? Let's say I came out with a lot of money. Not a whole lot, but enough to let you quit that fucking job. Would you? Quit the job?''

She was silent for a moment, and he turned back around and faced her.

"Well?" he asked.

"No. No, I wouldn't quit."

"Why not?"

"Because . . . because it's drug money, Bob. It's not like winning the state lottery or something, for God's sake. It's drug money." She tilted her head up at him and examined his large, dark face. "This is what I mean, about not knowing you anymore. No, you keep your drug money. Buy yourself a new car with it, if you want. Anything. But don't buy anything for me with it, or for the children. Just don't. As far as I'm concerned, you can throw it in the ocean. I don't want it touching me or my children, that's all."

"*Why*, for Christ's sake? What's the big deal it's illegal? Lots of things are illegal and we do them."

"Like what?"

He hesitated a second. "Well, you know. Little things. Drinking and driving. You know what I mean. And what about Eddie, for Christ's sake? You think *he* wasn't doing anything illegal? And *Ave*? You didn't seem to mind it when what Eddie or Ave did ended up benefiting you."

"They're not you, Bob. And Eddie's dead. Ave's in jail. But even if that wasn't true, even if they were still out there, still getting away with it, like you think you just did, it'd be the same. Look at me, Bob. I'm not crying. Not anymore. And I'm not yelling. Not that anymore, either. I'm just saying. I'm not upset, and I'm not angry. I'm just saying."

"Saying *what*, for Christ's sake? You don't love me anymore? Is that what you're saying? I'm too stupid, or . . . or I'm too illegal, or . . . or immoral? Or what?"

"No. Not that, none of that. Something else. It's more complicated." She seemed genuinely puzzled. "I don't know . . . something worse, maybe."

"What could be worse?"

"To love you and not know you, I guess. That'd be worse. For me."

"Jesus H. Christ, Elaine! You know me."

"No. Not anymore. And I don't know why, if it's because you've changed who you are since we left New Hampshire, or because things have happened to you since then. Bad things. Things I didn't even know were happening, some of them. All I'm sure of is I don't know who you are anymore."

"You know me."

She smiled. "I'm going to be late for work. Let me have the keys. We can talk later if you want."

He gave her the keys. "I hate that fucking job. More than you can ever imagine. That you have to do that."

"I hate it too, Bob. More than *you* can ever imagine. But it's legal. And right now, it's the only job we've got." She turned and started toward the car.

"Elaine! What . . . what can I *do?*"

She kept walking.

"Do you want to go back to New Hampshire?" he called out. "Is that what you want?"

She stopped, turned and said, "Yes. Yes, I do." Then she opened the car door and got in. A few seconds later, she was gone, and it was dark. Slowly, Bob crossed the yard and went inside to his children.

ELAINE CAME HOME AT ONE-FIFTEEN, STOPPING ONLY FOR A moment in the living room, as if to give Bob a chance to look up from the David Letterman show and ask her to sit down, have a cup of tea, talk things over. He didn't. All he did was glance at her when she came through the door and then look back at the TV screen as she crossed the room. She called from the kids' bedroom, " 'Night, Bob," and he answered, " 'Night,' " and that was it. They no longer slept together.

He watched the TV screen inattentively, as if instead it were watching him, until the National Anthem was played at two-thirty and programming ceased. A half hour later, he realized that the blue eye in front of him was dead, and he reached over and flicked it off. With the lights on, he lay back on the sofa and tried to sleep. He squirmed and bent and unbent himself, but his body felt like a sack of nails to him, painful in any position, until finally he gave up trying, sat and smoked cigarettes, finished all the beer in the refrigerator and read *People* magazine twice, until it disgusted him, and he threw it on the floor. All those happy, pretty, successful people—he hated them because he knew they didn't really exist, and he hated even more the magazine that glorified them and in that way made them exist, actors, rock musicians, famous writers, politicians. Those aren't *people,* he fumed, they're *photographs*.

At six, he heard the baby wake, burble and yap to himself a few minutes and then cry to have his diapers changed. Bob rose slowly from the couch, got the bottle of apple juice from the refrigerator and headed down the hallway toward the children's room. Elaine appeared at the door, crossed the hallway silently, as if alone there, and went into the bathroom, closing the door tightly behind her. As he entered the bedroom, softly gray in the predawn light, he heard the splash of the shower behind him. Ruthie and Emma, accustomed to their brother's morning howl and the sounds of a parent tending to him, slept on, grabbing at the last, fat hour of sleep before they themselves had to get up.

Ruthie lay curled away from Bob, facing the wall, her thumb jammed into her mouth; Emma, in the other bed, slept on her belly, arms and legs splayed, as if swimming underwater. In the crib, which was squeezed between the dresser and the back wall of the small, crowded room, Robbie lay flat on his back, scowling and red with discomfort, until suddenly he saw Bob towering over the crib and ceased to cry.

Bob handed him the bottle, and while the baby noisily sucked at it, proceeded to strip away the sopped, plastic-lined paper diaper. When he had the baby's bottom naked, he stopped for a moment and thought, almost amazed, as if seeing it for the first time, My God, he has a penis. Just like me. An ordinary, circumcised penis. A doctored tube coming out of his digestive tract, that's all. It was contracted and short, shrunken to little more than thimble-sized from the cold and sudden exposure to the air. Below it swelled the testicles in their tight pouch, like the breast of a tiny, pink bird. There was no mystery, no power, no sin, no guilt. Just biology. It was terrifying for that, and for an instant, wonderful.

"Oh, Robbie," Bob whispered.

The baby, large blue eyes peering over the cloudy bottle, looked up at his father, and though his lips and cheeks yanked furiously at the rubber nipple, the baby seemed to be smiling. Bob returned his son's gaze for a moment, then began to examine his own hands, huge against the infant's tiny, smooth torso, legs and feet. They were coarse hands, scratched and hairy across the tops, with thick veins zigzagging over the surface like blue bolts of lightning, and suddenly his hands looked like weapons to Bob, weapons with wills of their own, like stones that could hurl themselves, and he hauled them out of the crib and jammed them into his pockets.

Once again, his left hand felt the money, but this time, instead of pulling away from it, the hand grabbed onto the packet and held it for a long moment. "Robbie," Bob whispered. "Robbie, your father is a terrible man. Look what he's ended up doing," he said, and his voice sounded like a cold wind rattling a shutter. "Just look at it."

The baby gurgled and smiled, kicked his bare feet in the air. Across the room, Ruthie twisted in her sleep, while Emma, blinking open one eye, saw her father and instantly dove back into sleep as if into deep, warm waters.

With his hands still stuffed into his pockets, Bob slouched from the room, peering back over his shoulder as he went out. He passed down the hallway, the bathroom door still closed, and left the trailer. Outside, the air was cool and almost still, as a thin, low fog drifted off the sea and caught against the Keys, shrouding the islands in a soft, silvery mist. He could hear the water lap against the shore, as if speaking to it, but he couldn't see the water at all.

He got into his car, and with the headlights on, drove slowly, not much faster than if he'd walked, over to

Islamorada, where once again he bought newspapers. In the parking lot, inside the car, he unfolded the *Miami Herald* and spread it over his lap and read, for the first time, the article about the drowning of the fifteen Haitians.

15 HAITIANS DROWN OFF SUNNY ISLES

MIAMI, Feb. 12 (UPI)—Fifteen Haitians, mostly women and children, drowned this morning in choppy waters off Sunny Isles just north of here after being forced into rough seas by the captain of what Coast Guard officials said was probably an American fishing boat engaged in smuggling Haitians into Florida. The unidentified boat escaped into the darkness while crew members of the U.S. Coast Guard cutter *Cape Current* attempted to save the Haitians.

Immigration authorities said it was one of the worst such incidents recorded since the waves of immigrants from the impoverished Caribbean country began heading for the United States 10 years ago. Gov. Bob Graham called it "a human tragedy which has been waiting to happen," and said he would press the Federal Government to work with Haiti to stop the flight to these shores.

In Miami, a Coast Guard spokesman said of the drownings, "It's just such a tragedy," adding, "It's subhuman, what some of these smugglers will do for a few dollars." When the fishing boat was first hailed by the *Cape Current* at 2:30 this morning, it was a half mile off the beach at Sunny Isles. According to the Coast Guard spokesman the captain of the fishing boat frightened the Haitians off his boat by firing a gun into the air.

The Haitians, most of whom apparently could not swim, drowned in the six-foot chop almost immediately. It's thought that several of them may have made it to the beach. Authorities are urging anyone who may have survived the tragedy to come forward and help identify the individuals who abandoned them to the sea.

The bodies of five men, six women and four children were taken to the Dade County morgue. A spokesman for the Medical Examiner's office said that autopsies would be performed and that attempts would be made to identify them. "Then," said the spokesman, "the bodies will have to be disposed of in some respectable and tasteful fashion. I don't quite know how we're going to do that yet."

Bob's chest tightened into a fist, then opened and emptied, and he wept, sitting in the shadows inside his car, surrounded by a milk-white fog, in a parking lot on an island in a sea, lifetimes and whole continents away from where none of this could have happened to him.

AN HOUR LATER, HE WAS SITTING AT THE KITCHEN TABLE, and he read the article again, studied the photograph accompanying it, read and studied as if decoding a secret message from an ally, while the girls ate breakfast in silence and gathered lunches in paper sacks and milk money for school, and Elaine in housecoat and slippers, without uttering a word, made breakfast for them all, served it and cleaned up afterwards, and the baby, on his belly in the playpen in the living room, watched.

Finally, the girls have left for school, Elaine has put Robbie back into his crib for his morning nap, and she stands at the sink, her hands in soapy water, and she looks up from the dishes every now and then at her husband bent over the newspaper.

"Awful, isn't it?" she says, her flat, expressionless voice cracking the silence.

Bob's face comes up as if from the bottom of the sea, white, bloated and whiskery, eyes like holes, mouth a bloodless slash, thin and drawn down, his long chin trembling.

"What is it, Bob?" she cries.

He shakes his head slowly from side to side, a sea beast shedding water in a fine spray, and opens his mouth to speak, but cannot.

"Oh, God, what's the *matter?*" Elaine rushes over to him. She holds his cold face and says again, "Bob, what's the *matter?*" She looks down at the newspaper, then back at his face. "I know, the poor Haitians. I read it when you first came in. . . . I was . . . I was looking for Ave. There wasn't anything. . . ." She makes her gaze drive down into her husband's, and she sees through films, membranes, veils, curtains, doors, walls, all the way into the secret man at the center.

She knows now. She knows what he has done. She knows at last who he is. She pulls back in horror. Then an instant passes, and she comes quickly forward and cradles his head against her breast. "Oh, my God, Bob. My God."

Suddenly, she pushes him violently away from her. His body flops back against the chair, and he says, "I . . . I don't . . . I can't . . ."

"Shut up! Just shut up! Don't say anything!" Slowly, as if afraid she will break, she moves to the other side of the table and sits down opposite him. In silence, they sit there, staring at each other, husband and wife and the third person their marriage has made of them and who, at this moment, stands before them, a monster.

BY NOON, THEY HAVE DECIDED WHAT TO DO. IT COMES OUT slowly, without argument or discussion, sentence by sentence, cell by cell, like a healing. First Bob quietly announces, "We should leave here." Then, after several minutes, Elaine says they should go back to New Hampshire, where Bob has a trade and can find work.

A little while later, Bob says they should pack up and leave now, as soon as possible, before they spend all their money here in Florida. Elaine agrees. She should quit her job now, pick up her pay this afternoon and take from the bank the few hundred dollars they have left in the checking account.

For a long time, they say nothing more, until Elaine says that the money Bob took from the Haitians should not leave Florida with them. "It's worse than drug money," she says.

"No. You're right. I don't know what I should do with it, though. I can't turn it in to the police. It's a lot of money, though," he adds.

They are silent for a while, then Elaine says, "Shouldn't you give it over to Ave somehow? That's where it belongs. It's evil money. Or what's-his-name, Tyrone."

"No, what I should do is give it back to the Haitians. If I could figure out how."

For the first time, as they make their plans, they are

speaking of "should" and "should not," and they do it stiffly, awkwardly, for these are words that make it difficult to mingle fantasy with hope. The sentences fit clumsily in their mouths and stumble over tongue, teeth and lips, as if either the words and grammar or the mouths were not their own. But Bob and Elaine struggle on, for they know now that this is the only way a new life can be made. And they must make a new life; the old one has died and is rotting. They are living on a corpse that has begun to stink.

They can't afford to rent a U-Haul, so they decide to pack and carry north only their clothes, bedding, linens and kitchenware. They will leave the rest of their belongings—except for the baby's crib and playpen, which can be tied to the roof of the car—in exchange for the rent they'll owe for not giving a month's notice to Horace. "Should we tell him what we're doing?" Bob asks.

Elaine says, "No. We shouldn't tell anyone. Once he sees the stuff we've left, he'll be happy we're gone."

By the time the girls come home from school, Bob and Elaine have begun packing in earnest. When Ruthie and Emma learn that they are moving back to New Hampshire, and Daddy will get his old job back, and they'll find a nice place to live, just like they used to have, the girls are visibly pleased, even Ruthie, and immediately they go to work packing their favorite toys, dolls, games and books into the boxes that Elaine brought back when she went out to close the bank account and pick up her paycheck at the Rusty Scupper.

For supper, because all the dishes, pots and pans have been wrapped and closed into boxes, Bob takes everyone out to McDonald's in Key Largo, and though he still cannot eat—the very sight of the Big Macs and fries makes him suddenly nauseous—Bob enjoys his family's pleasure in a way he has not for months. Their fussing and noisy delight, their impatience, their innocent, shining faces, make for him a world that, for once, is sufficient unto itself.

On the short drive back to the trailer, rain starts to fall, large, swollen drops that spatter against the windshield. Bob flips on the wipers and defogger and lights a cigarette. He's thinking intently and has said nothing since leaving McDonald's.

"You all right?" Elaine asks. "Want me to drive?" Robbie lies asleep on her lap.

"No. I'm okay." The overcast sky and now the rain have brought on an early dusk, and Bob switches on the headlights.

"You should go to bed when we get home. Really, Bob. I'll finish the packing."

Bob exhales jets of smoke from his nostrils, and the windshield, despite the defogger fan, clouds over. Reaching one hand forward, he rubs away a square that lets him see the road directly before him. "No. I couldn't sleep even if I wanted to. And I dont want to."

"You must be exhausted."

"Yeah, sure. Of course." He glances into the back seat. The girls are slumped in opposite corners, lost in their private thoughts. "Listen," he says in a low voice, "I'm going to drop you and the kids at the trailer. I guess I've figured out what I should do with the money. And I have to do it tonight, if I'm going to do it at all. Okay?"

Elaine stares straight ahead at the windshield. After a few seconds, she reaches out with her free hand and wipes a head-sized circle clear.

Bob asks, "Don't you want to know what I'm going to do?"

"No. Not especially, no. So long as you get rid of it, and we don't take it with us away from here."

"I'm going . . ."

"Bob, I don't want to know. I don't. Really. I don't know why, but it feels . . . cleaner not to know. Better, for the future. Our future. Okay?"

"Okay. Good."

She asks when he'll be back, and he says he can't be sure, by morning anyhow. Sooner, if he's lucky. "And I feel lucky," he says. "For once."

They pull up and stop in front of the trailer, and the girls are alert as puppies again, complaining about the rain. "Just run inside. The door's unlocked," Elaine tells them, and they scramble from the car and splash through puddles to the trailer.

"Drive careful," Elaine says, hefting the baby to her shoulder. "The roads are wet. I don't want you dead."

"You don't?"

"Don't joke about stuff like that, Bob. No, I feel like our life is over, though. The old life, I mean. The one we imagined when we were kids. That old me and that old you are dead already, I think. Maybe it's good they are. I don't know. No, I don't want you dead, Bob. I want to grow old with you."

"Didn't you always want that?"

"I guess I didn't. I just wanted to be young with you. You know? And that's what I've been, until now."

"Yeah. Me too. I feel so old now. Old as my father. It's strange, isn't it?"

"Yes. Be careful," and she opens the door. She gets out of the car, grunting with the effort, slams the door closed and disappears behind the clouded glass. Stretching across the seat, Bob rubs the window clear and watches his wife climb the steps, where, as she opens the door, she shifts the baby to her hip, and then the door is closed, and she is gone.

AN HOUR AND A HALF LATER, BOB TURNS LEFT IN KEY Largo at Blackwater Sound, crosses the bridge and leaves the Keys on the Route 1 causeway to the mainland. The rain has passed over, scudding northwest across the bay toward Naples and Fort Myers and on up the Gulf Coast, and now, ahead of Bob and slightly to his right, an egg-shaped moon droops in the purple sky over Miami. He follows the moon, its yellow light reflecting off the old canal alongside Route 1, through the Everglades to Florida City, where he picks up the Dixie Highway north through alternating suburbs and truck farms, until the suburbs take over altogether and the huge orange glow from the city, blotting out the moon and stars, fills the northern sky from east to west.

Though the land is flat, a mere three feet above sea

level all the way in from the Keys to Miami, Bob feels, as he enters the gleaming city, that he's descending from a high plateau. Along Brickell Boulevard, south of the Miami River and north of Coconut Grove, he passes between tall royal palms, and on either side, the pink mansions of deposed Latin American politicians and generals hide behind poinciana bushes and chain-link fences. Across the bay on his right is Key Biscayne. He passes terraced luxurious high-rise condominiums that house heroin and cocaine couriers from Colombia whose million-dollar cash deposits help keep Florida bankers happy, and then he drives between the banks themselves, clean white skyscrapers with window glass tinted like the sunglasses of a small-town sheriff.

When he crosses the Miami River in the center of the city, he's downtown and can see Miami Beach across the bay, where people live in hotels and live off hotels, a city where there are no families. Then north along Biscayne Boulevard, past the grandstands from last month's Orange Bowl parade, empty and half demolished and throwing skeletal shadows over the grass of Bay Front Park, until he passes out of downtown Miami and enters dimly lit neighborhoods where there are no more white people—no white people on the sidewalks, no white people in the stores or restaurants, no white people in the cars next to him at stoplights. This is where he wants to be. He knows, from what newspapers and boatmen on the Keys have told him, that he's in Little Haiti now, a forty-block section of the city squeezed on the west by Liberty City, where impoverished American blacks boil in rage, and on the other three sides by neat neighborhoods of bungalows, where middle-class Cubans and whites deliver themselves and their children anxiously over to the ongoing history of the New World.

He parks the car on North Miami Avenue one block beyond Fifty-fourth Street, in front of a small grocery story open to the street and still doing business, despite the late hour. There are burlap sacks of what look like flour stacked on the sidewalk and crates of rough orange yams, plantains and red beans. Several women inside the store talk to one another, while a man with spectacles pushed up on his shiny, mahogany-brown forehead totals their purchases. Bob takes a step inside, listens to the swift, soft Creole the women are speaking, and when, at the sight of him, they go silent, he steps back to the street.

Farther down the block, he comes to a record shop, speakers over the door shouting music onto the street, and he opens the door and walks inside. Everyone in the shop—three teenaged boys, a pair of young women, a bearded man behind the counter—stops talking and proceeds to examine a product, records, needles, plastic disks for 45s, microphones, until Bob leaves, when they resume their loud, quick conversations, and the music plays raucously over and over.

He enters a restaurant on Fifty-fourth with closed venetian blinds facing the street. A slender brown woman holding long, narrow menus greets him at the door and in French-accented English politely asks how many people are in his party. Bob peers across the room, sees large, beefy black men in three-piece suits, fashionably dressed women, a few children at table, and he says, "I'm . . . I'm looking for someone." He pretends to search the room for a friend, then says, "No, sorry, he's not here yet, thanks," and ducks out.

In a bar, seated on a stool at the far end, Bob orders a Schlitz from a short, stocky, mustachioed man wearing a cream-colored silk vest buttoned tightly across his belly. There are a dozen or more booths and small tables behind him, where three or four women, young and pretty, wearing heavy makeup and miniskirts and glittery, low-cut blouses, sit alone, one woman to a table, drinking. At the bar, four or five young men, boys almost, who seem to know each other and the bartender as well, talk, drink, smoke cigarettes and snap fingers in time to the music blatting from the jukebox in the corner by the open door. It's what brought Bob in from the street in the first place, the music, Haitian, loud, friendly, warm and available to anyone willing to listen.

The bartender brings the beer and glass and sets them down in front of Bob without once looking at him.

"How much?"

"One dollar fifty."

Bob hands two ones over. "Keep the change."

"Thanks," the man says, and starts to move away.

"Quiet tonight."

"Yes. Well, Wednesday, you know. It's late."

"Say, listen. Ah . . . I was wondering," Bob says.

"Yes?"

"You're Haitian, right? That's a Haitian accent, right?"

The man examines Bob for a few seconds, this battered white man, large, unshaven, eyes in caves, clothes dirty and rumpled, and he says, "Yes, I am Haitian."

"Cigarette?" Bob says, pushing his pack forward.

The man hesitates, then takes one. "Thanks."

Bob lights his cigarette. "You probably know about those Haitians that drowned day before yesterday, right?"

The man steps back. "Well, yes. From the newspapers." He eyes Bob warily.

"Me too. From the papers, I mean. Sad, isn't it?"

"Ah, yes. But it happens. Such things happen."

"But some get through anyhow, right? Some of them make it to shore. I read that."

"I suppose so." The man starts to leave. Farther down the bar, the young men have ceased talking and have taken up watching Bob and the bartender. There are four of them, two with bushy Afro haircuts and long sideburns, the other two, younger, with short haircuts. All four are dressed up for a night out, billowy nylon shirts cut and unbuttoned to expose their chests, tight, bell-bottomed slacks, slip-on shoes with pointed toes. Two of them wear heavy gold chains around their necks and copper bracelets on their wrists. All four are faceless to Bob, kids out looking for some action. He supposes they have a car parked outside, a beat-up Olds or Pontiac with elaborate hub caps, the dash and rear deck covered with pile carpeting.

"Listen, friend, can I ask you something?"

The bartender returns, and Bob slides a ten-dollar bill

across the bar. "I was wondering . . ." he says in a low, confidential voice, "if you could tell me something."

The bartender palms the ten and pockets it without changing his expression of calm, mild curiosity.

"Those Haitians who drowned the other day. I wondered if there were any survivors. You know?"

"I think not. No survivors. The sea was rough. Why do you ask?"

"Well, see, I got a friend, Haitian guy who works for me, out on the Keys, and he's looking for his people, his family, see, and he was wondering."

"Why will he not come and ask himself, then? Why do you ask?"

"Yeah, I understand that, I realize how it looks, me doing the asking and all. But, y' see, he's got to be careful about that sort of thing. You know. Because of his papers not being so good. You understand."

"Ah. Yes." The man turns away again. "I am sorry, mister, I know nothing of the people from the boats."

"Wait!" Bob says. Reaching into his pocket and drawing out the packet of money, he peels off a twenty and lays it on the bar.

The bartender stares for a second at the thick wad of bills in Bob's hand, then at the twenty before him. "I know nothing of those people. You should drink your beer and go. We close soon," he says, and walks slowly but emphatically away.

Bob picks up the twenty and wraps it around the others and shoves the money back into his pocket. Finishing off his beer in one long gulp, he slides off the stool and makes for the door. As he passes the young men at the bar, they turn and watch him.

"Hey, mister!" one calls. He's tall and broad-shouldered and wears a thick denim cap nested in his huge, bulbous Afro.

Bob turns and says, "Yeah?"

"You want something? Maybe you want a girlfriend, eh?" he says, winking and flashing a wide grin.

"No, thanks," Bob says, and he steps outside to the street. Behind him, the youths laugh and start talking in

Creole to the bartender, who ignores their questions and proceeds to grab up their glasses and empty bottles and hurry them out the door.

Down on Fifty-fourth, a few blocks east of where I-95 soars overhead, Bob spots in the distance a small clot of people, a few women and children, but mostly old men, shaky, decrepit-looking, dressed in rags and ill-fitting castoffs. The people have gathered on the sidewalk beside the open side door of a large brown and white Dodge van. Attached to the top of the van and running the length of it, like a political poster, a large, hand-painted sign cries: *The Kingdom of Heaven is at hand! Repent! Matthew 10.:7*.

As Bob nears the group beside the van, he sees at the center a tall young white man, blond and wearing jeans and a hooded gray sweatshirt with FLORIDA STATE emblazoned across the front. Inside the van, a woman, also in jeans and sweatshirt, with the hood pulled over her head like a monk's cowl, hands the young man, in sequence, parcels wrapped in brown paper and then what appear to be paper cups of hot soup. The young man in turn passes the goods to the people gathered around him, first a parcel, then a cup of steaming soup, which the recipient, tucking the parcel under his or her arm and stepping away from the van, slurps down in relative privacy and furtiveness, as if hunger were a slightly embarrassing secret.

Bob edges up to the van, hears the young white man speak Creole to the people, who remain silent, who simply reach out, take the parcel with one hand, the soup with the other, and back away to make room for the next person to come forward. And in a few moments, Bob himself is the next person.

The white man is in his early twenties and extremely tall, several inches taller than Bob. He's gaunt rather than skinny, a physically strong man overworked, and his short, straight hair is thin and already disappearing at the temples, giving his face an unnatural boniness for one so young. His bright blue eyes are small and deep-set, a Swedish or Norwegian face, with large bones and delicate skin. Holding a parcel in one long hand and a cup of soup in the other, he says to Bob, "Praise the Lord, brother," as if it were a command, the price of the gifts.

"Praise the Lord," Bob murmurs, but he refuses the gifts and steps aside to let an old, bewhiskered fellow behind him take them. "I want to talk to you a minute."

"Oh?"

"Yes. It's important."

"Okay. Sure. Jennie," the man calls to the woman inside the van. "Can you handle the rest yourself? There's only a couple more."

The young woman sticks her head outside, examines Bob, then the remaining Haitians. "Okay, sure, Allan. No problem." She's a pretty young woman, Bob notices, with freckles on her face and neck. She pushes back her hood, revealing long, pale brown hair tied in a ponytail that swishes heavily, healthily, as she hands out the parcels and ladles the soup from a large stainless-steel drum.

Allan walks around to the rear of the van, pulls open the door and sits wearily down inside, his feet up on the bumper. "Hi. My name's Allan," he says, extending his hand.

"Bob."

They shake hands, and Allan says, "You wanted to talk. You look worried, brother."

"I am. I need some help."

"Of course. We all do. Are you saved, Bob?"

"What?"

"Do you know Jesus, Bob?"

"Jesus? Know him? Well, I guess not, no. I mean, I'm . . . no."

"You haven't given your life over to Jesus yet?"

"I guess not. No, not really."

"That's okay," Allan says brightly. "You will, Bob."

"I will?"

"What church do you belong to, Bob?"

"Well, none, I guess. I mean, I was raised Roman Catholic. But I haven't been in a while. You know."

"Things are pretty bad, though, aren't they, Bob?"

"Yeah." Then, impatiently, "Listen, I have to ask you how to do something for me . . . for these Haitians and all."

"Okay, sure, Bob."

"Well, you sort of specialize in helping out the Haitians, right? I mean, the refugees."

"They're the lost sheep of Israel. But we do the Lord's work everywhere, Bob. Jesus said, 'He that receiveth you receiveth me.' So there you are. But yes, we're helping the Haitians especially. They need food and clothes, so we find Christians who'll pay for it, and then we give it out to them. Jesus said, 'The kingdom of heaven is like a net that was cast into the sea and gathered of every kind.' Do you know your Bible, Bob?"

"No. Not really."

"Read it, Bob. It's God's word."

"Yeah, I will. Look, Allan, I got some money here, a lot of money, and I want you to give it to the Haitians. These people here, people like them."

"God bless you, Bob! That's incredible, brother. Praise the Lord!" The man claps Bob on both shoulders. "God bless you!"

"Well, no, it's not my money, exactly. It . . . it really belongs to them, see. The Haitians. And I'm trying to get it back to them somehow, that's all."

"How's that, Bob?"

Bob studies the man for a second, then says, "You guys are like priests, right? I mean, I tell you something, it's confidential, isn't it?"

"I am a servant of the Lord, Bob, yes, but a far cry from a Catholic priest, I'm afraid." Allan laughs. Then seriously, "Whatever you tell me, brother, I'll hold in strictest confidence. Unburden yourself, Bob."

Bob takes a deep breath. "Well, I'm a fisherman, see, and I brought some Haitians over from the Bahamas . . . a while ago. They paid me for it. Anyhow, well, some of them didn't quite make it, if you know what I mean. . . ."

"No. What do you mean?"

Bob lowers his voice almost to a whisper. "Some of them drowned. Coming ashore."

Allan looks into Bob's dark eyes for a long moment. "Some of them drowned? Coming ashore?"

"Yes."

"You brought them over in your boat? And some of them drowned?"

"Well . . . yeah."

"Then you . . . you're that man in the papers with the boat, up at Sunny Isles?"

"Yes. I am."

Allan brings his large hands to his mouth, lifts them to his forehead, and cries, "Oh, my God! That's *awful!*" He gapes at Bob and whispers, "Lord have mercy on your soul, Bob." He studies Bob's face for a moment, as if to determine his sanity, then says, "I . . . I don't know what to tell you. Except that you should get down on your knees, you should give yourself over to Jesus, Bob. Save your soul, brother," he pleads. "Now, before it's too late."

"Look, I don't want to talk about that right now. I got enough problems without worrying about my soul too. I got a wife and three kids. What I want is for you just to take this money and make sure it goes to some people who need it. Some of these Haitians." He pulls out the wad of bills and shows it to Allan. "It's way over a thousand dollars. Maybe two. I haven't even counted it. See? I don't care how you do it, spend it on soup or clothes, or just dole it out, I don't care." He pushes the money at the man.

Allan recoils and slides farther back into the van. "Put it away! People'll see it!" He looks over Bob's shoulder and repeats, "Put it away!"

Bob turns. In the distance, thirty or forty feet behind him, the youths from the bar are talking to one another under a streetlight, smoking cigarettes and lounging against the brick wall of a windowless building facing the street. They ignore Bob and Allan and the van, acting as if they're alone on the street and bored and don't want to go home yet. The largest of the four, the man with the denim cap who spoke to Bob in the bar, has his back to Bob and chats easily with the others, making large gestures with his arms as he talks.

Bob turns to Allan and shoves the money at him. "Here, for Christ's sake, take it. Please, take it. I don't know what I should do with it anymore."

"Just pray, Bob. I can't take the money. And I can't help you, only Jesus can help you. You must pray, and then Jesus will tell you what to do. Bob, I'll pray with you, if you want. Come on," Allan says, and he slides forward from the van and stands up. "Let's get down here, right here on the street, and pray to Jesus. He's here with us now, I know it, I can feel His presence. Come on, Bob," he says, grabbing Bob's arm.

Bob wrenches free. "No! Just take the damned money, will you?" He waves the bills in front of the man's face.

"Bob, no!" Allan cries. "Just pray, that's all you have to do. Pray to Jesus for forgiveness and guidance, and repent. That's all you need to do. Repent. You don't need me, Bob. You need Jesus. We all need Jesus. You're no different than anyone else, in spite of what you've done."

Bob steps back. "You won't take it, then."

Allan looks at the money clutched in Bob's hand. "No. Lord forgive me, but I can't. I can't. Not unless we both pray to Jesus and *He* tells you it's the right thing to do, and also tells me I should take it." Allan gets down on his knees in the street beside the van. "Fall on your knees, Bob!" He's sweating, and his blue eyes glisten. "Pray! Jesus will hear you. Jesus loves you, Bob."

Jamming the money into his pocket again, Bob wheels around and walks swiftly away. When he looks up, he sees the four young men from the bar watching him. He briefly hesitates, then keeps coming, and as he passes them, the leader of the group smiles and says, "Still out, eh? Sure you don't want no black pussy, mister? Plenty black pussy around here."

Bob looks into the young man's face. "You know what I'm looking for."

"Me?" He breaks into a warm smile, and his bushy sideburns spread like wings. "I can't know what you are looking for, mister, until you have told me."

"Are you Haitian?"

"Born there, yes, but American now. All of us," he says, still smiling. "All-American boys, eh?" he adds, and he steps back and slings his long arms over the shoulders of the other young men. They all smile now, as if for a group portrait.

"You guys were at the bar back there," Bob says. "The bartender tell you what I asked him?" The young man's act irritates Bob and makes him nervous. He can't see the reason for the act, can't figure out what kind of impression the man is trying to make on him. Bob thinks he may be making fun of him somehow.

"He only say you a nice fellow," the young man says. Then he moves in close and in a low voice adds, "He say you looking for somebody. True?"

"True."

"Well, then, maybe we know how to find this some-body, eh?" Again, he's expansive, arms spread, broad grin on his face. "Everybody here know everybody else, like a country village. Eh? You know that? You a smart man, I see it right off," he says, crossing his arms over his narrow chest. Then he says, "So."

Bob is silent a moment. Then he, too, says, "So," and smiles. The other three are followers of the first, their expressions and postures merely weak imitations of the tall, thin man with the Afro and sideburns, so now all five men are standing with their arms crossed and smiles on their faces. This is a game, Bob thinks. They know who I'm looking for, and they know who I am too. They know my whole story. In a minute, when they're through playing with me, when this one has finished showing off his English, they'll surround me, show me their knives and take the money from me.

Bob doesn't want that. The money is no more theirs than it is his. If he lets them take the Haitians' money from him, it will be like throwing it away, burning it. He says, "I happen to know that somebody got to shore from that load of Haitians that drowned off Sunny Isles the other night.''

"Ah! How do you know this, mister?''

"I'm . . . I'm a fisherman. There were fifteen bodies recovered, and I heard there were sixteen Haitians on the boat.''

"You heard this, eh?''

Bob studies the man's eyes, but he can't penetrate them. The man seems purely and simply amused. "Yes. In a bar, on the Keys.''

"Oh. Well, then, you heard the truth," he says. "A woman, sister to a man in the neighborhood, she get through to the land and get to her brother.''

Suddenly Bob's chest fills as if with a large, hard, metal-skinned balloon, and his breath comes in short, rapid bursts. "You . . . do you know where she is?''

"In bad shape, I hear. Very bad shape.''

"Can you take me to her? I'll . . . I'll pay you.''

The man turns to his comrades and murmurs in Creole for a moment, then returns to Bob. "One hundred dollars.'' He's no longer smiling.

"Fine, that's fine.''

"You got to pay now, mister.''

"Oh. Oh, sure, okay.'' Bob reaches into his pocket, turns away from the group and draws the money out. Carefully, he peels off five twenties, replaces the packet of bills and hands the hundred dollars to the man. "You sure you know where this woman is?''

"No problem, mister. Like I say, this place is a neighborhood, a country village. Her brother is a well-known man here, and my friend is friend to him, too. We hear all about this woman this morning. Everybody who wants to know about her knows about her. If you don't want to know, you don't. If you do, you do. Simple, eh? We know where she is right this minute, too. Not far from this spot.'' He's grinning again.

Bob says, "All right, then. Take me to her.''

"You got somet'ing for her, give it to me, eh? I take it to her for you, save you trouble.''

"No. I'll give it to her. I need to talk to her.''

"She probably don't speak English."

"That's okay. Just take me to her."

"Suit yourself," he says.

They start walking, a shapeless group of five men, four black and one white. Shadows in moonlight of palm trees, parked cars, fences, lampposts, fly up like dark flames and lie down behind the men as they stride down Fifty-fourth Street. All the storefronts and shops are blocked and barred by iron gates and shutters; the restaurants and bars are closed, dark, empty. There is no traffic on the streets, Bob suddenly realizes, no cars or buses moving.

They leave the sidewalk, cross a junk-strewn vacant lot on a corner of Fifty-fourth and come out on a dark side street, which draws them at once into a maze of side streets. Bob is frightened now. Two of the men are in front of him, two behind. Bob imagines coming to a sudden halt, yanking the four men to attention and holding out the packet of money to them. That's what they want. If they take the money, all of it, just take and pocket it, and if they don't stab him, which he knows they could easily choose to do, then he'll be alive, safe, free to go home to his family. But he'll have given away his only and last chance to make the first, small attempt to purge himself of the consequences of his crime. He knows that it will take years, possibly a lifetime, for him to forgive himself, but he also knows that it is essential to the process, the necessary first step, that he somehow return the money unasked, that he not merely get rid of it by giving it to four strangers who just happen to be black and Haitian. He was wrong to try to give the money to the Christian back there, he knows now. He has to give it back to the people he took it from. That won't make him clean again; possibly nothing will. The deaths of the Haitians will still be his fault, his crime, but he will not have traded their lives for a pocketful of ten-, twenty- and fifty-dollar bills. Instead, he will have traded their lives strictly for freedom, freedom to pack up his car and drive his wife and children back north to New Hampshire and get his old job back and rent an apartment for his family and try to build them a new life out of the scattered, cast-off pieces of their old lives. He will have done something bad, not for money, but in order to do something good. Maybe, then, if he gives the money back, he won't be any worse than a lot of good people are, and then he will be able to start hoping for a kind of redemption.

If he simply loses the money, however, if he gives it over at knifepoint to four young muggers on a dark back street of Miami, Florida, there will be no hope for any kind of redemption. No hope. He's got to have hope. Hope is what must replace fantasy in his life. Without it, he'll end up like Eddie, dead in his Eldorado, or like his father, drunk and dreaming to "Destiny's Darling," or like Ave Boone, cynical, small and cheap, and in jail. A dead man, a foolish man, a shallow man—these will be his alternatives. Bob wants to be a good man. And then he can begin to hope for redemption.

They're now deep into Little Haiti. From throat to groin, his body feels like a cold steel beam, his arms and legs hardening into cast iron, his head—eyes, mouth, nose and ears—seeming to shut down bit by bit, as if a bank of switches were being flicked off one by one. He's panting, taking quick, shallow breaths, and knows that if he had to speak, he could not. He can barely hear their footsteps click against the pavement, cannot smell the oleander and orange blossoms, the cold cookfires from the backyards, and when finally they pass out of the maze of crosshatched streets and lanes onto an open boulevard, which he recognizes, Miami Boulevard, where he parked his car, his peripheral vision has left him altogether, and it's as if he's looking down a tube.

They cross the boulevard and soon turn left and pass down a shadowed alley between two long, flaking white cinder-block warehouses. At the end of the alley, they come to another that crosses it, and at the crossing a silvery sheet of moonlight falls over them. A long-unused, rusting railroad siding sinks into the trash-littered passageway between still more old, boarded-up warehouses. They are walking slowly now and with care through splotches of darkness and moonlight, picking their way over the tracks to the farther side, where they move in single file alongside the wall of a building, touching it with their fingertips as if seeking a place to hide. Bob is aware of the Haitians' speaking now and then to one another in Creole, but he doesn't so much hear them speak as remember a few seconds afterwards that they have spoken.

Suddenly he realizes that they have stopped, the tall man in front, then Bob, then the three others, and the tall one is talking in a low voice to Bob and pointing across the alley to a warehouse where a loading platform extends like a pier to the railroad tracks. A rickety wooden staircase leads from the ground to the platform, and at the end of the platform there is a large, closed cargo door. Next to it, a smaller door with a piece of old plywood over the top half lies open a few inches, as if unlocked and left ajar mere seconds ago.

Bob steps over the railroad tracks with careful haste, like a man crossing an ice floe. He puts one foot on the crumbling steps and looks up and sees that there are people standing above him on the platform, people looking down at him, people waiting for him. They are black, three men and a woman. One man, dressed all in white with a scarlet sash around his waist, has positioned himself slightly ahead of the others and has folded his arms over his chest, like an impresario. The second is slight, wearing dark trousers and a white dress shirt, and looks downcast, like a prisoner whose confession has been extracted by torture. Behind him looms the third, a man tall as a column, sepulchral, tautly drawn to his full and amazing height and dressed in a morning coat and striped trousers and wearing sunglasses and a top hat. Holding lightly to his elegantly bent arm, like his consort, is a woman in a white frock, a very dark woman whom Bob recognizes at once. She's the woman from the boat, saved from drowning to come back and move among the living and, when the white man presents himself, to name him to himself, that he may be judged. She's the woman whose fate now is to say his fate to him, that he may live it out. It's she who must endure the sight of the sign of his shame, the money clutched in his outstretched hands, and must hear him beg her to take it from him, "Please, take this from me, take the money, take it," while bills fall like leaves from the pile in his hands, get grabbed back up from the ground and get thrust at her again and again, as he pleads, "Take it, please! Take the money!" And she's the woman who must refuse to remove the sign of his shame, who must turn away from him now, and leading the three others, walk back through the door to the darkness beyond, leaving him alone out there, the money still in his hands, and behind him, waiting, the four young wolves who led him to this place.

Bob turns and faces them. The leader takes a single step forward and extends his hand, palm up, for the money. Bob shakes his head slowly from side to side. Then, crushing the bills together, he stuffs the money back into his pocket. All four wolves step carefully over the railroad tracks toward him. The leader, his right hand still extended toward Bob to receive the money from him, holds a short knife in his left. The other men hold knives also.

With a coarse shout that stops the four, Bob cries, "No! This money is *mine!*" And abruptly, like a boy in summer diving off a pier into a lake, he puts his hands before his face and steps forward, and at once the four men pounce on him, stabbing at him until he falls— spinning, arms and legs outstretched, spinning slowly as he falls, almost weightlessly, like a pale blossom in a storm of blossoms, filling the air with white, a delicate, slowly shifting drift through moonlight to the ground.

And so ends the story of Robert Raymond Dubois, a
decent man, but in all the important ways an ordinary
man. One could say a common man. Even so, his bright
particularity, having been delivered over to the obscu-
rity of death, meant something larger than itself if only
to him and to those who loved him. Normally, to the
rest of us, the death of a man like Bob Dubois signifies
little more than the shift of a number from one column
to another, from the lists of the living to the lists of the
dead: one of those who make their livings with their
hands becomes one of those who die at the hands of
others; one of those who have lived to the age of thirty-
one becomes one of those who have died by thirty-one;
one of those who perpetrate crimes becomes one of
those who are the victims of crimes. The larger world
goes on as before, quite as if Bob Dubois never existed.
In the vast generality, a statistic is merely a statistic,
regardless of the column it's in, and once an ordinary
man is dead, all possibilities of his ever becoming his-
torical, of his becoming a hero, are gone. No one will
model himself on Bob Dubois; no one will reinvent him
and remember the man in order to invent and make

419

*memorable himself. Even Bob's children will forget him
and the shape of his brief life. Elaine Dubois, his widow,
will return to Catamount, New Hampshire, where she
will devote herself to raising her three children; from
here on out, it will be the whole point of her life, until
long after the children have become adults. And she will
never ask them to emulate their father, nor will she
herself deliberately emulate him. He will be to her as
Bob's father, brother and best friend eventually became
to him, an example to avoid. And the degree to which he
avoided patterning his life on theirs is the degree to
which his wife Elaine and his three children will avoid
patterning their lives on his. Elaine will work on the line
at the cannery until she retires at sixty-five, the first
signs of emphysema starting to close in on her. Ruthie
will not graduate from high school; she will marry at
seventeen a boy of nineteen who works for the telephone
company, and in six months she will give birth to the
first of her five children, a boy she will name Sam, after
her new husband's father. Emma, after a six-week course
in cosmetology, will become a beautician, and she will
move into her own apartment in Catamount, buy a new
red Japanese fastback coupe with number plates that
say EMMA, and she will spend her winter vacations in
places like Jamaica and Barbados, smoking lots of marijuana and sleeping with the local hustlers for two wild
weeks before returning to Catamount and work at the
beauty parlor and long nights at the bars. By the time
she's thirty, she'll be alcoholic, gaining weight fast, looking worriedly for a husband. The baby, Robbie, will
enlist in the navy after graduation, and when he completes his basic training in San Diego, he'll be assigned
to an aircraft carrier, after which he'll return to Catamount and become a plumber. Everything that happens
in their lives after Bob Dubois's death in Miami will
seem to have happened as if he never existed. Yet surely,
if he had not existed and if his life had not taken the
shape he gave it, then the particulars of the lives of his
wife and children would have been different. Just as
Bob's own life, without his father's drab life behind it,*

would have been different. It's those particulars that give meaning to the life of an ordinary man, a decent man, a common man. And the lengthy, detailed history of such a man must celebrate or grieve, depending on whether he lives or dies, even though nothing seems to happen as a result of his life or death—even though the Haitians keep on coming, and many of them are drowned, brutalized, cheated and exploited, and where they come from remains worse than where they are going to; and even though the men in three-piece suits behind the desks in the banks grow fatter and more secure and skillful in their work; and even though young American men and women without money, with trades instead of professions, go on breaking their lives trying to bend them around the wheel of commerce, dreaming that when the wheel turns, they will come rising up from the ground like televised gods making a brief special appearance here on earth, nothing like it before or since, such utter transcendence that any awful sacrifice is justified. The world as it is goes on being itself. Books get written—novels, stories and poems stuffed with particulars that try to tell us what the world is, as if our knowledge of people like Bob Dubois and Vanise and Claude Dorsinville will set people like them free. It will not. Knowledge of the facts of Bob's life and death changes nothing in the world. Our celebrating his life and grieving over his death, however, will. Good cheer and mournfulness over lives other than our own, even wholly invented lives—no, especially wholly invented lives—deprive the world as it is of some of the greed it needs to continue to be itself. Sabotage and subversion, then, are this book's objectives. Go, my book, and help destroy the world as it is.

About the Author

A native New Englander, Russell Banks has lived and worked in Florida, Jamaica, and other parts of the Caribbean. His fiction has received numerous prizes and awards, and he has been a Guggenheim, National Endowment, and Fulbright Fellow. He is the author of THE BOOK OF JAMAICA; FAMILY LIFE; TRAILERPARK; SEARCHING FOR SURVIVORS; THE NEW WORLD; HAMILTON STARK; THE RELATION OF MY IMPRISONMENT and SUCCESS STORIES. He lives in Brooklyn, New York.